Also by Susan Sizemore
and coming soon from Pocket Books

Primal Heat
Master of Darkness

Primal
Desires

SUSAN SIZEMORE

POCKET
BOOKS

LONDON • SYDNEY • NEW YORK • TORONTO

First published in the USA by Pocket Star Books, 2007
An imprint of Simon & Schuster Inc.
First published in Great Britain by Pocket Books UK, 2007
An imprint of Simon & Schuster UK Ltd
A CBS COMPANY

3 5 7 9 10 8 6 4 2

Simon & Schuster UK Ltd
Africa House
64-78 Kingsway
London WC2B 6AH

www.simonsays.co.uk

Simon & Schuster Australia
Sydney

A CIP catalogue record for this book
is available from the British Library

ISBN: 978-1-84739-115-5

Printed and bound in Great Britain by
Cox & Wyman Ltd, Reading, Berkshire

Dedicated to the
fond memory of Fern Anderson

Prologue

Central Europe, Winter 1943

Jason Cage enjoyed the company of wolves, but the trio of creatures surrounding him in the clearing had to be werewolves. No wolf had ever looked at him out of glowing gold eyes with intelligence that rivaled his own. Being surrounded by members of the Gestapo wouldn't have surprised him, nor a touch on his shoulder from the vampire Prime who also hunted him. But this pack was the last thing Jason had expected to find in the deep forest tonight.

Then again, the moon was full, the woods were remote. If he were a werewolf, he'd consider this countryside perfect for running free. Freedom was a thing every creature desired, be it mortal or otherwise evolved.

"Good evening," he said, mostly because it

was something he'd heard a vampire say in an American movie.

He hoped the largest werewolf's answering snarl was a form of laughter.

"I mean no harm to you," he went on.

He spoke calmly, without making any effort to reach the minds of the werewolves telepathically—mostly out of politeness, but also because every time he tried psychic communication lately, the other Prime somehow focused in on his use of mental energy.

The werewolves circled him, silver moonlight outlining their dark shapes. In morphed form they must be huge men, *he thought.*

It occurred to him that they *meant him harm,* which was not generally the way it went between werewolves and vampires.

"Why?" he asked as the trio drew closer.

They began to circle, growing one step nearer with each turn around the clearing. Clearly this was a dance, a ritual. Was there meant to be a sacrifice at the end?

While his ancestors might have participated in such Old Religion nonsense, Jason was a Prime of the twentieth century.

"There's a war on, you know," he reminded the circling beasts. "We should be fighting the Germans instead of each other."

Chapter One

Las Vegas, Spring, Present Day

"One more show, and then two months off—I can hardly wait!"

Jason understood his assistant's enthusiasm as they waited backstage. During their hiatus, she was going to get married and honeymoon on Bora-Bora. He had no particular plans or destination in mind.

Or he hadn't until a few minutes ago.

"Of course, I'll miss the critters. Do you think they'll miss us?"

The tigers and lions they used in the Beast Master magic show were going to be spending their holiday at a very exclusive private nature reserve. The wolves, of course, never left his side.

"They won't want to come back to work after two months of running free," Jason answered.

He fingered the talisman he'd put in his vest pocket. He'd recognized the gold coin instantly, even though only half of it had been sent to him.

Out front, the applause was beginning.

Even with his powers, it was never wise to be distracted during a performance. He wished he hadn't opened the padded envelope until he was alone in his dressing room after the show. He certainly wished he hadn't read the note.

Now he had somewhere he absolutely needed to be, and an obligation he could not refuse to fulfill.

But at this moment, the lure of the audience called him.

Northeast of San Diego, Spring, Present Day

Sofia Hunyara was aware of the weight of the pendant resting at the base of her throat. Nothing else felt like gold. It was heavy and rich, and *there* whether she could see it or not. The crescent-shaped half of an ancient coin, which she wore on a leather cord, was tucked discreetly beneath her blouse. She traced the coin's outline beneath the soft silk. Once upon a time the coin had been all she'd had, and she'd fought hard to keep it. In the last few years, she'd kept it in a safety deposit box and hadn't thought about it much—not until the message arrived last week.

She peered out of her windshield at the house on the hilltop and shook her head. The impressive mansion looked completely out of place in the California desert.

Why am I doing this? she asked herself yet again.

Probably because of her grandfather, and her great-grandfather.

She pressed her palm against the pendant.

And the fact that, except for a distant cousin, she was alone in the world and the world did not make sense. At least the past didn't make sense.

"This should go to your father," her grandfather had said, handing her a small leather bag. *"I am so sorry this burden must go to you."*

She tugged the bag open and spilled its contents into her cupped hand. It was what she expected, yet different. She looked at the dying man propped up in the hospital bed. "Where's the other half?"

"Your father should be the one to teach you," he said. *"He should be here now."*

Her father was serving three consecutive life terms at Seal Bay. She was never going to see him again, and she didn't want him teaching her any-

*thing. She'd seen what he'd done. But this was
no time to take her bitterness out on her grandfather. All she could do was wait for the old man
to go on.*

"*Someday you'll know what must be done.
Someday your teacher will be found. Until then,
be patient. Someday . . .*"

His last word had been *someday*. Sofia had
waited a long time. Much of that time had not been
pleasant. She'd stopped expecting explanations,
or even wanting them. But now here she was.

Another vehicle pulled up behind hers at the
end of the long drive. Sofia got out of her car at
the same time a man exited the white SUV behind
her. Tall and lean, he had very broad shoulders
and lots of wavy brown hair. She was struck by
the coiled energy and animal grace in the way he
moved as he came toward her. She'd have to be
dead not to stare, and she couldn't help but lick
her lips.

Okay, the guy looked delicious, but that was
no reason to be rude, or blatant. Sofia managed to
get the spike of lust under control by the time he
reached her, but felt awkward and embarrassed.

She turned her attention toward the Gothic
pile of stone in front of them. "Do you think it
comes with its own madwoman in the attic?" she
asked. "Or do they have to rent one?"

"And do Heathcliff and Cathy have a guest-house out back?" he answered.

Wow, a guy who knew *Jane Eyre* from *Wuthering Heights*! His voice was deep and rich as cream, and she couldn't help but look at him and smile. She was immediately caught by the bluest eyes she'd ever seen.

She almost stuck her hand out and said, *My name's Sofia. Can I have your babies?* The odd, powerful reaction unnerved her, and all her usual mistrust and wariness rushed back. She immediately turned and walked toward the house. Who this guy was and what he was doing here didn't matter. She had her own fish to fry.

Jason waited a moment before following the dark-eyed Hispanic beauty, appreciating her long legs and the curve of her behind as she walked away. He also needed the time to recover from the psychic whirlwind that had hit him when they'd looked into each other's eyes. He'd gotten the impression that beneath the skin, she was a creature of fire. He also knew a caged animal when he saw one. He doubted this mortal knew the first thing about her psychic gifts, or knew that she'd unconsciously thrown up one of the strongest psychic shields he'd ever encountered.

He supposed he'd have to go inside to find out who she was and what she was doing here.

He joined her as she rang the doorbell. When no one came to the door after a couple of minutes, she muttered, "Now what?"

There was an ornate brass knocker in the shape of a gargoyle in the center of the heavy wooden door. Jason tried it. No one answered this summons, either.

He was prepared to force the door open, but the knob turned easily. "Shall we?" he asked.

"Isn't this breaking and entering?" the young woman asked.

"I have an invitation to be here," he answered. "Don't you?"

"Yeah," she agreed, not sounding at all happy about it. "All this mystery is *so* annoying."

He nodded and pushed open the door. The gentlemanly thing would have been to stand back and let the lady enter first. But a protective instinct kicked in, and he went into the house ahead of her.

The entrance hall was huge, and deeply in shadows, but the darkness didn't keep him from seeing the enormous werewolves waiting in the corners. Jason turned to slam the door on her, but the mortal had already followed him inside.

"What's the mat—" she began as the beasts charged forward.

"Get out!" he ordered, and put himself between her and the werewolves.

The beasts snarled and leapt, and Jason took them all on at once. Claws slashed him across the face and teeth sank into his calf, but he was the one left standing when it was done. It was then that he turned toward the door and saw the young woman staring at him. Her back was pressed against the door, her eyes huge with fear, and she was pale and trembling.

He took a step toward her, but turned as someone began to clap behind him. Jason didn't recognize this old man, but he looked at him in disgust. "Haven't I already passed this test?"

The old man smiled, though it was more of a sneer. "Who says the test was for you, vampire?"

Chapter Two

San Diego, Spring, Present Day

Sidonie Wolf took a sip of orange juice and looked across the restaurant terrace at the sun sparkling on the calm water. The fresh breeze that ruffled her short blond hair was scented with salt from the ocean and jasmine from the pots of flowers lining the edge of the terrace.

On the other side of the table, Tony Crowe was drinking tomato juice. His dark eyes held a twinkle that said he knew exactly how ironic the sight of a vampire drinking blood-colored liquid looked in this setting. "Hey, I like the flavor," he said when he put his glass down.

"Did I say a word, Daddy?" she asked.

Tony took a quick look around, but no one was sitting near enough to overhear. "Daddy?" He raised an eyebrow. "Sid, darling, what are you up to?"

To any mortal watching, they certainly wouldn't look like father and daughter, but that was what they were. Both looked to be in their twenties. He was dark, handsome in a sharp-boned, Central European, how-Dracula-should-have-looked-if-he'd-really-been-a-vampire way. She had the blue eyes and blond hair of her mother's side, but had inherited Tony's elegant cheekbones.

Sid smiled enigmatically and ate a few bites of omelet. Then she waved a finger at him. "Paranoia from the male parental unit? I'm hurt. How was the drive down from Los Angeles?"

"The drive was fine. Why are you calling me Daddy?"

They were Clan vampires, meaning that their culture was both matriarchal and matrilineal. Sid was a female of the Wolf Clan, the daughter of House Antonia. Tony was a Prime of the Corvus Clan, son of House Berenice. Technically, since Tony and Antonia were not a bonded pair, their child had no reason to call him "Daddy." But Sid was quite close to the Prime who had sired her and frequently referred to him in mortal terms.

"Okay, maybe *Daddy* is a bit much," she conceded. "How are you doing, Pop?"

He grimaced. "Let's just go with Dad, okay? I'm fine."

"Good." Sid sat back in her chair. She was finding this far harder than she'd thought it would be. "Are you still running security for the clinic? How's Dr. Casmerek? I suppose he's busy doing important research to help the diurnally challenged."

"I suppose he is," Tony answered. He looked very suspicious, but at least he wasn't trying any telepathic probing for her ulterior motives. "What are you up to, girl? Your daylight drugs don't need adjusting so soon, do they?"

She shook her head. "I was just wondering if he'd come up with any new wonder drugs lately. Or if he might be interested in other medical problems we have."

"He and his teams better be, with all the money the Clans and Families invest in their projects."

"Good. David Berus is in town, did you know that?"

"Is he?" Tony asked.

"Lady Juanita asked me to come to dinner tonight," she rushed on. "David Berus is going to be there."

The Clan Matri actually didn't ask, she commanded. Sidonie Wolf hated being ordered around. Even for something as ostensibly pleasant as being a guest at a dinner party for a respected Prime of the Snake Clan. Sidonie was not like other Clan daughters. At least she wasn't going to be if she could help it. Open rebellion was not an option, but guile . . . now, guile could work wonders.

As ever, Tony was quick on the uptake. "Lady J. wants you to mate with David. Congratulations. I look forward to being a grandfather soon."

"Oh, please!" she complained. "Not that I object to having a baby," she went on. "Or even several babies. I'll do my duty to the Clan. But I want the choices to be mine, without attachments and emotional complications."

"Then what's wrong with David? He's still heartsore from having lost his bondmate, so he's not likely to want emotional complications, either. Genetically—"

"He and I are first cousins," she pointed out. "His sire's Wolf Clan."

"I forgot that."

"The Clans need fresh blood."

He gave her a stern look. "Yeah, but the fresh blood you're interested in sprouts fur and a tail at least once a month."

"How's Rose?" she snapped back.

There was fire in his eyes when he answered. "She's eighty and just moved into a nursing home."

Sid hated herself for reacting so unkindly to his having touched a sore spot. "I'm sorry," she told her father. "But I think we just made the point that because of duty to the Clans, neither of us can have the ones we really want."

He looked thoughtful. "You have a plan. You always have a plan. You, my dearest, would make Machiavelli look like an amateur, and old Nick was one hell of a Family Prime."

"We females are always the smarter ones," she said, grinning.

Tony smiled back. "You want me to approach Dr. Casmerek about something, don't you?"

Sid decided she might as well be blunt and hope that the storm would pass quickly. "Artificial insemination. My egg, a donor's sperm—"

Tony shot to his feet. "Are you out of your mind?"

Everyone on the terrace was staring at them.

"Calm down." She gestured. "Sit down. Hear me ou—"

The cell phone in her purse rang before she could finish. Frustrated by the interruption, Sid flipped it open and demanded, "What?"

The answer from her partner at the Bleythin detective agency sent all her own problems right out the window.

"I'll be in as soon as I can, Joe," she said, and hung up. "Sorry, Dad," she told Tony. "We're going to have to have this argument later."

"What's the matter?" he asked.

"Cathy's gone missing. She's our office manager," she added.

"This sounds more serious than just calling a temp agency to cover the phones."

"Oh, yes." She nodded. "It's extremely serious when a werewolf who can't control the change goes missing so close to a full moon."

Chapter Three

Hollenbeck, Los Angeles, Summer 1991

The scrambling of sharp claws on hot concrete was louder in Sofia's ears than the sound of her own ragged breathing.

They were right behind her.

She could feel the heavy bulk of furred bodies close behind her.

They were faster than she was.

Why didn't they catch up with her?

Were they enjoying the chase?

Her heart pounded as she ran as fast as she could. Her feet slipped in the flimsy flip-flops, but they'd surely bring her down if she stopped to kick the shoes off. She dug her toes into the soft plastic and kept going. Traffic slid past on the street, people loitered on stoops and at storefronts as she ran by, but no one seemed to notice that she was being chased by three enormous dogs. The sun hadn't quite set yet. Why didn't they see?

She didn't have the breath to call for help.

She did cry out when one of the dogs moved up to nip her bare leg, and a warm trickle rolled down her calf.

The animals smelled the blood and began to howl.

She spotted an alley and remembered that there was a fence at the end of it that she could climb, and the dogs couldn't. One of her shoes slipped off when she made the skidding turn and she stepped on a shard of broken glass, but she kept running.

She was nearly at the end of the alley when she saw that she'd made a wrong turn. There was a wall where she'd thought there'd be a fence.

She slammed into the brick wall before she could stop herself, scraping her palms and jarring her arms from wrists to shoulders. She turned around and fell to her knees, putting her at eye-level with the dogs.

They had big heads, and huge teeth. Their eyes glowed, cruel and fierce, and full of hunger.

Their eyes glowed!

She grabbed a broken bottle from the ground.

They formed a half circle around her and stared at her for a while.

They wanted her to drop her weapon, but she wouldn't!

Then the largest one growled as if to say very well, and all three of them began to move in for the kill.

Northeast of San Diego, Spring, Present Day

"She's not with us," the old man said.

Jason put his hands on her shoulders and saw a nightmare in the woman's dark eyes. "You think?"

She was trembling and her heart was racing faster and faster. The woman needed help, but none of the mortals were going to step in to halt their stupid *tests*.

Jason tried gently shaking her, then calling to her, but he knew he'd have to go where she was— even though interfering with mortal thoughts was dangerous.

For him.

"You're having a panic attack. It'll be over in a minute," he reassured her.

But tears welled from her big brown eyes. What was a Prime to do? He pulled her closer and into a tight embrace. Then he kissed her.

Fire shot through him, and their minds joined

at the moment their lips touched. There was a moment of urgent passion, then . . .

The tangy scent of the blood of a terrified child assaulted his senses.

Anger overrode desire, and he was filled with an overwhelming sense of protectiveness. She was his! She needed help.

The shape of the world shifted, and Jason stood at the entrance of an alley. It was like looking down a long tunnel. At the end of it was a trio of beasts. Facing them was his Sofia on her knees.

He moved forward until he was in among the beasts. They turned claws and fangs on him, and he answered them in kind, keeping himself between them and the girl as he fought her attackers. After he turned them into bloody piles of fur at his feet, he turned and helped Sofia to stand.

When his hands touched her, she wasn't a little girl anymore and she came into his arms, warm and trembling.

And their lips touched . . .

Sofia was aware of the mouth pressed demandingly against hers and the sensual heat rushing through her, threatening to melt her bones. Her kiss was equally demanding; she wanted to taste all of him. His palm splayed across the small of her back, pulling them close, hip to hip. He was all hard muscle, and she melded to it. His other hand cupped the back of her head, possessive and protective at once. His thumb stroked down the back of her neck, sending a shiver through her. Her hands fiercely clasped his shoulders, never wanting to let go. He permeated her senses. He smelled male, and tasted male, and *felt* so male, it drove her mad with need. She had no idea how anything could feel so right so fast, yet their bodies fit perfectly together.

She'd never believed in perfection, and skepticism rose to pull her out of the nonsense of believing in this perfect kiss.

"What the hell are you doing?" she demanded as she pushed the man away.

She tasted copper and wiped the back of her hand across her sensitized lips. A drop of blood smeared across her hand and she stared at it. Hers or his? Hers, she thought, remembering that her tongue had touched one of his very sharp teeth. Some of her annoyance faded with the realization that she'd been as much involved in the kiss as he'd been.

His eyes twinkled. They were very blue. "You can't tell me you didn't enjoy it."

Oh, he was a cocky one. She had to fight not to be charmed by his insolence. "You started it. Why?"

He shrugged. "Seemed like a good idea."

Vague memories and nightmare images swirled around her. She had no interest in remembering the details. "I saw a dog. I hate dogs. I must've overreacted."

A flash of annoyance crossed his features, but all he said was, "Yes."

From his sudden coldness, Sofia sensed he was a dog lover. Well, that doomed any possible relationship. Which brought her back to . . .

"*Why* did you kiss me?"

"To calm you down."

"Aren't you supposed to slap someone when they get hysterical?"

"That's not my style." He cocked an eyebrow and crossed his arms.

A stern voice spoke from behind them. "Jason Cage, Sofia Hunyara, you have been summoned. It is time for you to learn why. Come."

Chapter Four

"Shall we, Sofia?" Jason asked, and took the mortal woman by the arm.

She resisted for a moment. He caught the thought, *What the hell am I doing here?* Then her curiosity got the better of her and she let him lead her forward.

"Do you know what this is about . . . Jason?" she asked as they followed the old man down a long, ill-lit hallway.

"Not really."

He could tell that she wanted his reassuring touch on her arm, yet feared any dependence; she fought the craving by deliberately stepping away from him. He shouldn't resent her lack of trust, but he did.

They were led to a large room lined with tall

bookshelves, most of them empty, and shown to a pair of threadbare wingback chairs. The old man sat behind an ornate but battered desk. Jason noted that much of the damage to the furniture looked like the marks of animal claws, and the wooden floor was marked with long, deep gouges. It looked like generations of wolf pups had run wild in the place.

"Show her," the old man told Jason.

"Show me what?" Sofia asked.

"Who are you?" Jason asked the mortal male.

The old man sighed and folded gnarled hands on top of the desk. "So much to explain—I don't know where to start."

Sofia glanced at her watch. "Talk fast."

The old man said, "Sofia, I am your great-uncle Pashta Hunyara."

Her expression went hard. "I don't have any uncles."

"Great-uncle," he repeated. "And there is a great deal about yourself you do not know."

Pashta? Jason smiled, remembering a fearless toddler in the Romany camp who used to climb onto his lap and demand stories. How quickly they aged.

"You know me, Prime," Pashta said. "Show the girl the one thing she can believe in."

Jason remembered what had drawn him to this

odd meeting and took the gold coin out of his pocket.

"Where did you get that?" Sofia demanded when he held up the heavy half circle of gold.

"It belonged to a friend of mine," he told her.

"It belonged to my grandfather," she said. She reached beneath her blouse and brought out the other half of the coin, hanging on a leather cord. "What are you doing with my talisman?"

Jason tilted his head toward Pashta. "He sent it to me, I think."

"I did," the old man said. "Are you going to snatch the other half away from the Prime and run away, Sofia? Or would you like me to explain everything to you?"

Sofia liked to think that six years in the navy had made her a logical, methodical, and disciplined person. Yet here she was, the wild child she'd fought to tame was trying to claw out into the open again at the first painful mention of family. She had to get herself under control—though being hit with equal parts lust, terror, and weirdness in the last few minutes was enough to rattle anyone.

She sat back down and made herself concentrate on the man who claimed to be her relative, instead of on the man holding the other half of her heart. It took all her willpower to remain polite. "Please explain."

Pashta smiled, and for a moment he looked just like her grandfather. "First, let me say that we have been searching for you for a long time. For you and your cousin Catherine. Where have you been all these years?"

Her suspicions heightened, and the mention of Cathy shook her. "*You're* the one offering explanations."

"What do you know of our family history?"

Sofia said nothing, waiting him out.

He sighed. "Our family is different. We have secrets, very deep secrets. We are blessed with great powers, and cursed as well."

Not to mention being full of bullshit, she thought.

Hear him out, Jason advised, his voice so clear it felt like he spoke inside her head.

Sofia turned sharply to look at Cage and was caught by his soothing, reassuring gaze.

This is hard stuff to explain. Harder to believe and accept. Give it a chance. Give Pashta a chance.

His calm voice caressed her soul; she couldn't be afraid with him beside her.

And *that* made no more sense than the old man's talk of curses and blessings.

"We are a tight-knit and insular people. We have to be. Your great-grandparents are the ones who made the decision to bring our people to America after the war. They wanted to start over, to escape the curse, to pretend that we are normal people."

"I *am* a normal person."

"You don't really believe that," Cage said.

She glared at him.

He smiled and pointed toward the old man. "He's beating around the bush because he doesn't know how to explain that a werewolf bit one of your ancestors, and your whole tribe has been hiding from the natural-born werefolk ever since. That about sums it up, doesn't it, Pashta?"

"Were . . . wolf?"

Pashta nodded.

She smiled. "This is where Marty Feldman shows up and says, 'There wolf,' right?"

Jason smiled at her reference to *Young Frankenstein,* but Pashta said, "What?"

"There are no such things as werewolves," she told the old man.

"Just because you've never been formally introduced to any doesn't mean they don't exist," Jason told her.

How did one get formally introduced to a werewolf? Shake paws?

That would be a polite way to start.

Jason sounded amused and calm, which helped her hold her temper. She didn't know why she found him reassuring when he might be as crazy as Pashta.

"What do you think those animals in the hallway were?" Pashta asked.

She didn't want to think about those slavering monsters. "Hounds of the Baskervilles," she said. "Go on about my family. Promises of information are how you got me into this nuthouse."

"We finally found you through the blog where you post about books and films on Live Journal." The old man chuckled. "It amazes me how anyone can be Googled these days. Some secrets are becoming too hard to keep, don't you agree, Prime?"

Jason nodded. "But we have to keep trying."

That's what she got for using her real name online. She sighed. "Go on, *Uncle* Pashta."

"Neither your father nor Catherine's mother wanted anything to do with our heritage, though they both had the gift. She wouldn't use it, and he . . . he misused it tragically."

Sofia made a sharp gesture. She didn't want to know anything about her good-for-nothing father, but she'd put up with hearing about him if she could learn other things. Her grandparents and great-grandparents had always been secretive and mysterious.

Maybe because they were hiding from nutty relatives who believed in werewolves.

"Once we finally tracked down you and your cousin, we asked you both here to explain your heritage to you. We asked Jason Cage to come because his skills are necessary to train you."

So where was Cathy? She glanced at Jason. "What skills?"

"I'm an animal trainer and stage magician," he said.

"You are the Beast Master!" Pashta proclaimed.

This sounded familiar. "Haven't I seen you on Leno?"

Cage gave a modest shrug.

"You work in Vegas, right?"

"Pay attention!" Pashta demanded. "This is important!"

"It's not our fault that you're making such a botch of the explanations, Pashta," Jason said.

The old man gestured at Sofia. "I've never had to explain this to a stranger before. We need her to lead the hunt, we need her to train the ferals, but she is not one of us!"

"Nor will she ever be, if you keep thinking

of her as an outsider. I can feel you reluctantly pulling out every word you say. It's giving me a headache."

"The truth is difficult."

Sofia seethed at knowing her relative wanted her only for some skill she supposedly possessed, even if he was a nutjob. Angry at herself for holding out hope again for some family connection, she got up. "That's it."

"Wait!" the old man called.

She heard his desperation, but walked out anyway.

Chapter Five

Jason rose, needing to go after her, and held up the coin. "What is really going on here?"

"Do you remember what happened during the war?"

"The experiments? Is that what you meant by 'It's started again'?"

Pashta nodded. "Some of our people have been taken. Perhaps they have Catherine, as well. She went missing soon after we found her. They may be looking for Sofia after today." He banged his fist on the scarred wood. "We need that girl. We need you to show her how to tame the beasts those bastards make." He gave a bitter laugh. "Though first we have to find the beasts, and rescue them."

Or destroy them, Jason thought, remembering back to 1943. "Who is doing this? Why?"

Pashta spread his hands out before him. "We don't know very much yet, but we have to act quickly. I'm trying to assemble a team, which is why I need Sofia and you." He gave him a hard look. "You will honor your vow, won't you?"

When he put it like that, Jason couldn't point out that American werefolk had their own system for dealing with problems. Besides, Pashta's people were not proper werefolk. They were as likely to be hunted as they were to be helped.

"I'll protect the girl," he said. "I'll train her."

Pashta pointed to the door. "Then go after her."

Because he could move faster than a mortal, Jason reached Sofia before she got into her car. He put his hand over hers as she began to open the door and said, "Let's start over, shall we?"

He was almost overwhelmed by the warmth and softness of her skin.

"You seemed like a sane person," she said as she turned to him. "I don't know why I thought that."

"It's probably because I'm so handsome and charming."

"Good Lord, I hope I'm not that shallow."

He ran his hand up her arm, delighted by the faint shiver this sent through her. "I notice that you aren't denying the attraction."

"The attraction isn't the problem. The fact that you're a nutjob who believes in werewolves is the problem." She glanced past his shoulder as an eerie sound filled the air. "Your SUV is howling."

He sent a soothing thought toward his wolves. "That's just George and Gracie," he told the suddenly tense woman. "You'll like them once you get to know them."

"You may have noticed that I don't do well around dogs."

"They aren't dogs. And neither were those creatures in the house."

She paled and swallowed hard. "Wolves, then."

Jason shook his head. "You don't *really* believe that."

"Of course I do!" Her denial was sharp, and genuine.

"You're a Hunyara. Some instinct in you knows the difference between dogs and wolves, natural-born werefolk and your own lycanthropic relatives."

She tried to back away from him. And who could blame her? He was going about this as poorly as Pashta. He wanted her badly and that was clouding his thinking.

"Let me tell you a story," he said, and lifted his hand to touch her temple.

Central Europe, Winter 1943

He went with the Romany to a small encampment far deeper in the forest. It was nearly dawn when they showed him into the shelter of a hut. Inside, a large group of people sat around a small fire. Smoke swirled around the low ceiling. The air was acrid, and hardly warmer than outdoors. Energy permeated the room, almost as visible to Jason as the smoke, and he was aware of being in the presence of several powerful mortal psychics.

Werewolves and psychics? He wondered what was going on, but waited for the others to speak.

One of the younger males bent forward and peered at him closely. "Are you as young as you look, Prime? What are you doing out on your own?"

Jason would have been offended had the questions come from one of his own kind. Now he only shrugged. "There's a war on."

The old man clipped the younger man behind the ear. "My son is rude, Prime. His name is Grigor. That little one skulking in the shadows when he should be in bed is my youngest, Pashta. I am Sacha Hunyara. And we"—he gestured around him—"are the Outcasts. People not of the mortal world, nor fully members of the super-

natural world. We live in hiding, we keep our secrets, but now we need help."

Being an outcast and fugitive himself, he was prone toward instant sympathy for them. But being softhearted toward mortals was what had gotten him in trouble in the first place.

"Explain," Jason said.

"What do you know of werewolves?" Grigor asked.

"That most werefolk are born with the ability to change shape to wolf, bear, or whatever they become at will, and keep sane while doing it. But a mortal bitten by one of the werefolk turns into a creature forced to shift into a maddened animal during the full moon."

"Precisely," Sacha replied. "Our people, Prime, are somewhere in between. The natural-born see the bitten as diseased, and a threat to their own existence. They are more likely to hunt down and murder the ones their own renegades are responsible for making, than they are to try to help them."

"Is there help?" Jason asked. "I'm sorry, but I don't know very much about shape-shifters."

"We tame them," Sacha told him. "The Hunyara took on that responsibility long ago."

"We had to," Grigor added. "It is better to tame than it is to kill members of our own family."

"Some of us carry the disease," Sacha said. "An ancestor was bitten, and the tribe cared for him. He escaped during a full moon and bit his own wife and son. She became a werewolf. With the son it was different. Instead of turning him, the attack brought out the skill to reach into the werewolf's mind. Ever since then, some of our people become werewolves, and others are able to control them. I am the current Wolf Tamer of the tribe."

Northeast of San Diego, Spring, Present Day

"Does that explanation work for you?"

Sofia heard the question as though it were asked from a very long distance, then she realized that Jason's hands were on her face, his body pinning her against her car.

The chill of winter faded, along with the firelight and the faces and words that filled her head. She blinked as the hot, bright afternoon came sharply back into focus.

"What happened?" She looked sharply at the man holding her. He was an illusionist, a stage magician. "How did you do that?"

"Never mind," he said, and took a step back. His hands moved to her shoulders, warming her more than the sunlight of the fading day. "I'm sorry that you're being asked to take a lot of things that sound like nonsense at face value."

The screwy thing was that, coming from him, she half wanted to believe this nonsense. Sofia shook her head. "One of us has got to be crazy. You, specifically," she added.

He laughed. "The supernatural is perfectly normal to me, but I understand your skepticism. Think about what I showed you." He glanced at the sky and sighed. "We'll talk later."

"What's wrong with talking right now?"

This was stupid! She should want nothing more than to run away from this guy, yet a knot of loneliness squeezed her heart at the prospect of him leaving. She was never going to see him again, was she?

"Don't look so sad." He stroked her cheek, cupped her chin in his palm, and looked deep into her eyes. She wanted him to kiss her again. "I want to kiss you, too. May I?"

He lifted her hand to his lips.

So I can find you again, his voice whispered in her mind.

She thought he was going to kiss the back of her hand, a romantic but terribly old-fashioned gesture. But she didn't mind because she'd been reading a lot of Jane Austen lately.

Instead, he bit her wrist.

Chapter Six

**Wolf Clan Citadel, La Jolla, California,
Present Day**

"How long do you think we'll have to stay?"
Eden asked as they approached the Moroccan-
style mansion Lady Juanita called home.

Sidonie Wolf knew that her sister-in-law wasn't
comfortable around large numbers of vampires,
and she certainly didn't blame her, considering
Eden's family history. Normally she might tell
Eden to just suck it up and live with the shame of
being born into an ancient line of vampire hunters. It wasn't like anyone was going to bite her
or anything. Tonight, however, Eden's attitude
was tinted more with impatience than paranoia,
and Sid was in complete agreement. She was even
more anxious to get this duty over with than her
mortal friend.

"Let's try to get in, smile at everybody, and get out."

"Roger that," Eden answered.

At least Eden carried her and Laurent's daughter, which assured her welcome. Sid hoped that little Toni would be the center of attention and darling of everyone's eye for the evening. Toni was going to grow up mortal, which meant that she wasn't going to help the vampire population problem, but she was an adorable toddler, all blond curls and pink cheeks and dimples. She got the dimples from her dad, Sid's brother, Laurent. Who didn't have to be here tonight because, after all, *he* was Prime.

"Putz," Sid muttered.

She deeply resented the fact that even at the dawn of the twenty-first century, thems with penises still got to have all the fun. She didn't blame Laurent, who was out on the streets searching for Cathy, but she seethed with fury at Lady Juanita for not allowing the female members of Bleythin Investigations to join the hunt.

"What?" Eden asked as they went up the wide steps leading to the carved double doors.

"Just pouting because I have to go in and be nice to everyone. Do you want to take a turn?"

"Yes, please," Eden said. "I could be hacking into the old laptop we found in Cathy's closet right now if not for this command performance. It's not that I don't love your Clan, but—"

"You don't."

"I love your mother."

"As well you shou—Hello, Matri," Sid said as Lady Juanita opened the door.

The Matri nodded regally. "Welcome, Wolf daughters. You will always have a place in my citadel."

Whether we want it or not, Sid thought, using many layers of mental shielding to keep her opinions to herself.

Besides, the Matri had spoken to them aloud instead of issuing a telepathic greeting. That set the ground rule for this evening. Sid understood why when another female appeared beside Juanita at the door.

"Hi, Mom," Sid greeted Lady Antonia, head of her house of the Wolf Clan.

Antonia had lost her ability to use telepathy, and it would be rude and cruel to use this sense when she couldn't. Besides, Eden didn't have a lick of psychic ability.

Antonia held out her arms, and Eden dutifully handed Antonia's namesake over to her grandmother. Then Lady Juanita ushered them into her home with an elegant, imperative gesture.

"I hear your sire was in town," Antonia said

as Sid walked beside her down the long entrance hall.

"He stopped by to pay his respects this morning before he returned to Los Angeles," Juanita said before Sid could answer.

She hoped he hadn't said anything about the conversation they'd had to the Matri, since he'd been livid about her suggestion of using modern medicine to assist their population problem. He had calmed down enough to say he'd talk to the people at the Los Angeles clinic, if and only *if* she could come up with a Prime who'd agree to the procedure.

She knew this was because he didn't think she had a snowball's chance in hell of finding a suitable candidate, since Clan Primes were so stupidly old-fashioned and macho.

And speaking of macho . . .

Sid was aware of the males waiting for them before they reached the garden courtyard. The energy that hit her senses was hot and spicy, filled with dark undertones of challenge and rivalry. The males of her own species always reminded her of cinnamon and pepper, black coffee and dark chocolate. They made her hungry. She couldn't stop the primal thrill of excitement that shivered through her.

But the call of male to female was normal

and natural, and Sid was able to acknowledge it without letting a rush of lust go to her head. She smiled at her sister-in-law when they reached the waiting males in the courtyard, and Eden grinned back.

"I might be bonding with my own gorgeous vampire," Eden whispered to her, "but I can enjoy the window shopping."

"It's too bad Laurent isn't here to defend his mating rights when the boys start hitting on you."

Eden's grin widened. "I'm not sure what's more fun: watching Laurent get jealous, or the way he stands back and smiles and lets me defend my own honor when the Clan boys gather. I'm not sure if that's because he accepts me as an equal, or because he's as lazy as he claims to be," she added.

"I think it's a bit of both," Antonia said. "Eden, come with me, there's someone I want you to meet. Sidonie, mingle."

"Aw, Mom," Sid complained at being left alone.

Eden gave her a sympathetic look, but dutifully accompanied the woman holding her baby.

"Motherhood makes us weak," Sid grumbled as she faced the crowd. Oh, well, it was best to get the social obligations over with so she could get back to hunting for their missing associate.

As she stepped onto the tiled courtyard, she glanced at the sky. Instead of seeing the beauty of the moon, she was gratefully aware that it was several nights away from being full. They had some time before Cathy was helplessly trapped in her lycanthropic form, but not much. They had to find her before then, because if she killed or bit a human as a werewolf, according to werefolk law she'd have to be executed.

To Sid this was brutally unfair. What was even worse was that the person who had to carry out the sentence was someone who cared for Cathy very much. Sid knew that if she lived the circumscribed life of a proper vampire female, this wouldn't be any of her business.

But she couldn't live like that, all cosseted and safe. It wasn't that the Clan women didn't have incredible power—personal, spiritual, sexual, financial—a Matri's word was law among her Clan, and only the Matri could override the decisions of the Mother of a House. But these powerful women weren't *involved* in the greater world outside their own domains.

Boring.

But this wasn't the time or place to proclaim her feelings. She took a deep breath, forced a smile, and walked through the crowd of males in

the courtyard to stand next to the bubbling fountain in the center. There she turned and waited to
be adored.

A pair of handsome Primes showed up before
she finished moving.

"Mortals think they invented speed dating, but
they're wrong," a richly amused male voice said
behind her. "You boys move along," he went on.
"The lady is here to meet me."

When the Primes smiled sheepishly and moved
away, Sid knew the Prime behind her could be no
one but the legendary David Berus.

Chapter Seven

The civilized rules of vampire society required that he be here, and Jason was scrupulous about obeying the rules since his youthful run-in with the law. He approached the mansion carrying a bottle of wine and two dozen bloodred roses, George and Gracie pacing at his side. He buried his own impatience and mentally soothed the wolves, even though he shared their restlessness. It was important to get the formalities over with, even if he was anxious to be somewhere else, with someone else.

As he expected, the door opened before he could ring the bell. He hadn't expected it to be opened by Lady Juanita herself, who wore the necklace of the Wolf Clan Matri.

She smiled, her eyes glinting in amusement. "Who might you be, night child?"

"A stranger in your territory, but a friend." Jason introduced himself, his family, and his house and bowed formally.

"I've heard of you," she answered.

"My bad reputation tends to precede me." He smiled and held out the wine and roses. "But I bring nice presents."

"Did I say I'd heard bad things?" She took his gifts and stepped back to let him enter. "You are welcome in my home." She glanced at George and Gracie. "The wolf may be our Clan's symbol, but some of my guests tonight are mortal and might find your companions disturbing. Will they be all right if you leave them in the library?"

"Perfectly all right," he replied smoothly. "I didn't mean to crash your party, Lady Juanita. I came to pay my respects."

"But you must stay. Let me introduce you to my guests."

What did one say to the most famous Prime of them all? Sid felt like an idiot, but all she could manage was, "Hi."

She had not planned on being impressed with David Berus, but some things simply couldn't be helped. He had an aura of sadness and hard-won wisdom that was instantly intriguing. Besides, he smiled at her in that appreciative, flirtatious way Primes had, yet she didn't sense any of the usual desperation that accompanied Primes meeting females. He didn't instantly want her simply because she was a girl. She couldn't help but like that.

"You are a perverse creature," he said.

"Tell me about it."

"Oh, I know all about you. Lady Juanita has been singing your praises since I arrived."

She had no intention of letting any other vampire know all about her, but she smiled as if she were flattered by the comment.

"Are you in search of rescue?" he asked when she glanced around.

"Not at all. I'm looking for—" She waved as her mother came into the courtyard. "Mom, over here."

She realized that she'd practically shouted while all other conversation among the hypersensitive guests was being conducted in murmurs and whispers. This brought stares and frowns, which were answered by a fierce smile from Berus.

"I only lost my telepathy, darling," Antonia said, coming up to her. "I'm not deaf."

It always amazed others that Antonia accepted a devastating disability with such matter-of-fact aplomb. But as she had once said to Sid, *"You can be alive or dead, and anything but dead can be dealt with."*

"Unless they're zombies," Sid had reminded her. *"But zombies aren't our problem."*

Werewolves weren't supposed to be, either, but Sid's worry for Cathy reasserted itself, and she was suddenly very anxious to leave.

Cover for me, please!

She sent the thought into her mother's mind, hating the necessity as she saw Antonia wince in pain.

But Antonia rallied, smiled at her, and came forward. "Hello, it's so good to see you again, David," she said, holding out her hands.

David Berus took them, and Sid moved away as Antonia imperiously demanded his complete attention.

Only to have another Wolf Clan Prime instantly step up to her. A second male put a hand heavily on the first male's shoulder. The first one's fangs came out. A scuffle began.

Sidonie sighed.

These meet-and-mate evenings were always the same; it was an ancient ritual overseen by the Matri and Mothers. Available females were trotted out for available Primes to vie for their favors in secure surroundings, away from any mortal eyes. A little blood might be shed for the sake of impressing the ladies and cooling the Primes' more violent urges. By the end of the evening, the females would choose one or two Primes as sexual partners. It was not unusual for the Matri to orchestrate which Primes the younger females mated with. Perhaps a child would be conceived, or the spark of a bond might ignite. Since there were far fewer females than there were Primes, it was always hoped that a female would produce several offspring with different fathers before she found a bondmate to settle down with. This was how it had always been done. For the continuation of the species, this was how it had to be.

Sid wasn't so sure.

Fifty years ago, vampires couldn't go out in the daylight. They couldn't tolerate garlic. The touch of silver brought agonizing pain. Modern medicine changed all that; why shouldn't it be used to change the culture, as well? What Sid needed was a volunteer to prove her point.

"I'll take him," she said as a stranger approached at Lady Juanita's side.

He had wavy brown hair and very blue eyes. You could probably seat six around the width of those shoulders. Long legs, trim waist. Assured, graceful walk. Beautiful hands.

Sid wouldn't mind having a kid with beautiful hands.

She smiled and stepped around the Primes fighting over her, even though the Matri gave her a disapproving look as she approached.

The tension level in the place went up when the blond woman smiled at him, and Jason would have preferred not to have the attention. Having a Clan female look favorably upon a Family Prime while surrounded by males of her own kind was not a good way for him to be welcomed into Wolf Clan territory. All he wanted was to get out of here and get back to Sofia.

Lady Juanita stopped and put herself between him and the other woman. She closed her eyes and touched his cheek, and the Matri's mind sliced through his shielding with gentle, determined skill. He could tell that he was the stronger telepath, but he suffered the intrusion politely. She was equally polite, taking only information important to the moment. And at this moment, Lady Juanita's mind was on matchmaking.

She was quite pleased when she said, "Blood sings in you, and calls."

He couldn't deny he'd tasted a mortal recently, but he wasn't so sure about that other stuff. "There is a woman who needs my help," he said.

"She's the reason I've entered your domain, Matri. I have a duty to her family that goes back several mortal generations, and I must fulfill my obligation." Clanfolk liked hearing about things like honor and duty and protecting mortals; their old-fashioned ethics came in handy for him.

"Does this mortal know what you are?"

"Not yet," he admitted.

"Does she know about us?"

"My obligation to her in no way compromises the secrecy and safety of your Clan. I ask permission to dwell in your territory for a time, and to hunt if I must. But I swear that my being here will bring no harm or attention to you and yours."

Jason spoke so that everyone within earshot could hear. He didn't want any of the Primes having even the faintest suspicion he was a threat. So he really wished the Wolf female would stop peering over the Matri's shoulder with a look like she wanted to eat him up. He wasn't in town to give the Primes competition in any form.

Lady Juanita studied him intently for a time herself, then finally nodded. "I thank you for seeking me out. I value your intention to honor your mortal debt. I grant the permission you ask for." She spared a moment to give a stern look to the other female, then added, "And I congratulate you

on finding the one every Prime is born to seek."
She dropped her formal attitude then and said,
"You arrived just in time for dinner. You will stay
for dinner, of course?"

She seemed genuinely welcoming, but Jason
wasn't tempted to spend the evening among his
own kind. "Sofia needs me," he said, though he
certainly hadn't meant to make any sort of desperate declaration about the situation. He was a
Prime who usually knew how to keep his business
to himself.

"And you need her as well." Lady Juanita's
smile was knowing.

Might as well let the Matri think whatever she
wanted. "With your permission?" he asked.

She gave a regal nod. "Go, for now. Know that
you are welcome in my citadel. Take my greetings
to your own Matri, Prime of Family Caeg."

"I will." He hurried out of the courtyard to
collect his wolves and get away before the female
he could feel still watching him put any moves
on him.

"Imagine that," Sid murmured as the Family
Prime made for the exit. "There's somebody here
who doesn't want me. Isn't that interesting?"
Since the last thing she wanted was to be wanted,
she followed him.

Only to be stopped by her sister-in-law as she reached the hallway that led to the entrance of the house. "Did you get a look at that guy?" Eden demanded.

"I'm trying to get a better look," Sid answered.

"Talk about melodramatic—he travels with a pair of wolves. I've never known any vampire to call attention to himself like that. Pretentious, no?"

Eden was descended from a long line of mortal vampire hunters. Before she'd become the bond-mate of a Clan Prime, she'd been more likely to sneer at vampire behavior than participate in it. She still had bouts of being terribly unimpressed with the culture of the ethnic group she'd married into.

Eden's news about Jason Cage set off alarm bells in Sid's head. "Wolves?" she asked. "Or werewolves?"

"I think I know the difference between wolves and werefolk by now," Eden answered a bit testily. "He called them George and Gracie—wait a minute. Do you think he knows something about Cathy's disappearance?"

"He said he was in town to help some mortal damsel in distress," Sid said. "No names were mentioned, but I don't believe in coincidences. I think we need to check this guy out."

It won't hurt to find out all I can about the sperm donor of my future child.

"Right now, we'd better get back to the party," Eden said, taking her by the arm and turning her toward the courtyard. "We've got at least an hour more of being dutiful Clan females before they'll let us skip out and get back to work."

Chapter Eight

The wolves snapped and poked their long, hard noses against her skin. They pushed her this way and that between them, playing an evil game. She knew it was a game by the way they grinned, showing huge, glistening fangs. She whimpered, blinded by tears. Deep down under the fear, she was furious for showing the weakness she knew they wanted from her. Sofia hated the animals as much as she feared them, but she hated the helplessness even more. Finally she got up the courage to beat against one's flank, but it took no notice of the blows. The fur was warm and soft, but she was more aware of the hard muscle underneath. These creatures could easily tear her to shreds.

Then a shadow materialized at the head of the alley, and Jason was there and . . .

* * *

Sofia shook her head and the drab motel room came back into focus. They were just dogs, she told her child's memory. Don't be so melodramatic.

And it had been her great-grandfather who appeared at the head of the alley, not some stranger she'd only met today.

The old man had saved her, and he'd died the same night. The exertion had killed him. She still blamed herself.

She didn't blame herself for what happened after that. Oh, no, only her crazy father was responsible for the next tragedy of that horrible day.

Stay, Jason ordered the wolves when he parked in the lot behind the small motel. *I know it's hard to teach a wolf tamer her trade without having the real thing to work with, but this has to be handled delicately. You want her to like you, don't you?*

He wanted Sofia to like them, even if that wasn't really necessary to the training. He wanted his wolf companions to accept the mortal woman as an alpha member of their pack, and the realization that he wanted these emotional commitments shook him. He was fulfilling an obligation with Sofia Hunyara, not looking for permanence, right?

He must be having some sort of weird reaction to the Matri's reading his mind. Maybe Lady Juanita had even put the notion of finding a mortal bondmate into his head to keep his attention away from the Clan female who'd been eyeing him. Whether it was obligation or sexual interest, he was anxious to see Sofia again.

He was all too aware of her presence calling out to him from inside a nearby ground-floor room. Heat raced through him, fueling the urge to be near her.

Gracie gave a jealous snarl and George glared when Jason got out of the SUV, but the wolves settled down as he left them.

He was nearly at the door when once more he found her memories flowing easily into him.

"Go to the hospital. Grigor needs you," Daddy *said. He continued loading the gun she hadn't known he had, while Grandpa stood in the middle of the living room, staring at him.*

They both stared at him, Grandpa's dark skin pale with worry, she barely aware of the aches of the cuts and bruises covering her face and body. She was so cold her teeth chattered. She didn't understand why she was freezing on such a hot day. Her muscles were tense with dread. The things she forced herself to focus on were crystal clear, but everything outside that small circle of reality was fuzzy and full of shadows.

"Why do you have a gun?" she asked.

"What are you going to do?" Grandpa asked.

"Protect my daughter."

Grandpa gestured at the weapon. "You know that isn't our way."

"Those bastards aren't our people. The old ways don't mean a damn thing to me. Go to the hospital," he ordered Grandpa. "Take Sofia with you."

She wasn't going anywhere with Grandpa. Her father was so intent on his own business, he didn't notice when she followed him out of the house.

He went to the motorcycle shop two blocks from their house. Even the local gangbangers had learned to steer clear of the bikers who'd recently started hanging out there. But her father showed no fear when he turned down the back alley and walked into the open garage in the back.

Shaking with dread, Sofia crept along the back of the building and peered cautiously inside the doorway just as the first shot filled the air with noise and the smell of sprayed blood.

She watched three men die, one after another. Then her father took out a knife—

"By the Goddess of the Moon, you are one messed-up woman."

Sofia heard the words, felt the warm strength of the arms surrounding her, and realized she'd been sobbing against Jason's shoulder long enough to get his shirt wet. "I'm not this bad normally," she answered between sniffles. "I've just had a rough day and—"

She pulled away from Jason. For a moment she was totally disoriented. Nothing looked right. The only thing that felt right was . . . him.

Then she realized they were seated on the bed in the room she'd rented for the night. Strangers, in a strange town, at the end of a very, very strange day. It seemed to have somehow gotten stranger still.

"How did you get in here?" she demanded. Somehow, she couldn't question how he'd found her. Having him with her was too disturbingly natural.

"I'm a professional magician. I always carry lock picks." This answer seemed too smooth and pat. She started to protest, but he added, "Can I buy you a cup of coffee?"

She didn't want coffee, but the walls of the room closed in on her like a prison. And the thought of a prison cell conjured up an image she never wanted to think about. Jason Cage's presence was reassuring, steadying, though she didn't understand why. The man claimed to believe in werewolves, for God's sake. And he'd broken into her room. Yet she trusted him.

If anyone was crazy here, it probably wasn't him.

She rose to her feet and held out her hand. "Let's get out of here."

He touched her fingers, and the contact was electric. Heat raced through her when he stood close to her.

"Lust is definitely clouding my judgment."

Had she really said that out loud? His smile was all the answer she needed.

"Let's save the coffee for later," he said, and kissed her.

She'd never needed anything as much as his mouth pressed against hers, devastating and demanding. The need that blazed in her burned away all doubts; sensation took her.

She clutched at him, ran a hand through his thick brown hair. *Such beautiful hair.*

His laughter flowed through her like champagne. *Shouldn't I be saying that to you?*

Your hair's prettier than mine.

His fingers tangled in her thick curls. *Eye of the beholder, darling.*

She wasn't so sure about this *darling* thing, but it sounded good coming from him.

Sound? What sound? Their lips were locked together and their tongues were busily twined around each other.

You're thinking too much. Don't.

The thought was commanding and cajoling at the same time. Then his clever fingers and lips worked magic on her skin.

It was only a step back to the bed, and they fell onto it in a frantic rush to pull off each other's clothes, eager for the touch of skin to skin. She'd never wanted anything as much as to touch and taste every solidly muscled inch of his body. She needed his claiming touch on every inch of her. Nothing had ever felt so right or real, and her body came to life like it never had before.

"I've never thirsted like this before." He spoke in a rough whisper, his lips brushing her ear. The heat of his breath sent shudders through her, as did the touch of his tongue gliding down her throat a moment later.

She suddenly felt sharp teeth pressing against tender skin and closed her eyes, waiting breathlessly. The urgency of his need pounded against her senses. This moment was important, imperative, though she didn't know why or how. Instinct urged her to flee or to submit, and submission was really the only choice. What would come next would be terrifying or wonderful, or both, but she didn't want to run.

You're braver than you think. Braver than I knew. Be mine.

Not a question but a demand.

She opened her eyes and stared into his, saw a soul as lost as her own, on fire with consuming hunger. Then she saw the sharp, bright fangs. Arousal ran through her, far stronger than the instant of fear.

She held on tight. "Yes."

Chapter Nine

Jason hadn't meant for this to happen, hadn't known he needed it to happen. Of course he'd intended to make love to Sofia from the first moment he saw her, but this . . .

I've found you at last.

He hadn't known he'd been searching for a bondmate, but here she was in his arms, his body covering hers, his mouth pressed against her warm, yielding flesh, her heartbeat matching his. Her need matching his.

It terrified him, but it seduced him even more. He couldn't pull back. He couldn't stop. She belonged to him.

And he took her, fangs sinking deep to draw the sweetest blood he'd ever tasted, heaven and honey and fire. Her life filled him, her soul sang in him.

Orgasms rushed through her as he took her blood and slammed through Jason with the force of lightning strikes. Soon his body was demanding more than the taste of her. He needed to be inside her.

He gave her one swift, fierce kiss, sharing the last drop of blood on his tongue with her. Then he knelt over her and she lifted her hips, urging the deep, hard thrust that took him into her. He gasped at the sweet, surrounding heat and moved in a slow building rhythm that brought them both to a long, shattering climax.

Jason rolled onto his back and flung an arm over his eyes.

Oh, Goddess, what have I done?

He had never been more satiated, or hungrier for more of the same. The woman slept beside him, curled against his side. He was all too aware of the pleasure and peace he had brought her.

It made him happy—and worried the hell out of him.

Had this been a normal sexual encounter with a normal mortal, he would be content with the mutual satisfaction they'd shared. The Families weren't out to protect mortals the way their Clan cousins were, but they did believe in fair exchange in all their mortal dealings.

If Lady Juanita was correct—and Matris always were in these matters—Sofia Hunyara was his fated bondmate. Not that he needed the Matri's opinion. He knew in his gut, in his groin, and most of all in his soul that Sofia was his destiny, his completion.

"Damn it all to hell," he complained to the ceiling. "Why now? Why her?"

She belonged to her own people. They needed her whether she knew it or wanted it. It was his duty to make her accept her gift, to train her and—

Let her go.

"You belong to me," he whispered, turning to her and kissing her on the cheek. "Always and forev—"

"What?" She sat up and groggily ran a hand across her face. A flash of fear went through her, and she stared at him for a moment as if she didn't recognize him. Then she said, "Oh, it's you." And yawned.

Jason had never felt more deflated in his life. Here he'd been making a declaration of his undying devotion and she—

"Oh, it's *you*," he repeated sarcastically. "We just had the best sex of our lives and you act as if—"

"How do you know it was the best sex of my life?"

"Believe me, I know."

"Arrogant, aren't you?" She pushed her heavy curls out of her face and grinned at him. "Arrogant with good reason. It *was* the best."

He gave her an acknowledging nod. No Prime could ever be accused of false modesty.

Sofia still didn't know what Jason Cage was doing in her motel room, but she supposed it made about as much sense as everything else that had happened today. Though she wasn't in the habit of going to bed with someone on such short acquaintance, getting all huffy after the fact would be hypocritical. She'd wanted him from the first instant she saw him.

And now she wanted him again. But the question was, now that she'd had him, what was she going to do with him?

Had he actually said something like 'You belong to me' when she'd woken up? If he had, what did he mean by it?

Something in her gut and the back of her brain told her she knew very well what he meant, and that she liked it, but she told it to shut up. She'd lost too many people already to expect any permanence in her life. Giving in to the faint hope of

connection was what had begun this whole crazy
day in the first place.

She got up and went into the bathroom. The
first thing she noticed when she glanced in the
mirror was the love bite on the side of her throat.
She touched it, remembering the delicious pleasure that ran through her along with the slight
pain when he bit her.

What an interesting man, and what interesting
reactions she had to him. Interest like that could
be dangerous—probably *was* dangerous. Maybe
she should tell him to get dressed and get out.

Instead, when she came back into the bedroom
she said, "Didn't you offer to buy me a cup of
coffee?"

"Don't scream."

Sofia froze a step away from Jason's SUV. As
his hand tightened on her arm, a stray breeze en-
hanced the shiver that went up her spine. She was
alone in an empty parking lot with a stranger.

Oh, God, what had she gotten herself into!

What was he going to do to her? What did
he . . . ?

"Don't show any weakness if you want them
to respect you."

"What?"

"They always need to know who's the boss.

They'll keep testing you. It's the pack mentality."

"I have no idea what you're—"

Then she saw the malamutes in the backseat. "Oh."

They raised their huge heads to regard her.

"George and Gracie," Jason said. "Meet Sofia."

She looked back at the animals for a moment, then she glared at the man beside her.

"I do not panic at the mere sight of dogs," she informed him. "What kind of wuss do you take me for? Slavering beasts attacking me tend to put me on edge, but I'm perfectly capable of sharing the planet with man's best friend. Most of the time." She looked at the animals again. Their steady regard wasn't hostile, but it was disturbing. "Let's take my car," she suggested.

"Wuss."

She wasn't going to let this man think she was a coward. "Fine," she grumbled, and let him open the door for her. A cold nose touched the back of her neck as she fastened the seat belt, but she refused to flinch.

Cage noticed. "A point to the lady, Gracie," he said to the animal. "Oh, and they aren't malamutes," he added to Sofia as he put the car in gear. "They're Arctic wolves."

Chapter Ten

"You might have mentioned what those animals were before letting me into the car with them."

"Did they hurt you? No," he answered for her. "And you learned a valuable lesson about self-discipline."

She supposed he was referring to the fact that she hadn't jumped out of the SUV at the first stoplight and run away screaming. She had merely sat in frozen silence until he'd parked and escorted her into the coffee shop. Now, safely seated at a table with a large foamy latte cupped in her hands, she was finally able to voice her objections.

"Do you have a license for those things? Why would anybody want a pet wolf in the first place?

Shouldn't they be locked in a cage instead of—"

"They have a very comfortable traveling pen in the back of the truck," he answered. "But they'd rather be near me, where they can shed in the backseat."

She couldn't help but smile at this. She noticed a few silver hairs on the black jacket he wore over a white shirt. "And on you, too."

He nodded and dusted fingers across the front of his jacket. "Fur is my constant companion. The dry-cleaning bills alone sometimes make me question my choice of profession."

"What is the Beast Master doing in San Diego anyway? Shouldn't you be doing two shows a night in Vegas?" *Bare-chested and in skin-tight pants that show off your package?*

The heated look he gave her made her blush and worry that she'd spoken out loud. "I mean—"

"This started out as a vacation, became an obligation, and now . . ." He shrugged. "It's gotten very complicated—or maybe very simple. I'm not sure yet."

She wondered why she had this almost overwhelming urge to find out everything there was to know about this man. Everything she hadn't learned from looking him up on the Internet, that is. It was an odd compulsion for a loner like herself, but she'd been having odd compulsions since the moment she'd first laid eyes on him.

"If you were really a loner you wouldn't have come when your family called."

Anger shot through her. "They didn't call, they sent an e-mail. And stop reading my mind."

He just smiled. "I'm glad you finally noticed. You're taking it well," he added.

She banged a fist on the table. "You're being insufferable."

He bowed his head contritely before looking up at her through impossibly long lashes. "Smugness is one of my prime traits. I can't help it."

It was hard not to melt at the sight of those big blue eyes, but she tried her best. She sipped her latte and realized that she was very tired. She put the cup down as she fought off a yawn. "It's been a long day."

"And the strangest day of your life?"

Her gaze flashed back to his. "Not by a long shot."

He reached across the small table and took her hands in his. They were big, strong, capable hands, hands that had made love to her not long ago. She wanted them on her again soon, but right now she fought the urge to let his touch be comforting.

"Tell me about that day," he urged in a gentle whisper. "Tell me about you."

She was sure he could have made her tell him anything. Though it was insane, she truly believed he could invade her mind. She didn't know why his power excited her rather than frightened her.

Since he didn't take what he wanted, she decided to tell him. "Well, apparently I come from a family of insane people."

He shook a finger at her. "Facts first. We have a lot to correct about your opinions later."

She frowned but went on. "I'm an American mutt from east L.A. My mom died when I was little. This left me the spoiled only child, and female, in a run-down house with my father, grandfather, and great-grandfather. I guess the family came from someplace in central Europe. My father didn't let my grandfathers discuss it with me. I learned a few words of what I later found out to be a Romany dialect, but I've forgotten them."

"And you weren't curious about finding out more about your ancestry until recently?"

She shook her head. "Until recently I was concentrating on putting some kind of normal life together."

"Survival does tend to take up all of a person's attention when things get rough."

"You sound like you know all about what it's like when life goes down the toilet."

"Oh, I do. But we're concentrating on you right now."

His gaze caressed her, making her go hot all over. It was hard to go on with a sudden spike of lust zinging through her.

Sofia cleared her throat. "We didn't have much, we didn't do much, but it wasn't a bad childhood. I was loved and protected. Even when—"

This time she had to clear her throat because of the sudden welling of pain. She'd long ago stopped crying over the memories, but now her eyes blurred with tears. She ran the back of her hand angrily across her face.

"Then one day my grandfather came home with the news he'd been diagnosed with cancer. That same day, the dogs chased me. My great-grandfather chased them off, then had a heart attack and died."

"Your great-grandfather was Grigor Hunyara?"

"Yes."

"I knew him when he was young."

"*What?*"

"Go on," he urged.

The look in his eyes was too compelling for her not to. "My father—my stupid, idiot, hot-tempered bastard of a father—reacted to all this by going to the garage where the dogs' owners hung out and shooting three men in the head."

She'd watched her father then barbarically cut out his victims' hearts, but she wasn't about to add that gruesome detail to this already lurid tale, no matter how much she wanted to confide in Jason Cage. Some things couldn't be talked about. The pain of thinking about them was still almost unbearable after all these years. She could still see brain matter splattered against dirty gray walls. She could still smell the blood.

The nausea that always welled up in her when she let herself remember churned in her stomach. She tried to control it, but had to run to the bathroom to throw up like she always did.

Jason watched the bathroom door anxiously while Sofia was gone.

I will never again think I've had a hard life, he thought, miserable for her.

Why hadn't anyone told her the truth, he wondered angrily. Why hadn't Pashta told her about her father?

Jason knew why her father had killed those three men. At least, he was almost certain of the reason. Did he have the right to tell Sofia? She certainly wasn't ready to believe him yet.

It couldn't be easy to be mortal in this modern era. So many things that had once been sureties about the supernatural world had been taken away from them. Very few *believed* anymore, even fewer *knew*. His kind had helped push the changes to the mortal psyche, triggered by the scientific age. Scientific discovery had benefited everyone, vampires perhaps even more than mortals. Because of science, his kind could now live in the daylight, and because no one believed in them, they could hide in plain sight as long as they were careful and circumspect.

But it also made it very difficult to explain reality to those who had a need to know, he thought as Sofia returned from the washroom.

"Better?" he asked, and handed her a cup of mint tea he'd ordered while she was gone. "This will help."

She took a sip, breathed in the scented steam, and sighed. "Thank you."

He very nearly melted from her grateful look. Jason wanted to tell her then and there that he would do anything to comfort her, to protect her, to give her pleasure. She had him.

Why the hell did her people have to need her now, when all he wanted was her?

"What happened next?" he asked. "After your father—"

"He took a plea bargain and went to prison instead of getting a needle in the arm." Her dark gaze flashed fiery anger. "He got better than he deserved."

"Aren't you being a bit harsh on your own—"

"Why do you want to know, anyway?" Her fingers clamped tightly around the cup.

"Your family lost track of you. I was wondering how that happened."

"My father went to prison. My grandfather died two months after being diagnosed. I ended up in foster care."

"That had to have been unpleasant."

She smiled at his dry tone. "Understatement's a gift with you, isn't it? I got lucky eventually," she went on. "I eventually ended up living with a retired Navy SEAL and his family. I joined the navy when I finished high school, and spent the last six years mostly on sea duty and reading books. Now I'm a civilian, I'm going to college, and for no good reason I'm using my spring break to meet up with a bunch that claim to be relatives— and turn out to be crazier than my murdering old man." She folded her hands together on the tabletop. "How about you, Jason Cage? Where do you come from? What is there to know that I didn't find out about from your Beast Master website? How did you end up on the other side of this conversation? *Why* did you end up in this conversation?"

He pried her hands away from the cup and took them in his again. "At first I didn't want to be here. Now I can't imagine being anywhere else."

Chapter Eleven

Sofia snorted rudely. The fact that he sounded serious scared her to death. When he looked offended, she couldn't help but laugh. "I don't need romantic drivel," she told him, then ducked her head. "But that did sound—nice."

"I see," he said. "You tell yourself that you don't need what you want."

"I learned early that it's not wise to harbor expectations. And so far, this trip to meet the family has been a complete waste. Even my cousin Cathy isn't answering her phone or e-mail, so I probably won't get to see her while I'm in the area."

"Complete waste of time? How can you say that after meeting me?" He gave her a teasing smile. "You wound me. Ah, I've made you smile. I don't suppose suggesting your uncle Pashta would like to see you would do the same."

"You'd be right."

"I'm glad. This way I get to have you all to myself."

She wasn't sure what he meant by "this way," but the incident at the creepy house swirled around in confusing images in her head. "Let's not talk about it."

"All right," he said. "We don't have to talk about it."

He definitely meant something by that, but Sofia let it go. She couldn't stop the yawn that suddenly reminded her that it had been a hell of a long day. Let's see, travel, trauma, treachery, and great sex. Yep, she had every reason to be this tired.

"I have to go to bed. To sleep," she added at the sparkle in his bright blue eyes. When they rose to leave, she said, "I'll walk. It's only a block back to the motel."

"George and Gracie won't like being deprived of your company."

"I'm not interested in spoiling your pet wolves."

His arm came around her waist as they stepped outside. "That's a very good attitude. You always have to be the one in control. However, never make the mistake of thinking that a wild animal is your property."

This was doubtless good advice from a man who made his living sharing a stage with tigers, even if she wasn't ever going to need it. "Thanks. You're not planning on saying good night when we get to your truck, are you?"

"A gentleman always walks a lady home."

She couldn't bring herself to object, even though it scared her to feel so secure in his embrace. His warm touch fended off the cool evening air. Maybe it wasn't permanent, but being with him felt nice for now.

They stopped in front of her motel door. When he turned her toward him, she expected him to kiss her. Instead, he looked her in the eye and said, "There are things I have to tell you."

Annoyance shot through her. "I said I didn't want to talk—"

He touched her cheek. "We aren't going to talk."

"The Nazis treat the Romany the same way they treat the Jews. They send captured Rom to their death camps."

"I know," Jason answered Grigor. If he hadn't tried to help some Romany friends, he wouldn't be a fugitive from his own kind.

"*They have scientists in those camps who conduct horrible experiments on the prisoners.*"

"*So I've heard.*"

"*One of these torturers discovered the Hunyara secret. They decided that a racially degenerate characteristic is responsible for turning us into beasts. They despise us, but they're eager to exploit us. Now the Nazis are hunting the Hunyara and taking them to a very secret camp. They're trying to make werewolves they can control and use. At first, they used other prisoners to find out how the curse is transmitted. They caged them with our werefolk during the moon madness. Now they have soldiers volunteering to be bitten.*" He laughed bitterly. "*Can you imagine the damage an army of Aryan werewolves could do?*"

Jason had no trouble imagining the bloody havoc it could cause. "*This has to be stopped.*"

"*We must rescue our people and the other Rom they've infected,*" Grigor agreed. "*But there are too many newly made werewolves for me and my father to tame.*"

Much more than simply rescuing the werewolves needed to be done. The whole operation had to be obliterated—no evidence, no Nazi survivors. He needed to tell somebody in authority about these experiments, before all supernatural *beings were discovered and targeted. But he was a fugitive with no one he could turn to.*

It looked like he and a small band of Romany were going to have to save the world all by themselves.

"We did it before; now we have to do it again."

Sofia heard Jason's voice as though from a long distance away. What he said made no more sense than the minimovie that had been running in her head.

She blinked and found herself standing outside her motel room door. She could make out the parking lot past Jason's wide shoulders. There were streetlights, and a little traffic. She was in San Diego, not Nazi Europe.

She focused on Jason Cage. "How do you do that?" she demanded.

He kissed her on the forehead. "Think about what I just showed you. Think about it happening again, here and now. And that your missing cousin might be in danger."

"But—"

The next thing Sofia knew, she was inside her room with the door closed behind her. He was gone, she was alone—lonely and confused—and wondering which one of them was actually crazy.

Chapter Twelve

"Show me."

Smiling, Jason took her hands. "Just remember that you're the one who came to me in your sleep. I don't want you pissed off at me when you wake up."

Sofia wasn't sure where she was or how she'd gotten here, but she was certain that here was the right place to be. "I had to find you. My gut tells me—"

"Your awakening psychic ability tells you."

"—that this is all true. Cathy needs my help. I need your help. She's in danger, and it has something to do with werewolves."

"I do believe you are correct, my darling. What does your cousin know about werewolves?"

"Pashta said that he tried to get hold of both of

us to explain our heritage. She knows less about our Romany background than I do. We never discussed werewolves in our e-mails, but—"

The world twisted and changed before she could finish.

"Dreamscapes," she complained upon suddenly finding herself standing among a group of people in a fire-lit cave.

Jason stood in front of the group. He seemed younger. He was pale and thin to the point of gauntness, all cheekbones and shadows and burning blue eyes. The people around her were thin as well, their clothes threadbare and hopelessly old-fashioned. There was something familiar about each face she saw in the flickering light.

"Your people," Jason said. No one seemed to hear him but her.

She realized she was somewhere long ago, when her great-grandfather was that tall, grave man to her left, and her grandfather was the strikingly handsome teenager beside him.

"You're giving me a past I never knew I had," she said to Jason.

"Yes, but that's not why we're here."

"Why are we here?"

"To save the world from Nazi werewolves. Your attention, please," he said to all of them.

She'd been through basic training; she knew when to listen to a drill instructor.

"Somewhere deep inside every moonchanged creature there is a human mind. If you think you should feel compassion for them, then you are dead wrong. Or, I should say, you will be dead. Show anything but strength and dominance and you will rightfully end up with your throat ripped out."

"How can you *know* this?" the youthful version of her grandfather asked.

"Do you think my kind start out as sane and reasonable beings?" Jason shook his head. "Our males go mad when we come of age. We crave violence, blood, and females. We live to hunt. We seek out combat. We delight in fighting our brothers until the strong win and the weak die. Civilization has to be imposed on us with a will and hand of iron. The moonchanged are no different than our young." He smiled. "Except that they are easier to control."

One of her relatives snorted cynically and spoke up. "Teach your revered granny to suck blood, Prime."

"Right. You guys already know how to control crazy werewolves." Jason turned his intense blue gaze on her. "But you don't."

The world rippled and changed again; she and

Jason remained the only constant things in it. The link that bound them together circled around and through them. It filled her with bright hot sparks that pooled in her heart and her soul and set her insides ablaze.

"That feels—wonderful," she told him.

He held her close. "I know. But it's not helping."

"Depends on what you want to help." She traced her fingers up his back and through his hair. "You feel so good." Sofia touched her tongue to the base of his throat. "You taste good."

"Sweetheart, you have no idea how good I taste, but I promise sometime soon, you will. I want you," he told her. "All of you, body and soul—but right now it's your mind I need to pay attention to me."

"Isn't this attention enough?" She continued to kiss a line across his throat and felt the pulse racing beneath his skin.

He made a small, needy sound that triggered the strangest urge to sink her teeth into his neck. Animals growled behind her before she could give in to the impulse.

Sofia glanced back to see the snarling George and Gracie. "Shoo," she commanded them. "Who invited you into this dream?"

"I did."

"I'm not getting naked in front of your mutts," she informed him.

"It's nice to have your attention back on business."

Before she could ask him what he meant, the world changed again.

Damn it, I wish you'd stop doing that! she thought.

"Pay attention," he replied.

From that point on, the concept of words disappeared altogether.

"You do realize that you're in a lot of trouble, don't you?" Cathy Carter asked the younger of her captors.

She sneezed as she finished speaking, which lessened her statement's dramatic impact. She was having a terrible allergic reaction to whatever they were spraying on her and themselves.

The beefy teenager laughed, but she sensed his unease. He looked toward the locked door. "I'm not supposed to talk to you."

She'd been working on this one's fear from the moment she'd been kidnapped. "Then listen, and remember that this is not a threat. It's not long until the full moon. Come the change, you are going to get your throat ripped out."

He sneered. "Not by you."

She could feel the moon madness creeping closer to the surface. A taste for blood was starting to burn the back of her throat. She licked her lips and fought back the anticipation.

"Maybe it won't be me," she agreed with him. "But your pack is still going to die."

Handcuffs fastened her to a chair. The chair was inside a sturdy cage. The cage was in a warehouse that also contained trucks, vans, and motorcycles. She'd woken up in the cage after a trio of ferals snatched her outside her apartment building as she was leaving for work. Her captors had been coming and going all day, mostly ignoring her except for the kid they'd left to guard her. She didn't know how many of them there were, and it bothered her that they seemed to be getting ready to leave town.

She hoped the Bleythins showed up to save her soon, or that she figured a way out of here herself. Wherever the bad guys were going, she didn't want to go with them.

"When my pack—"

"You don't know anything about *your* pack!" the boy shouted. "We're your real family."

His reaction startled her. Surely the blond biker types she'd seen coming and going all day weren't the Romany relatives she and Sofia had been exchanging e-mails about? This bunch had a kind of Aryan Nation vibe going for them. Several of them sported shaved heads and swastika tattoos, one of them on his forehead à la Charles Manson. Creepy.

"You're not my family," she said.

"You're a werewolf just like us," he snarled.

"That will do."

Cathy shifted her attention to the man who had spoken. She hadn't seen him before, but she knew a pack alpha when she saw one. Instinct told her to avert her eyes and submit to his least whim, but she wasn't about to give in to instinct.

"That's right," he said, stepping forward and looking deep into her eyes. "The moon doesn't control you yet."

Cathy was furious at the heat that shot through her. "Who are you?" she demanded.

"Your destiny."

She made a gagging sound.

He laughed. "Call me Eric. I've been searching for you for a long time."

"And why is that?"

"Because we are meant to be together, Catherine, my love. I'm the reason you are what you are. It was because of me that you were turned."

Hatred seethed through her, along with complete disbelief. "The feral that turned me is dead."

Eric nodded. "He was a good friend and a

loyal follower. His sacrifice is greatly appreciated."

This was sick and weird, and sent a chill through her. "Sacrifice?"

Eric smiled at her gently, but the look in his eyes was possessive. "There's so much you have to learn about our kind. It's important to know that incest is taboo. We never mate with one that we have turned. I wanted you above all others, so a friend brought you into the pack."

Cathy's free hand flew to her throat, to the spot where she could still feel hot breath and sharp teeth sinking into her flesh. She remembered bright gold eyes, soft fur, and a heavy body pinning her down. She'd thought the wolf was going to kill her, but what had happened had been infinitely worse.

At least for a while.

Mike Bleythin had rescued her, from the terror and from the moon madness. He'd given her a pack, and protection. She still couldn't control the monthly transformation into a beast, but at least she no longer dreaded the change quite so much.

She focused every bit of hatred she could summon on the smiling Eric. "You *deliberately* forced me to become a werewolf?" He nodded. "You bastard."

He shrugged. "We should have been mated a long time ago, but the natural-born Tracker interfered with my plans for you. Now we only need one more thing before we can abandon this stinking mortal world and return to the wild, where we belong."

Cathy had no intention of running off to live in the woods like an animal. She had to find out all she could, think of a plan. "What thing do you need?" she asked.

"Your cousin Sofia, of course. Once she's turned as well, we'll have both of the Hunyara females bearing our offspring. You can't imagine the strength that will bring to the pack."

She didn't want to imagine it. She wanted to be sick. Even more than that, she wanted to rip out this smug asshole's throat.

Chapter Thirteen

"Who would have guessed Cathy had a secret life?" Sid commented as she peered over Eden's shoulder at the computer screen. Eden had easily cracked the security on Cathy's laptop and now they were sitting at her kitchen table going through her e-mail.

"You're not referring to the secret life where she's a werewolf, are you?" Eden responded.

"That secret life isn't secret from us," Sid pointed out. "But we didn't know about Cathy's having a family."

"We all come from somewhere—with baggage," Eden said.

Sid nodded. "You speak truly, my sister. But Cathy has never talked about where she came from before Mike saved her from the feral that turned her. It's strange to find out that she's kept up with her relatives. I thought we were her family," Sid added a bit forlornly.

"Maybe you should think of Cathy as a little sister who hid her diary from you. We all need privacy, werefolk and vampires even more than mortals." Eden gave Sid a very discerning look. "We all have secrets. Some more dangerous than others."

Sid knew that Eden wasn't at all psychic, but she was far from stupid or unobservant, and all the vampires, werewolves, and mortals at the firm's office spent a lot of time interacting with one another.

"I have no secrets," she said as lightly as she could.

"Oh, no, a daughter of the Wolf Clan like yourself is too noble and forthright to ever scheme, lie, conspire, or connive to get exactly what you want, while denying yourself the one thing you don't think you can have."

"There are a lot of things I know I can't have. Vampire females have to tread very carefully and you know it."

"And yet, you are a career woman with all the perks of a Prime—in most things."

"In most things," Sid echoed hollowly. "And I shall continue to scheme, conspire, and connive to get what I want—for all the good it will do me in the long run."

Eden shook her head. "You don't have to be a prisoner of your gender."

"For the sake of the continuation of the species, and the honor of my Clan, in the end, I will be. I'm just trying to put off the inevitable as long as I can."

"And you'd never openly rebel?"

"You know I won't."

"You Clan folk are such hopeless, selfless romantics. Not that I'm complaining," Eden went on before Sid could argue. "If you hadn't decided to go searching for your long-lost brother, neither he nor I would have ended up as part of the Bleythin-Wolf menagerie. He was terrible at being a villain and I made a lousy vampire hunter, so Laurent and I have a lot to thank you for. You and Joe, and Mike and Harry and Marj and Daniel, and Cathy, our lost feral sister."

Sid noticed the slight emphasis Eden put on Joe Bleythin's name, and her heart pricked just a little with knowing that here was one more person who shared the knowledge Sid could never share with him.

"Let's concentrate on Cathy." She firmly called their attention back to the far more important subject. "Read on."

Eden opened up another saved message in the Sofia file, but Daniel Corbett came into the kitchen before Sid could read the e-mail.

"See anything?" Sid and Eden both asked.

He blinked from behind his glasses and ran a hand through unkempt blond hair. They'd left him sitting in Cathy's bedroom doing his psychic thing while they searched the computer.

"I doubt it," Daniel answered. "I'm not sure if what I caught was glimpses of the past, or scenes from a horror movie set in World War II." He scratched his jaw, where faint stubble of a beard showed how long he'd been up. "Somehow I don't think Cathy's disappearance has anything to do with rescuing gypsy werewolves from evil Nazi scientists."

Sid looked at her retro-psychic mortal cousin in disbelief. "What did you eat before going into your trance?"

"My gift's obviously no use this time," he said. "I think I'll see if Joe and Mike need help. Has Laurent picked up any news from his sources?"

It sometimes came in handy that Laurent Wolf had not always walked on the good-guy side of vampirekind. He knew a lot of dubious characters out on the streets who wouldn't talk to anyone else at the Bleythin agency.

Sid tapped a finger on her forehead and held up a cell phone. "Not a word so far."

Eden sighed, in the way of a female missing her bondmate. "I really hate not going along for backup when he's dealing with scum."

"I'm sure he wishes you were there, too," Sid said.

Laurent was probably the only living Prime who didn't object to having a mortal female as a fighting partner. Eden and her brother were definitely the black sheep of the Wolf Clan.

"Try checking for temporal connections at the office again," Sid suggested to Daniel. "You might have more luck without the rest of us around contributing psychic white noise."

He nodded and left. This time her cell phone rang before she could read the e-mail. It was Joe.

"Still not a trace of a scent," he reported.

"Could a vampire be involved?" Sid asked her werewolf partner. "You know how we can mess up your sensing."

"What would a vampire want with a werewolf?"

What indeed? "I have no idea. But there was a Family Prime at Lady Juanita's tonight. I've got a feeling he's involved in this somehow."

"But what *is* this?"

"I don't know. But my senses tell me that there's somebody out there who wants Cathy for a really evil reason."

Joe growled. "You think it's this vampire?"

"I think he's involved, but I don't know why. Not yet."

"It's best to let vampires handle vampires," Joe said. "Mike and I will keep looking for the werewolf connection."

Eden gave Sid a skeptical look when she put the phone down. "I was under the impression you liked this Cage guy."

"I like his genetic potential," Sid answered. "That's not the same thing."

Finally, as dawn neared, she started reading Cathy's e-mail correspondence.

Chapter Fourteen

$\mathcal{T}$o save the world from Nazi werewolves," Sofia murmured as she woke up from the long and complicated dream.

How did the subconscious come up with stuff like that? She chuckled and stretched out along the comfortably warm length of the man in the bed beside her.

The man in the bed beside her?

Wait a minute.

Her head rested on a bare shoulder, and an equally bare arm was wrapped protectively around her. When she opened her eyes she saw Jason Cage, and for a moment joy flooded through her.

Then she recalled that she'd gone to bed alone and sat bolt upright. "What the hell are you doing here?"

He opened one eye and grumbled, "Trying to sleep."

She didn't remember him arriving in her room. She knew she hadn't answered a knock on the door and let him in. Yet, she had the impression of having welcomed him into her . . .

Into her what?

Sofia rubbed her temples. Her mind felt stretched, and different. There was a lot of jumbled-up information swimming around in there and—

"You'll have a migraine if you try to make your conscious mind straighten it all out."

"Confusion seems to be turning into the normal state of things, and I don't like it," she told him.

"I don't blame you. But let it go. Relax." His deep voice was oh so soothing.

He sat up and began to knead her tense shoulders with his strong fingers. She couldn't help but close her eyes and lean back into the pressure.

"What am I going to do with you?" she asked. "I didn't ask you to be here. I don't know how you got here. I—"

"Don't want me to be anywhere else," he finished for her.

His hands moved down to cup her breasts and her nipples went instantly hard against his palms.

As desire pulsed through her, Sofia knew she couldn't argue with what he'd said.

Making love made more sense than the sorts of conversations they had, anyway.

She turned in his arms and drew his mouth down to hers. Her tongue explored and grazed across sharp canines. For a moment she tasted the metallic tang of her own blood, bringing her to the brink of orgasm. Then his hands on her took her over the edge.

He'd known he couldn't keep from making love to Sofia again, but he'd sworn that he'd keep from tasting her. That promise flew right out the window when he accidentally drew blood merely with a kiss. Her pleasure resonated through him. He'd never known a sharing of desire and fulfillment to match this. He needed more. To give her more, to take more.

I want you in every way. Want me. Need me.

Only you, was her answer.

He tasted her all over then, a drop from each soft breast, from her warm, pulsing throat and each wrist, her belly and the inside of each thigh. His tongue worked magic, soothing and caressing each place where he marked her as his. She panted and writhed as orgasms burned through her blood, and he tasted them on his tongue.

* * *

What was the man doing to her? How could anything feel so good? She clutched at him and clawed and begged for more, though she didn't know how there could possibly *be* more sensation.

Then he came inside her and she rose to meet every hard, fast thrust. Orgasms rippled through her, but—

More!

In response to desperate need, she lifted her head and bit down hard on his shoulder until the taste of molten pleasure filled her.

Jason shouted as her teeth sank into his skin. His body stiffened, and as he came, Sofia went with him, the explosive force of pleasure taking them down into the dark together.

"You bit me," he accused, and moaned. "I really wish you hadn't bitten me."

Sofia became slowly aware of the voice that whispered in her ear and slowly processed what Jason had said. It took her a bit longer to assess her surroundings. Their arms and legs were all tangled together. Pleasant aches and aftershocks pulsed through her. She was sticky with sweat, and thoroughly happy.

She didn't remember many of the details of

what they'd done, but that one, she did recall.

"You bit me first," she defended herself.

"It's all right for me to—"

"You *bit* me!" She untangled herself from his embrace and sprang out of bed. She clapped a hand over a spot on her bare breast.

He sat up on his elbows and stared at her. "Yes?"

"You said that people became werewolves by being bit. Am I going to turn into a werewolf?"

"I'm not a werewolf."

Relief flooded her for a moment.

Then he added, "I can't even turn you into a vampire. It doesn't work that way."

She stared at him in shocked disbelief for a moment, then she threw back her head and laughed. "Oh, you had me going for a minute. I'd almost started to believe this werewolf stuff." She looked at him and sternly shook a finger. "Let's not add vampires to your weird tales, okay?"

His expression turned guarded, and it took him a while to answer. "Okay."

She became aware that a sexy naked man was in her bed, he was staring at her, and that she was just as naked as he was. How did this keep happening? It had to stop. Okay, he was great in bed, but the guy was crazy, and increasingly making her think she was. If she wanted to deal with crazy people, she could return to her relatives' desert lair.

She glanced at the clock on the bedside table, then edged toward the bathroom. "I would like you to leave now."

He touched his shoulder, drawing her gaze to beautiful, bare skin. "You bit me."

"I'm sorry."

"I'm not."

There was something very important going on here, important for *them*, but she wouldn't let curiosity get in the way of her sanity. There was no *them*.

"Please leave, Jason. There's somewhere I have to be. Something I need to do."

"You're going to go looking for Cathy. You need my help."

He was wrong about her needing him. She couldn't afford to let herself need anyone.

"Please leave," she repeated, and walked into the bathroom, locking the door behind her.

Chapter Fifteen

Jason stood up and stretched and considered where to go from here. His lady had asked him to leave. Honoring her wishes would be the chivalrous thing to do.

"Screw that," he muttered.

He heard the shower go on, and within moments her scent came to him on a warm current of air. He got up and went into the bathroom.

She spun around when he joined her in the shower, and he had to grab her around the waist to keep her from falling. Her eyes went wide and she opened her mouth, but he didn't give her time to speak.

"Meeting one's bondmate is supposed to be a joyous but fairly simple stage of life. It's supposed to go down like this: True lovers look into each other's eyes, recognize kindred souls, share blood and sex, and settle down to live happily ever after," Jason informed the woman who had been born to be his.

"Say what?"

"The Prime involved shouldn't have to have obligations to the female's family that could keep her from him, but that's how our story goes."

"Our story?"

He cupped her wet face in his hands. He wanted to kiss her, but he had too much to get off his chest first. "The female half of the bond shouldn't be so prickly and terrified of trusting anyone."

"Are you talking about me?"

"I'm talking about us."

"There isn't any—"

"Let me finish. When you bond with a Prime, you're supposed to instinctively recognize your true love—that would be me. I recognize you. And I think you recognize me."

"But—"

"There sure as hell aren't supposed to be were-wolves involved."

"You're a nutjob," she told him. "Please get out of this shower."

Despite her words, he knew she wanted to believe him.

Her instincts just need a little kick-starting. Or maybe she and I need to concentrate on us, instead of her family's problems.

Except that her family's problems could easily turn into deep, dark problems for the supernatural world, and the wider mortal world as well. If there was a pack of feral werewolves out there, bodies were going to start turning up in growing numbers. It was going to take as many wolf tamers as they could find. Which meant he had to train Sofia as quickly as possible without letting romance get in the way.

"I shouldn't be talking like this," he said.

"Like a crazy person?"

"You didn't think I was crazy last night. And I'm not talking about the sex," he assured her. "Those weren't dreams. I was teaching you, sharing knowledge."

A spike of fear ran through her. "You really were in my head?" Anger followed the fear. "How dare you?"

"Because you and I cannot let it happen again."

"Let *what* happen again?" Her shout rose above the rushing water in the shower.

Jason reached around her to turn off the faucet. When she tried to dodge past him he picked her up and carried her back to the bed, even though they were both soaking wet. He held her close while she struggled futilely. When she started to scream, he stopped it with a kiss. She both responded and rebelled, her lips clinging to his while she still tried to strike at him. He rolled her onto her back and held her down until she stopped struggling, at least physically.

The only excuse he could give himself for his behavior was that she had asked for his help and she was going to get it, no matter how much she fought against it.

It's so much easier to deal with tigers than stubborn mortals.

Her mental reply was so profane that he threatened to wash her brain out with soap. The woman swore like a sailor.

I was a sailor.

For some reason this struck her as funny, and her amusement rippled through her and into him. The feeling was almost as delicious as lust, but he forced himself to ignore the urge to explore this connection any deeper. He already knew she was the right mate for him. Why delve deeper into the bond now when any hope of having a future together might be futile?

Do you want to help your cousin? he asked.

You know I told you I do. I remember now, what happened in our dream. You taught me something dark.

How to harness the dark.

How did you—?

Lesson time again, Jason interrupted. *Watch. Learn. Come play with me if you can.*

Sofia knew a challenge when she heard one.

I don't play games, she told him.

No?

She knew he was aware of the eagerness coursing through her that gave the lie to her words. It amused him, but not as much as it surprised her. She had never been interested in competition before encountering Jason. What was this man bringing out in her?

Are life and death stakes enough for you? he asked.

Are there any other kind? she replied.

Then come with me.

It was dark here in the forest, and cold. She looked up at a sky full of stars, and the huge full moon terrified her. She reached out and Jason's hand closed comfortingly around hers.

"This is not a good idea," she said.

"I agree," he answered.

"Then why go tonight," Grigor asked, "when they're all moonchanged?"

"None of us are werefolk," Jason explained.

"It's easier for us to recognize them in wolf form."

"It's going to be bloody," Grigor complained.

Jason's eyes lit with anticipation and he gave a dangerous grin. His voice was a silky purr. "Oh, yes."

Sofia had never been so turned on in her life.

They stood in woods at the top of a hill. The camp was in the center of the valley below. Wolves howled inside the fenced compound and stalked along the fence line. Soldiers stood at the gate and inside the watchtowers on the four corners of the site. The cleared ground surrounding the place was brightly lit by the moon. Anyone approaching would be an easy target.

"The beasts know we're here," Grigor said. "But they can't tell the Germans."

"The racket the wolves are making tells them something's up," Sofia said. "I wonder if they're going to let the monsters loose to hunt us?"

"That would be fun," Jason said. "For us, not the beasts," he added when she gave him a skeptical look. "But the Germans won't risk letting their prize experimental weapons loose on the world until they're sure they can control them."

"Those experimental weapons are people!" Sofia complained.

"Most of the time," Grigor said.

"Let's go get them and see what we can do with them," Jason said. "Wait here while I take out the guards."

He gave her a swift kiss, then he was gone.

Despite the bright light, all she could make out was a blur of movement. Then she saw men go down and she knew they wouldn't be getting up again. Sofia's heart twisted at knowing Jason was a killer, but necessity kept her from dwelling on it.

A muffled scream came from one of the guard towers. Jason appeared at the tower opening as the sound died, and waved. She imagined that the shadows around his mouth were blood.

"Let's go," Grigor said.

He loped down the hillside, and she followed.

Deadly danger lurked inside, but Sofia didn't hesitate. She kept repeating to herself that the beasts were people and they needed her help. Knowing this helped fight off the fear.

Until she saw the huge furred bodies, the snarling muzzles, and glowing eyes of the creatures she'd come to save. They surrounded her, trapping her between the fence and the wall of a building.

They didn't want to be saved. They wanted to feed.

"Oh, crap."

You know how to do this, *she told herself as she was backed against a rough wooden wall. She saw the malevolence in their eyes. Hot breath steamed in the air; the stench of it blew across her skin and burned in her nostrils.*

She wanted to scream, but knowing the beasts relished her fear kept her quiet.

Take power over them, *she remembered Jason telling her.* You have to be in control. Look them in the eye until you make them yield.

Since she couldn't flee, she had to fight. The beasts were mindless killing machines armed with fangs and claws and thick, heavy muscles. All she had was her mind, which Jason assured her was enough.

Believe in me, *his voice whispered from far away.* Believe in yourself.

With no other choice, and no other armor, Sofia glared around the circle of approaching monsters. Her heart hammered in her chest and her knees threatened to buckle, but she couldn't let any fear show. These creatures accepted only strength. She had to be stronger than they were, in her heart and in her soul.

She put all of her will into looking at the beasts, not just at them but into them. Madness batted at her senses, wildness as sharp as claws ripped at her sanity. She knew their lust to taste her flesh and blood and threw it back at them, shaped into defiance and scorn. Who were they to think they could kill her?

"I am alpha here!"

She said it aloud, and into the werewolves' perceptions as well.

One of the werewolves lay down and rolled onto its back. A second one sat on its haunches. But a third one, the largest and fiercest, growled and took a menacing step forward. Another rushed from the side to nip at her leg.

The pair of them distracted her enough to break the hold she had on the others.

When they rushed toward her as a pack, panic took over and all she could do was scream.

Chapter Sixteen

*I*t's all right. It's all right, sweetheart. You know I would never let anything hurt you."

"You were going to let them kill me!"

Jason held Sofia close and rocked her while she sobbed. She clung to him so tightly her nails bit into his shoulders, even though vampire skin was tougher than mortals'. He didn't mind the pain. He did mind her accusation.

"You have to do this on your own," he told her. "You have to have confidence in your abilities. You were doing fine."

"They were going to kill me! They always try to kill me!"

"You are getting the hang of how to control the beasts. You have to believe that you can save yourself."

She lifted her face to look at him, and the look in her eyes tore his heart, touching every primal, protective fiber of his being. The connection and desire that rushed through them when their lips met could not be denied.

He soothed her with kisses, and long, lingering caresses. Her fingers moved over him frantically, bringing fire wherever they touched.

"I want to build it slowly for you, let pleasure wipe away the fear," he told her, kissing her navel and then moving down to her clit. It was already swollen and moist.

She gasped and arched against his mouth. "No!" Her hips lifted insistently. "Now!"

Possessive delight went through Jason, heightening desire into a storm. "Happy to oblige your every wish, my lady."

Everything came down to the need to make love to her. Everything came down to becoming one with her.

He moved onto his knees and she guided him inside. He took a moment's pleasure at being sheathed within her soft heat before settling into hard, swift strokes. Her cries of pleasure drove him into a wild frenzy.

Sensation, pure explosive waves of it—it was all she wanted or needed for the longest time.

Sofia didn't know how long it was before she fell back into the real world, if indeed that was where she actually was when she finally opened her eyes. She saw a plain white ceiling above her, felt the bedding beneath her. Jason Cage was lying on top of her, and nothing had ever felt so right or natural against her skin as he did.

Amazing.

Fantastic, was his reply.

This time she didn't doubt for a second that he spoke inside her head. He began to stroke her breasts and tease her nipples, which distracted her for a while.

Is all we think about sex? she finally asked, not bothering to speak aloud either.

At least you included us both in the question.

But there are other things. Important things. We're being selfish.

We're bonding. The instinct tries to drive out everything else.

Well, tell it to stop.

Why do you think it's called an instinct?

We should be able to control it.

The way you're able to control werewolves?

Not fair!

She pushed his shoulder and he rolled onto his back. Sofia sat up, bunching the sheet around her, and looked down at the glorious man in her bed. It was *her* bed.

"I distinctly remember asking you to leave." It seemed like hours ago. She glanced at the bedside clock. It had only been a few minutes. "Didn't we just make long, lingering passionate love?"

With a smug smile, Jason propped his hands behind his head. "It's all subjective, isn't it?"

Sofia thought back over everything she'd experienced—in the last few minutes. "It really happened, didn't it? My great-grandfather was there, only no older than I am, and you, and me." She ran a hand over her suddenly aching forehead. "I was with you when you raided the German prison camp."

He reached out and took her hand. He kissed her palm, then answered, "Yes. The rescue mission really happened, and Grigor and I were successful, though that was only the beginning. This time I brought you along as a training exercise, and to show you what we might be up against again."

She was beginning to believe him, despite how crazy it all sounded. It was other aspects of their telepathic sharing that disturbed her. "It actually happened—sixty years ago."

"Over sixty."

"How old are you?"

"Obviously over sixty." He flashed a bright white smile at her. "Well preserved, aren't I?"

She wasn't susceptible to his snarky charm at the moment. In fact, she found him irritating, and disturbing. "You killed a lot of people that night."

He sat up and turned serious. "There was a war on, Sofia. You have a military background; you should understand the necessities of war."

Maybe she should, but she never had. "I joined the navy to pay for my education. I served on an aircraft carrier, but nowhere near the flight deck where all the testosterone flowed. I don't understand killing."

He touched her cheek. "Yes, you do."

She jerked away. "You enjoyed killing. I could feel it."

He looked at her intently, his gaze boring into her soul. "What did you feel?"

She closed her eyes and the sensations all came back. "Darkness running through you like a rushing river threatening to flood. Blood—not bloodlust, but . . . a craving, a craving for human blood."

"That is part of my nature."

"I don't understand. You said you're not a werewolf. What are—"

"What I was at the time was arrogant but

idealistic. The craving was also stronger then; I wasn't as much in control." Jason shrugged. "I was very young during that war."

She could accept that Jason had psychic powers, but she couldn't deal with the fact that he liked killing people. She knew she should fear him, but even knowing what she knew about him, her attraction to him was as strong as ever. What kind of sick fool was she? Just how badly had watching her father murder three men warped her?

"About your father," he said suddenly.

"Stop reading my mind!"

"I can't really help it," he answered. "I'm not influencing your thoughts," he added hastily, "but I am using telepathy to teach you."

"I know that," she snapped back.

He smiled at her annoyance. "You trust me."

It was probably stupid of her, but for some reason she did. "I don't think you'd abuse your power."

"Not now," he said. "Not ever again, but I have to tell you that I did once. And I was deservedly punished for it. That's why I want to talk about your father—because I understand his situation."

"You don't understand *anything* about my father."

"I know it hurts you to think about him. I don't want to hurt you, but—"

"Then shut up about it."

"You mean about *him*. You don't know how lonely his life is, how hopeless. But I've been in prison; I do know what—"

"Damn it, you're a criminal, too?"

She most definitely did not need a man like this in her life. There was nothing a violent ex-con could teach her. Nothing she wanted from him.

Except sex. God, what the man did to her in bed!

But she could and would live without it. The important thing was finding her cousin, making sure Cathy was safe. She certainly wasn't going to introduce a psychic psychotic werewolf hunter to her nice cousin Cathy.

"Get out," she said. "I mean it this time."

"You meant it the last time," he reminded her. He didn't look like he was going to budge.

She sneered. "What about all that 'happy to oblige your every wish'? Or does that only apply to sex?"

He looked very much like he wanted to argue with her. Anger crackled from him, and for a moment she felt vulnerable and scared.

Then he sighed and got out of bed. "All right, I'll go."

Once he said it, every fiber of her being ached for him to stay. The thought of losing him devastated her, but Sofia fought off this crazy reaction and bit her tongue. She turned her back on him as he dressed. She stared at the wall until she heard the motel room door close behind him. She wanted to run after him and beg him to come back, but she reminded herself that it was better for her to be alone.

Once she got herself under control, she picked up her cell phone and tried dialing Cathy's cell phone one more time.

Chapter Seventeen

ho are you people?" Cathy demanded. "Other than feral werewolves, I mean?"

Eric laughed arrogantly as he gestured around the warehouse. "We're the Master Race, of course."

He sounded like he really meant it.

"Of course you are," she told him.

His smile disappeared at her sarcasm. "You are one of us," he informed her. "Your place is by my side. You will be one of the mothers of a new breed destined to conquer the world."

The fanatical light in his eyes was nearly blinding, and she decided it was safer not to argue about it.

He unlocked her cage and brought another chair inside. "I have so much to tell you," he said once he'd taken a seat in front of her.

Cathy studied their positions and the distance to the open door behind him. Her chair was bolted to the floor of the cage, and her raw, bloody wrist was proof that the handcuffs weren't going to come off. About all she could do would be to kick Eric in the shins. While antagonizing him would be fun, what good could it do her at the moment? She'd play along with him for now.

"I've got the time if you want to talk," she told him.

"First, let me ask you a question," Eric said. "How much do you know about your Romany ancestry?"

She didn't want to discuss her personal life, but she suspected Eric knew more about some things than she did. "My mother didn't talk about her family."

"I can't blame her for wanting to deny her bad blood."

"You make her sound like a muggle or something."

He frowned, obviously not getting the reference. "Your family isn't from the typical rabble of gypsies. Your tribe have magic in their blood."

"So we're not muggles."

"During the war, scientists in the Reich discovered uses for the blood of your tribe. Much of the knowledge about the experiments was destroyed, but I am descended from a man who brought all the information that was left about werewolves to America." His chest puffed out proudly. "It's taken decades and three generations of volunteers to achieve the results my ancestor intended."

Cathy stared at him. "Let me get this straight— you *volunteered* to become a werewolf?" He nodded. She was appalled. "Why would anybody volunteer to turn into a mindless monster once a month?"

"Anyone who loves their race will gladly volunteer to defend it. My men and I are soldiers for our cause."

She'd been through a lot in the last couple of years—being turned into a monster, being rescued by a natural-born werewolf, being integrated into that werewolf's pack, discovering that the world contained not only werefolk but vampires and God knew what other kinds of supernatural beings—but this, this took the cake.

"I've been kidnapped by a gang of white supremacist werewolf bikers? Oh, for crying out loud!" she shouted. "There's only so much a woman can be expected to put up with, and I've had it up to here."

Eric merely smiled.

Cathy got herself under control. Just because

the situation was ridiculous, that didn't make it any less dangerous.

"What did you mean, about the Hunyara having magic?" *And how do I use it against you?*

He grinned enthusiastically. "There's so much I have to tell you. How long does it take for a bitten werewolf to learn to retain sentience during the change?"

"We bitten can learn to control the murderous rage eventually, but that's not the same as being sentient in wolf form. Only natural-born werefolk are sane and themselves in human or animal form."

"And yet you are already starting to come out of the moonchange easier and faster than a normal feral, aren't you?" He grinned again. "And how long does it take a bitten to learn how to change form at will?"

"Never." Only those born as werefolk had the skill to change from one form to another whenever they chose. "A mortal who's bitten by a werewolf is infected with a disease, not blessed, like you seem to think." She lived with the disease every day, and it was this bastard's fault. Her fingers curled, and she fought down a snarl.

"Your natural-born friends have told you you're cursed. They are wrong, but they aren't lying to you. You see, the natural-borns don't know about the Hunyara strain of werewolf."

"Strain? That does sound like a disease."

"Perhaps I should have said the Hunyara breed. Your family has gone to great lengths to hide themselves from the natural-borns—who would destroy them. Ironic, isn't it, that you found yourself in the clutches of Michael Bleythin, the werefolk's fearsome Tracker? He'll execute you without a moment's hesitation if he finds out who you really are. He's a ruthless, pitiless defender of *his* own kind."

How dare this bastard talk about Mike like that? Mike had bent werefolk rules when he killed her maker but let her live.

"You'll be safe with us," Eric assured her. "I'll never let anyone hurt you."

She was chained and in a cage, so it seemed as if he was more interested in keeping himself safe from *her.* "And in turn for this protection, I give you what?"

He gave her a salacious once-over. "Offspring."

"That's what I figured."

"And the other Hunyara gifts you don't yet know you have. The Hunyara and the Movement have so much shared history."

She feigned enthusiasm. "Tell me about the Movement."

"Of course, much of our research was lost

because of a partisan raid of our facility during the war. Your ancestors who were being used as specimens escaped during that raid, and mine had to start looking for viable subjects all over again, in a new country with very little support. We had to hunt your family for decades. The Movement wasn't even aware of the existence of natural-born werewolves when research began in America. We had to learn the same caution as the Hunyara to keep our efforts secret from the natural subrace."

Cathy didn't think this guy had any clue how disturbing the things he said actually were. He was so *proud* of the current success of these experiments, and the means and results obviously didn't matter.

"The natural-borns will be the first subrace we destroy. There can only be one dominant wolf pack."

She understood pack hierarchy and territoriality with every fiber of her being. She also knew deep in her being that this loser's pack wasn't going to be the one that came out top dogs.

"You have a great-aunt Maria," he went on.

"Never heard of her."

"Your family thinks she died in a car crash. She was the first werewolf we managed to capture. I should say that she was the first Hunyara;

we succeeded in capturing a feral in the early seventies. We began to build our army from this stock. Your aunt managed to teach all the recruits to obey orders while changed into wolves. But only the offspring she bore learned the ability to change at will. We needed more Hunyara, so Maria's three sons took on the task of tracking down more of your family. They found the Hunyara living in Los Angeles."

"Sofia's family," Cathy guessed.

Eric nodded. "Our men would have brought Sofia to us when she was still a child, but it turned out that one of the old wolf tamers was still alive. Our people died, and Sofia and her family disappeared."

What a shame.

"But we were patient. A new generation grew up; we learned more. And now we have you. Soon we'll have Sofia. Then a new day will begin for the Master Race."

One of Eric's minions came up to the cage. "Walt's here."

Eric's manic smile grew even wider. "Now we can get started." He stood and gestured a newcomer over.

Cathy didn't like the looks of this Walt at all. He was big and blond and gorgeous, about six feet four inches of hard-muscled Teutonic perfection. Worst of all, he had the burning gold eyes of an überalpha wolf. There was nothing natural about his scent. Walt reeked of deadly danger, and cold calculation. If Eric was the brains of this operation, Walt was the enforcer. Walt sent a jolt of terror through her.

"What do you mean by 'get started'?" she asked.

Eric pulled her cell phone out of his pocket. "Show her," he said to Walt.

While Eric pressed buttons on her phone, Walt took off his clothing.

A fear worse than of being raped gripped her when he did something completely unexpected. Before her eyes, the huge human male turned into a yellow feral werewolf.

She'd often watched natural-born werewolves shift shape, but seeing a bitten do the impossible brought a scream to Cathy Carter's throat.

Chapter Eighteen

Jason stood outside Sofia's room for a few minutes before he knocked. He would have heard her frustrated shout even if his hearing wasn't better than a mortal's.

She flung the door open with such force that it bounced against the wall and flew back to hit her in the shoulder. "Ow! Don't you understand the word *leave*?"

Despite Sofia's very real fury, her eyes were happy to see him. He refrained from kissing her, putting his hands behind his back to fight other temptations as well.

"I do understand, and I will go," he told her. "I need to explain something first. May I come in?"

"No."

Had he been the traditional vampire of fiction,

that one word would have kept him from crossing her threshold. He stepped inside.

"I want to tell you something."

She backed up, and he saw her considering throwing the phone in her hand at him. Instead, she tossed it on the bed and rested her fists on the lovely curve of her hips. She'd gotten dressed, which he thought was a pity since he loved her naked body. Still, her tank top did a very nice job of outlining her bosom and slender waist.

"If you're done looking at my rack," she said after a long pause and a significant rise in the room's temperature, "I suggest you say what you have to and go."

"I'll never be done looking at you," he told her.

His response caught her between a smile and a grimace and he took another step closer. *Stop that bonding!* he ordered himself.

Jason forced down the lust and said, "I want to explain to you why I'm protecting you and teaching you, and generally interfering in your life."

"It's something about keeping a promise, right?"

"I'm a Prime of my word."

"What the hell's a Prime, anyway?"

"First things first."

With that, he moved forward and touched her.

* * *

"This month has to be better than last month," Jason said to Grigor. "We lost three during the last moonchange, and I'm sorry for it."

"What an odd Prime you are," was Grigor's answer. "Those beasts could never live as men; I'm not sorry for their deaths."

"I don't mind killing," Jason said. "I relish what I can do to the enemy. But I do hate having to destroy those who have already been victimized."

Grigor nodded. "My father made a wise choice when he chose to reveal our secrets to you."

"I may be a friend, but I'm not as effective an ally as I'd like to be."

"You've been a great help in training the ferals. I'm certain Maria and Yaros will be able to control the change on their own this month. We'll find out come sunset, I suppose."

Tonight was the first night of the full moon. Jason had been with the Hunyara for three months now.

"And," Jason continued, "my most pressing concern is that I didn't get all of the Nazi bastards responsible."

"We burned down the camp, and the bodies of every German that was there."

Jason nodded. "But partisan intelligence thinks that the top-ranking officers weren't in camp that night. I didn't notice any of the bodies wearing a uniform with a higher rank than captain."

"Half of them were in their pajamas." Grigor chuckled. "Though I suppose German officers would be the sort to wear their medals to bed."

"I'm not sure the civilian scientists were—"

"You have trouble, my friend," Grigor's father said as he came into the hut.

Jason knew instantly that he wasn't talking about werewolves. "He's found me." He stood. "I have to go. I'm sorry, but I can't be of any more help to you."

"You don't think we can stand against a vampire?" Grigor asked.

"No, you can't. And there is no reason for you to. I won't put anyone else in harm's way because of something I did."

"Very noble," Grigor said, putting a hand on Jason's shoulder. "Are you sure you're not a Clan Prime?"

He shook his head. "I almost wish I was. Then maybe I wouldn't be in so much trouble. How close is he?" he asked the Rom patriarch.

"I've had my people searching for a vampire's scent since you arrived and today is the first sign we've had. How he got this close without our knowing, I don't know. I wanted to give you an early warning."

"I'm grateful."

"After all the help you've been to us, do you think we'd let you just run?" Grigor asked. "We've planned for this."

Jason was appreciative of his friends' loyalty and kindness, but he had no intention of putting them in danger. "It's only an hour until sunset. I better go."

"You can't travel now," Grigor protested.

"It's a cloudy day and the woods are thick," his father said. "If you're careful, you'll be all right, Jason." He spoke to Grigor. "We'll set up our ambush to cover Jason's retreat."

Jason looked from one Rom to the other in shock. They looked back with stubborn determination. He knew they couldn't stop a vampire, and so did they. He also knew arguing with them would do no good. There was no way he could express the gratitude that filled him.

"What's your plan?" Jason asked.

"To buy you as much time as we can," Grigor answered. "Come nightfall and the moonchange, we'll set the German ferals free on your hunter. If he kills them, he'll be doing us a favor."

The enemy soldiers who'd allowed themselves to be bitten by captured werewolves and brought out of the camp with the rest of the moonchanged pack weren't interested in the training the Hun-

*yara and Jason offered. The Hunyara were being
kinder to these prisoners than the Germans had
been to them, but kindness could only go so far
during wartime.*

*"Crazed ferals won't slow a vampire down for
long," Grigor went on. "But the sane members of
the pack can lead him on a long dance after the
ferals have tired him out a bit."*

*"We'll give you at least a few hours' start," the
old man said.*

*"I'll take whatever you can give me," Jason
answered. "And I want you to know that if you
ever need my help again, I'll do whatever I can
for your people."*

*Both men nodded, solemnly accepting this
offer.*

*With that, Jason gave them each a quick hug,
put on his heavy, hooded coat, and stepped out
into the excruciating light of day.*

Chapter Nineteen

You were being chased by a vampire?"

He ignored her skepticism. "That's not the point."

This man kept showing her the craziest things, but what the hell did it all mean? "Why were you being chased by a vampire?"

He brushed his thumbs across her temples. "I was being chased by a vampire cop, if you must know."

Sofia tried to take this in, and not be distracted by his gentle touch. "I'm still not sure I believe in werewolves; now you're adding Dracula to the mix. Why was Dracula after you?"

"His name is Matthias, not Vlad Dracul, and your family put themselves at risk to keep him from capturing me."

"But why . . . ?"

He sighed. "Because I did the wrong thing for the right reasons. The point is, I wanted you to know why I'm protecting you, why I'm training you. I made a promise to the Hunyara and I keep my promises."

She understood why he would be indebted for their trying to keep him from being captured, but he seemed to expect her to find her family's behavior admirable.

Sofia shook her head.

"You don't get it, do you?" she asked Jason. "You were a fugitive, and they helped you avoid capture. People who commit crimes are not sexy outlaw heroes—they are evil. People who help them are wrong. Wrong, wrong, wrong! I don't care that you're sworn to protect me now, because they helped you then. It's not my job to give you redemption, or pay your blood debt."

Jason took a step back. "Whoa. You don't have to be so melodramatic about it."

"I'm Rom and Hispanic—drama comes naturally." Actually, she'd been living a quiet life and avoiding drama for years. Jason brought out the unwanted wilder side of her nature, which was another good reason to get him out of her life.

"Now that you know that I don't find your

vows and crimes to be romantic, will you please leave?"

"Would it help if I told you your family's sacrifice didn't do me much good? Matthias caught up with me a week later, and I spent the next twenty years in prison."

The shadow that came into his eyes when he told her this twisted her heart. No, no, no! She was not going to feel sympathy for any con. Or any ex-con, no matter how fascinating and sexy she found him to be.

"Stop trying to manipulate me."

He sighed. "Point taken. That wasn't fair."

"Besides, don't you have to go feed your wolves, or something?"

"Thank you for thinking about them."

He seemed genuinely pleased, and when he touched her cheek, the ice around her heart nearly melted.

"All right, all right, I'm going," he said after they stood looking at each other for an unknown time.

The next thing Sofia knew, Jason was gone, but she had no memory of his leaving her room. She didn't remember the kiss either, but she still felt the effects of it, from the tingling top of her head to her toes curled on the thin motel carpet.

"Whew." She touched her sensitized lips and

sat weakly on the bed. Only when her hand brushed across the cell phone there did she recall what she should be doing.

"Sorry, Cathy," she murmured contritely. "With that man around, I can't seem to keep my mind on your emergency."

Cathy shut her mouth. Her panicked scream didn't last more than a few seconds but left her terribly embarrassed. Werewolves might howl occasionally, but Cathy hated being caught screaming like a girl.

So she glared at the captors staring at her and asked, "How the hell did he do that?"

Eric smiled at her with proprietary pride. "It's your right to know, Hunyara."

"My name's Carter," she said as the feral changed back into human form with the same ease as when he'd become a wolf.

This time she didn't scream, but she did watch his transformation carefully. Somehow her muscles seemed to almost understand the process. She'd never had this response when watching any of the Bleythin brothers change their form. She needed to learn this! She needed time to think about it, and to practice. She had to get out of this cage.

She looked to Eric. Damn, but she hated asking

anything of this bastard. "Tell me." She wasn't quite ready to say "Show me."

He still regarded her with that smug smile. "Research has revealed that, like any mortal, those with the Hunyara mutation must first be bitten to activate the changes that make you special. Once bitten—"

"Twice shy," she grumbled.

His smile widened somehow, and he made a gesture with his empty hand that took in her whole form like a distant caress. The naked guy looked her over as well, his eyes shining with hunger. Her hackles would have risen were she in wolf form. Still, she was unbearably curious.

Eric sensed her interest. "Can you guess why the Hunyara are different? Do you want me to tell you?"

The other feral's hand landed on Eric's shoulder. He seethed with impatience. "What about the other female?"

"Soon," Eric told him. His gaze never left Cathy.

Cathy finally gave in to that look. "Go on. Please."

"Vampires," he answered. She gaped, and he laughed. "Yes, you have vampire blood in you as well as werewolf."

"Not possible," she said.

"Vampires mate with mortals."

"Yeah." Among her friends and coworkers were Laurent and Eden, a vampire and mortal couple. "But vampires do not mate with werewolves." She wrinkled her nose. "That would just be wrong."

She'd never been attracted to any vampire she'd met, and both Sid and Joe had told her that it wasn't possible for the two of them to be more than just good friends. Really, really good friends who gave each other longing looks when the other wasn't looking, from what she'd observed.

"The researchers want more proof," Eric went on, "but we think that once upon a time a vampire and a werewolf produced a child and began the Hunyara line."

"I realize you're trying to impress your future mate," the shifter said. "But I came here to collect the second female."

"I know," Eric said, and flipped open the cell phone. "You have quite a few voice mails," he told Cathy. "The natural-borns are quite anxious to have you back under their influence."

"You mean my friends are worried about me."

"Your cousin certainly is. Sofia has left as many messages as all the others put together. Family is so important, isn't it?"

Cathy sneered, "I suppose the plan is for me to call Sofia so you can lead her into a trap. I don't care what you threaten me with, but I won't do that to family."

Eric shook his head. "Trust you with a telephone? I don't think so." He began pressing buttons on the cell phone's keypad. "Not when text messaging can be used to trap her instead."

Chapter Twenty

Jason left the motel reluctantly, but Sofia was right about George and Gracie needing some attention.

"I'm sorry this isn't the vacation I promised you," he told the wolves when he let them out of the pen in the back of the SUV.

They jumped down to the crumbling parking lot concrete and George let out a howl while Gracie bumped her head against Jason's thigh. He rubbed her head while carefully looking around the area one more time. Sunlight warmed the cracked concrete and reflected off the pastel walls of the single-story motel buildings that stood on three sides of the parking lot. The street beyond was lined with almost identical motels and fast-food restaurants. The traffic moving by was light. It was all very worn-down and sad. He caught no sense of danger yet, but knew it was coming.

"Come on," he said to the wolves, and set off on a run with the animals at his side. Running with the wolves was good for him. They were mortal and he had to keep pace with them, because they could not keep up with him. Continual practice in being among mortals was necessary. And now he had a mortal woman to protect and cherish and bring into his world.

Kicking and screaming, no doubt. Jason smiled.

After a few more blocks he stopped at a fast-food place and bought a lot of hamburgers. He fed most of the burgers to the wolves, who complained because they preferred their meat raw. Then he headed back to the motel.

Once again he had to leave George and Gracie penned up in the SUV, but it was safer for them this way. A small generator provided them with air-conditioned comfort, which he envied as he climbed onto the roof over Sofia's room in the blistering Southern California sunlight.

There, Jason closed his eyes and opened his mind.

Sofia's restlessness reached him first. And the awareness that she missed him. He couldn't help but smile. What was righteous indignation at his supposed sins, compared to the draw of the bond?

She was stubborn, and determined to see the world in terms of black and white and right and wrong. She'd put him firmly into the black and wrong categories—but down there in her lonely room, she wished he was there.

The same way he wished to be with her. How much better it would be if they spent the day making love. She wouldn't be so self-righteous once he'd worn her out with hours of pleasure beyond bearing, now, would she?

After allowing himself a few moments of smugness, Jason tamped down that part of his Primal nature and went back to shameless telepathic spying on the woman he was sworn to protect.

Chapter Twenty-one

"Do you want to know what she has to say about Dracula on her blog?" Eden asked.

"No." Sid looked up from her computer to glance around the office of Bleythin Investigations. Eden was at her desk researching Sofia Hunyara, and Daniel sat on a chair behind Cathy's. He held something belonging to their missing friend cupped in his hands and closed his eyes as he psychically searched.

Joe, Mike, and Harry were off checking out an address out in the desert where Cathy had been asked to meet with some mysterious relatives.

Laurent was still following his own line of investigation, and hadn't checked in by telephone or telepathy for quite a while.

"The place seems so empty," Sid said.

"But at least no one's shedding on the furniture." Eden sighed. "I miss my husband and kid. At least Antonia is having a good time babysitting her only grandchild."

"I heard the slight emphasis on 'only.' Don't you start, too," Sid complained. "I'm working on the baby thing."

"With David Berus?"

Sid did not want to get into this subject. "So, what does this Sofia person have to say about Dracula?"

Eden cleared her throat and assumed a pedantic tone. "I quote from the wisdom of Sofia Hunyara: 'When I first read the book, I thought Stoker was the worst writer in the history of the English language. The story was full of too many characters, too many plot holes, and far too much overblown prose.

"'Of course, I was thirteen at the time. Reading the book again after puberty set in, I came to the revelation, "Oh, that's what it's about." Why didn't the guy just say all that exchanging of fluids between dark foreign strangers and fair English flowers was about forbidden sex?

"'I now understand what makes the story so timeless and evocative, but it's still full of plot holes. And why must there be fanatically loyal gypsies running around doing this vampire's bidding in Stoker's book? Why are Romany always portrayed as being on the side of the Dark Occult Powers in Western literature?' "

Eden stopped reading and chuckled. "I hope I meet this Sofia Hunyara sometime, so I can fill her in on the real history of vampires."

Sid boggled at her ex-vampire-hunter sister-in-law. "Are you saying Stoker *didn't* have it all wrong?"

"I'm not sure you have a need to know on that one, oh, Daughter of the Clan." She scrolled through several more screens of Sofia's blog. "She's really into old writers. She goes on and on for pages about *The Scarlet Letter*. I thought that was a Demi Moore movie."

"You don't read anything that isn't put out in comic book form from Marvel."

Neither did Laurent. Sid had even heard her brother and Eden refer to each other fondly as Gambit and Rogue.

"I'm a geek, I'm entitled. And don't tell me you've actually read *The Scarlet Letter*."

"Point taken. Tell me, does any of what this woman says bring us any closer to finding Cathy?"

"Probably not," Eden replied. "But you're

right about the place seeming empty, and I'm trying to keep my mind off worrying about Cathy
while we wait to hear from the guys."

"Me, too. My research isn't getting anywhere."

"What are you researching?"

"Not what, but who. I'm trying to figure out
what Jason Cage has to do with all this. Not that
there's much about him in the data I can access. Not
without bringing a liaison between the Clans and
Families into this already overpopulated mess."

"Why not call up the Caeg Family Matri?
Aren't the vampire Clans and Families close allies?"

"We're close because we make a point of stay-
ing out of one another's business as much as possible. You saw how Jason had to ask permission
to hang out in Clan territory, but didn't explain
to the Matri what he's doing here, and she didn't
press him for details."

"I wasn't actually there for that."

"Right. Oh, mighty hunter." *And please tell me
he's decent genetic material,* she added to herself.

Eden looked thoughtful and rubbed her chin.
"Let's see, I know that the Caegs are the largest
and most influential of the vampire Families. I
think Jason is the grandson or great-grandson of
the current Matri. He's from one of the Eastern
European branches of the family that came to

America after the Communist takeover of their home territory." She rubbed her chin again. "There's something I should remember about him—something I read in his dossier that I thought was cool and romantic, but—"

"You have dossiers on all of us?"

"Not all of you," Eden responded calmly to Sid's outrage. "I never heard of you before we met, or Laurent, but I did know a little about Antonia. Mostly the hunters concentrate on keeping tabs on the Tribe vampires," she reassured Sid.

Sid couldn't blame the mortal vampire hunters for spying on the Tribes. Tribal Primes were nothing but bad news for mortals and immortals alike.

"So, what did you think was cool and romantic about Jason Cage?"

Eden thought for a few more seconds, tapping a finger on her chin. "Oh, yeah, I remember. He got into trouble for trying to stop World War II. I guess he telepathically brainwashed some high-ranking Nazi. That's the kind of interference my kind goes after vampires for. Good intentions or not, your kind doesn't mess with our heads and get away with it."

"Messing with people's minds is bad," Sid agreed. It was evil and wrong and not to be tolerated; she believed this with all of her being, even though she'd done it herself—with good intentions. At least she hadn't been caught.

"I can't believe the hunters let Cage get away with brainwashing."

"We wouldn't have, except that the Families sent their own cop after him and put him away in solitary for a good, long time. I remember thinking that he was all cool and tragic for trying to save the world and getting in trouble for it. He sort of combined the Clan Primes' idealism with the pragmatism of the Families."

The Clans could use a bit more pragmatism, Sid thought. Maybe Jason Cage's DNA could help with that.

"But what does his past have to do with our present situation?" she wondered.

"Well, Cage used to hang out with Romany," Eden said.

"This Sofia Hunyara is Rom, Jason Cage is involved with Sofia, and Sofia is Cathy's cousin. Maybe they kidnapped Cathy."

"We don't yet have any proof that Cage is involved with Sofia."

"I'm psychic; I—"

Her phone rang and she answered it instantly. "Harry! Have you found her?"

"I'm not sure what we've found," the senior werewolf partner of the firm said. "When we reached the house there was nobody here, but the traces left behind are like nothing I've ever smelled before."

Harrison Bleythin had the best nose in the business. Harry's twin, Michael, had the ferocity, and their younger brother Joseph was one tenacious scent hound, but Harry was the elite bloodhound of the pack.

"Tell me," Sid said.

"Werewolves have been all over the place. And mortals. And a vampire. Most of them are related to Cathy."

"We knew that her family had contacted—"

"The werewolves are kin to Cathy," Harry interrupted, speaking slowly and distinctly.

This made no sense. "Please, Goddess, don't let her have been biting people when we weren't looking."

"That isn't possible," Harry reminded her. "You know she hasn't been out of our sight once during her moonchange."

Sid had a moment of relief, for Mike's sake as much as Cathy's. Mike Bleythin had another job besides private detective. Among werefolk kind he was known as the Tracker. It was his duty to take down the ferals and rogue werewolves. He'd spared Cathy from execution once. Sid knew it would destroy him if he had to kill her after all.

"The werefolk and the mortals that were in this house are *all* blood relations to our Cathy," Harry said.

"I so do not understand that." Had Cathy lied about how she'd been turned into a werewolf? "Mike rescued her from a feral. Didn't he? What about the vampire scent? Anyone you recognize?"

"Male," Harry said. "Not Wolf Clan, that's all I can tell. There was also a pair of true wolves here."

"Jason Cage travels with wolves," Sid told him. "I knew he had to be involved! He's with Cathy's cousin Sofia."

"The mortal female's scent will be hers," Harry said. "The Hunyaras have scattered. There's a dozen trails we could follow. What do you think, Sid?"

"Jason and Sofia," was her immediate response. "My gut tells me they're the clue to finding Cathy. We can solve the other puzzles once we have Cathy home safe."

"Agreed," Harry said.

He hung up on her, but Sid sent a telepathic *Stay in touch* his way.

Chapter Twenty-two

Sofia read the text messages from Cathy again and shook her head. She didn't like this—whatever this was.

"Too much mystery," she grumbled.

First there'd been the crazy relatives and the sexy stranger attaching himself to her. Now the missing cousin had reappeared but was being obtuse.

My senses are just about on overload. Got to get it together. I've got to get it under control.

But why do I feel the sudden need to be the one that's responsible? I'm not an alpha type, I'm a lone wolf.

And why am I using that sort of analogy?

She paced the motel room restlessly, the tension building in her making her want to scream. She needed a clear head. She needed a plan.

Sofia did not for one moment believe that her cousin was on her way to meet her here.

She missed Jason, missed him with every thought and breath. She missed him with her soul and every cell of her body. She missed him so much she couldn't stop herself from picking up the pillow his head had rested on and breathing in the scent of him that lingered there.

"Crazy."

Maybe she'd been too hard on him.

And maybe this was no time to obsess over her personal problems. She had to make sure Cathy was all right before she let herself worry about Sofia.

She noticed her laptop sitting on the motel room desk and smiled. She knew of one sure way to focus her thoughts. She might as well use the time spent waiting to get her head in order.

She sat down at the desk and switched on the computer. "Thank goodness this place has WiFi," she said, and soon began to type.

"Well, look what just popped up on Live Journal."

"What?" Sid asked Eden.

"A fresh posting from our girl Sofia. Let's see

what she has to say. *While sitting here waiting for a werewolf—*"

"What?" Sid bounded to her feet.

"Hush." Eden waved her back down. "Listen. 'I can't help but think about Jane Eyre.' "

"What does Jane Eyre have to do with—"

Eden gave her a withering look, and Sid subsided.

" 'It's one of my favorite books,' " Eden read on from the blog posting. " 'I love Jane's strength of character, her independent spirit, her resiliency. I guess I've unconsciously identified with her—a poor orphan girl making her way in a cruel world, with pride and dignity intact, and all that.

" 'But I never understood her and Rochester. I never understood that whole "passionate soul mates meant for each other" rubbish.

" 'Rochester tried to trick her into marrying him when he already had a mad wife up in the attic (and btw, the first thing I said to the person I'm really writing about was a reference to Jane Eyre). Anyway, Rochester lied to Jane, tried to trap her into a bigamous marriage, fell apart and felt sorry for himself when his nefarious plan was thwarted, and just generally acted in an irresponsible, selfish fashion.

" 'I believe in honesty and restraint. Unbridled passion creeps me out.

" 'But, still—I think I'm beginning to understand why she couldn't stay away from him despite her own self-respect and pride. Jane couldn't stop herself from running back to Rochester. He called to her and she had to answer the call.

" 'Maybe when you love someone, you forgive them. Maybe pride and love have nothing to do with each other. Maybe Rochester couldn't help what he did because he needed Jane to be with him, no matter what. I begin to get it, this call of passion despite one's better judgment. It sucks.' "

"I wonder what she's talking about?" Eden asked.

"It sounds like the beginning of a bond to me."

Eden wasn't the only one who jumped at the sound of David Berus's voice. She hadn't seen, heard, or felt him come in, but there he stood, large and blond and handsome, beside Eden's desk.

He turned a smile on her. "I met Charlotte Brontë once; she was quite old at the time. The lady certainly knew what she was talking about."

"I thought Charlotte Brontë died young," Sid said.

"That was the cover story that took her out of the mortal world," David answered. "She was bonded to a Prime. So of course she understood about soul mates and passion."

He looked away suddenly, and an awkward silence stretched out.

Sid noticed Eden almost shrinking in on herself in the hope of not being noticed. Eden had been born into a family of vampire hunters, and mortal hunters were responsible for the death of David's vampire bondmate.

Back in the bad old days the hunters had concentrated on killing vampire females, knowing that few daughters were born to vampires and only female vampires could give birth to vampire children. Sid knew her people had good reasons for the protected, circumscribed lives led by their women, despite her rebellion against the old ways.

David Berus had survived the loss of his bondmate, but the scars of that loss on his soul were still there in his eyes when he looked at Sid again.

She fought the urge to hug him and say "There, there." If she let herself get close to him, Lady Juanita's plan to hook her up with this very admirable Prime might succeed. Oh, no, that wasn't going to happen. She had plans of her own.

"Do you think Sofia is bonding with the Cage Prime?" Eden suddenly asked.

Not until I get my hands on a paper cup full of his sperm, Sid thought.

"Lady Juanita thinks so," David said.

"Cage and Sofia just met, so if they're bonding that quickly, that means Cathy's cousin is strongly psychic," Eden said. "I wonder what Sofia's being psychic has to do with werewolves?"

"I bet it means something," Sid said. When David came to stand by her desk, she stood and almost moved backward. Instead, she kept the desk between them and asked, "What can Bleythin Investigations do for you, David?"

He smiled. "I'm hoping I can be of some help to Bleythin Investigations. Lady Juanita suggested I apply for a position with your firm."

She'd been afraid he'd say something like that. "She wants us to work together, does she?"

"You know she does." He moved around the desk to stand close beside her. "The question is, what do you want?" His voice was rich and deep, and utterly seductive.

She didn't respond to him at all, and almost wished she could. If only she could feel something for one of her own kind! Sid met his coffee-dark gaze and tried to let his searching look spark something inside her.

Nope.

Chapter Twenty-three

Sid tried to think of something to say, but thankfully the office door opened and her mother came bustling in with Toni in her arms.

"Mommy!" Toni called. The toddler held her arms out to Eden.

"You do know she can walk?" Eden asked as she came to take her daughter. Her actions did nothing to prove this as she balanced the girl on her hip.

"I know you're very busy, Eden," Antonia said. "But I thought you could use a Mommy break."

"You are so right," Eden said, hugging Toni close. She began to stroke her daughter's cheek.

Sid noticed the fond look David gave the women and child, which she thought was sweet.

But she didn't appreciate it when he put his hand on her shoulder.

She slipped away from his touch and approached her mother. She barely managed not to growl when David followed close behind her. Maybe she had been hanging out with werewolves too much.

"What's Danny doing?" Toni asked, staring hard at the man seated behind Cathy's desk. *Oh, he's time walking,* the little girl added telepathically.

When Antonia winced, David put a hand comfortingly on her shoulder and said to Toni, "Use your out-loud voice, honey. You have quite a gifted child," he said to Eden.

Antonia brightened with pride and grinned with anticipation. "You don't know the half of it. Show Mommy, Toni."

Toni obediently turned her head and bit her mother's thumb.

Sid caught the sweet scent of blood as Eden shouted in pain and almost dropped her daughter.

But she held on, and so did Toni, suckling like any proper baby vampire. Eden started to pull her thumb out of Toni's mouth, but after a moment she gave a contented sigh and let the girl draw small sips from the bite.

"Nothing as good as mother's blood," Antonia said.

Sid was totally confounded. "But Toni's not—one of us."

"She's a daughter of the Clan," Antonia stated firmly. "Lady Juanita and I have suspected she'd make the change, and when her baby teeth popped out this morning we were sure."

"But how?" Sid asked. "Children born to mortals and Primes are always mortal themselves."

"Not always," Antonia said. "Why don't you explain, Eden? Hunters understand the process, don't they?"

"Yeah. But I never expected my own kid would be—"

"Explain!" Sid demanded.

"Most children born from any kind of vampire matings are male," Eden said. "Vampire genetics are inherited strictly from the female side. So, a son born to a Prime and a mortal woman is going to be mortal."

"There have been exceptions," David said.

"Granted," Eden said. "Maybe five or six sons of mortal matings have gone Prime in the history of the world, and they all had really funky powers, but the odds are astronomical for a male to turn vampire. Daughters of mortals and vampires can make the change, but only if the girl's mother has a vampire somewhere in her own ancestry."

"I've heard of mortal women who made the change when they were bonded to a Prime," Sid said.

"But they still have to be descended from a vampire." Eden looked thoughtful, then she laughed. "Of course, I'm from a hunter family."

"Hunters and vampires have been mating as long as there've been vampires and hunters," David said.

"But we hunters don't like to talk about certain *special* relationships. It's anathema to admit that our enemies sometimes turn out to be our destined loves." She laughed again. "I wonder which one of my grandpas had fangs and his own opera cape?"

"Watch the stereotypes," Sid told her. "And congratulations."

Eden didn't look quite like she was ready to be congratulated on this surprise turn of events, but Sid wanted to crow with glee. The vampire population was dangerously small, so every female added to their gene pool contributed to the species survival.

"I have to tell Laurent," Eden said. She slipped her thumb from her daughter's mouth. "Mommy needs to leave Daddy a voice mail now."

"Why?"

"Because Mommy isn't a telepath like you are."

Before Eden could turn toward her desk, Daniel suddenly stood up. "We have to go," he announced. It took his eyes a moment to focus on all the people suddenly staring at him. "They need our help," he told them. "Their minds are"—he shook his head as if trying to toss something out of it—"being messed with."

"Who?" Sid asked. "When?" After all, Daniel's peculiar psychic gift was for reading the past.

"The Bleythins," he answered. "All of them." He was pale, and he shuddered and took a deep breath before he went on. "We have to help. Right now."

"What did you see?" Sid demanded. She was skeptical, but she didn't question his urgency or his belief.

"I'll tell you on the way," he said. He headed toward the door. "Hurry!"

Sid and Eden looked at each other. "Do we go with this?" Eden said.

"We go," Sid decided.

Eden kissed Toni's forehead and handed her over to the waiting arms of Antonia, then headed after Daniel.

David would have come with them, but Sid

pointed to her niece. "That is a future Clan Mother. She needs guarding, Prime."

"You are a future Clan Mother," he reminded her.

Sid showed him her fangs. "It isn't only Primes who can grow these."

"Sidonie, be polite."

"Sorry, Mom." She drew in her fangs and nodded curtly to David. "Prime of the Snake Clan."

Antonia put a hand on David's arm. "I trust my daughter to take care of herself. Let her go. Stay here with me."

He didn't like it, but said, "As the Lady Antonia wishes."

Thanks, Mom, Sid thought as gently as she could to her telepathically null mother, and hurried after Daniel and Eden.

Chapter Twenty-four

Sofia had never thought of herself as impatient, but right now the waiting was killing her. Her only consolation was knowing that not being patient might get her killed.

Maybe.

Suspecting that she was acting like a delusional idiot about to be made a fool of was also killing her.

Any minute now, Cathy will show up. She checked her watch. *She's five minutes late, so she'll show up any second now. And then I'll know that all this werewolf stuff is crazy family folklore, and I'll feel like an idiot for my current behavior.*

Or . . .

From her car, Sofia stared at the door to her room and tried not to think about the "or."

She checked her watch one more time, then saw movement out of the corner of her eye. It was large, slinking carefully from shadow to shadow, keeping close to the wall. It was padding very carefully forward, stealthy and purposeful.

Damn!

Her stomach clenched with fear and she wanted to scream, but she would not give in to automatic fear.

She watched the wolf's careful approach and was glad that she'd taken a walk all over the motel buildings and parking lot. She'd carefully touched every door, every car, leaving her scent everywhere just in case she needed to confuse a creature she'd hoped wasn't really coming and didn't really exist.

That's probably one of Jason's pets.

She shook her head and ignored the voice of sanity. The wolf she watched was bigger than George and Gracie combined. They were gray and white; this one's fur was yellow.

She also doubted that George and Gracie were capable of doing what this wolf did when it reached her door. It reared up on its hind legs and banged its head against the wood.

There was a wolf at the door, and it was knocking.

Okay, now she had a certain amount of proof

that werewolves were real. But she had no idea how to ask a monster about her cousin. So she waited, hand poised over her keys.

When the door went unanswered, the wolf snarled. Then it backed up, ran forward, and hit the flimsy wood with the force of a battering ram. The door flew inward and the wolf rushed in.

Sofia had the car started before the werewolf bounded outside again. She had the car in gear by the time the creature saw her. His head came up and their eyes met; Sofia froze in terror.

His soul was evil and cruel, and she'd looked into eyes like those before.

Though her brain might've been frozen, her foot stomped on the gas pedal. The car sped forward but the werewolf easily jumped aside. Sofia was barely able to jerk the steering wheel hard to the left before slamming into the side of the building.

The monster was nowhere in sight when she headed toward the street.

The doors of her car were safely locked, but that did her no good when the werewolf jumped through the rear windshield.

Hot breath burned across the back of her neck, and Sofia threw open her door and rolled out. She hit the pavement hard while the car continued to move out into the street. She heard the crunch of metal and squealing tires behind her as she took off in the opposite direction.

She dodged into an alley behind the motel, hoping that a truck had flattened her car with the werewolf inside it.

No such luck, she realized within seconds when she heard the creature racing up behind her. The sound of claws scrambling on pavement sent a chill up her spine.

I'm repeating history. I need to be out in the open, among people. That thing won't draw attention to itself by attacking in a crowd.

Repeating history?

"Damn it!" she shouted. Consumed by sudden fury, she turned to face the onrushing beast. "Look at me, you bastard!" Her voice had never been so full of command and conviction before.

The beast did. Their gazes met and it came scrambling to a halt a few feet away from her.

The animal snarled, baring huge fangs.

Sofia glared, putting a lifetime's worth of anger into it.

She felt power gather in her. It was like nothing she'd ever known before; she was in control here.

Keep your distance, she thought at the werewolf. *Sit, and stay. How dare you look me in the eye?*

The werewolf snarled and snapped. Its whole body shuddered in resistance to her command.

After long, tense seconds, it began to slowly sink to its haunches.

Sofia concentrated as hard as she could, beginning to tremble, sweat beading on her forehead.

The werewolf continued to stare at her, defiance boiling in its gold eyes, its hard will boring into her determination.

She began to grow cold, though sunlight flamed against her skin. A dark tendril of fear began to twine through her, and a voice began to whisper in her head. She could make out no words, but the sound was sinister and distracting.

She took a shaky step forward.

He was calling to her, wasn't he?

How did he get into her head?

Her own thoughts distracted her, and shadows came up dark around her.

The alley changed. She changed.

She slammed into the brick wall before she could stop herself, scraping her palms and jarring her arms from wrists to shoulders. She turned around and fell to her knees, putting her at eye-level with the wolf.

He had a big head, and huge teeth. His eyes glowed, cruel and fierce, and full of hunger.

His eyes glowed!

He began to move in for the kill.

Chapter Twenty-five

Sweetheart, you were doing so well, too, Jason thought as he jumped off the roof behind the werewolf.

He'd kept his fury in check while monitoring Sofia's confrontation with the werewolf. Pride and hope warred with anxiety until she absolutely needed him.

Now he gave in to the fierceness of his nature and grabbed the creature from behind. His claws dug into soft fur and tough skin as he lifted the werewolf high over his head. It snarled and bucked in his grasp.

He ignored the struggling creature while he looked at Sofia's blank expression. "Come back, hon. You're fine."

She blinked and shook her head. Then she

looked up at the werewolf before meeting Jason's gaze. Puzzlement and anger replaced the shadows of the past that had consumed and crippled her.

"Try again," Jason said, and dropped the werewolf.

It instantly leapt at Sofia.

He hadn't expected the animal to be so fast. When he grabbed it again, he broke its neck. It was inches away from Sofia's throat.

"Nobody touches that neck but me," he said as he dropped the werewolf.

Sofia looked from the body at her feet to Jason. "You killed him."

Jason took her by the shoulders and drew her close. He gave her a hard, tight hug, then turned her, keeping an arm around her waist. How good she felt next to him! She quivered with tension, radiated shock and growing disgust, but she didn't try to pull away from him. Whether she acknowledged it or not, she needed him as much as he needed her.

"Look," he said. He leaned so that his cheek touched hers. "Watch."

Her attention was riveted by the large body stretched on the concrete in front of them.

The transformation of the yellow wolf took place with quick, magical grace. Reality stretched and briefly blurred, and became different. The sharp muzzle and pricked ears melded into a human head covered in long blond hair.

The human body that emerged was hard-muscled and huge, the same size as the wolf's but a different shape. She could clearly see him breathing.

"He's not dead."

Sofia looked over her shoulder at Jason. "You didn't kill him?"

"It takes a lot more than a broken neck to take out one of the werefolk."

He let her stare at her unconscious attacker for a few moments. She shuddered and he pulled her closer. A police siren sounded in front of the motel.

"You wanted me to see it—him—change."

"You needed proof." He turned her to face him. "You needed to believe."

She closed her eyes for a moment. They flashed with anger when she opened them. "You knew I'd be attacked." She sneered, "You wanted the chance to act the hero."

"No!" Her accusation stung. "I gave you the chance to save yourself. To prove to yourself that you could—"

She tried to struggle out of his embrace. "You let me face that—" She gestured wildly toward the werewolf.

He realized that she was still on the edge of panic and nothing would be settled until she calmed down. And they weren't going to be alone for long; there was a great deal of excitement about the wrecked car out in the street. He heard people shouting about having seen a huge dog running from the wreck.

Jason let Sofia go and bent to sling the werewolf over his shoulder.

"What are you going to do?" she asked.

He didn't ask her to come with him, but was glad when she followed him to the other end of the alley. He'd left his truck parked where Sofia wouldn't notice it when she left her room. He carried the prisoner to the vehicle and shoved the werewolf inside the empty wolf pen. The wolves were happy to keep away from the prisoner.

"The lock ought to hold him when he wakes up," Jason told Sofia. "I can't question him until he comes around."

"We've got to find out what they've done to Cathy."

"Right now, we have to get out of here." He took her arm, but she shook him off before he could lead her to the truck cab. He gestured back toward the motel. "We don't need mortal interference."

"I need my stuff," she answered, heading off.

He caught up with her. "Why?"

She gave him an angry look. "I need my laptop for school. I left it in my room. At least I wasn't stupid enough to have it in the car."

"Waiting in the car was a good plan," he told her. "I wondered what you were up to when I saw you running around marking the place."

She blushed.

"You did great, Wolf-Tamer-in-Training," he assured her. "And right now, you have to keep thinking like what you are and get out of here."

She shook her head. "Do you think I can afford to run off and leave what little I have? Even if I'm supposed to save the world, I'm still on a budget."

Jason supposed that telling Sofia that he could fulfill her every material wish wasn't the way to win this independent woman's heart.

"Fine," he said, and took her into an empty motel room, with the wolves following at their heels.

Once inside he couldn't stop himself from kissing her, and after a moment her mouth opened beneath his and her arms came around his back. They clung together in an eager, hot embrace for a few moments before Jason reluctantly drew away.

"I'll get your stuff for you. Stay right here," he ordered. "All of you."

"Wait a second," she insisted as he started to leave. He glanced back. Arousal stretched across the room between them. She touched a finger to her sensitized lips, but her gaze was sharply questioning. "How did you get that door open?"

He smiled. "It's just a little trick my people have."

"You're not a werewolf, right?"

"Right."

"I saw how fast you moved, how strong you are, and you've got all that"—she tapped her forehead—"telepathic talent. What are you?"

Jason knew he'd put this off too long, but he couldn't help but smile wider and show a great deal of fang. "I'm a vampire, sweetheart."

He closed the door behind him, but he still heard Sofia's stunned whisper. "Vampire?"

He laughed out loud as he ran toward her room.

Chapter Twenty-six

Sofia looked at the wolves that had jumped up on the bed. "He's a vampire. Did you know about this?"

Not that the wolves answered. They were, after all, just plain fierce, huge Arctic wolves, not vicious telepathic mean werewolf scum. One of them yawned at her.

She turned away from George and Gracie, unable to muster any fear of natural canines anymore.

Sofia began to pace around the small room, seething. She had to get rid of all the pent-up frustration and confusion somehow.

Not to mention anger. *I've got quite a few things to say to that man. Vampire.*

"What does he *mean*, he's a vampire?"

The wolves refrained from commenting.

Why did she believe him? And where was he? Why wasn't he back yet?

Oh, please, it's only been about thirty seconds.

Her back was to the door when the wolves began to howl. As she turned, they jumped down to cower beside the bed.

"Just what the hell do you think you're doing?" Sofia shouted at the three black werewolves that rushed through the doorway.

For the first time in her life, she was too angry to know any fear. "I am *not* putting up with this anymore!"

She swept them with a glare. All three beasts had bright blue eyes, full of intelligence. Sofia's were full of determined fury when she took them on. They surrounded her in an arc and began to stalk slowly forward.

She stomped her foot. "Oh, no you don't." She pointed to them one at a time. "Stay right where you are."

She repeated the order as a thought, a firm mental command spoken directly into their minds.

They froze.

Two of them looked surprised. The third growled and bared his fangs at her.

She felt him trying to change, and she stopped him. She wasn't sure how she did it, but the control came as naturally as breathing. They fought her, pushing at her mental control, and she pushed back. She smiled as the tug-of-war accelerated.

She was utterly and completely pissed off, and that was a good thing. Jason paused outside the door to savor the triumphant fierceness of his soul's equal. Her power and strength filled him with a pride and love he'd never experienced before. What a woman!

And she was his.

Every possessive fiber of his being insisted on the truth of their bonding.

But right now, police officers were going from room to room looking for the owner of the squashed vehicle in the street. A small crowd was gathered in the parking lot. Jason had already had an encounter with a female officer whom he'd telepathically convinced hadn't seen him, and that the room where Sofia waited had already been searched.

They needed to deal with the latest batch of werewolves, get back to the prisoner, and get out of here. He tucked her suitcase and laptop under one arm, and eased into the room.

Sofia didn't glance around when he entered, but all three werewolves growled. George and

Gracie whimpered from the far side of the bed.

"Wimps," Jason told his wolves. He looked at the big, black werewolves and spoke to the snarling one in the center. "Hi, Mike."

Mike Bleythin snapped his jaws angrily.

"We haven't been introduced, but I assume you two are Harry and Joe," Jason went on.

"Do you know these creatures?" Sofia asked without taking her attention off her captives.

"This is Sofia Hunyara," he told the Bleythins. "She's Cathy Carter's cousin, and I just now realized who Cathy must be."

"What do you mean?" Sofia asked.

Two of the wolves tilted their heads curiously, as well.

"I'll explain when we can all have a civil discussion."

He put Sofia's stuff down by the door and came up to put his arm around her slender waist. Her head barely came up to his shoulder, but her newfound strength of will filled the room.

"She's mine," he informed the Bleythins, who knew better than to mess with a vampire. "You can let them go, sweetheart," he told Sofia. "These are the good guys."

Sofia was trembling enough for him to feel it even as she showed a brave front to the werewolves.

"Good guys?" she questioned. "They're werewolves! They broke in!"

"Which was quite rude of them," he agreed. "I'm sure they'll apologize if you let them turn back into humans."

It's all right, he whispered into her mind. *It truly is all right. They're Cathy's friends.*

She hesitated, but decided to trust him.

He held on to her when she let go of the mental leash. The rush of released energy would have knocked her to her knees if he hadn't been there to hold her. She closed her eyes and leaned her head against his shoulder, spent and breathing heavily.

It was too bad her eyes were closed, because she missed the quick transformation of Mike, Harry, and Joe, and the looks of shocked outrage they turned on the woman who'd held them at bay.

Jason smiled proudly. "Yep, she's good. Her people would call her a Wolf Tamer."

Chapter Twenty-seven

Jason's words were a soothing balm to her soul. She had a family. She had a place in the world. A purpose. And it was Jason who had brought her to this place.

But it was a stranger's angry shout of "What the hell is going on here?" that brought Sofia's attention back to the situation.

When she opened her eyes she saw three naked men. Large, well-made, black-haired men with the blue eyes she'd stared into when they were in wolf shape a few moments before. Two of the men looked so much alike they had to be twins. The third was younger and more slender, but enough alike the twins that he had to be their brother.

The one who'd shouted was standing right in

front of her, body tense, fists clenched. His fury was barely held in check, and for a moment she wanted to slink behind Jason.

She lifted her chin and asked the werewolf, "Are you really Cathy's friend?"

"I'm Mike Bleythin," he said. His next words were low and threatening. "I've never heard of a Tamer, but perhaps you've heard of the Tracker?"

Jason's embrace tightened protectively, but it wasn't the reassurance of his being there that kept her calm. Though she did appreciate having him beside her.

"No, I haven't heard of any Tracker. I just found out about werewolves, actually. I take it Tracker is a werewolf title," she said to Mike. "You haven't answered my question."

"What was your question?" Mike's twin asked. He shouldered his threatening brother aside. "I'm Harrison, the sane member of the family. Let's talk."

"We're looking for our friend," the youngest werewolf said. "So far, following the trail to you has been all we've been able to do."

"My lady was attacked by a werewolf before you arrived," Jason said.

"One of the Hunyara pack?" Mike asked.

"I seriously doubt it. A Hunyara would recognize a vampire's scent, but this feral had no clue I was around. Don't tell me you didn't pick up his scent? It must be all over the neighborhood."

All three Bleythins looked shocked. Harry shook his head. "Not a whiff."

"You're kidding."

"I wish we were. That's why we haven't been able to find Cathy. There's no fresh scent of her anywhere."

"What happened to this invisible werewolf?" Mike asked.

"I have him locked up in my Denali," Jason said.

The brothers exchanged looks. Harry spoke to Sofia again. "To answer your question, all of us are friends of Cathy's. More than that, we're her pack brothers. May I now ask you some questions?"

Sofia wanted more explanations, but nodded.

"Do you know why you were attacked?"

After thinking about it for a moment Sofia came to a dreadful conclusion. "He wanted to turn me into a werewolf." She looked at Jason. "Why would he do that?"

"I think I'll go ask him," Mike said, and suddenly the big naked man turned into a huge black wolf.

"Mi—" Harry began, but Mike was out the door before he could finish.

"He's the Tracker," Joe said. "Let him do his job."

Sofia waited for an explanation, but all Jason said was, "I hope he doesn't leave any blood in my truck."

Sofia decided she didn't want any more information. If she thought about it she might be sick, which she did not want to do in front of the werewolves.

Harry reclaimed her attention when he asked Jason, "What did you mean about knowing who Cathy must be?"

"I just remembered that the name of the woman Mike brought to my cousin's wedding was Cathy. I hadn't associated her with the woman Sofia is looking for, until the three of you showed up. To tell you the truth, I've been thinking so hard about not getting Mike involved in Hunyara business that I forgot he's based in San Diego."

Sofia's head spun with confusion once more. "Vampires have cousins? Werewolves go to weddings?" She looked into Jason's amused gaze and telepathically said *I don't know anything about your world.*

And now isn't the time to discuss it, he answered as the door burst open again.

* * *

Sid would not let Daniel drive.

"Becasue I've seen you do it with your eyes closed," she told him when he protested that he knew where they had to go.

Daniel gave directions while Sid sped her sleek black Mercedes skillfully through heavy traffic. He did it with his eyes closed.

"I hate having one more thing to worry about," Eden said from the backseat.

Sid gave a quick glance back at Eden's worried face. "I'm sure we can get the boys out of whatever trouble Dan's seeing."

Eden sighed. "I was talking about finding out my daughter's going to be a vampire."

Sid couldn't see this as anything but an occasion for rejoicing, but she tried to get a mortal mother's perspective on it. Especially a mortal who'd been trained to hunt vampires. She couldn't do it.

"You object to a miracle?" she asked after making a quick left turn at Daniel's direction. Tires squealed and horns blared in her wake.

"I can't object to biological fact," Eden said. "But I need some time to wrap my mind around it."

"We all do," Sid said. "As soon as we get Cathy home."

"Right," Eden agreed. "But Laurent and I aren't

your average vampire couple, and if Lady Juanita thinks we're going to raise our kid as a proper little vampire princess—no offense—"

"None taken."

"—she's got another thing coming."

"Spoken like a true hunter." Another turn. More offended drivers. At least no cops had noticed yet. "I'll do what I can to help. So will Antonia."

Eden reached forward to pat Sid's shoulder. "Thanks—we'll take all the help we can get. Speaking of Lady Antonia," she added, "I approve of that bit of matchmaking you pulled on her and that dishy Berus Prime, even if you did use my daughter as your excuse. Your mom could use someone nice."

Sid drove in flabbergasted silence. She'd only been trying to duck out on a date with destiny with David Berus herself. She hadn't been trying to dangle her own mother as bait to attract the Prime's attention away from herself.

Though come to think of it, that wasn't a bad idea.

No, no, no! Sidonie Wolf, you will not think like that!

Daniel broke in, "Traffic will be blocked up ahead. Turn right at the next light. We'll come around from the back." After a couple of minutes he said, "Left here. Stop."

She barely had the car parked behind a long, one-story structure when Daniel jumped out and ran toward the front of the building.

"I think his eyes are still closed," Sid said as she and Eden followed him.

She overtook him in a couple of steps, being faster and stronger and far more dangerous than her mortal relative. She felt Joe and the others' presence and she was the first one through the door, ready for any danger waiting inside.

Instead, the first person she saw was Jason Cage. She came to a quick halt and cheerfully said, "Hi!"

Chapter Twenty-eight

A new trio of people rushed in, led by a gorgeous blonde woman.

Somehow, Sofia was certain none of this trio were werewolves. She expected them to attack, but instead the blonde's eyes brightened at the sight of Jason and she looked like she wanted to eat him up.

Jealousy boiled through Sofia, but the woman took no notice of her.

Instead the blonde put her hands on curvy hips and looked at the naked men. "So, Harry, do you need rescuing, or is this about to turn into an embarrassing situation?"

"We needed rescuing about ten minutes ago," Harry answered.

"See, Dan's getting better," said the other

woman who'd come in. "He's up to seeing ten minutes into the past, instead of two hundred years."

When she heard the name Dan, Sofia looked hard at the blond young man wearing glasses and the striking woman with dark curls next to the tall blonde. Realization dawned at last.

She pointed at the dark-haired woman. "You're Eden." To the blonde. "And you're Sid. And Mike and Harry and Joe—I should have remembered about you when you told me your names. But having three more werewolves come at me scared me to death."

"You didn't act scared," Joe said.

"Oh, God, I'm sorry!" Sofia told her cousin's coworkers. "Cathy's told me all about you— except for the werewolf stuff."

"That's understandable," Sid said. "Except Cathy never told us about you."

"I'm sorry about what I did to your brains," Sofia said to Joe and Harry, carefully not looking below chin level.

Sofia wondered if she was the only one who cared that there were a couple of naked men in the room.

Not men, Jason thought at her, *werewolves. And I'd rather you didn't look at anyone but me.*

Right, she thought back.

She wouldn't mind looking at him naked. She didn't think Sid would mind, either. And why the devil couldn't she get her mind off having sex with Jason, when there were more important things to deal with?

This reminds me of a scene in A Night at the Opera, Jason continued in her head as the new-comers and naked men began talking among themselves. *More and more people and luggage and things keep piling into this tiny ship state-room, until eventually no one can move, and finally it's so crowded people start falling out the door.*

A Night at the Opera? she asked.

"It's a Marx Brothers movie," Jason explained. "It's a comedy from the 1930s."

"Oh." *I want to have sex with you,* she thought.

I know.

I can't help it, and I don't like that I can't help it.

You don't like the sex?

She very much liked the sex. She craved the sex. She wanted him covering her and inside her, and her body was burning just because his arm was around her. Why didn't these people go *away*?

I don't like this—compulsion. Is it because you're a vampire and drank my blood that I want you constantly? Anger sizzled through her, but the need for him didn't abate any. *Are you forcing me to feel like this?*

Sweetheart, I feel the same way you do.

While the others talked, Jason whirled her around into the bathroom and closed the door.

"I'm not going to kiss you," he said, though he held her close and she automatically pressed her body against his. He could feel the hard swell of her nipples through the fabric of her shirt. "Stop tempting me for a moment."

"How?"

"I don't know." He lifted her chin to look into her eyes even while the sweetness of her lips beckoned to him. "Although I very much want to kiss you, instead I'm going to tell you some things, and I want you to listen to me without any argument. Promise me that you'll listen and think about everything, and we'll discuss it or argue later."

"You're a vampire. A vampire ex-con. But everything you've told me so far has turned out to be true, so all right," she said. "I promise to keep my mouth shut and listen."

"I am a Prime, which means I am an adult male vampire. Vampires are people," he said. "Some vampires are good, some are bad, most are somewhere in between. We have our own cultures and history and problems. We aren't the dead brought back to life; we're born vampires. We don't turn people into vampires when we bite them."

"Only werewolves do that?"

"Right, but I'm explaining my own people now. We can't fly without airplanes, or change shape like the werefolk can. We do suffer from some of the problems you see in the movies—allergies to sunlight and garlic and silver and certain types of wood, but we take medicines for these allergies.

"We don't fear religious symbols. Or sleep in coffins, or need to rest in the earth of our homeland, or have trouble crossing running water.

"We are telepathic, we are faster and stronger and longer-lived than mortals. We do need to drink blood, for nourishment and for psychic reasons, and especially to enhance sexual gratification—but we don't have to kill when we taste mortals.

"I'm not saying we don't have tendencies for fierceness and violence, but we channel those tendencies—at least most of us do, most of the time—into acceptable pursuits. I control tigers for a living, for example.

"We're highly sexed and we love making love, to our own females and with mortal women. If we're very lucky, we find the one woman that is destined to be our bondmate. A bondmate is our perfect sexual and psychic partner, and we are the perfect partner for our bonded. The mortal term is probably soul mate.

"You are my soul mate, Sofia, and I am yours. You can deny it and fight it, but it is the truth. You want me, I want you, and every issue that stands in between is just bullshit. Normally we could and would work it out. But right now we have the complication of your being needed by your people, and my giving you up if I have to in order to fulfill my obligation to your people, and I have no idea of how we're going to get around that."

He paused. "You can talk now."

As she opened her mouth to say something, a knock sounded on the bathroom door.

"Come along, you two," Harry called. "It's time we got back to hunting for Cathy."

Chapter Twenty-nine

Cathy's captors kept spraying themselves and her with the stuff that blocked out scent. It made her eyes water and she kept sneezing. She knew an allergic reaction was the least of her problems. As time crept by, Cathy also tried to keep her mind off the bad things that could happen to Sofia.

Sofia was an innocent mortal in town simply to meet family. Cathy was terrified her cousin would walk into an ambush and be turned into a werewolf, just as she had been.

She tried to assuage her guilt over involving Sofia in this by envisioning all the ways she'd savage and mutilate her captors as soon as she broke free, but such thoughts only made her want to gnaw at her shackled wrist to facilitate her escape. Two things kept her from the stupid move. One was the fact that she was still a sane human being until the moon was full and not a raging, insane werewolf.

Come the full moon, though . . . She kept unconsciously smiling about that, and flexing her fingers as though they already sported strong, sharp claws.

The other drawback was that if she somehow managed to bite off her own hand, she would still be locked inside a cage. And oh, yeah, bleeding to death.

She tried not to believe any of the things Eric had told her about his plans, her people, and especially her werewolf and vampire friends. But his ideas gnawed at her.

Don't think about gnawing.

Her only distraction came from studying everything around her. There were a great many people coming and going from the warehouse. They were bringing in supplies and loading them into shiny new vans and trucks and Hummers, while Eric supervised and gave orders like a general preparing a campaign. Some of those supplies were weapons and ammo, which gave her a very bad feeling.

"What do werewolves need with guns?" she

asked as Eric strolled her way after slapping a subordinate.

"It takes more than werewolves to take over the world, darling," he told her.

"Superpowers have nuclear weapons," she said. "What have you got? Fleas?"

He grinned at her. "I take my Top Spot every month. We're working on getting the nukes."

Cathy's heart sank. "You're joking."

"Only about the flea medicine."

She got the distinct impression that he wanted her to be proud of his plans for world domination.

"Am I supposed to bat my eyelashes and say, 'Oh, you're so alpha'?"

He laughed. "Oh, no. I want you to know that I'm worthy of having an alpha bitch like you for myself."

In a werewolf way, this was the most romantic thing anyone had ever said to her. Mike certainly never—

"Do you really believe you and I are members of the master race?" she asked. "Or are you just power hungry?"

"Yes," he answered, flashing that sharp-toothed grin again. "And we won't *be* the master race until we wipe out the naturals and then the vampires, but one thing at a time. First we absorb the Hunyara genetics into our own. Then we must build up our ranks and expand our territory. We must gain more allies and exploit their weaknesses when they are no longer useful. The war hasn't begun yet, but the buildup is well under way." He looked at his watch. "I wonder what's taking Walt so long." He chuckled. "He's probably taking his time with a female he knows he's not fit to bed in her proper state. I would do the same, if I knew it was my only chance with an alpha female. Not that I'll let him breed her. Or you," he added to Cathy.

"I love it when you talk like that," she said, but doubted Eric recognized her sarcasm.

Their conversation was interrupted by the warehouse door swinging open to allow a new van to drive inside. Eric went over to greet the newcomers.

"We got a couple of them!" a bearded man shouted as he got out of the van. He gave a triumphant laugh. "It was as easy as you said it would be. All we had to do was follow those natural-borns and they led us to the Hunyara hideout. After the naturals gave up and left, a pair of Hunyara males came slinking back to the house. They're as feral as we are and put up a good fight. We stunned them and came straight here." He glanced toward a second man who'd come around from the passenger side and looked sheepish. "Well, not quite straight back."

"I stopped for a girlfriend along the way," the other man said. He faced Eric squarely, making eye contact for a few crucial seconds. When Eric didn't slap him down, he went on. "Nobody saw the pickup. She won't be missed. We can always eat her if she doesn't take to being turned."

Cathy fought down the urge to throw up.

"We sprayed everybody down mostly," the first man went on.

"What the hell does that mean?" Eric demanded.

"We ran out of deodorant, but not until everybody'd been sprayed," the other man answered. "At least enough."

"Define *enough*?" Eric asked, voice low and threatening. All activity had stopped, and his people stared at him. "Pack up," he ordered. People sprang into action without any questions, while Eric turned his attention back to the newcomers. "That was good work snatching the Hunyaras," he said, getting grateful looks from the pair. "But did it occur to you that the natural-borns might have returned to the Hunyara house, too? Maybe they're trailing the Hunyaras right now. If they are, and there's the faintest trace of scent to follow, you'd be leading them back here."

Cathy could only hope.

The driver shook his head. "No way. We got the stink off of all of us. But it wouldn't hurt to spray everything down again anyway."

"You do that," Eric said. "Everything and everyone." He rubbed his hands across his face and rolled his head to relieve tense muscles. "Things are moving faster than I'd like, but we'll be okay." He gestured two men over. "Tanner, I want you to get the caravan moving north, right away. Call Nathan when you're out of the city to give an update on the situation. Make sure you get the Hunyaras back to base in good shape. John, your team and two vehicles will remain here with me. Make sure at least one of the team can operate the vampire zapper, and break out some silver rounds for one of the modified AKs. We've got one more delivery. I'll wait here for it. Send out a couple of men to track down Walt."

Cathy did not like this evidence of her captors' efficiency.

Tanner gestured toward her. "Do we take her?"

"I'm not trusting transporting the bitches to anyone but me. Get moving."

Cathy watched the increased activity with growing dread. One of the men came over and sprayed her cage full of the deodorant chemical, and she started to cough and sneeze, her eyes watering so much that everything became blurred.

To get her mind off the discomfort, she focused her attention deep inside. Maybe, if she tried hard enough, she could figure out how to shape-shift on her own before the full moon forced the change—whether she wanted it or not.

Chapter Thirty

"You didn't have to break into my truck," Jason complained as Mike entered the office. "I would have given you the keys."

The big werewolf ignored the Prime and looked Sid's way. "Status?" he growled.

She was more interested in what Mike might have learned, but she saw that he wanted time to get his seething anger at Jason under control. Since he was a dear friend, and she didn't want the office wrecked if the Tracker and Prime got into it, she answered his question.

"Harry and Joe decided to follow the trails of any Hunyara werewolves they can find."

"None of my relatives know where Cathy is, either," Sofia spoke up. She was sitting at Cathy's desk, with Daniel standing next to her.

"But we'd still like to talk to them," Sid told her.

"Oh, yes," Mike said softly, focusing his blue laser stare on her. "I certainly intend to talk to them."

Fear crossed the mortal's face, followed by a flash of determination. Sid wondered if Mike was deliberately trying to make an enemy of a woman who could control werefolk. More than likely he was still upset about what he'd had to do to the feral werewolf, and was taking it out on Sofia.

"What do you mean by that?" Sofia demanded of Mike.

"Daniel has been showing Sofia what he does," Sid continued quickly. *Keep it together, Tracker,* she sent telepathically. "And Sofia and Jason have been trying to see if the glimpses of the past he pulls up make any sense to them."

"Nothing so far," Daniel said.

Mike continued to glare at the mortal. The Prime didn't like it. Damn, this could go bad.

"Still no word from Laurent," Sid went on. "I sent Eden home to be with Toni—more on that situation later. And I have been catching up on our casework while waiting for you." *I have also been telepathically looking for Cathy,* she telepathically told Mike. *But I think whoever has her is using a psychic damping device like the vampire hunters use.*

Do you think those Purist bastards have her?

I certainly hope not. Are you calm enough to talk yet?

"No." Mike turned toward Jason. "Why the hell didn't you tell me about these Hunyara ferals?"

Jason rose and faced the Tracker's fury quite calmly. "They're a very private people, and it's not my story to tell. What did *you* find out from the feral?"

"*Everything* about werefolk is my business," Mike growled. "What am I supposed to tell the governing council about a gang of mavericks we've never heard of before? What do we do about them?"

"The Hunyara aren't the problem," Jason said. "It's the ferals that are preying on the Hunyara that are our problem. What did the feral tell you?"

Mike's fists clenched at his sides. "My species has been put at risk and—"

"Cathy! Remember her?" Sofia suddenly put herself between Mike and Jason. "I thought you cared about her. I know she cares about you, but you aren't doing anything at the moment to show me why she should."

Mike's attention switched to the small mortal

woman, and the tension that flowed between them filled the room.

Sid saw how Jason prepared to spring forward to protect his woman. She admired the Prime's effort at restraint. He had Sofia's back, but encouraged her independence. She liked that in a Prime, especially since it didn't come naturally to them.

At least a minute stretched out before Mike scratched his jaw and nodded to Sofia. She nodded back. Air came back into the room, and Jason stepped forward to put his hand on Sofia's shoulder.

The opening chords of Coyote's "Tempting Fate" began to play, and Sid quickly answered her cell phone. That was the ringtone she'd programmed for Tony Crowe.

Everybody looked her way.

"Hi, Dad. I can't talk right—"

"I asked Dr. Casmerek about that thing you wanted to know about," Tony interrupted. He sounded cranky. "I didn't like it, but I asked."

"Thank you." She couldn't keep from looking Jason over. Sofia noticed. "What was his response?"

"He said it's possible. He wants you to give him a call. Don't."

"You know I have to."

"You're a stubborn child."

She wanted to dance with elation. She wondered if Jason would let her lead. She smiled. "Thanks for doing this for me. I'll get back to him as soon as I can."

"What's that about?" Mike asked when she hung up. Werewolves' hearing might possibly be better than vampires.

"Nothing involved with any of our cases," Sid answered. She folded her hands on top of her desk, all prim, proper, and professional. "What did you learn from the feral?"

Mike concentrated on Sofia. "He was sent to bring you over to his kind, the way they did with Cathy. They want female ferals."

"I suggest you moderate your tone," Jason said. "You sound like you're blaming the victims."

Mike gave Jason a long, hard look, but went on coolly. "He didn't know where they're keeping Cathy. They kept him out of that loop by blindfolding him and driving him everywhere—just in case he got caught. I learned a lot of things from him, but not how to find Cathy. We'll discuss those things after we find her," he told Sofia.

Chapter Thirty-one

Sofia did not like this guy, and couldn't see why Cathy constantly raved about Mike in her e-mails. Okay, he was big and strong and handsome, but he wasn't very nice. Was Cathy's life in danger from him now?

"Do you want to find her because she's your friend, or because she's a danger to your species?"

Mike walked away without answering and went to talk quietly with Sid.

Sofia watched him carefully, worried.

On the drive to the Bleythin office, Jason had told Sofia what he knew about natural-born were-wolf society, and how hard her family had worked to keep their existence from the natural-borns. He explained that the werefolk consisted of all sorts of shape-shifting predators—foxes, cougars, bears, and more—but werewolves were at the top of the food chain. The natural-borns were a paranoid lot with *rules,* and Mike Bleythin's job was to enforce them.

Though she was new to the idea of·having a family, she'd developed a fierce need to protect all the Hunyara. Now she might have to protect them from Mike Bleythin, the Tracker, as well as from these ferals out to use the Hunyara family for their own purposes.

"Cathy first," Jason said.

He put his arm around her waist and she drew comfort from being near him, comfort from the way he knew her mind.

"I wish we hadn't come here," she whispered to Jason.

For one thing, she didn't like the way Sid kept looking at Jason with blatant, hungry interest that sent waves of jealousy through her.

I'm not interested in her, Jason thought at her.

You're flattered, though, she thought back.

I can't help it, sweetheart. I'm a Prime, and she's a female of our species. We Primes are vain—we love it when the ladies take notice. It doesn't mean anything.

Maybe not to him, but it sure distracted her. Finding out that Sid Wolf was also a vampire had shocked her, but she adjusted to the idea quicker than she would have a few hours before.

Detaching herself from Jason's touch—and bothered by how hard it was to do—she went back to stand by Daniel. Jason went over to Mike and Sid.

"Tell me about your father," Daniel said when she reached him. He adjusted his wire-rimmed glasses on his nose. "He and Cathy's mother are twins, aren't they? Multiple births are common in werefolk families."

"My *father*. Oh, my God!"

Sofia staggered to a seat as the room spun sickeningly around her. She was vaguely aware of Jason coming toward her, and of his turning to face the door when it opened.

She knows, Jason realized. Sofia's heartbreak ached in his chest. Her head dropped into her hands and he could almost taste the sudden tears welling from her eyes.

But when a pair of vampires entered, he automatically put himself between his mate and any potential danger. He relaxed when he recognized Sid's mother and the Snake Clan Prime he'd met at the Matri's party.

Sofia looked up, wiped the back of her hand

across her eyes, and put her feelings aside. Jason admired her resilience, but feared someday she was going to break apart.

"I came to renew my offer of help," David Berus said.

Sid stood and gave the Prime a wan smile. "Thank you. And Mom—"

Another Prime came through the doorway before she could finish. He radiated excitement and all eyes turned his way.

"Laurent!" Sid said eagerly. "You've got something."

"Who's the elf lord?" Jason heard Sofia ask Daniel.

"I think we're beginning to need a flowchart," he whispered back.

"I've got some information," the newcomer said. He flashed a charming smile at Sofia. "Don't be alarmed, miss, I work here. If I take the time to hit on you, as politeness requires, my sister over there will be annoyed, so I'll get on with what I have to say. Is that a wolf sleeping under my desk or a relative of yours, Mike?"

"You're easily distracted, aren't you?" Sofia asked.

He pushed hair out of his face. "I haven't slept in days, and I'm down a couple of quarts. Deprivation definitely affects me."

"What information, Laurent?" Mike demanded. "Where's Cathy?"

"I don't know."

Mike took an angry step forward. "You don—"

"Let me finish. I believe Cathy's disappearance is part of a much bigger plan." He paused for a moment for dramatic effect. "There's a werewolf revolution afoot."

"I know," Mike said.

Laurent lost some of his bright enthusiasm. "What do you mean, you know?"

"Never mind how he knows," Sid said. "Tell us what you found out."

"I found out that local illegal arms dealers have been doing a lot of business with some hard-core biker types in the last few days. I've convinced one of them to let us do a ride-along on a delivery."

"You used telepathy on this man?" David Berus asked.

Laurent gave Berus an incredulous look. "Hell, no, I bribed him."

Jason liked this Laurent. When Berus threw back his head and laughed, Jason decided he liked him as well.

Sofia was not amused. "How is this going to help us find my cousin?"

"The bikers are holed up in a warehouse," Laurent answered. "We find the warehouse, we find Cathy."

Sid's phone rang before anyone could ask more questions.

"Hello, Harry. I'm going to put you on speakerphone so everyone can hear."

"We had the scent of a couple of the Hunyara family," Harry Bleythin said, "but their trail disappeared. Then we picked up a faint whiff, followed that, then it was gone again. I remembered how there was absolutely no trace of the feral at the motel when we were within a few feet of him. So I want to ask Mike if he has any information about how the feral managed that."

Mike said, "They've developed a chemical they spray on themselves that completely masks all scent. They must've used it on Cathy when they picked her up at her apartment."

"And now I suspect they've used this chemical on the Hunyaras."

"Cathy's a Hunyara," Sofia reminded them. "They kidnapped her, tried to get me, and now they've abducted more of my family."

"That's my conclusion," Harry said. "But I think this lack of scent is finally starting to work against them—now that I know what not to sniff for."

"I'm having a brilliant idea," Laurent spoke up.

"You usually do," Harry said. "What is it?"

"We come at them from both angles." He quickly filled Harry in on his information, then outlined his plan.

When Laurent was done, Harry said, "Roger that. We'll be in touch when we're in position."

"Count me in on this rescue," David Berus said.

"The more the merrier," Laurent said.

"I'm in," Antonia said.

Laurent, Sid, and Mike nodded without showing the least surprise, so Jason didn't think it was his place to protest the involvement of either female. They were Clan after all, and he was Family. Their customs were not his, although his own Matri would never permit a female to put herself in harm's way.

David spoke up. "Lady Antonia, is that wise?"

"I don't have to be wise," she answered with a gentle smile. "I'm a grown-up. I get to make up my own mind."

He put his hands on her shoulders. "But . . ."

They gazed into each other's eyes.

Everyone else looked on and forgot to breathe while the silence stretched out to eternity. The pair smiled at each other, and their expressions were identical, totally in harmony, totally content.

"I think I've been in mourning long enough," he said.

"So have I." Antonia put her hand on his cheek, and David turned his head to kiss her palm. It sealed a promise.

And broke the moment.

"I see where your daughter gets her independence," David said. "I like it."

Antonia chuckled. "It seems that you're going to have to get used to it."

"Mom?" Laurent and Sid asked.

So that's what the beginning of a bond looks like, Jason thought. *Beautiful.*

He wanted to pick up Sofia, whirl her around, and kiss her until they were both crazy with desire. He wanted to lay her down and give her all the pleasure she deserved. He wanted to hold her close to his heart and make promises and plans, and simply just be with her. But now was not the time.

"We'll get back to this later," David said. With his arm around her waist, he turned Antonia toward her gaping children. "Right now we've got a rescue to carry out."

Chapter Thirty-two

I can do this, Cathy thought. *I can transform.* She wanted to take a deep breath and close her eyes to relax, but a deep breath was out of the question with the chemical hanging in the air. It didn't help that they had cranked up the zapper device that blocked vampires' awareness of them. While the subaudible whine didn't cause her pain, it was distracting.

Cathy closed her eyes and stopped trying to concentrate. For over a year she'd been trying to learn how to be a werewolf. Maybe instinct was the key to what she needed to learn.

Go with the flow.

Flow. Yes, that was it. She brought up the memories of Walt changing from man to wolf and back again, and of all the times she'd seen the

Bleythin brothers do the same thing. She'd always assumed she had no control over the change, because she'd been told so. She had no doubt the natural-borns believed what they'd taught her, but she now chose to believe they were wrong.

Cathy slipped off her shoes and flexed her toes. She ran her awareness along the muscles of her calves and thighs. She blanked out how they felt now and superimposed the feel of wolf muscle stretching over her bones. She thought of her bones, and what shape they needed to take to support wolf muscle and sinew. She thought of fur, warm and soft, protecting her skin. And of skin tougher and more protective than human.

Flow, she thought. *Change. Be.*

"Cathy! No!"

She heard the shout just as her vision changed. Though her hearing grew more acute, she couldn't make out the word. She understood the fear in the sound and reacted with a snarl, revealing her long fangs. She was not afraid; she was alpha and would prove it.

She sprang toward the wall of the cage, but something held her back. Something was wrapped around her leg. It wouldn't budge when she tried to free her paw. She snapped. Her teeth came down on metal but couldn't break the restraint. She had to be free!

She didn't mind the pain.

The cage rattled; the door opened.

"They've got a zapper all right," Laurent said, putting a hand to his forehead and driving slower.

Beside him, Sid grimaced and squinted. The sunlight hurt her eyes. She glanced behind her to where the others sat. Daniel looked sympathetic and Sofia puzzled, but the three other vampires looked as uncomfortable as she felt. Having been briefed on the effects of the zapper, they didn't complain. "At least this proves we've got the right place," she told them.

A guard stepped in front of the SUV when they turned into the parking lot behind the warehouse. He held up a hand and showed a weapon.

Laurent stopped the van and rolled down the window. "I've got a delivery for you, friend."

The guard shook his head. "Not now."

Laurent gestured toward a wide metal door at the back of the building. Then he caught the man's gaze and said, "Open up. I'm not unloading out here."

If he was trying to psychically influence the werewolf, it didn't work.

"I said not now."

"They've got a situation inside," Daniel said

suddenly, his eyes closed. "Cathy's . . . bleeding."

"Go, Harry!" Laurent shouted into his cell phone as he stepped on the gas. He opened his door and it slammed into the guard as they passed. "Bloodsuckers out!"

Sid heard her brother shout, "Mortals duck!" as she jumped from her side of the vehicle. The other vampires went out the back door.

Dodging bullets as she ran, she managed to get the entrance to the warehouse open just as Laurent drove up to it.

With the van inside, Sid joined the other vampires in fighting the well-armed werewolves outside.

The van crashed into a truck parked inside the warehouse, and both car alarms began to whine. Laurent jumped out and Daniel scrambled after him.

After that, Laurent moved so quickly, Sofia could only make out a blur. She did hear him yell, "Ow! God damn it, silver bullets!"

A moment later a weapon landed on the floor and a body sailed through the air, screaming.

Daniel headed purposefully toward the far side of the warehouse and smashed a large machine.

It must have been the zapper, because Laurent

shouted, "Clear!" and the other vampires moved inside.

Bullets were still flying when Sofia cautiously slipped out of the van and searched the room for wolf shapes.

She ignored the trio of black beasts that came bounding inside; the Bleythins wouldn't be here if they hadn't taken care of the guards stationed outside.

Then she saw the cage and the man bending over something inside it. When he stood, she saw what she'd come looking for. Sofia started forward.

Before she'd gone two steps, the cream and gold werewolf pounced, pinning the man against the bars of the cage. And as he reached to push it away, the werewolf ripped open the man's throat.

Chapter Thirty-three

The smell of blood brought Sid to a momentary halt as she rushed inside, and she licked her lips. She sometimes forgot how spellbinding mortal blood could be. It permeated the soul, called up ancient hunger, tried to strip away the civilized veneer.

She pushed down the ancient part of herself and continued into the room, where Laurent was taking down one of the bad guys. There was blood on her brother's arm, his own.

"Eden's not going to like that," she called to him.

"I won't tell her if you won't," he called back. "It'll heal in a minute." He looked around. "All looks clear."

Daniel stepped around from the back of the

truck. "They're all down." He sighed. "Now we've got a crime scene to clean up."

Sid knew they wouldn't have much time; someone nearby was sure to report the sound of gunfire. The cops would be on the way soon.

Daniel took out his cell phone to call in the waiting cleanup team. Antonia came up to him and they began to consult in quiet tones. Laurent found the weapon that fired silver bullets and put it in the back of their van.

Sid heard a growl and turned to see a huge black body arcing through the air. Two other black werewolves stalked behind Mike, a fierce guard for the Tracker. Then she saw what the werewolves were headed toward: Cathy in wolf form, crouched over a human body. Her pale fur was stained with blood and her muzzle was buried in her victim's throat.

Her heart sank. "Oh, no," Sid whispered. "Stay back, Sofia," she said as the mortal moved forward.

But of course the woman didn't listen.

Sofia didn't want to go closer, but that was where she had to be, where she was needed. Her heart pounded hard and her head hurt.

"Cathy."

The beast looked up. It growled and tried to stare her down.

Sofia said, "No."

Then the Bleythin pack were there, and she automatically put herself between them and her cousin.

Mike changed into human shape in a quick blur. Behind Sofia, Cathy snarled.

"Get out of my way," he ordered.

"Leave her alone," Sofia replied. "Let me help her."

"There's no help for a killer feral. She dies right now."

"The hell she does!"

"You don't know our laws."

"You can't just put her down without knowing why—"

"She's moonchanged! That's why!"

"She's not," Jason said.

The calm in his voice soothed Sofia's anger; it seemed to have a similar effect on Mike.

Jason stood beside Cathy, his hand resting on top of her head. The beast shivered, but most of the insane fierceness had gone out of her eyes.

"You don't want to do this," Jason went on. "I've been inside your head, Mike. I know how much you love this woman."

"Shut up!" Mike shouted. He threw back his head and let out a rough-voiced howl that should never have come from a human throat.

Sofia finally realized that it wasn't fury driving the Tracker, but heartbreaking pain. Prepared to fight him, now she wanted to help him.

"The moon isn't full yet," she said. "We don't know why she changed, or how. We don't know why she killed." She pointed at the body. "He was her captor. What did he do to her? Was he a werewolf?"

Mike sniffed. "He was."

"Your world has changed," Jason said. "Your laws might not apply to this situation. If you act on instinct, you'll never forgive yourself."

"I can't think about myself. I can't do what *I* want."

Mike was stubborn, but Sofia sensed that his resolve was wavering. She said, "Cathy needs help. Please let me help her. There's a lot going on here. We need to find out what these bastards were up to. Let me get into Cathy's mind."

"She doesn't have a mind right—"

"We came here to rescue her," Sid said, stepping in front of Mike. "My vote is to take her home."

"I second Sid's vote," Laurent put in.

"This is werewolf business," Mike said.

"Your kin is affiliated with the Wolf Clan,"

Antonia pointed out. "We do not rule werewolf kind, but our Matri has some say in advising your kin. This is a complicated situation. I think you need Lady Juanita to mediate it."

Harry morphed into human and put a hand on Mike's shoulder. "They're right, bro. You know they are."

Mike stared at Cathy for a moment before his hard expression cracked into one of utter pain. "All right," he said. "Let's get her out of here."

Chapter Thirty-four

"You'll be all right?" Jason asked.

"I'll be all right," Sofia replied.

"You will be all right. I'm trying to reassure myself more than you, you know."

"I know. Trust me."

Jason sighed, brushed his lips across hers, then stepped back and closed the metal door. It was covered with gouges and scratch marks.

Sofia locked the door and looked around. The walls of the windowless room were thickly padded. She'd been told it was soundproofed as well. The room was in the rear of the Bleythin office building, and it was where Cathy was kept during the days she was in wolf form during the full moon.

The wolf Cathy was curled up in one corner.

Her head rested on her front paws and her eyes were half closed. Sofia was pretty sure Jason's mental influence was the reason Cathy wasn't currently raging around like a maniac.

"You look tired," Sofia told her. She stretched aching muscles. "I sure am."

Cathy had emptied large bowls of water and raw meat before lying down.

Sofia looked at the empty dishes and said, "You know, I can't remember when I ate last, or slept." She settled slowly onto the floor and leaned her back against the door. She kept her gaze on her cousin. "It's been a rough couple of days, hasn't it?"

Cathy lifted her head and showed a mouth full of fangs. A snarl rumbled low in her throat.

Sofia scratched her earlobe and fought off a yawn. "I'm too tired to be scared." Cathy's head dropped back to her paws. "You, too, huh? I'd like to be able to trust you not to attack, and leave you alone. Maybe with time you could figure the change out on your own. But your boyfriend is off consulting with his superiors, and I'm told that some vampire queen wants to have a talk with us. So, let's get to work proving that we Hunyara are a viable addition to the werewolf community."

She knew it was dangerous, but Sofia had to close her eyes to concentrate.

She heard Cathy move and shouted, *Stop!*

Cathy whimpered as Sofia invaded her mind. The action sent a wave of pain through both their heads, but Sofia didn't flinch away from what she had to do.

Cousin, we're going to make this up as we go along, but I promise you we're going to be okay.

If she was going to succeed, she couldn't doubt this for a moment herself.

"You have to trust her," Sid said. She pulled a chair up beside Jason's in the hall across from Cathy's room.

"I do trust her." He didn't look away from the door. "I also worry about her."

Sid took a seat and passed a steaming mug of coffee to Jason. He took a deep gulp. Only then did he look at her. She appreciated his blue eyes and sharp cheekbones, in an aesthetic way.

His eyes narrowed. "Just what are you thinking, daughter of the Wolf Clan?"

She took the mug out of his hand and took a drink. Jason's eyebrow shot up. She laughed. "I know sharing liquids has great symbolism among our kind, Prime of the Caegs, but mostly I wanted a hit of caffeine."

"Mostly?"

"It's complicated. Why is it that suddenly

everything to do with werefolk is complicated?"

"What the werefolk didn't know about for several generations hasn't done them any harm," he said. "No, that isn't true. The Hunyaras and the mortals trying to use them have been a ticking bomb. But I think your concern is very personal—and not just because Cathy Carter is your friend. You're not here to sit vigil, are you?"

She'd been bearing this secret alone for several years. She didn't want to be alone with it anymore. Besides, if anyone deserved an explanation for what she was about to ask, it was Jason Cage. There wasn't a Bleythin in the building, and Laurent had gone home to his wife and child. Sid felt safe enough to talk.

"No," she answered him. "I have been looking for an opportunity to talk to you alone. I think you're the only one in our world who could understand." His eyebrow canted questioningly once again. "I know what you did back in the forties, and why, and I don't think you were wrong."

Pain and regret flashed in his eyes. "I intruded into a mortal's mind and made him do things against his will. How is anything I did right?"

"You were trying to serve the greater good. To help mortals you loved."

He waved her words away. "Excuses."

"Reasons. Good ones." Sid took a deep breath

and plunged on. "I would have done the same. I have done the same."

She waited for his reaction, but all Jason Cage did was look at her and wait.

Sid put the mug on the floor and twisted her hands together in her lap. She hated the guilt and nervousness coursing through her. She was a person who worked hard to get what she wanted, for Goddess's sake! She was strong, independent. She shouldn't feel like a child in need of comfort and absolution.

"It's a long story," she said. "I need your promise to keep it to yourself."

"I'm not a Clan Prime," he reminded her. "It's not up to me to judge you. You have my silence," he added. "You're in love with a werewolf, aren't you?" he asked before she could blurt it out. "Which one? Harry?"

"Of course not! Harry's happily married to a mortal—a vet, actually. And please, no jokes about having a doctor in the family, because we've made them all already. I'm babbling, aren't I?"

"Yes. Young Joe Bleythin, then."

Sid closed her eyes until she got the naked longing under control. "Yes."

She'd just admitted to falling in love with a male who was not a Prime. It was the most dangerous thing a vampire female could do, and she waited with her breath held to see how the Prime would take it.

"You could get him killed."

She let out her breath. "I know." The fear gnawed at her every day. "He doesn't know. He's never going to know. I've seen to that, for his own good."

Jason's hands landed hard on her shoulders and he brought them both to their feet. "What have you done?"

His urgency ripped into her. "I—"

"Is there a bond between you? Is that possible?"

"No!" Not exactly. Some things were too private, too dangerous to share. "I messed with his mind, that's all." She gave a bitter laugh. "That's bad enough, even though I did it for his safety. When I realized how attracted we were to each other, I knew it had to be stopped. Werewolves disapprove of their people mating with mortals, though they don't outright forbid it. Harry's been ostracized by just about everyone but his brothers since he married Marj. I don't want Joe to have to choose between his people and me. Besides—"

"Your Clan Primes would kill him if he dared to touch you."

"Yes." She felt the familiar wave of dread for

Joe's safety. "At least, they'd kill him if they knew I wasn't interested in mating with anyone else."

"And you would lose your freedom if they found out about this love."

"Whatever I feel, I keep to myself," she told him. "I've made Joe believe that neither of us can be interested in being more than friends, that our species are too different to be attracted. I psychically brainwashed him, going against what the Clans stand for, but I did it for the right reasons."

"That was my defense six decades ago, and they put me in prison anyway. Of course, I was also sixteen and stupid. You're neither. Why are you *really* telling me about this?"

Chapter Thirty-five

Sofia continued thrusting her consciousness into her cousin's trapped mind.

Talk to me. Come on, I know you're in here somewhere. I'm getting tired of telepathically stomping around in a head filled with insanity and vicious cravings. I refuse to believe you really prefer dripping entrails to chocolate cheesecake.

Stop snarling at me, Catherine Sigornie Carter, or you'll have to put up with my rant about Great Expectations *again. Even worse, I'll start dissecting* The DaVinci Code. *When I posted about it on my blog, we argued about it for a month. Come on—wake up and argue with me again. Help me find your brain. Once you find your brain, you can find your way back to your human body. You made yourself into a wolf. Now take the next step—come back to yourself. Come back to me.*

All right, I'm going to say it, even if I really don't like the guy—come back to Mike. Come back for Mike. The two of you need to have a long talk. Maybe what you need is a good fight. Or to screw. But you can't do anything with him until you show him you're just as much a werewolf as he is. He may be the Tracker, but you're Hunyara, and that's just as good. Maybe even better. *Definitely* better. *He doesn't deserve you.*

Does . . .

You said something! Sofia responded to the faint, faraway whispered word. *Thank God! Do you know how sick I am of hearing my own voice, even if it is all in your head? Say something else.*

Sofia was answered by the usual snarl and growl from the beast dominating Cathy's mind. *Well, if you have a weapon, use it.*

Mike sucks, Sofia stated.

Does not, Cathy countered, the thought faint but adamant from behind the beast's fury.

Cathy, come back, Sofia called. *Come back . . .*

To Mike? For Mike?

A faint trace of hope reached Sofia.

For you. You have to do it for you. Face Mike as an equal. Love him as all you are.

"Good point," Cathy said with a human voice, a human woman once more.

Sofia sighed in utter weariness. Her shoulders rested against the padded wall, and Cathy's head rested heavily on her shoulder. It took all of Sofia's energy to raise her hand and stroke her cousin's cheek, which was wet with tears. Sofia realized that her cheeks were wet, as well. Tears, or sweat?

"I'm human," Cathy said. "How did you do that?"

"We did it together. From now on, you can do it on your own. Right?"

"Yeah," Cathy said after a long pause. "I think I can."

"Good. I need to sleep now."

"Me, too. Does your head hurt, too?"

"God, yes."

"Try meditating."

Sofia thought a bottle of aspirin might work better, but she didn't have the strength to move. "How does one meditate?"

"Open your mind," Cathy said. "Don't think."

That sounded easy enough. Go blank. Go to silence.

Jason . . .

Jason dreaded whatever was coming, but he

had to ask, "Why are you really telling me about this?"

"I owe my Clan children," Sid answered. "My Matri wanted me to have a child with David Berus, but I wasn't interested. Imagine my relief when he and my mother hooked up."

He knew Sidonie Wolf was different than other vampire females, but her attitude shocked him deeply. "You don't want to have children?"

"Of course I do!"

Her outrage pleased him. "But—"

"I accept my duty to my Clan and to my species. More than that, I very much look forward to being a mother. But I have a very big problem when it comes to the biological mechanism required for getting pregnant."

"You're infertile?"

"No. I simply can't bear the thought of having sex with a Prime. It would be wrong."

"So you're bonded to Joe."

"Only a little, and that's not the point. It's really very simple," Sid said. "I want you to father my child."

"But—you said you couldn't have sex with a Prime. I'm a Prime."

"Sex is not necessary for what I have in mind."

Chapter Thirty-six

The door across the hall flew open before Jason could say another word. He didn't know how to react to Sid's outrageous proposal, anyway.

"Jason?"

Sofia staggered out into the hall and he forgot all about Sid, scooping Sofia up in his arms. He kissed her forehead, then gently touched his lips to hers.

"You look terrible," he told her.

Her arms came around his neck. "I smell, too."

"I wasn't going to mention that. Come on, sweetheart, let me take you away from all this."

"Somewhere with a bed, I hope."

"Excuse me." Sid eased past them and went

into Cathy's den. Jason ignored the look she gave him before she closed the door.

The mattress was wonderfully comfortable. The sheets were smooth and soft, and smelled of vanilla and lavender. The blanket felt like velvet. She had to be dreaming, because this couldn't be the bed in her motel room. A warm body lay along the length of her back and thighs, making her feel safe and comforted. She'd had lots of dreams. The shadows of dark and fantastical images still spun inside her brain, but all was well while they were side by side.

Sofia sighed and came fully awake. She didn't recognize the room when she opened her eyes, but she'd never been anywhere so luxurious before.

"Jason?"

When she sat up and looked at the body beside her, she was disappointed to discover that George and Gracie were the ones keeping her company in the king-size bed.

"Jason?" she called again, and heard the sound of running water from a nearby bathroom. Naked, she got up and padded through the ankle-deep carpet toward the bathroom door.

The door opened before she reached it and Jason stood there wearing a plush black robe. He looked good in black, and she liked the way the robe gapped open to show his ripped chest and abdomen.

"Hello, beautiful," he said.

She was too aware of aches and pains all over to feel beautiful, but her body still reacted to his burning gaze. Heat flooded her insides and her nipples stiffened. He stepped forward to brush his thumbs across the hard peaks.

"What you do to me," she murmured.

"Just wait," Jason said. Then he glanced over her shoulder. "Excuse me." He crossed the room and opened a patio door that faced a courtyard garden. "Out," he ordered the wolves. "And don't do anything to embarrass me," he added as the animals ran outside. Jason closed the door and drew a curtain across it. "Alone at last," he said, turning back to her.

"Where are we?" she asked. "And how'd we get here? Vampire magic?"

"I drove," he said. "You fell asleep on the way over."

She blinked. "Yeah. I sort of remember that."

"We are guests of Lady Juanita at the Citadel of the Wolf Clan. Actually, it's a mansion in La Jolla."

"Lady Juanita's the vampire queen?"

"Not mine," he answered. "She's the head of the Wolf Clan. I'm a Family Prime. She isn't my Matri, but I do have to defer to her in her territory."

Sofia listened to this and rubbed her forehead. "I guess I have a lot to learn about vampire and werewolf social structures."

"You'll have a chance to learn this evening. We've been invited to the Council of Elrond after supper."

"The book or movie version?" she asked. "The council is actually my favorite part of *The Lord of the Rings*."

"Mine, too," he answered. "I was never fond of Tolkien's antitechnology stance, but I love his world-building and the history and mythology—"

"Keep talking sexy to me like that, and I'm going to throw you on the bed and have my way with you." She grinned.

"I'm all in favor of ravishing and being ravished." Jason gestured toward the bathroom. "But first I've run you a hot bath."

She sighed gratefully. "I can certainly use one."

Jason took her hand and led her into the huge bathroom, which was bigger than her entire apartment. It was all pale marble and glass bricks, highlighted with indirectly lit mirrors and matte chrome, and furnished with stacks of thick, royal blue towels.

She stared at the bathtub. "Does this thing come with a lifeguard?"

"I'm your lifeguard." He lifted her and eased her into the wonderful warm water. She leaned her head back against the marble rim and watched appreciatively as Jason shed his robe. What a magnificent body the man had!

"Yes, I'm hot," he said with an ironic smile. When he climbed into the water with her he added, "It's a wonder it doesn't sizzle and steam."

Sofia held her arms out to him. "I think I'm in charge of doing that." But even as he came close and their lips touched, her concerns began to surface.

Take this time for yourself, he whispered in her mind. *For us.* His hands moved through the water and over her.

His thoughts eased her and his touch stimulated; the combination sent her into a blissful haze. "I can't remember how many days it's been since we met," she said.

"Does it matter?" he asked.

His mouth came down on hers and nothing mattered but sensation for a long time after that. At some point her tongue brushed across the sharp points of his teeth, and they shared the heady taste of a drop of blood.

He drew away from her then, even though she whimpered and tried to pull him back.

He chuckled and said, "I like you this way, Wolf Tamer, all needy and hungry." She bared her teeth and Jason laughed. He picked up a sponge and a bottle of bath gel. "Lean back and relax. If I can bathe tigers, I think I can manage one grubby wolf tamer."

"Grubby?" She splashed water at him, even though it was true. "How hard can it be to give tigers a bath? They like water."

"But they don't like soap."

"I like both."

She relaxed in the deep, warm water as Jason's deft hands worked magic on her with sensual touches and creamy, flower-scented lather from her toes to the top of her head. His fingers skimmed along her skin and kneaded away all the soreness in her muscles. His gentle care both soothed and stimulated. When his fingers moved between her thighs, and then inside her, she shuddered with an orgasm at this first intimate touch.

He kissed her throat, nibbled on her ear, and whispered, "If I make love to you now, I'll just have to wash you all over again."

She pressed against him. "I can live with that." She closed her hand around the cock pressing against her belly, stroked the length of it, then guided him inside her. She wrapped her legs around his hips in the buoyant water and he positioned her against the side of the tub.

He made love to her then in long, slow strokes that took her up and over the edge many times, before he joined her in a final explosive orgasm.

Chapter Thirty-seven

When she first stepped into the courtyard and saw Mike playing with the wolves, Cathy paused and smiled. He was a pain in the ass, but she couldn't help but like the big man when she caught him not acting all dour and dangerous.

The moment didn't last long, of course. He sensed her presence and waved the animals away. Turning a frown on her, he said, "You shouldn't be here."

"We're living under vampire rules right now." She snorted. "I now understand what you meant when you said being around vampires plugs up your psychic nose. I don't exactly have a headache, but I don't exactly not have one, either. And our hosts won't let me see my cousin. I was informed that 'the bonding pair needs privacy'—as if we don't have more important things to deal with than Sofia's sex life! Since I couldn't see her, I decided to work things out with you."

"We have nothing to work out." His look dared her to approach.

She took the dare.

The wolves, being sensible creatures, slunk away from a confrontation of two werewolves.

When they were standing toe to toe in front of the garden's central fountain, Cathy pointed up at the clear blue sky. "There's a full moon hidden up there," she told him. "You will note that I'm not wearing a fur coat."

He said nothing.

"Come with me," she said.

She turned around and walked to the entrance of the room she'd been given. She knew he tried hard not to follow her, to be stern and unbending. She also didn't doubt for a moment that he would give in. When he grudgingly came inside, she closed the patio door and drew the curtains.

"Now that we're alone . . ." Cathy pulled her dress over her head. She wasn't wearing anything underneath.

Mike stared.

He was looking at her as a man, which pleased her, but that wasn't what she aimed for at the moment.

"I've been practicing this all day," she told him, and changed into a wolf.

Mike tensed as though he expected her to attack. It took all of her newfound control not to snarl at the insult. She took a step back and sat, carefully not looking into his eyes. She wasn't here to play dominance games, at least not of the traditional kind. She didn't want to be more alpha than Mike Bleythin.

"I'm trying to prove a point," she told him when she turned back to human, and he continued to stare.

"Prove whatever it is to the council," he answered, his voice rough.

"Don't you want to know?"

"It won't matter."

She wanted to grow claws and rake them across the stubborn fool's chest. But full moon or not, she was in control of her volatile werewolf emotions. She stomped one bare foot into the thick carpet to vent her frustration. "This is between you and me, and it matters."

"There isn't anything betw—"

"Then why are you looking at me like that?"

"You're gorgeous, and you're naked. What else am I supposed to do?"

She put her hands on her hips and thrust her breasts out. "You could make love to me. It's all

I've wanted since the day we met. You've never told me you love me or that you even care, but I know you do."

"I can't," he said. "I won't."

He started to turn toward the door but Cathy grabbed his hand and pulled him closer. He gasped as their thighs brushed together.

"It's just lust," he said. "Ordinary, healthy lust. It doesn't mean anything."

"It could. It will. We can be together now, Mike." His eyes closed when she pressed her body against his. "I feel how hard you are. I can smell how much you want me. Stop fighting what you want, what you need. You're a lonely man, Michael Bleythin, but I'm here for you."

"I'm not a man," he ground out. "And you're a feral." His hands grasped her shoulders; she could feel them shaking. "I will not mate with someone I may have to kill."

"You won't have to kill me."

"Are you trying to seduce me to go against the council?"

"Oh, screw the council! This is about *you*. I know you, and I know exactly what will happen if you kill me."

"What?"

"The guilt and grief will drive you crazy. And when you go crazy, you fall off the wagon.

There's nothing more dangerous than a drunken werewolf. This time, you won't make it into rehab—you'll go feral. Then your poor brothers will have to hunt you down and kill you. Since I am very fond of your brothers, I intend to spare them that."

"How kind."

"Not to mention the fact that I have too much to do to let you kill me." She grinned. "Oh, yeah—and I love you."

He stroked the back of his hand across her cheek. She grabbed it and kissed his palm, then placed his hand on her breast.

"Woman . . ." he growled.

"Mate," she answered. "I'm no feral. I'm no danger to werefolk. I am what you want and who you need, and it's time you faced up to it and took me to bed."

She put her hand behind his head and brought his mouth down to hers. The kiss they shared was eager, fierce, and hungry, just the way it should be between alpha mates.

I love you, I love you, I love you, he told her.

I know.

He drew away to look at her. "What about the council? What about what happened to you? What about your fam—"

"Later." She began to unbutton his shirt. "I'll

explain everything and take care of the council later. Right now, let us take care of each other."

All the fight went out of him; only the desire remained. "All right."

Cathy whooped with joy when he finally picked her up and carried her to the bed.

Chapter Thirty-eight

Sofia smiled at herself in the mirror as she brushed out her damp curls.

"You look like a cat that's been into the cream," Jason said.

He stood framed by the doorway, once again dressed in the black plush robe. She had a huge towel wrapped around her.

"I feel like one, too." Their gazes met in the glass, making her tingle inside and out all over again.

"Speaking of cream," he went on. "Are you hungry?"

"Yes," she answered promptly. "In more ways than one, and you know it."

He grinned. "Me, too. But I was thinking of breakfast right now." He glanced into the bedroom. "And some very kind person has left us a tray of goodies. Do you by any chance like baklava?"

"Baklava," she said eagerly, and abandoned her hair without another thought.

"I see you can be seduced by honey and rose-water."

She smiled at him. "Dip yourself in honey sometime and see what happens."

"I'll do that."

The tray of food sat on a small table near the patio doors. She surveyed the selection of pastries, glasses of orange juice, and a carafe of coffee, and rubbed her hands together in delight. "I like vampire room service."

Jason held out a chair for her before taking the chair on the other side of the table. "A peaceful citadel does have a five-star-hotel quality to it." He gestured toward another door. "In there will be a closet full of clothes in many styles and sizes. A Matri never knows who is going to drop in, why, or for how long, so she prepares for all sorts of guests. We're trained quite strictly as children that courtesy and hospitality are part of the glue that holds a civilized culture together."

"Why 'quite strictly'?"

"Because vampire babies are spoiled rotten

little savages." He poured her a cup of coffee. At the same time he ran a bare foot up the length of her calf.

She clasped the fine china cup in her hands as a shiver of desire ran through her. Sofia gave Jason a firm look. "Breakfast first. Then I intend to have my way with you."

"Eat faster," he suggested. He glanced at her throat and his lips uncovered fangs. "But eat a lot. I need you to keep up your strength."

She stuck her tongue out, far more turned on than daunted by the idea of a vampire longing to taste her. Her insides tightened and her nipples hardened at the very thought of it.

Everything was fresh and delicious. The texture of the delicate china dishes alone made her feel like she was going to be caught out at any moment and sent to the kitchen to do the dishes.

"Think of yourself as a lost princess who's been found," Jason said, catching her thoughts.

"The luxury is almost overwhelming," she said as she looked around.

"As children, we are also taught to invest wisely. If you're going to live a long time, it's best to live well."

That made a great deal of sense. Then again, she was so attracted to this man that just about anything he did or said was fine with her. She stood, let the towel drop to a blue puddle around her feet, and held out her hand.

He took it without a word and followed her to the bed, where she took off his robe and they lay down together.

Then he made her feel like far more than a princess. He made her feel like a goddess, worshipped, adored, and satisfied.

"Satiated?" he asked after he'd brought her to orgasm more times than she could count.

Sofia gazed up at the ceiling and let out a long breath. "Hell, no," she answered.

Jason rolled onto his side and patted her hip. "That's what I like to hear."

She looked at him through half-closed eyes. "Though I think I've had more sex today than in all the rest of my life combined." She yawned and stroked a hand up his thigh. "I bet the same cannot be said for you."

Jason gave an unapologetic shrug. "Sex with you makes me forget every other time, place, and person."

Sofia was willing to go with that romantic explanation. A memory of the conversation she'd overheard between Jason and Sid Wolf returned—but she might well have dreamed that, so she let it go.

Jason pulled the sheet up over her. "Excuse me a moment."

He got up and opened the patio door. The wolves came bounding in and jumped up on the end of the bed. Sofia considered shooing them off, but decided it wasn't worth the effort. How her world had changed. She not only had a family and a purpose and a lover, but not very long ago she hated and feared every canine in the world. Now she was becoming fond of George and Gracie.

"Remember that they aren't pets," Jason said, getting back into bed beside her.

She turned to face him. "What are they, then?"

"Friends." He glanced at the animals and smiled. "A reminder."

There was sadness in his words, a hint of loneliness and old pain in his eyes. Sofia began to suspect why wolves were so important to Jason Cage, and she moved closer to him. His arm came around her shoulders.

Sofia rested against him for a while, basking in the heat of his body and the masculine scent of him. It would kill her if she had to leave him. *Take this time for yourself,* he had said. *For us.*

"It's good to just *be* together," Jason said.

Sofia was certain that he hadn't read her thoughts, yet he seemed to know her, body, mind, and soul. There were too many things about him she didn't know.

"Are some things too painful to talk about?" she asked.

"Yes. But that doesn't mean you don't have the right to know about me. All you have to do is ask."

Awed by Jason's emotional generosity, Sofia almost remained silent, but curiosity finally got the better of her. "What's it like? Being in a vampire prison?"

He gave her a gentle, lingering kiss, letting her know that lack of physical contact had been a devastating part of his punishment.

"They took my name from me," he said, then brushed his lips across hers again. "Belonging to our Family, our Clan, or our Tribe is very important to us. Exile can be permanent, but my Family took me back after I'd learned my lesson. I spent much of my time alone. It nearly drove me crazy."

"You are the farthest thing from crazy that I've ever met."

He caressed her cheek. "Thank you, even if you didn't think so at first."

"Having learned that every crazy thing is true, I now know that I'm nuts and you're the lucid one."

"But you didn't know me in my youth, not after the glimpses of the past I've shown you. Maybe if you'd been born all those decades ago, I would have found you when I first went hunting."

"Hunting for what?"

"I don't know if it was something my guards allowed me to do, or something I got away with. But when I couldn't take solitary confinement anymore, I sent my spirit out of my body. My people are all telepathic, but I've always been more psychic than most. Though I couldn't physically leave my prison, I learned how to psychically be free—at least for a little while. I think the mortal term for what I did is astral projection. To me it was my only means of escape. I'd learned my lesson and stayed away from mortal minds, but I'd always been comfortable with wolves, so I telepathically found the pack I used to play with as a child and ran with them whenever I could. I became a wolf. It was very good for me: I learned a great deal about cooperation and leadership; when to run and hide and when to stand and fight." He looked at George and Gracie. "I owe the wolves a lot."

Sofia rolled over to lean on his chest and look down at him. "So I guess running with the wolves helped you learn how to tame the Wolf Tamer."

A sly smile lifted his lips. "Are you tame?"

"Want to find out?" she asked, and straddled his hips.

She leaned forward to kiss him, and his hands cupped her breasts.

But a knock sounded on the door before they could do anything else. "Excuse me," a voice called. "But you have half an hour until dinner."

Resisting the urge to scream in frustration, Sofia called back, "Thank you."

Jason continued to caress her breasts. "Do you think half an hour's enough time?" he asked with a wicked smile.

She smiled back as she positioned herself over his erection. "Let's find out."

Chapter Thirty-nine

I've never seen a more beautiful night." Sofia lowered her gaze from the magnificent full moon to Jason's face, which she found even more magnificent.

"Neither have I," he said. "And I've seen a lot of nights."

"I could howl at a moon like that."

"The werewolves might think it rude," he warned. "I'd prefer laying you down in the jasmine and making love to you."

"I'd like that, too. Though I still might howl with passion if we did."

He sighed. "If only we had time to find out."

They were standing in the courtyard garden with their arms around each other's waist. Dinner was over and they were waiting to be called inside to the meeting. The air was scented with night-blooming flowers, and the murmur of the central fountain added its soothing sound. Peace permeated her senses out here.

"You see this differently than I do, don't you?" she asked the vampire. "This place is arranged to be at its best in the dark."

"Yes," he said. "Lady Juanita doesn't take the daylight drugs, so darkness is her world."

"Why not?" Sofia asked.

She dreaded the upcoming meeting with werewolves and vampires, with the Four Horsemen of the Apocalypse playing bridge in the corner, for all she knew. She welcomed any knowledge she could get and appreciated any distraction.

Dinner had been friendly enough. Their hostess had been gracious, everyone had flirted with everyone, there had been no serious conversation. She'd been able to tell which ones were werewolves, but she still couldn't tell the differences between vampires and mortals. Everyone had seemed normal. Almost everyone present had been wearing black, but since she'd picked a black dress out of a multicolored selection in the closet for herself, she couldn't even count that as odd.

"At dinner," she said, "I kept expecting unicorns or house elves to show up to clear the dishes."

"Were you disappointed? Maybe Lady Juanita's chef is named Igor. Shall we ask?"

"No. But do you know why she doesn't take medicine so she can go out in the daylight? Is she allergic?"

"Some of us are allergic," Jason said. "But taking the drugs is a personal choice. Lady Juanita believes in living a natural, unenhanced life. She doesn't forbid the rest of her Clan from benefiting from modern science, but she doesn't encourage it, either. Since we don't know the long-term effects of—"

"Excuse me, but you are wanted inside now," a young man said, stepping silently out of the darkness. He gave Sofia a quick once-over and an inviting smile, and disappeared just as quickly.

"That," she said, "was a vampire. I'm beginning to be able to tell the boys, at least, because you're all horny all the time."

Jason took her hand to lead her inside. "We're called Primes," he reminded her. "And you are absolutely correct."

"This is not going to be pleasant," Mike whispered as they took their seats on a leather sofa in the large central room. There were no windows and only one door, with Clan Primes standing guard on either side.

"Scared?" Cathy asked. She took it as a good sign that he sat beside her. It was a bad sign that every werewolf in the room glared at him when he did so.

She twined her fingers with his as he gave her a nod.

Sofia and Jason Cage were the last people to enter. Once they were inside, the door was closed and the Prime guards moved to stand in front of it.

"I guess no one's leaving until the vampires say so," Cathy whispered to Mike.

"You know how they always like being in charge," he whispered back. "And I'm not sure that's a bad thing right now. I might have killed you if they hadn't interfered."

"We've talked that through already. Just don't try it again."

He patted her on the knee. "Yes, dear."

Sofia and Cage joined them on the sofa, and Cathy wondered, *Now what?* as the stares from every point in the room grew even more fierce.

"I welcome all of you to my citadel," Lady Juanita said, drawing everyone's attention. "First, Jason, will you please explain what you know about the Hunyara to everyone."

Cathy was deeply interested in this. "Yeah, Jason, Mom never told me anything."

"Wait for it," Sofia whispered. "It's like going to a movie, only—"

"Ladies, please," Jason said. "Since I can't touch everyone in the room, I must concentrate very carefully to communicate telepathically to all of you."

Chapter Forty

Cathy found out what Jason meant as his memories of everything he knew about her mother's family filled her mind. Everything she found out tallied with what she'd learned from Eric.

When Jason was done, Cathy stood up. "My turn," she said.

She explained about how she'd been captured and what her captors wanted from her. She didn't tell them everything, since there were people who needed to be rescued, and she wasn't sure if the werefolk would want to help or destroy the Hunyara. There was certainly plenty of hostility from the werewolves as they listened.

"The people who took me are a threat to all of us," she continued. "They aren't just a gang of crazed feral werewolves. They're organized, fanatical, well funded, and high-tech. They want to destroy werefolk and vampires and anyone else who stands in their way. They have their own agenda, but I have the impression that they're working with allies. Supernatural kind has enemies, but we Hunyara aren't among them.

"There's a full moon tonight, and as a mortal who suffered a werewolf attack, I should be howling at that moon right now. Everyone knows that bitten werewolves turn into mindless monsters during the full moon.

"Thanks to Sofia Hunyara's wolf-taming gift, I've learned to control the madness. I am now no different than any natural-born."

Her claim was greeted with hostile silence. Maybe she shouldn't have put it quite like that, but damn it, it was true!

"What is the matter with you people?" she demanded. "The Hunyara aren't the problem."

"Tracker," one of the werewolf elders finally said. "Why is this creature still alive? It admits to being feral, but you do nothing."

"Even worse," another werewolf said, "you have shielded a feral and protected it. You of all—"

"What a bunch of jerks," Sofia interrupted.

"Destroy the feral!" the elder shouted at Mike.

"The hell I will!" He sprang to his feet and

looked around, challenging all the others. Most looked away. "Our world has changed, and I'm not your damn Tracker anymore."

"Haven't you listened to a word Cathy's said?" Sid spoke into the sudden shocked silence. The vampire female walked out of a shadowed corner of the room to stand beside Cathy and Mike. She glanced toward Lady Juanita. "With your permission?"

"Say what you wish," the Matri answered. "The opinions of all are welcome."

Sid knew very well that the werefolk resented her interference, but no one was going to argue with the Matri.

"I respect werefolk," Sid said. "I work with the Bleythin pack and count them as my friends."

She forced herself to remain calm and reasonable in the face of building animosity. She even sensed Joe's anger at her.

"I am an outsider to the pack structure, but because I am a vampire of the Wolf Clan, which is affiliated with werewolves, I've observed and studied werewolves my entire life. I know that while vampires and werewolves are longtime allies, our methods of coping and dealing with the mortal world have taken drastically different directions in the last century. We agree that hiding from mortals is the safest means of protecting ourselves. Vampires have turned to science and technology as a means to hide in plain sight. Werefolk have taken a very different road. I think that it is a narrow, dangerous road that will lead to your extinction."

"Ain't that the truth," Harry chimed in.

"Traitor!" a female elder snarled at him.

"I've never done anything against the laws of our kind," Harry pointed out. "Marrying a mortal is not forbidden."

"It should be," the elder shot back.

"Why?" a white-haired representative of the werefolk chimed in.

"Continue, Sidonie of House Antonia," Lady Juanita commanded.

"Werefolk have hidden so long and so deeply that I don't think even they know what they're hiding from anymore. You don't allow werefolk to change their mortal lovers; you even discourage them from having mortal lovers. When mortals do somehow get bitten, you don't allow the bitten mortals into your packs, even though the natural-born birthrate gets lower every generation—"

"The bitten can never be trusted!" an elder proclaimed.

"They're abominations," said another.

"Bullshit!" Cathy yelled.

"History shows that bitten werefolk can learn

to be calm during the moonchange given time," Sid went on.

"It isn't the *law* to kill the bitten just because a feral attacked them," Mike pointed out. "But it has become the custom. A custom that I've been expected to carry out. I've become sick of killing people who were victims themselves, and you're angry with me because I stopped doing it."

"Your council has decreed the destruction of all ferals, even the ones that could be tamed," Sid said. "But you can use the Hunyara to—"

"We have to protect ourselves," an elder interrupted. "These Hunyara are outsiders." The elder pointed at her. "You're an outsider. Vampires have no business interfering in our dealings with these Hunyara."

"I think you might be wrong about that," Cathy spoke up.

She turned to Lady Juanita. "My captor told me something that I didn't believe at the time, but the more I think about it, the more sense it makes. He told me that the Hunyara are descended from an offspring of a vampire and a werewolf."

"That's not possible," Joe declared.

"We don't know that," Juanita answered. "Continue."

Cathy noted that the vampires looked as stunned at this revelation as the werefolk. They didn't look as offended, though. Primes, she concluded, would make it with anything that moved.

She gestured at Sofia, who stood and looked around. There was telepathic power in that look that registered on every psychic in the room. None of the werefolk could meet her gaze for more than a few seconds.

Cathy let out a long breath and rubbed her forehead. "Werewolves can't do what she just did, but vampires can. She used the understanding of werewolf instincts and the psychic power of a vampire to save me."

"Maybe the Hunyaras are a cross between the best of both our kinds," Sid said, taking up Cathy's argument. "We need to study them to find out how their gift works. More important, the werefolk need to start thinking like they live in the twenty-first century and let the Hunyara use their gift for the good of all of us. In the meantime, I request that the Matri of the Wolf Clan grant the Hunyara protection."

This sent the werefolk into a frenzy of argument. Cathy, Sid, and Sofia looked at one another and silently agreed to stay out of it. Jason and Mike stood protectively next to them.

"Nothing's getting resolved," Sofia whispered.

"I know," Sid replied. "But we've made a beginning. There's so much that has to be brought out into the open, it's going to take a long time to settle."

"In the meantime, we've got more pressing matters to deal with," Cathy said.

"What aren't you telling us?" Jason asked.

"That most of the bad guys got away with Hunyara hostages."

Sofia swore; Mike roared. Suddenly everyone in the room looked their way. The psychic interference from the vampires as well as the others' shouting had kept their conversation quiet, but Lady Juanita wasn't the only one to give them shrewd, suspicious looks.

When the Matri spoke into the heavy silence, everyone paid attention. "Since there is clearly so much more we need to learn from these Romany, I grant all members of the Hunyara bloodline the protection of the Wolf Clan." She looked around, but nobody was stupid enough to argue. Her gaze settled on Jason. "Will my protection be enough to bring the Hunyara out of hiding?"

"I believe it will," Jason answered.

"But how—" Sofia began.

"It's the twenty-first century, remember?" He took out his cell phone. "I've got Uncle Pashta on speed dial."

Chapter Forty-one

Sofia didn't like it when the Matri took Jason off for a private chat after the meeting; being separated from Jason was almost physically painful for a few moments. Annoyed with herself for being so needy, she went outside in search of privacy, cutting through the garden on the way back to their room. She noticed Sid Wolf sitting on a bench by the fountain and started to pass by with only a nod of greeting.

But the vampire woman looked so forlorn, Sofia couldn't help but stop and ask, "What's the matter?"

She'd always made a point never to pry into other people's business and had avoided making friends, but a lot of her emotional barriers were melting away lately. As for never falling in love—well, she'd certainly screwed up that intention. Damn.

"You're scared," Sid answered. "Terror is coming off of you in waves." She patted the bench beside her, and Sofia took a seat.

"You don't look so happy yourself." She glanced around the garden. "Who are you hiding from?"

Sid sighed. "It's a long story."

"Sordid?"

"Completely. What are *you* scared of? You can't lose Jason, you know. That's what bonding's all about."

"But do I want to keep him? Or anyone? What if I have to spend my life defending the Hunyara from all those werefolk?" The prospect of battles to come made her doubt any possibility of settling down and living happily ever after.

"You might have to do that," Sid agreed. "But does doing your duty really have to interfere with you and Jason? Do you think he'll let it?"

"I don't know. No. But what about what I—"

"Mortals have free will, don't they?"

Sofia nodded.

"Primes do, too. You two will be fine."

Sofia didn't know if that was true, but she still found it reassuring. They sat in companionable silence for a few minutes. Sofia enjoyed the jasmine-scented evening breeze and the splashing of the fountain. "Do you live here?" she asked after a while.

"No. I've got my own place. That might change soon, though."

Sofia sensed that Sid didn't want to pursue that subject. She recalled Sid's part in the meeting and said, "You're quite the politician, aren't you? I was impressed by the way you worked the situation around so that the Matri offered to protect my family."

"That was more Cathy's doing than it was mine. She provided the vital information; I used it. I was raised to be a diplomat. I'd rather be a warrior, but I'm likely to end up being a Matri."

"Then watch out, world." Sofia grinned.

Sid gave her a conspiratorial smile. "Maybe. I need to have a few kids first, start my own house." She shook her head. "That's going to be complicated, but having children is important."

Sofia considered the vampire for a moment. "I like you, Sid," she said. "But I won't if you try to play me. Why don't you tell me straight up what you want?"

Sid smiled at her. "I'd hate to sit across a negotiation table from you."

"Isn't that what we're doing? Your conversation with Jason about wanting his baby wasn't something I dreamed, was it?"

Sid looked around as though frightened of being heard. *How much of this "dream" conversation do you remember?*

I want you to father my child. Sex is not necessary for what I have in mind, Sofia remembered. "You're looking for a sperm donor."

Sid nodded. Then she proceeded to telepathically whisper her reasoning into Sofia's head.

It gave Sofia a great deal to think about, but they were interrupted by Joe Bleythin's arrival before she could ask any questions.

"I've been looking for you, Sidonie."

He sounded calm, but the furious wolf Sofia sensed beneath the surface made her skin crawl.

Sid stood. "I thought you might be." She looked like she was prepared for the worst.

Sofia knew she didn't belong here. Dealing with this werewolf was Sid's business.

As she walked away, she heard Joe say, "Lucy, you got some 'splainin' to do."

"What can I say?" Sid asked. "I'm as surprised as you are."

"Do you know that you blink when you lie?"

"I do not!"

Joe gave a harsh laugh. The air around them seemed to grow colder. "So you are lying."

He knew her too well—except for the things

she'd made him forget. Sid turned away. "I do not want to have this conversation with you, Joseph Bleythin. At least not here and now."

"What *did* you know?" he demanded. "When did you know it, and for how long? And exactly what have you *not* been telling me?"

"About the Hunyaras? I don't know any more than you do about the bad guy's claims about Cathy's family." That was true, even if . . .

"Your species didn't seem repulsed by the idea of mating with members of my species when the subject came up. Why was I the one who protested?"

Sid shrugged. "Well, you know Primes . . ."

"How much have you lied to me? Why?"

His anger was shredding her. "It's complicated." She sighed. "Maybe the lesson should be to never do anything for anyone else's own good—because it'll only come back and bite you in the ass."

"Explain that to me."

"Okay." She looked up at the moon rather than at Joe, then took a deep breath. "I love you."

He was silent for a long time. She heard him pace around the fountain, then come back to her.

"I don't love you," he said.

Sid made herself look him in the eye. "Yes, you do. You just don't remember."

After that, the shouting started.

Chapter Forty-two

Sofia was surprised to find Jason already in their room when she reached it. He'd changed into black silk pajama bottoms, in which he looked mighty fine, and was lying on the bed reading a book. She instantly wanted to climb on beside him and toss aside the book.

"And you a lover of literature," he said, looking up and raking her with a hot gaze.

"Some things are more important than a good book." She chuckled. "That would be considered heresy if I posted it on my blog. Then again, it would be considered porn if I posted what I'm currently considering—and I'd get a lot more hits than I do talking about books."

He put the book on the nightstand and patted the mattress beside him. "Come here."

"Give me a minute."

She smiled and went into the walk-in closet. If he could wear black silk, so could she. She found a sexy, lacy confection in a lingerie drawer and quickly slipped into it. She gave a brief glance in the full-length mirror to check the effect, then shook out her long curls so that they rested on her shoulders and framed her face.

"How do I look?" she asked, stepping back into the bedroom.

He looked her over, eyes lighting with lust. "Wanton," was his response.

"What a lovely, old-fashioned word." She slinked forward, and he rose to meet her. "George and Gracie aren't likely to disturb us, are they?"

He took her in his arms. "They're kenneled up, and the evening is ours." He nuzzled her throat, kissed across her collarbone and down between her breasts.

Sofia curled her toes in the deep carpet. "That feels sooo nice." She ran her hands over his shoulders and arms, relishing the feel of sculpted muscles and warm flesh. "What did the Matri want with you?"

He gave her a look that said this wasn't the time or place for conversation, but after a moment he gave in to her curiosity. "She's concerned about Sidonie. She wanted to know if I knew any Prime among the Families that might spark Sid's interest."

"What did you tell her?"

"That I'd think about it."

"Um . . ."

Jason drew away from her. "What?"

"Can we talk? About Sid."

He looked almost panic-stricken. "I don't know what you overheard, but—"

"I know she wants to have your baby. Rather, she wants you to father her baby."

Jason sat down on the bed and stared at her. "You're taking this calmly."

He wasn't. The agitation that boiled off him made her head hurt.

"I begin to suspect a cultural problem here that I have no clue about." She pulled up a chair to sit down, rested her folded hands on the smooth silk of her nightgown, and kept her tone reasonable and as academic as she could manage. "Walk me through this, please. I have been given to understand that vampires are matrilineal." Jason nodded. "Women are heads of households, and all children belong to the mother and are part of the mother's Clan, no matter who the father is, whether they're bonded or not."

"That is correct."

"And it is not only customary, but necessary for the viability of the species, for vampire women to have children with several vampire males. They reproduce this way until they acquire a bondmate, and after the bonding they only have children with the Prime who is their bondmate."

"Yes."

"Okay, so, Sidonie is not bonded."

He gave her a hot look that made her shiver all over. "I am."

Sofia refused to give in to the strong urge to forget about everything and throw herself on the man. "You're working on being bonded. I believe the process of mind-soul-body integration takes some time."

"*We're* working on being bonded," he answered. "You and I. Sidonie Wolf has nothing to do with it."

"No, she doesn't. She doesn't want to have anything to do with you sexually. I'd cheerfully kill her if she did. She simply wants you to contribute your DNA to conceiving a child that will be totally hers. She wants to take the sex out of an ancient custom and put a modern spin on it. She wants a sperm donor—that's all."

"All?"

He stood, with grace that barely covered his outrage. For a moment Sofia shrank back in her chair. It was like having a furious giant standing over her, but she didn't give in to the intimidation for long. She met his gaze, Wolf Tamer to Beast Master, and after a few seconds of mutual glaring Jason resumed his seat. He hadn't calmed down at all, though. This was *so* not going well.

"I really don't understand why you're angry."

He crossed his arms over his bare chest. "You want to pimp me out to stud, and you wonder why I'm angry?"

"Oh, please. That's just male ego talking. I thought you were better than that."

"I am Prime!"

"Good for you," she snapped as her own temper flared. She shot to her feet and glared down at him this time. "Aren't you the person who recently pointed out that this is the twenty-first century? What's wrong with vampires using alternate fertility methods?"

"That's sick and disgusting and utterly—"

"Mortal?" she questioned sarcastically.

"Yes," he snarled back. "If Sid wants a baby, let her do it the right way—instead of using you to try to get to me."

It wasn't that she really wanted him to be Sid's

sperm donor, but she saw the other woman's point, and her desperation. "Jason, you're being old-fashioned."

"In this, yes. I belong to you." He grabbed her shoulders hard. "And you're mine. Conversation closed. Do you understand?"

Chapter Forty-three

Jason knew instantly that he hadn't phrased that right. He took his hands off her shoulders, terrified that he'd left bruises, and clasped his hands tightly behind his back. "I'm sorry. I—"

Sofia turned away from his apology. She walked to the patio door and he let her go, realizing that the hurt he'd caused her wasn't physical.

"You aren't my property," he said. "I didn't mean it like that."

She stopped and rested her head wearily against the glass door. "I am not ready for this. I am *so* not ready for this."

He moved up behind her and put his arms around her waist. Though she tensed at his touch, he took it as a good sign that she didn't move away. He buried his face in her thick hair and breathed in the scent of her. He didn't understand why being near her brought him peace, even now, when she was so agitated, but he accepted this gift she brought to his life. He hated that the last thing Sofia was feeling right now was peaceful and longed to help her.

"I'm not ready for this," she repeated in an anguished whisper.

"For us?" he asked, dreading the answer.

"For everything. For life. Everything's changed so fast. Everything is so different! I'm used to being alone, to being unwanted, to having a father who's a murderer and . . ." Her voice trailed off into a long, strangled moan.

Her tense muscles went suddenly limp, and she threw her head back with a tortured wail.

Jason quickly turned her around and pulled her close.

She shook like a tree in a storm, sobs racking her.

My father! Daddy!

I know. I know.

She cried and cried, a lifetime's worth of grief pouring out of her. She bled inside, battered by pain.

Her pain cut through him. He wanted desperately to make it stop—but no. She needed this.

Sometimes pain could be a gift, no matter what

it felt like at the time. So he held her, and loved her and waited, hoping she could come to terms with all she'd lost.·

When she sagged against him, he picked her up and sat on the bed with her cradled on his lap.

After one last huge shudder, finally Sofia lifted her head. "My father went to prison for killing feral werewolves."

"Yes." Jason used a tissue to wipe her wet face.

She took the tissue from him and blew her nose. Then she scrubbed her hands across her cheeks. When he rose to carry her into the bathroom, she said, "I can walk."

He ignored her and didn't put her down until they got to the sink. He stood back while she splashed cold water repeatedly on her burning face and handed her a towel when she straightened.

"You're too good to me," she said. "I'm a blubbering fool."

"You needed the release. Feeling any better now?" He already knew the answer to that; her broken heart beat inside his body. He would do anything to make her whole.

She looked at him, her dark eyes full of bleak hopelessness. "He did the wrong thing for the right reason."

Jason nodded.

"He's serving life in Gull Bay Supermax." She swallowed fresh tears. "He did it for me." The bleak expression left her eyes, but the hurt remained.

Jason crossed his arms. "I see. You won't let yourself grieve anymore, but you will blame yourself for the choice he made. Don't do that, sweetheart. He wouldn't want you to."

"That selfless bastard," she spat out. She threw down the towel and marched out of the bathroom.

He followed her into the bedroom and watched her pace restlessly around the room. He knew a caged tiger when he saw one. An angry caged tiger.

"What are you thinking?" he asked.

She turned to him. "Can't you read my mind?"

"Sometimes it's wiser not to."

"This isn't justice," she said. "This isn't fair. What am I going to do?"

"Visit your father," Jason suggested. "Let him know you know why he did what he did. Let him know you forgive him, and that you love him."

"Of course I love him. I've hated his guts, but I haven't stopped loving him. Believe me, I tried." She went back to pacing. "I wonder if I could hire a lawyer and get the case reopened with new evidence."

"You can't mean that."

"Why not? Even if every werewolf in the world comes after me for outing them, I don't care."

"I'd care. I'd have your back, sweetheart, and I'd have to kill a lot of nice werewolves defending you."

She saw his point and kicked a chair leg in frustration, then winced. He felt the blood racing through her and the wild pounding of her heart.

"This is life and death we're talking about, Sofia. You are in my world now, and our secrets cannot be revealed."

She nodded reluctantly and began pacing again. "I know. But something has to be done! I cannot—*will* not—leave an innocent man in that place."

"He is not innocent," Jason reminded her.

She stopped moving, her fists bunched at her sides. "Why did he have to kill them? Why couldn't he have—"

"He was a father defending his child. I'd kill any monster that threatened my child."

"All right. Maybe the question is, why did he have to get caught? Where was his cleanup crew to make sure the police didn't know anything supernatural occurred?"

"That was—unfortunate."

"Something has to be done," she declared. "We have to do something to help him."

"I don't know what." He hated the way she felt, desperate and close to breaking again, her control a brittle and fragile shell. "We'll think of something," he promised.

"We could break him out of Gull Bay."

He might have laughed had this not been so deadly serious. "Sweetheart, this is real life, not some show on the Fox network."

She countered, "Vampires, werewolves, skinhead biker bad guys? Don't talk to me about *reality,* Jason Cage."

"Okay. Point taken. But how could we—"

"Wait. I think I've got an idea. Vampires. And werewolves." Sofia laughed. "It's crazy, but it just might work. Of course it'll work! It *has* to work."

He caught her enthusiasm. "What have you got in mind?"

"Do you know anything about the security at a place like Gull Bay?"

"Do you?"

"I know as much as anyone on the outside can know about Gull Bay." She shrugged. "As much as I tried to forget about my father I couldn't stop myself from doing websearches about where he is. I didn't want to know, and I couldn't bear not to."

"That is understandable."

"Is it? Anyway, Gull Bay was built specifically to house Level Four offenders—the worst of the worst. It's located in an isolated spot in northern California. My father's in the Security Housing Unit, which means he spends twenty-three hours a day alone in a cell. Only the staff are allowed into the SHU, except for routine searches by drug-sniffing dogs. The dogs and their handlers are brought in from police units outside the prison. Do you see where I'm going with this?"

Jason shook his head. "No."

"You and Cathy in wolf form can go in as one of those canine units."

He began to get an inkling of what she had in mind. "You want to use our strength and telepathic abilities to break your father out."

She nodded. "I remember how you psychically made the cops at the motel go away. All you have to do is go into Gull Bay, make everybody in the place forget Daddy ever existed, and bring him out."

By the Goddess, the woman didn't know what she was asking! But she deserved to have her father. And he would do anything for her happiness. He wasn't going to tell her what it might cost him, though.

He forced a confident smile. "It's so crazy it just might work."

"Good. Let's go talk to Cathy."

When she started toward the door, he turned her around and pointed her toward the bed. "You're exhausted. I'll go talk to Cathy. You get some rest."

Chapter Forty-four

Sofia lay with her eyes closed while Jason got dressed, and she tried to go to sleep after the door closed behind him. She'd never felt so drained; her muscles burned with weariness. Yet her mind raced, and after a while she couldn't take the thoughts chasing around in her head any longer. She wanted Jason to come back and began counting the seconds he was gone.

When she grew disgusted with her neediness, she got out of bed, put a matching short robe on over her black nightgown, and went out onto the patio. A few breaths of brisk night air helped clear her head. She stared up at the beautiful night sky until she heard a footstep.

"Can't sleep?" Sid's voice asked out of the darkness. The vampire stepped onto the patio.

"Me, either. With all the psychic turmoil flying around the place, I doubt if anybody's asleep."

"You've been crying," Sofia observed.

"You, too."

Sofia nodded. "I hate living on an emotional roller coaster."

"It's been a rough week."

Sofia recalled their earlier conversation by the fountain. "I talked to Jason about fathering the baby. It didn't go well."

Sid wasn't disappointed. "That's okay. I think that plan's pretty much on hold for the moment, anyway." She looked concerned. "Did you two have a big fight over it? Is that why you've been sending out so much hysterical energy?"

"There was a bit of stress during that conversation," Sofia answered, "but my hysteria came from something else."

Sofia explained to Sid about her father, and the plan to save him. She thought Sid would be pleased by what she told her, but the vampire woman looked worried when Sofia was done.

"What's wrong?" Sofia asked. "Don't you think it will work?"

"I think that Jason Cage might be the wrong person to ask to break your dad out of Gull Bay."

Sofia was confused. "Why? He agreed with the plan."

"He's Family, and the Families have different rules about dealing with mortals than the Clans do. The Families do not directly interfere in mortal matters. He got in deep trouble for trying to save the world once already. I don't think his people will take kindly to his interfering again."

Sofia sank weakly onto a patio chair and she swore—at life, at herself. What had she done?

Totally miserable, she looked up at Sid. "I saw how determined he looked when he left. I don't think I could stop him now even if I begged him. How much trouble have I gotten him into? What do I do?"

"Talk to Lady Juanita," Sid advised. "Maybe she can think of something."

"If you're looking for Jason, he just left," Cathy said when Sofia entered the central meeting room.

"I know." Sofia tapped her forehead. "It's impossible for me not to know where he is."

There were several others in the room with her cousin. Mike and Harry Bleythin, Antonia, and David Berus were there, along with Lady Juanita and several people whose names Sofia couldn't remember.

"I'm glad you're here," Cathy told her. "We

were discussing a plan to rescue our missing relatives."

"Cathy's come up with something we believe will work," Harry said. "We want to know what you think of it."

Of course they had more than one crisis to deal with. Sofia felt almost selfish for putting her concerns first, but Jason's well-being meant more to her than anything else—even more than her father's freedom. She closed her eyes and tried to bury the pain of the loss beneath its usual layer of scar tissue.

"Are you ill?" David Berus was suddenly beside her.

"No."

Everyone's concerned attention was now on her. She tried to smile reassuringly at them, but couldn't manage it. Cathy, Mike, and Harry all came toward her, but she gestured for them to sit down.

She wasn't used to asking for help, but for once, she didn't hesitate. She looked to the Matri. "Lady Juanita, I did something that's going to get Jason in terrible trouble, and you have to help me stop him. Please."

The Matri didn't show any surprise. "But the plan to help your father sounds workable."

"After we made a few suggestions and alterations to it," Mike added.

Cathy gave Mike an annoyed look. "Mike means he insisted he be the one to go into the prison with Jason."

Mike brushed a hand through Cathy's hair. "I'm not letting my mate anywhere near a bunch of dangerous convicts. Besides, I owe Jason one."

"You don't understand," Sofia said. "Jason will be in terrible trouble if he does this. His people will punish him, and he knows it. He's being noble, which is lovely, but I can't let him go back to jail for breaking somebody else out."

"Of course, he's Family," Lady Juanita said. "He's so much like one of us that I'd forgotten the restrictions he lives under." She looked steadily at Sofia. "My dear, because he is Family and I am Clan, I have no authority to forbid him to do this."

"He's doing what's right," David said.

"His Matri won't see it that way," Mike said.

"True," David looked at Sofia sympathetically. "You and I may not approve of the way the Families choose to deal with mortals, but they have their own good reasons for their policies."

"Well, I think my uncle deserves to be broken

out of jail," Cathy spoke up. "Come on, people! Let's think of a way to get this done."

"The solution is perfectly simple," Antonia said. "Isn't it, David, my love?"

David looked at her and laughed. "I *am* Clan Prime. Rescuing mortals is what I do." He told Sofia, "I am not as strong a telepath as Jason, but my ability will suffice for the assignment. May I offer myself as the means for righting the wrong done to your father?"

Sofia's heart sang with gratitude, and she threw her arms around the big, blond vampire. "Thank you! Thank you, thank you!"

"She agrees," Antonia said. "Now get your hands off my bondmate, young lady."

Sofia quickly stepped away from David. "But what do I tell Jason? He isn't going to back off from going through with this mission."

"You need not tell him anything," Lady Juanita said. "All you have to do is go back to your room and do what comes naturally to a bonding couple."

Everyone laughed, but Sofia protested, "I can't lie to him. That wouldn't be right."

"You don't have to talk to him at all," Cathy said. "All you have to do is screw his brains out until the mission's accomplished."

"You're already dressed for it," Mike pointed out.

Sofia had forgotten she was only wearing a skimpy nightgown and robe, and she blushed. Jason had told her that the reason they kept being distracted by lust from other matters was because of the bonding. She hadn't understood at first, then the need had proved as inconvenient as it was wonderful, and now she saw how this distraction could help them. This wasn't manipulating him, it was saving him.

"All right," she told the group waiting for her decision. "I can do this."

"Bite him," Lady Juanita advised. "And get him to taste you, as well. Keep that up and neither of you will notice the time passing. Now go." She gestured toward the door. "Jason will be looking for you, anyway."

She nodded. "Yes. I'd better get him back to our bedroom, fast."

Chapter Forty-five

"I'm so sore, I don't think I can get out of bed." Sofia ran her foot up Jason's calf. "But then, I don't want to get out of bed."

She had no idea how long they'd been there. She'd hidden the clock in the nightstand drawer and had kept the curtains drawn. Time kept going in and out of focus as they made love again and again. Whenever they slept, they'd wake up to find food waiting for them, and eating always turned into lovemaking.

"Good." Jason caught her foot in his hand and started kissing her toes, which she found thoroughly erotic. He also tickled her instep, which got her giggling. The combination of sensations drove her crazy, and she became lost in them until—

"Ow! You bit my toe!"

"I did," Jason admitted, and did it again.

This time, the lightning bolt that shot through her was completely the opposite of pain.

"Do that again."

"Gladly."

He tasted her blood, and she writhed with orgasms from each little wound. When he finished with her foot, he moved to sink his teeth into the back of her leg, then to the inside of her thigh. Every touch took her higher.

His head moved higher still between her legs and his tongue began to make lazy cat laps across her throbbing, swollen clitoris. This delight took her out of herself in an entirely different sensual way, but it was no less intense. Jason's every touch brought her pleasure.

"My turn," she managed to gasp out after his tongue had worked wonders on her for a while.

He lifted his head to look into her eyes. His smile was teasing. "Sweetheart, was that an invitation?"

"It was a demand. I want to take you into my mouth."

He didn't need coaxing.

She took her time, slowly sinking her mouth onto his cock, then repeating the process again and again as she teased the swollen head and length with her tongue. She made him writhe and buck just as he had done to her, until she finally let him come.

When he was spent, she looked at him with an expression of triumph and not a little smugness. "I do believe you are wasted, Mr. Cage."

"Madam, you are wicked," he told her.

She batted her eyelashes. "I try."

"Come along." He got up and hauled her unceremoniously over his shoulder.

"Hey!" she protested as he headed toward the bathroom.

"You said you were too sore to walk."

"I said I couldn't get out of bed."

"Well, now you're out of bed." He took them into the glass-walled shower and didn't put her down until a pulsing, steaming stream poured over them. "And now you're *really* in hot water, mortal."

She picked up a thick bar of coconut-scented soap and washed his hair, then worked thick lather all over his long, muscled body. He took the bubbling bar and returned the favor, and they managed to make love standing up despite their slippery, soap-covered bodies.

When they were finally finished, Jason carried her back to the bed.

Just as he put her down, someone knocked on the door.

Jason swore, but went to answer it. She pulled on a robe and hurried after him, handing him a robe before he could open the door.

"Have you no shame?" she asked.

"None," he answered, but he did tie the belt as he called, "Who is it?"

"Lady Juanita requests your presence in the central chamber immediately," a voice on the other side of the door replied.

"Damn," Jason whispered. A Matri's request was the same as an order. He gave Sofia an apologetic look, and an affectionate pat on the fanny. "Of course," he answered the messenger.

Sofia hurried into the closet to get dressed; the eagerness that radiated from her served to clear Jason's head. He threw open the patio door curtains to discover that it was the middle of a brilliant day. He looked around the wrecked bedroom and scrubbed his hands over his face.

He remembered finding Sofia in the hallway outside the meeting room last night and their returning here. She'd said, *"I want you to make love to me as a Prime."* When she'd kissed him she bit his tongue and the sharing of blood drove him into a sexual frenzy.

That had been last night, hadn't it?

He looked at her suspiciously when she came back into the room wearing jeans and a red shirt, but she gave him such a deliriously hopeful smile, he couldn't bear to ask her what she'd done.

He had the feeling he'd find out very soon, in the meeting room.

Chapter Forty-six

Sofia barely noticed when the Prime who opened the meeting room door announced her name. The man standing by Lady Juanita's chair took all of her attention. Tears welled in her eyes and she could barely breathe.

He was taller than she remembered, and thinner. And when had he shaved his head? The wary expression on her father's face was anything but welcoming.

Instead of rushing headlong, she stopped in the center of the room and waited, awkward and unsure as silence stretched out around her.

It was Jason who finally said, "What's the matter with you, Hunyara? Don't you recognize your own daughter?" He gave her a slight shove and whispered in her ear, "He's all you want. Go to him."

Sofia was shocked into movement, more by the bitterness in Jason's tone than anything else. She began to turn to him.

Her father said, "Sofia?"

At the sound of her name, she ran forward and flung her arms around the man who'd spoken. His voice was so familiar. So was the way his arms came protectively around her.

After a while, she noticed that her embrace was just as protective of him, just as strong.

"You've grown up," he said.

She lifted her head and nodded.

"I'm sorry it was so hard on you," he said. "I didn't mean to hurt you."

"I'm fine," she said. "I really am." She looked around and saw David Berus smiling at her.

"Thank you," she said to the Prime. "I don't know how to thank you."

"The plan was yours; Michael and I merely carried it out. With your father's cooperation, of course."

"Wait a minute—" Jason began.

"I think we should leave these two alone to get reacquainted," Lady Juanita announced. "All of us," she added.

The tug of separation as Jason left was disturbing, but Sofia concentrated on her father.

"Where do we start?" she asked when they were alone.

He looked her over carefully, then met her gaze for a long time. "You're one of us," he said, and seemed disappointed.

"A Hunyara wolf tamer, you mean?"

He nodded. "I'm so sorry. All I wanted was to keep you from that curse."

She didn't feel cursed. But how could she tell the man who'd given up his freedom to protect her that he'd done the wrong thing?

"Now you're involved with werewolves and vampires, too, and the dangerous madness is going to continue through the generations."

"I can't deny it," Sofia told him. "We just have to cope. Can you—do what I do? Are you a wolf tamer?"

He shrugged. "I have the gift, though I never wanted it. I never used it after my father trained me. I passed it on to you, but I wouldn't let those old men raise my fragile little girl the way I was raised. Before your mother died, I promised her I wouldn't expose you to danger."

Well, that made sense. Mama was so girly.

"How did you learn the taming?" he asked.

"A vampire taught me." She smiled at the thought of Jason. "The same vampire who taught

Grandpa and Great-grandpa. So I've had the best teacher. I'm not afraid of what I can do. It can help people."

She explained to him about Cathy, and about everything else that had happened recently. He asked her about the years since they'd seen each other, so she told him what she'd done with her life. He didn't want to talk about life inside the prison. She supposed they'd have to probe those sore spots someday, but now was the time for happy reunions.

She had no idea how long they talked, but at some point, someone brought in a tray of sandwiches and tall glasses of iced tea. Long after they'd finished lunch, another vampire came into the room.

"Mr. Hunyara, if you could come with me, please?" he asked politely. "I'm here to help you work on your new identity, and I need to take some photos before I can go any further with the project. Sorry to take him away from you," he told Sofia as her father rose to go with him. "How would you feel about becoming a professional dog handler as your new profession, Mr. Hunyara?" the vampire asked as they left.

Sofia smiled, so grateful to the Wolf Clan for putting their well-organized resources at the disposal of her family. *I'm going to have to do something especially nice for them. Lady Juanita deserves much more than a thank-you for this.*

Once her father was gone, she remembered Jason and rose reluctantly to her feet. He was furious with her; she could feel it. No point in putting it off a moment longer.

She found Jason in the garden, sitting on the bench near the fountain. A warm breeze ruffled his brown hair. He was staring at the ground and didn't look up when he asked, "How's your father?"

His concern melted her heart. "Disoriented, I think. He's been out of the world for a long time."

"I know how that is," he said. "I'll talk to him, if you'd like."

"I'd appreciate that." She hated the strained sound of her own voice, and the hostility that was just under the surface of his. "Jason."

Blue eyes as hot as lightning suddenly met hers; the blaze of fury nearly burned her to ash where she stood.

Sofia took a step back, but fought off the urge to turn and run away. "I didn't come out here to tame a wolf," she told him.

"I'm a great deal wilder than a wolf when I let myself go." His tone was low and even, and really, really scary. "I am Prime."

"How am I supposed to translate that? Does it mean that I hurt your pride and you're pissed off at me?"

He nodded. "Very." He was standing in front of her before she could blink. "Why did you do that to me?" he demanded. "Why did you trick me while somebody else kept the promise I made to you?"

"Because I discovered how dangerous that promise was to you, and I wasn't going to let you go back to prison. I thank you for the promise. I truly appreciate your good intentions, but I had to protect you."

"It's *my* job—my duty and my privilege—to protect you, Sofia Hunyara."

"Back at you, Jason Cage," she snapped. "If we're going to have this connection between us, it has to go both ways. We have to be equals in this."

The fury slowly drained from his eyes, but his expression remained cold. "I don't know if I'm ready for this," he said. And then he left.

Chapter Forty-seven

"I can't believe he just stomped off to sulk and play with his wolves," Sofia told Cathy. "It's been three days, and I'm still upset about that conversation."

She kept her eyes on the busy freeway, trying to pretend that Jason's words didn't still sting. Every mile away from her pissed-off bondmate stretched her nerves, but this trip to Los Angeles was necessary. Maybe it was better for them to be apart, anyway.

"Men can be so melodramatic," Cathy commiserated. "He knows you did it for his own good, even if he doesn't want to admit it. Besides, it's not as if he didn't enjoy himself meanwhile—for days!"

"I hated hurting him. I should have done it a different way."

Cathy gave an earthy laugh. "How many ways did you do it?"

Erotic memories flooded her, and Sofia laughed as well. "More than I can remember."

"Jason's a Family Prime who thinks like a Clan boy. He needs to remember his pragmatic roots and learn to appreciate you."

The air conditioner in the borrowed car strained as the heavy traffic slowed. "Thanks for volunteering to help me pack up my apartment," Sofia said to her cousin.

"No problem," Cathy said. "It'll give us something to do after the vampire docs do the blood tests on us at their clinic."

"How many vampire clinics are there?"

"I have no idea. But I do know that this one in L.A. is where most of their medical research is done. I've never thought much about vampires until now."

"You had your own werewolf problems to deal with. Do you think this Hunyara werewolf-vampire connection is real?"

"I don't trust anything Eric told me," Cathy answered. "But I hope it is real, just for the sake of keeping the werewolves from coming after our Hunyara asses. Man, life has changed in the last few days! We've discovered family secrets, you got your dad back, I've got control of my shape-shifting, Mike's given up being the Tracker, and Sid's quit the firm and has gone to stay with her sire."

"Everything changes." Sofia saw the sign for their exit and moved over a lane. She sighed. "I never thought I'd drop out of college, but I posted it on my blog for the world to read about, so it must be true. So here I am, back in town to do just that. Along with a million other things."

"Blood tests and getting you moved are first on the agenda, though," Cathy said.

"So it would seem," Sofia said, and she and her cousin grinned wolfishly at each other.

"One very good thing about being a werewolf is that we heal fast," Cathy said as she removed the Band-Aid on the inside of her elbow.

"While I have a bruise the size of a quarter," Sofia complained, rubbing her arm. It felt like a half gallon of blood had been drawn by the vampire technicians. "And it itches."

"Whiny wimp," her cousin teased.

"You're buying my ice cream cone," Sofia declared as they reached the ice cream shop down the street from her apartment. There had been other medical tests, too, and the doctor who ran the clinic had asked lots of questions. They'd spent several hours there before returning to her university neighborhood. The doctor had wanted them to spend the night at the clinic, but they had other plans.

"How long before we know anything from the blood tests?" Sofia wondered as they waited in line.

"They told me several weeks, maybe months. DNA testing results really take much longer than they show on TV crime shows."

"I guess." Sofia was thinking of Jason, so she bought a double scoop of the deepest, darkest chocolate she could get.

When they had their ice cream, they went to the small park across the street. They found an empty bench under a tree and enjoyed their cones in silence for a while as they looked around the busy neighborhood a couple of blocks from the university. There was plenty of foot and car traffic to watch.

"I'm going to miss this place," Sofia said as she wiped her fingers with a napkin. "I've enjoyed school."

"Look at it this way," Cathy said. "The world loses a literature teacher and gains a wolf-taming superhero."

Sofia snorted. "I guess I can go along with that.

Except that I was majoring in electrical engineering. I read for fun."

"Whatever." A dangerous grin lit Cathy's features. "I think the bad guys read your blog and followed us to L.A. I recognize a couple of vehicles that are circling the park."

"Why, cousin dear," Sofia said as they stood. "Do you think we're about to get kidnapped?"

"I certainly hope so."

"About time," Sofia said. They began to walk toward the street. "Let's head back to my place. That ought to make it easier for them."

Chapter Forty-eight

"Good morning, ladies."

The unfamiliar voice roused Cathy to consciousness. The only scent she could detect, other than her cousin's, was that of coffee. The lack of smells told her they were in the presence of the enemy, but at least the bastards weren't complete barbarians—unless they didn't offer her a cup when she opened her eyes.

"Would you like a cup of coffee?" the man asked.

"No," Sofia answered. There was a hysterical pitch to her voice.

Cathy sat up and gave her cousin a frown. "Don't be an idiot—accept the man's hospitality."

Sofia looked their captor over carefully. He was tall and strongly built, with a long braid of blond hair and a heavy beard. His presence pretty much filled the one-room cabin.

"Not exactly a man," she corrected herself. "Werewolf."

He nodded.

"Oh, God, not another one!" Sofia had her arms wrapped around her drawn-up legs and was looking at their captor with wide, terrified eyes.

Cathy gave a disgusted shake of her head. "I bet you're Nathan," she told the werewolf. "Eric told me about you."

"Did he?" the deep-voiced male growled.

"May I have some coffee?" she asked.

He poured a mugful from a thermos and brought it to her. When she reached for the cup, he grabbed her by the hair and pulled her to her feet. "What happened to Eric?" he demanded. "What did he tell you?"

"Eric's dead," she said with a grimace of pain, leaving out the fact that she'd killed him herself. "He died when the Bleythin pack showed up to 'rescue' me. They didn't ask if I wanted rescuing," she added. "Then they made me go back to spending the moonchange locked in a cage. Eric promised me freedom. You didn't have to knock me out to get me here; I was hoping you'd come for me."

"You don't mean that," Sofia said. "You don't want to be a werewolf. *I* don't want to be one," she added in a bleak whisper.

Nathan let Cathy go and laughed at Sofia's fear. "You'll get used to it."

"You haven't bitten her yet, have you?" Cathy asked.

"No," he told her. "I'll let you do the honors to prove you really want to be part of the pack."

"Come the moonchange, I'll be delighted," Cathy said.

She didn't think he believed or trusted her for a moment, but he did finally hand her the coffee. She downed it in three gulps. "That almost helps the headache."

"Where are we?" Sofia demanded. "How did we get here?"

Cathy stood up. "Don't mind her," she told Nathan. "She's a whiny little thing who's never going to be a pack alpha." She approached Nathan. "I can see a pine forest beyond that barred window. It looks like the perfect place for our kind to run free."

He grinned. "It is."

"Why not take me for a walk?" She put her arm through his. "Show me around the place."

He didn't relax his guard, but he didn't say no. "There's food on the table," he told Sofia before leading Cathy outside. "And a guard on the door."

Once they were gone, Sofia returned to a conversation she'd been involved in since she fully awoke from the long, drugged ride. So far, she'd found out that they were being held in a large compound in a remote part of Oregon that was surrounded by an electrified fence. It was patrolled by armed guards. Their Hunyara relations and several other captives were locked up in a large central barracks, which was also guarded. The place was quite the fortress.

Am I as bad an actress as I suspect? Because Cathy's really good.

Are you sure your cousin's acting?

Please! This was all her idea. After a heavy silence filled her head for a few moments she went on, *Do not try to get me paranoid, Cage.*

All I'm saying is that sometimes you can't trust the ones you care for the—

All right, all right! I shouldn't have tricked you. How many times do I have to say I'm sorry?

Once.

Oh. Haven't I—

No.

Of course I'm sorry I hurt you. I just couldn't think of another way.

You could have asked me to let the Clan Prime go in my place. We could have talked it through.

Well . . . yeah. It didn't occur to me to be reasonable at the time. I was pretty hysterical that night. Sid said all the psychic turmoil was messing with everybody's brains.

And I've found out that Lady Juanita was messing with yours, Jason said. *Matris are born matchmakers. She saw suggesting you keep me in bed as a bonding gift to us. Due to all the blood we shared then, she pretty much arranged that we'd pass the point where we could ever leave each other.*

I don't want to ever leave you!

Nor I.

But you'd been thinking you might have to. I'd been thinking I might have to let you run off and hide with your people and stay away from you to cover your trail. We can't do that now. We didn't want to anyway.

Do you forgive me? Sofia asked. *I promise never to do it again.*

You'd better not be promising never to have an orgy again. I liked that part.

So did I. And if we want to do it again anytime soon, I suggest we get on with the rescue.

I agree. All our players are in position—even your Dad has shown up. I've been working with him on his wolf taming; he's rusty but talented.

I'm glad.

Okay, we're coming in. You and Cathy can do your thing now. See you soon.

I love you.

Love you, too. Get to work, Mrs. Cage.

Chapter Forty-nine

While talking to Sofia, Jason had been careful not to show her how worried he was for her. He kept reminding himself that she was brave and strong and resourceful, and he wanted her that way. But he would much rather lock her up somewhere safe and luxurious and keep her there. He couldn't follow those protective impulses with a wolf tamer for a bondmate, but that didn't stop him from having them.

He'd been terrified ever since he found out that she expected him to find her, no matter where she ended up or what condition she landed in. Everyone involved had assumed he'd follow the psychic trail to her, which he had. So her confidence had been well placed, but he'd still been scared he'd screw up. Now he intended to get her out of harm's way, and keep her there for as long as possible.

Coming up beside him, Mike Bleythin said, "Pashta's group is ready. Let's get this over with. I want Cathy out of there right now."

"I'm glad I'm not the only one thinking like a protective male."

"Our mates are altogether too tough for our own good," Mike answered.

Jason nodded his agreement as Laurent and Eden came up to them. The four of them gazed down from their hiding spot to the encampment below.

"I want to get my hands on the computers in there," the mortal woman said. "We need to find out what's really going on."

"I just want to kick some ass and get home to our kid," Laurent said. "Let's get moving, before the deodorant we confiscated from these jokers wears off."

"Roger that," Eden answered.

A second later, a hideous scream sounded in the compound below. They took this as their signal to move forward.

"I think Cathy's responsible for that," Mike said proudly as they ran for the fence.

The limitation to being a wolf tamer in this situation was that not everybody in this nest of dangerous lunatics would be a werewolf. When Sofia had mentioned the possibility of mortal bad guys, Cathy had come up with a solution. Everything now hinged on finding out what type of enemy was guarding her prison. Sofia stepped up to the door.

She wiped everything else from her mind and concentrated on the job at hand: she was supposed to be scared. "*Supposed* to be scared?" She managed to make herself cry and rapped on the door with both fists. "Help! Help!" she shouted. "Let me out! Somebody please help me!" She tried to mentally project that she was fragile and not a danger to anybody.

The man outside yelled for her to shut up. When she continued shouting and banging, he finally opened the door. "I told you to shut—"

She sniffled and wiped the back of her hand across her cheek. When he reached out to grab her shoulder, she looked him in the eye and latched onto a werewolf's mind. She'd taken him too much by surprise for him to put up much of a fight.

"Take me to the other prisoners," she told him.

With the guard as her escort, she crossed the compound to the barracks Jason had told her about. No one questioned their progress. When

Cathy made her move, everyone else in the compound rushed to find out what Nathan was screaming about. With this diversion under way, the attack from the outside began.

Sofia couldn't worry about the sudden gunfire from the defenders, or the huge truck that came careening down the hillside and crashed through the fence into one of the buildings. She only hoped nobody was driving it.

She had the werewolf under her control hold his weapon on her, and pretended to still be a scared captive when she went into the barracks. There, she saw five prisoners being watched by two guards. The prisoners, three men and two women, were each handcuffed to a bed frame set into the concrete floor.

"What's going on out there?" one of the guards asked. "Why'd you bring her in here?"

"You're both needed outside," her guard said, as she'd ordered him to. "Go on. I'll take over in here."

The men must have been bored, because they didn't question this order but ran out to join the excitement. Sofia hurried toward the prisoners after they left. "I'm here to rescue you," she told the staring prisoners. "If any of you is a werewolf named Hunyara, Uncle Pashta wants your help outside."

Two of the men raised their free hands, and one said, "You're cousin Sofia."

She nodded. "Help me free them," she ordered her werewolf.

He didn't have the keys to the handcuffs, but solved the problem by carefully putting a bullet through the chain on each prisoner's cuffs to break the links.

"Go to sleep," she ordered the werewolf when he was done.

She gave his gun to one of her cousins, and they went to join the fighting. "Stay here," she told the others, then ran outside, anxious to find Jason.

Once inside the compound, Jason headed straight toward Sofia. He moved too fast for any of the shooters to take aim at him, but bullets still buzzed dangerously close, hitting the dust as his feet flew by. He ignored them and happily tossed aside all those who tried to physically attack him.

Sofia's presence drew him like a beacon to the central building of the complex. She came through the doorway when he was just a few yards away, and her face lit with a smile that sent his heart soaring.

She didn't see the gunman taking aim at her.

That was all right, because Jason was on top of the shooter before he had time to fire.

When he let the body fall to the ground, Sofia looked at him with very wide eyes. "There was a time when I would have found that profoundly disturbing."

Jason grabbed her hand and took her back into the barracks, where they exchanged a quick, fierce kiss. "The operation's winding down," he told her. "Stay here until I come for you." Surprisingly, she didn't argue.

When he returned, he brought a crowd with him. Eden carried a confiscated laptop, and she and Cathy sat down to have a look at what was inside. Pashta and the other Hunyaras gathered around the three freed prisoners. Laurent and Mike stood guard over Eden and Cathy. Sofia's father stood back and warily watched everyone else, looking a bit lost amid all this activity.

Jason took Sofia aside. "You can debrief and take part later," he told her. "But first—"

Her mouth covered his, and they shared a long, lingering kiss. He held her close and she put her head trustingly on his shoulder.

"We'll have more adventures," Jason said. "But I promise you we'll always end up like this."

She looked up at him, her smile filled with joy and confidence. "Together."

"Together."

After they'd spent a few quiet moments holding each other, Jason asked, "So, how do you feel about working with animals?"

Chapter Fifty

Two months later

Sofia stood before the dressing room mirror and nervously assessed her brief, skintight costume.

George and Gracie restlessly stalked back and forth behind her, as if eager to return to the stage. The dressing room was overflowing with flowers sent by friends and family for her debut. The scent of the jasmine from Lady Juanita filled the room, blending sweetly with the yellow roses from Sid.

Jason stepped up behind her and put his arms around her narrow waist, which was emphasized by the boning in her scarlet and black costume. "How are you feeling, my beautiful lady?"

She met his gaze in the mirror. "I'm damned

glad I spent the last two months sweating with a personal trainer to get into this outfit, since I'm going to be seen in it in public tonight." Jason pulled her closer, and the reaction she picked up from her bondmate warmed her all over. "I can feel that you want to tear it off me, which isn't helping to keep me calm."

He ran his hands down her waist and around the curve of her hips. "I can't help myself. You're gorgeous."

She thought *he* was the gorgeous one, with the skintight pants that showed off his muscular thighs and the open white silk shirt that revealed his chest and emphasized his broad shoulders. It was enough to make her limbs go weak with lust—if they weren't already weak from stage fright.

"I'm going to be jealous when we go out there and all the women start screaming." The moment of truth was nearly here and Sofia was scared to death. "I was crazy to agree to this after your assistant e-mailed that she and her new husband had decided to buy a boat in Bora-Bora and sail around the Pacific. Anyone could have replaced her onstage."

"But it is a good job opportunity for you here in dull, mundane Las Vegas."

She smiled shakily. "Only a vampire would call Sin City dull and mundane."

"A vampire and a wolf tamer, you mean." He hugged her close again. "You and I know what *real* excitement is. Once you're onstage, it will be easy."

She had to admit, this should be much easier than chasing down evil werewolves bent on world domination. Since she'd begun rehearsals with Jason, her father had stepped into the role of main Hunyara wolf tamer.

"Did your father decide to come?" Jason must have sensed her thoughts.

She nodded. "Along with every Hunyara that Cathy and Uncle Pashta could dig up. I've learned that we used to be circus people. So in a way, I'm returning to my roots with this job."

"All of the Bleythins and many from the Wolf Clan are also in the audience to cheer you on."

"I'm delighted. But Sid sent her regrets from Los Angeles. She and Joe still aren't talking, by the way."

After an embarrassed moment, he asked, "Did she find a sire for—"

"Yes. I don't know the details though."

"And I don't want to know them." Jason turned her to face him. "I'm afraid I'm going to mess up your beautifully applied lipstick, my love."

A knock on the door and a call of "Ready for you" stopped him from kissing her. They touched noses instead.

"Come along, Mrs. Cage," he said, taking her hand to lead her to the stage. "The tigers are waiting."

Pocket Books
proudly presents

PRIMAL HEAT

Susan Sizemore

Coming soon
from Pocket Books

Turn the page for a preview of
Primal Heat . . .

"Not more Queen," a man said behind her.

The disgust in his voice amused her, and the deep British accent was intriguing. As the band played "Another One Bites the Dust," she took the water the bartender handed her, then turned around. She hadn't seen the man standing behind her before, though she was somehow already aware of his presence before he spoke. His hair was wavy and sandy brown, his eyes green and surrounded by laugh lines. He had a lived-in face; a dangerous face.

"I know what you mean," she told him. "If they play 'Fat Bottomed Girls,' I'm out of here."

"I'll join you," he answered.

"And, if they play a lot of Def Leppard, Jo will probably run away screaming."

The newcomer followed Phillipa as she edged around the dance floor toward the terrace.

"Who's Jo, and what's wrong with Def Leppard? I'm a proud son of Sheffield myself," he added. "Same hometown as the Lep—"

"Wait. What do you mean, *who's Jo?*" Phillipa stopped and confronted him. "You *are* a guest at the Elliot-Cage wedding, aren't you?"

smile was devastating, showing deep dimples and crinkling the lines around his eyes. "I'm the best man."

Irritation flared over the heat that had been roused by his smile. "You're Matt Bridger! You very nearly ruined this wedding!" she accused.

"It's not my fault my plane was late."

"You were supposed to have arrived yesterday."

He gestured at the boisterous people filling the crowded room. "It doesn't look like I was missed."

"One of my brothers stepped in as best man."

"Then it all turned out all right." He crossed his arms over his wide chest and moved close to her. "I don't know what you have to be angry about."

"I'm angry on my sister's behalf."

"Why's that?"

"She's Jo Elliot."

"The singer in Def Leppard?"

"The bride!"

Even as she indignantly stepped closer, Phillipa realized that Matt Bridger was teasing her.

Suddenly they were toe to toe and nose to nose. He put an arm around her waist, drawing her even closer. She was caught by the masculine heat and scent of him. "You're provoking me on purpose."

The back of his hand brushed across her cheek. "Yes."

Her knees went weak, and she almost dropped her glass. She didn't notice where it went when he took it out of her hand.

"Dance with me."

"Yes."

Of course. She never wanted to dance with anyone else.

He drew her onto the dance floor, and they started slow-dancing to the fast music. It was the most natural thing in the world to gaze into this stranger's eyes and press her body against his, soft and hard blending. They didn't share a word while the music played, yet the communication between them was deep and profound. She'd known him forever, been waiting for him forever. It was all too perfect to make any sense.

When the music stopped she would've kept right on dancing, but Matt Bridger turned them off the dance floor. Her arms stayed draped around his wide shoulders, and her gaze stayed locked on his. His palms pressed against the small of her back, large and warm and possessive.

Despite this intimate closeness, Phillipa tried to regain her sanity.

"We've just met."

"And you're really not that kind of girl."

"What kind of girl?"

"The sort who snuggles up to a stranger the moment they meet. And I'm not that sort of man." He flashed that devastating smile at her again. "Mostly."

"Then why are you and I—"

"We have more than snuggling in mind."

"Yes, but—"

"I have a theory."

She didn't want to hear his theory. "Kiss me."

Fingers traced across her lips. "Soon."

His touch left her sizzling. This was crazy! She should be embarrassed.

She took a deep breath, and made an effort to step away. She managed to move maybe an inch, making it a small triumph for public decency.

"Like calls to like," he said, pulling her back to him.

She lost interest in decency. "I'm a cop."

"Fancy that." As the music started again, he took her by the hand. The connection was electric. "Come on."

She held back. This was her last chance to stay virtuous. "I don't—"

"Listen."

She did, and laughed. "Oh, my God, 'Fat Bottomed Girls.'"

"You said you'd leave if they played it."

"Left alone with big fat Fanny—"

"Matt Bridger, let's get out of here."

They headed toward the door, but he stopped after a few steps. "One thing, first."

"What?"

"Your name."

"Phillipa Elliot."

Now, at least, she wasn't about to fall into reckless abandon with a *total* stranger.

He tilted his head and gave her a quick, thorough once-over. What he saw was a tall blond woman in a strapless, tea-length teal satin bridesmaid's dress.

"I know, I don't look like a Phillipa," she said. "But who does?"

"Pardon me for saying so, but that is an unfortunate name for a Yank, isn't it?"

"I'm used to it."

"Good. It suits you."

The band started to play louder, and they ran for the door.

"That was—" Phillipa sighed, unable to describe the experience. Now she understood why sex was called "the little death." Maybe it was just *great* sex that was called that.

Little sparks of pleasure were still shooting through her; she was exhilarated and exhausted at the same time. She was completely content to lie across Matt, her breasts pressed against the hard muscles of his bare chest. She rested her cheek against the warmth of his skin and breathed in the male scent of him.

"It certainly was," Matt answered.

She glanced up to see his hands propped behind his head, a smug smile curving his beautiful mouth. She caught the sparkle of green in his half-closed eyes.

"You look like a well-fed cat," she told him.

"Very well-fed," he answered. "But still hungry."

He pulled her up the length of his body for a kiss. His mouth was as insistent and needy as if they hadn't just made love. He made her hungry all over again. His hands began to roam, and her body responded.

This time she was able to keep her head long enough to say, "Maybe we shouldn't." His mouth circled a nipple. "Oh God! I mean—there's supposed to be photos—and—wedding stuff." Her mind was too into the pleasure to remember just what. "We'll be missed."

He nuzzled her, and his voice came muffled from between her breasts. "Do you really care?"

"Nooo—yes! We'll be missed. I should be there. She's my sis—" She suddenly became very aware of his erection, and her hand closed around it. She *had* to touch him, to stroke him. "I shouldn't be doing this."

"You better not stop."

His hungry growl sent a needy shiver through her. His voice was enough to make her melt. "But—"

This sort of thing happens at family gatherings all the time.

"What happens?"

People disappear to make love. It's a way to cel-ebrate the bonding.

"That's nice." It occurred to Phillipa that there was something odd about this conversation. "Did you just say something inside my head?"

Not that you'll recall. Relax, sweetness. Make love to me.

"All right." It was all she wanted to do anyway.

As a carousel version of "Ode to Joy" woke Phillipa, she thought, I belong with this man. When she came a little further awake, she realized that the noise was a cell phone ringing, and that she was lying naked in a dark hotel room with Matt Bridger. She couldn't think of anywhere better to be, and snuggled closer to him while Beethoven kept playing.

Eventually Matt rolled over and picked the phone up from the nightstand. "Mike, if you're drunk, you're a dead lobo."

Whatever the answer was, it made Matt sit up. His muscles bunched with tension. "Where and when? Right. I'm not alone."

Deciding to let him ride out this emergency in privacy, Phillipa slid out of bed and crossed the dark room to the bathroom. There she took her time using the facilities and drinking a glass of water.

Even as she stepped back into the bedroom, she was aware of the emptiness. The musky tang of sex was still in the air, but even before she turned on a light and saw the rumpled, empty bed, she knew he was gone.

Eternal Echoes
John O'Donohue

BANTAM BOOKS
London • New York • Toronto • Sydney • Auckland

ETERNAL ECHOES
A BANTAM BOOK: 0553 812416

Originally published in Great Britain by Bantam Press,
a division of Transworld Publishers

PRINTING HISTORY

Bantam Press edition published 1998
Bantam Books edition published 2000

1 3 5 7 9 10 8 6 4 2

Extracts from poems, entitled 'Do Mo Ghrā' and 'Idir an Paidrīn Pairteach', by
Caitlín Maude from *Dānta*, Coiséim, Dublin, reproduced by kind permission of
Cathal Ō Luain.

Extract from *Early Irish Poetry* translated by Myles Dillon, edited by James
Carney, published by Mercier Press, 1965, and reproduced by kind permission
of John Dillon.

Extract from 'Too Many Names' by Pablo Neruda translated by Alastair Reid,
from *Selected Poems* edited by Nathaniel Tarn, translator Jonathan Cape.

Extract from *C. P. Cavafy, Collected Poems*, translated by Edmund Keely and
Philip Sherrard, edited by George Savidis is reproduced by kind permission of
Hogarth Press on behalf of the Estate of C. P. Cavafy.

Extract from *Soul-shrine* by Carmina Gadelica, translated by Alexander
Carmichael, Floris Books, Edinburgh.

'Dear Angel of my Birth' copyright Kathleen Raine. First published in *On a
Deserted Shore*, Dolmen Press, Dublin, 1973; Agenda Editions, 1987.

Extracts from *Selected Poems: Fernando Pessoa* translated by Jonathan Griffin
(Penguin Books 1974, second edition 1982) copyright © L. M. Rosa
translations © Jonathan Griffin, 1974, 1982: 'I Know, I Alone' (p46, 8 lines),
'To Be Great, Be Entire' (p103, 6 lines), 'I See Boats Moving' (p49, 2 lines),
reproduced by permission of Penguin Books Ltd.

Reprinted by permission of the publishers and the Trustees of Amherst College
from *The Poems of Emily Dickinson*, Thomas H. Johnson, ed., Cambridge,
Mass.: The Belknap Press of Harvard University Press, Copyright © 1951,
1955, 1979, 1983 by the President and Fellows of Harvard College.

Set in 11/15pt Bodoni by Falcon Oast Graphic Art

Bantam Books are published by Transworld Publishers,
61–63 Uxbridge Road, London W5 5SA,
a division of The Random House Group Ltd,
in Australia by Random House Australia (Pty) Ltd,
20 Alfred Street, Milsons Point, NSW 2061, Australia,
in New Zealand by Random House New Zealand Ltd,
18 Poland Road, Glenfield, Auckland 10, New Zealand
and in South Africa by Random House (Pty) Ltd,
Endulini, 5a Jubilee Road, Parktown 2193, South Africa.

Reproduced, printed and bound in Great Britain by
Clays Ltd, St Ives plc

ANAM ĊARA

'John O'Donohue is a man of the soul. His scholarly meditation on the continuing relevance of Ireland's spiritual heritage has become a publishing phenomenon. . . This poetic meditation has become a bestseller on both sides of the Atlantic. . . A lyrical epic prayer'
The Times

'*Anam Ċara* is a radiant source of wisdom, a link between the human and the divine. This work is a blessed, rare gem'
Larry Dossey, bestselling author of *Healing Words*

'Words of wisdom. . . A heady mixture of myth, poetry, philosophy. . . Profound and moving'
Independent

'*Anam Ċara* is a rare synthesis of philosophy, poetry and spirituality. This work will have a powerful and life-transforming experience for those who read it'
Deepak Chopra, bestselling author of *The Seven Spiritual Laws of Success*

'This book is a phenomenon in itself. . . A book to read and reread forever, its style of varied narration responds to our times'
Irish Times

Also by John O'Donohue

ANAM ĊARA
CONAMARA BLUES
ECHOES OF MEMORY
PERSON ALS VERMITTLUNG

For the ones who inhabit lives
where belonging is torn and
longing is numbed.

Acknowledgements

I wish to thank: Brenda Kimber and Kate Melhuish, my editors at Transworld; Kim Witherspoon and her agency for her confidence in the work and its effective mediation; Laura Morris and the Abner Stein agency; John Devitt, who read the manuscript and offered a creative and literary critique; Benny Murphy for the excitement of question and conversation; Dr Lelia Doolan, who gave a wonderfully encouraging and rigorous critical response to the text; David Whyte for his brotherly care and our conversations about the world of the imagination; and especially Marian O'Beirn, who suggested this book on the theme of Longing and 'the hunger to belong' and who read and reread successive drafts, keeping a critical eye on structure and content and whose friendship and inspiration are generosity itself; the memory of my former teachers, Professor Gerard Watson, Professor Tom Marsh and Micéal O Regan, OP, for his wisdom of spirit; my family for their shelter and love; Connemara and Clare for their mystical spirit which awakens such longing and offers such a tenderness of belonging.

do mo cáirde a tug foscad agus solas.

'Stabant orantes primi transmittere cursum
Tendebantque manus ripae ulterioris amore'
(So they all stood, each praying to be ferried across first
Their hands stretched out in longing for the further
shore)

Virgil, Aeneid VI, 313

'Behold, I am the Ground of thy Beseeching.'
Julian of Norwich

'A single beat from the heart of a lover is capable of
driving out a hundred sorrows.'

Naguib Mahfouz

Table of contents

Matins

I

Somewhere, out at the edges, the night
Is turning and the waves of darkness
Begin to brighten the shore of dawn

The heavy dark falls back to earth
And the freed air goes wild with light,
The heart fills with fresh, bright breath
And thoughts stir to give birth to colour

II

I arise to day

In the name of Silence
Womb of the Word,
In the name of Stillness
Home of Belonging,
In the name of the Solitude
of the Soul and the Earth

I arise today

Blessed by all things
wings of breath,
delight of eyes,
wonder of whisper,
intimacy of touch,
eternity of soul,

urgency of thought,
miracle of health,
embrace of God

May I live this day

Compassionate of heart,
Gentle in word,
Gracious in awareness
Courageous in thought,
Generous in love

prologue

I remember as a child discovering the echo of sound. It was the first time that my father took me up the mountain to herd the cattle. As we passed a limestone cliff, he called out to the cattle in the distance. His call had barely ended when it was copied exactly and sent forth again by the stone. It was a fascinating discovery. I tried out my own voice and the echo returned faithfully every time. It was as if the solid limestone mountains had secret hearing and voice. Their natural stillness and silence suddenly broke forth in an exact mimic of the human voice suggesting that there was a resonant heart in the depths of silence; the stone responds in a symmetry of sound. Hearing one's echo in the lonely landscape of the mountains seems also to suggest that we are not alone, that we belong here on this earth. It is as if the symmetry of the echo comprised the radius of an invisible circle of belonging.

The hunger to belong is at the heart of our nature. Cut off from others, we atrophy and turn in on ourselves. Mostly, we do not need to make an issue of belonging; when we belong, we take it for granted. Merely to be excluded or to sense rejection hurts. When we become isolated, we are prone to being damaged; our minds lose their flexibility and natural kindness. We become vulnerable to fear and negativity. A sense of belonging, however, suggests warmth, understanding and embrace. The ancient and eternal values of human life – truth, unity, goodness, justice, beauty and love – are all statements of true belonging.

Our hunger to belong is the longing to bridge the gulf that exists between isolation and intimacy. Distance awakens longing; closeness is belonging. Everyone longs for intimacy and dreams of a nest of belonging in which one is embraced, seen and loved. Something within each of us cries out for belonging. We can have all the world has to offer in terms of status, achievement and possessions, yet without a true sense of belonging, our lives feel empty and pointless. Like the tree that puts roots deep into the clay, each of us needs the anchor of belonging in order to bend with the storms and continue towards the light. Like the ocean that returns each time to the shore, a sense of belonging liberates us and empowers us to trust fully the rhythm

of loss and longing. Like a welcoming circle of
friendship, it also shelters us from the loneliness of
life. Furthermore, when we belong, we have an outside mooring to prevent our minds from falling into
the abyss within us. Though we may not reflect too
frequently on the vast infinity that surrounds us,
such infinity can be threatening; it makes us feel
tiny, inconsequential and vulnerable.

Unknown to us, this sense of vulnerability intensifies our hunger to belong. Each one of us
journeys alone into this world – and each one of us
carries a unique world within our hearts. No-one
experiences your life as you do; yours is a totally
unique story of experiences and feelings. Yet no
individual is sealed off or hermetically self-
enclosed. Although each soul is individual and
unique, by its very nature the soul hungers for
relationship. Consequently, it is your soul that longs
to belong – and it is your soul that makes all belonging possible. No soul is private. No soul is merely
mortal. As well as being the vital principle of your
individual life, your soul is also ancient and eternal;
it weaves you into the great tapestry of spirit which
connects everything everywhere. Belonging does
not merely shelter you from the sense of being
separate and different; its more profound intention
is the awakening of the Great Belonging which
embraces everything. At the root of our hunger to

belong, therefore, is the desire to awaken this hidden affinity. It is only when we recognize this intimate unity that we know that we are not outsiders cut off from everything around us but rather participants at the very heart of creation. Each of us brings something alive in the world that is unique. There is a profound necessity at the heart of individuality. As we awaken to this sense of destiny, we can begin to live a life that is generous and worthy of the blessing that is always calling us.

In this post-modern world the hunger to belong has rarely been more intense, more urgent. With many of the ancient, traditional shelters now in ruins, it is as if society has lost the art of fostering community. Consumerism propels us towards an ever-more lonely and isolated existence. As consumerism numbs our longing, our sense of belonging becomes empty and cold. And although technology pretends to unite us, more often than not all it delivers are simulated images that distance us from our lives. The 'global village' has no roads or neighbours; it is a faceless, impersonal landscape from which all individuality has been erased. Our politicians seem devoid of imagination and inspiration, while many of the keepers of the great religious traditions now appear to be little more than frightened functionaries. In a more uniform culture, the management skills they employ would be efficient and successful. In a pluralistic and deeply fragmented culture, they are unable to speak to the complexities of our longings. From this perspective, it would seem that we are in the midst of a huge crisis of belonging. When the outer cultural shelters are in ruins, we need to explore and reawaken the depths of belonging in the human mind and soul that will lead us once again to unexpected possibilities of community and friendship.

In the Celtic tradition there was the beautiful notion of the *anam ċara*; *anam* is the Irish word for 'soul' and *ċara* is the word for 'friend'. In the *anam-ċara* friendship, you are joined in an ancient way with the friend of your soul; you form a bond that neither space nor time can damage. The friendship awakens an eternal echo of love in the hearts of the friends as they enter into a circle of intimate belonging with each other.

Yet, although the *anam-ċara* friendship afforded a spiritual space to all the other longings of the human heart, it is true that there exists a restlessness in the human heart which may never be finally stilled by any one person or place. There is a constant and vital tension between longing and belonging. Without the shelter of belonging, our longings lack direction and focus. As memory gathers and anchors time, so does belonging shelter longing. Belonging without longing would be empty and dead, a cold frame around emptiness. The arduous task of being human is to balance longing and belonging to work with and against each other – so that all the possibilities that sleep in the clay of the heart may be awakened and realized. In Greek mythology, this theme finds poignant expression in the story of Echo, a nymph who could only use her voice in reptition of another. Echo was one of the many who fell in love with the beautiful Narcissus. One day she secretly follows Narcissus as he goes out hunting with friends, and although she longs to address him she is unable to do so because she cannot speak first. Her chance to speak comes when Narcissus loses his friends. Alone and isolated, he calls out to his companions and Echo seizes the opportunity to speak by repeating his calls back to him. But when Narcissus calls to his friends, 'Let us come together here,' Echo misunderstands him and, rushing to embrace him, reveals herself. Narcissus brutally rejects her and she is doomed to spend the rest of her life pining in demented longing for him.

Narcissus, of course, finally beheld his beauty in his reflection in a pool and fell in love with himself. But this love was a torture to him, for in falling in love with himself he is caught in an unbearable contradiction. In the figure of Narcissus, self and other collapse into one; he is both lover and beloved in one body. Unable to endure the torment of such

desperate love that is its own object and can, therefore, never possess itself, he breaks the circle by
killing himself. Echo is there at his death to repeat
his desolate dying words.

In the subtle wisdom of Greek mythology it is no
accident that Narcissus and Echo are paired. It is as
if she externalizes the fatal symmetry of Narcissus's
self-obsession and his life path which is littered
with those he has rejected. The irony here is that he,
too, will have to reject himself with the same
ferocity. Trapped within a sealed circle of self-
belonging, his longing for himself leads to
self-annihilation; he is unable to build any distance
or otherness into his own self-love. It tells us much
about the nature of Echo that her fate is twinned
with his. She is totally vulnerable because she cannot speak first. Her name and nature are one. She
longs for him and when he rejects her she is doomed
and is reduced to little more than a lonely, desperate voice.

A book is barely an object, it is a tender presence
fashioned from words, the secret echoes of the
mind. This book attempts a poetic and speculative
exploration of the creative tension between longing
and belonging. The text has a dual structure: a first
layer of image, story and reflection, and underlying
this a more philosophical subtext which might
invite a more personal journey of reflection. The

modest hope is that in a broken world full of such eerie silence, this little reflection might clear a space in the heart so that the eternal echoes of your embrace in the shelter of the invisible circle of belonging may become audible. A true sense of belonging should allow us to become free and creative, and inhabit the silent depth within us. Such belonging would be flexible, open and challenging. Unlike the loneliness of Echo, it should liberate us from the traps of falsity and obsession, and enable us to enter the circle of friendship at the heart of creation. There is a resonant heart in the depth of silence. When your true heart speaks, the echo will return to assure you that every moment of your presence happens in the shelter of the invisible circle. These eternal echoes will transfigure your hunger to belong.

chapter I

Awakening in the World:
The Threshold of Belonging

The belonging of the earth

IN the beginning was the dream. In the eternal night where no dawn broke, the dream deepened. Before anything ever was, it had to be dreamed. Everything had its beginning in possibility. Every single thing is somehow the expression and incarnation of a thought. If a thing had never been thought, it could never be. If we take Nature as the great artist of longing, then all presences in the world have emerged from her mind and imagination. We are children of the earth's dreaming. When you compare the silent under-night of Nature with the detached and intimate intensity of the person, it is almost as if Nature is in dream and we are her children who have broken through the dawn into

1

time and place. Fashioned in the dreaming of the clay, we are always somehow haunted by that; we are unable to ever finally decide what is dream and what is reality. Each day we live in what we call reality. Yet the more we think about it, the more life seems to resemble a dream. We rush through our days in such stress and intensity as if we were here to stay and the serious project of the world depended on us. We worry and grow anxious; we magnify trivia until they become important enough to control our lives. Yet all the time we have forgotten that we are but temporary sojourners on the surface of an unknown planet spinning slowly in the infinite night of the cosmos. There is no protective zone around any of us. Anything can happen to anyone at any time. There is no definitive dividing line between reality and dream. What we consider real is often precariously dreamlike. One of the linguistic philosophers said that there is no evidence that could be employed to disprove this claim: the world only came into existence ten minutes ago complete with all our memories. Any evidence you could proffer could still be accounted for by the claim. Because our grip on reality is tenuous, every heart is infused with the dream of belonging.

Belonging: the Wisdom of Rhythm

O be human is to belong. Belonging is a circle that embraces everything; if we reject it, we damage our nature. The word 'belonging' holds together the two fundamental aspects of life: being and longing, the Longing of our being and the Being of our longing. Belonging is deep; only in a superficial sense does it refer to our external attachment to people, places and things. It is the living and passionate presence of the soul. Belonging is the heart and warmth of intimacy. When we deny it, we grow cold and empty. Our life's journey is the task of refining our belonging so that it may become more true, loving, good and free. We do not have to force belonging. The longing within us always draws us towards belonging, and again towards new forms of belonging, when we have out-grown the old ones. Post-modern culture tends to define identity in terms of ownership: possessions, status and qualities. The crucial essence of 'who' you are is not owned by you. The most intimate Belonging is Self-Belonging. Yet your *self* is not something you could ever own; it is rather the total gift which every moment of your life endeavours to receive with honour. True belonging is gracious re-ceptivity. This is the appropriate art of belonging in friendship – where friends do not belong *to* each

3

other, but rather *with* each other. This *with* reaches to the depths of their twinned souls.

True belonging is not, therefore, ownership; it never grasps or holds on out of fear or greed. Belonging knows its own shape and direction. True belonging comes from within. It strives for a harmony between the *outer* forms of belonging and the inner music of the soul. We seem to have forgotten the true depth and spiritual nature of intimate Belonging. Our minds are over-saturated and demented. We need to rediscover ascetical tranquillity and come home to the temple of our senses. This would anchor our longing and helps us to feel the world from within. When we allow dislocation to control us, we become outsiders, exiled from the intimacy of true unity with ourselves, each other and creation. Our bodies know that they belong; it is our minds that make our lives so homeless. Guided by longing, belonging is the wisdom of rhythm. When we are in rhythm with our own nature, things flow and balance naturally. Every fragment does not have to be relocated, re-ordered; things cohere and fit according to their deeper impulse and instinct. Our modern hunger to belong is particularly intense. An increasing majority of people feel no belonging. We have fallen out of rhythm with life. The art of belonging is the recovery of the wisdom of rhythm.

Like fields, mountains and animals we know we belong here *on* earth. However, unlike them, the quality and passion of our longing make us restlessly aware that we cannot belong *to* the earth. The longing in the human soul makes it impossible for us ever to fully belong to any place, system or project. We are involved passionately in the world, yet there is nothing here that can claim us completely. When we forget how partial and temporary our belonging must remain, we put ourselves in the way of danger and disappointment. We compromise something eternal within us. The sacred duty of being an individual is to gradually learn how to live so as to awaken the eternal within you. Our ways of belonging in the world should never be restricted to or fixated on one kind of belonging that remains stagnant. If you listen to the voices of your own longing, they will constantly call you to diverse styles of belonging which are new and energetic and mirror the complexity of your life as you deepen and intensify your presence on earth.

Why do we need to belong?

 hy do we need to belong? Why is this desire so deeply rooted in every heart? The longing to belong seems to be ancient and is at the core of our nature. Though you may often feel isolated, it is the nature of your soul to belong. The soul can never be separate; its eternal dream is intimacy and belonging. When we are rejected or excluded, we become deeply wounded. To be forced out, to be pushed to the margin hurts us. The most terrifying image in Christian theology is a state of absolute exclusion from belonging. The most beautiful image in all religion is heaven or nirvana: the place of total belonging, where there is no separation or exclusion any more. A Buddhist friend once gave a definition of nirvana: the place where the winds of destiny no longer blow. This suggests that it is a place of undisturbed belonging. We long to belong because we feel the lonesomeness of being individuals. Deep within us we long to come in out of separation and be at home again in the embrace of a larger belonging. The wonder of being a human is the freedom offered to you through your separation and distance from every other person and thing. You should live your freedom to the full because it is such a unique and temporary gift. The rest of nature would love to have the liberation we enjoy. When you suppress your wild longing and opt for the predictable and safe forms of belonging, you sin against the rest of nature that longs to live deeply through you. When your way of belonging in the world is truthful to your nature and your dreams, your heart finds contentment and your soul finds stillness. You are able to participate fully in the joy and adventure of exploration and your life opens up for living, joyfully, powerfully and tenderly. Conversely, when you are excluded or rejected, your life inevitably tends to narrow into a concern, and sometimes an obsession, with that exclusion and the attempt to change it.

The shelter of belonging empowers you; it confirms in you a stillness and sureness of heart. You are able to endure external pressure and confusion; you are sure of the ground on which you stand. Perhaps your hunger to belong is always active and intense because you belonged so totally before you came here. This hunger to belong is the echo and reverberation of your invisible and eternal heritage. You are from somewhere else, where you were known, embraced and sheltered. This is also the secret root out of which all longing grows. Something in you knows and, perhaps, remembers that eternal belonging liberates longing into its surest and most potent creativity. This is why your longing is often wiser than your conventional sense of appropriateness, safety and truth. It is the best antidote to the fear of freedom which is second nature to many people. Your longing desires to take you towards the absolute realization of all the possibilities that sleep in the clay of your heart; it knows your eternal potential and it will not rest until it is awakened. Your longing is the Divine Longing in human form.

Restless and lonesome

HERE DO WE GET OUR IDEA OF BELONGING from? What is true belonging? It seems that the whole origin of belonging is rooted in the faithfulness of place. Each one of us awakens on the earth in a particular place. This place was, and remains, full of presence and meaning for us. As a child one of the first things you learn is your name and where you live. If you were to get lost, you would know where you belong. When you know where you belong, then you know where you are. Where you belong is where you inevitably continue to return. In some strange way you long for the stability and sureness of belonging which nature enjoys. As you grow you develop the ideal of where your true belonging could be – the place, the home, the partner and the work. You seldom achieve all the elements of the ideal, but it travels with you as the criterion and standard of what true belonging could be. You travel certainly, in every sense of the word. But you take with you everything that you have been, just as the landscape stores up its own past. Because you were once at home somewhere, you are never an alien anywhere. No-one can survive by remaining totally restless. You need to settle and belong in order to achieve any peace of heart and creativity of imagination.

We live in times of constant activity and excitement. Media present endless images of togetherness, talk-shows and parties. Yet behind all the glossy imagery and activity there is a haunted lonesomeness at the vacant heart of contemporary life. There is a desperate hunger for belonging. People feel isolated and cut off. Perhaps this is why a whole nation can assemble around the images of celebrities. They have no acquaintance with these celebrities personally. They look at them from a distance and project all their longings on to them. When something happens to a celebrity, they feel as if it is happening to themselves. There is an acute need for the reawakening of the sense of community. It is true that neighbours are not necessarily close to you. They do not need to be friends. But there is a strong sense that humans who live in clusters with each other are meant to look out for, and look after, each other, rather than living in such isolation while near each other. This is a primal sense of duty. You often notice, when something happens to someone on the street or in the village, neighbours who had never been in the house before come to help and support. In Ireland this is especially apparent at a time of bereavement. People simply gather around so that you are not left alone with the shock and silence of death. While drawing little attention to itself, this support brings so much healing and shelter. It is something you would never forget; and the beauty is how naturally it happens. During times of suffering the shelter of belonging calms us. The particular shape of belonging must always strive to meet our longing.

The voices of longing

VERY human heart is full of longing. You long to be happy, to live a meaningful and honest life, to find love and to be able to open your heart to someone; you long to discover who you are and to learn how to heal your own suffering and become free and compassionate. To be alive is to be suffused with longing. The voices of longing keep your life alert and urgent. Yet if you cannot discover the shelter of belonging within your life, you could become a victim and target of your longing, pulled hither and thither without any anchorage anywhere. It is consoling that each of us lives and moves within the great embrace of the earth. You can never fall out of the shelter of this belonging. Part of the reason that we are so demented in our modern world is that we have lost the sense of belonging on the earth.

If you were a stone, you could remain still, gathered in silent witness in the same landscape. The horizons and the infinity would never trouble you. Nothing could draw you out. As a human, your daily experience is riven with fracture and fragmentation. Like a nomad you wander from event to event, from person to person, unable to settle anywhere for too long. The day is a chase after ghost duties; at evening you are exhausted. A day is over and so much of it was wasted on things that meant so little to you, duties and meetings from which your heart was absent. Months and years pass and you fumble on, still incapable of finding a foothold on the path of time you walk. A large proportion of your activity distracts you from remembering that you are a guest of the universe, to whom one life has been given. You mistake the insistent pressure of daily demands for reality and your more delicate and intuitive nature wilts. When you wake from your obsessions, you feel cheated. Your longing is being numbed and your belonging becoming merely external. Your way of life has so little to do with what you feel and love in the world. But, because of the many demands on you and responsibilities that you have, you feel helpless to gather your self; you are dragged in so many directions away from true belonging.

I was at a wedding once where an incident occurred, in fact, it was more of an event. The wedding breakfast was over and the music had begun. There was an older woman there. She was a quiet person who kept to herself, a shy country woman who was there because she was a next-door neighbour of the bride. Everyone knew that her husband was an upright person, but mean and controlling. They suspected that she had a very hard life with him. There always seemed to be a sadness around her; though he was quite wealthy, she never seemed to have anything new to wear. She had married young in a culture, and at a time, that if you made a huge mistake in your choice of partner there was no way out. You continued to lie on your bed of thorns and put a brave face on things for the neighbours. At the wedding she began to have a few drinks. She had never drunk alcohol before and it was not long until the veneer of control and reservation began to fall away. The music was playing but there was no-one dancing. She got up on her own and danced. It was a wild dance. It seemed that the music had got inside her and set her soul at large. She was oblivious of everyone. She took the full space of the floor and used it. She danced in movements that mixed ballet and rock. Everyone stood back, watching her, in silence. Her poor dance was lonesome, the fractured movements, the coils of gesture unravelling in the air. Yet there was something magical happening in it too. Often there is a greater kindness in gesture. Here she was, dancing out thirty years of captive longing. The façade of social belonging was down. The things she could never say to anyone came flooding out in her dance. In rhythm with the music, the onlookers began to shout encouragement. She did not even seem to hear them; she was dancing. When the music stopped, she returned to her table, blushing, but holding her head high. Her eyes were glad, and there was a smile beginning around the corners of her mouth.

Ⴆhe ꜰeeliNG that something is missing

he human heart is inhabited by many different longings. In its own voice each one calls to your life. Some longings are easily recognized and the direction in which they call you is clear. Other voices are more difficult to decipher. At different times of your life, they whisper to you in unexpected ways. It can take years before you are able to hear where exactly they want to call you. Beneath all these is a longing that has somehow always been there and will continue to accompany every future moment of your life. It is a longing that you will never be able to clearly decipher though it will never cease to call you. At times it will bring you to tears; at other times it will set your heart wild. No person you meet will ever

13

quell it. You can be at one with the love of your life, give all of your heart and it will still continue to call you. In quiet moments in your love, even at moments of intimacy that feel like an absolute homecoming, a whisper of this longing will often startle you. It may prod you into unease and make you question your self and your ability to love and to open yourself to love. Even when you achieve something that you have worked for over years, the voice of this longing will often surface and qualify your achievement. When you listen to its whisper, you will realize that it is more than a sense of anti-climax. Even when everything comes together and you have what you want, it will not stifle this un-welcome voice.

What voice is this? Why does it seep with such unease into our happiness? Deep down in each of us is a huge desire to belong. Without a sense of belonging, we are either paralysed or utterly restless. Naturally, when you enter times of belong-ing, you would love to anchor and rest there. At such times your heart settles. You feel you have arrived, you relax and let your self belong with all your heart. Then, the voice whispers and your belonging is qualified. The voice always makes you feel that something is missing. Even when every-thing you want is on your table and everyone you love is there in your life, you still feel something is missing. You are not able to name what is missing. If you could, you might be able to go somewhere to get it. But you cannot even begin. Something that feels vital to you lies out of your reach in the unknown. The longing to fill this absence drives some people out of the truth and shelter of love; they begin a haunted journey on a never-ending path in quest of the something that is missing. Others seek it in the accumulation of possessions. Again, this small voice leads other people into the quest for the Divine.

The voice comes from your soul. It is the voice of the eternal longing within you and it confirms you as a relentless pilgrim on the earth. There is something within you that no-one or nothing else in the world is able to meet or satisfy. When you recognize that such unease is natural, it will free you from getting on the treadmill of chasing ever more temporary and partial satisfactions. This eternal longing will always insist on some door remaining open some-where in all the shelters where you belong. When you befriend this longing, it will keep you awake and alert to why it is that you are here on earth. It will intensify your journey but also liberate you from the need to go on many seductive but futile quests. Longing can never be fulfilled here on earth. As the Un-Still Stones sang so memorably some decades ago: 'I can't get no satisfaction.' The beauty of being human is the capacity and desire for intimacy. Yet we know that even those who are most intimate remain strange to us. Like children, we often 'make strange' with each other. This keeps our longing alert.

Our longing to be loved

NE of the deepest longings in the human heart is the desire to be loved for yourself alone. This longing awakens you completely. When you are touched by love, it reaches down into your deepest fibre. It is difficult to realize actually how desperately we need love. You inhabit your life, you seem to be in control. You live within an independent physical body. From the outside, you seem to be managing very well. Because you present this face to the world, no-one suspects that you have a different 'inner body' called the heart which can do nothing for itself if it is not loved. If our hearts were our outside bodies, we would see crippled bodies transform into ballet dancers under the gaze, and in the embrace, of love. It is difficult to love yourself, if you are not first loved. When you are loved, your heart rushes forth in the joy of the dance of life. Like someone who has been lost for years in a forgotten place, you rejoice in being found. When you are discovered, you then discover yourself. This infuses your whole life with new vigour and light. People notice a difference in you. It is nice to be around you. Love somehow transfigures the sad gravity of life. The gloom lifts and your soul is young and free. Love awakens the youthfulness of the heart. You discover your creative force. It is quite touching to see love bring someone home so swiftly to themselves. The Connemara poet Caitlín Maude writes:

 is little beak
Under his wing
The thrush of our love.

(Translated by the author)

Even without the outside lover, you can become the beloved. When you awaken in appreciation and love for your self, springtime awakens in your heart. Your soul longs to draw you into love for your self. When you enter your soul's affection the torment ceases in your life. St Bonaventure says in *The Journey of the Mind to God*: 'Enter into yourself, therefore, and observe that your soul loves itself most fervently.'

Soul: the beauty of the broken circle

The one who dreamed the universe loved circles. There is some strange way in which everything that goes forward is somehow still travelling within the embrace of the circle. Longing and belonging are fused within the circle. The day, the year, the ocean's way, the light, the water and the life insist on moving in the rhythm of the circle. The mind is a circle too. This is what keeps you gathered in your self. If you were just a point in space, you would be forever isolated and alone. If your life were simply a line through time, you would be always trapped at this point with all past and future points absent. The beauty of the mind is its circular form. Yet the circle of the mind is broken somewhere. This fracture is always open; it is the secret well from which all longing flows. All prayer, love, creativity and joy come from this source; our fear and hurt often convert them into their more sinister shadows.

This breakage within us is what makes us human and vulnerable. There is nothing more sinister than someone whose mind seems to be an absolute circle; there is a helpless coldness and a deadly certainty about such a presence. When you discover this inner well of longing, it can frighten you and send you into flight from yourself. If you can be tranquil, amazing things can flow from it. Your body is open physically to the world and the well of your mind flows out of ancient ground. This is reminiscent of the mountains here in the Burren where there are many wells. The face of the well is on the surface; it is such a pure and surprising presence. Yet the biography of the well is hidden under eternities of mountain and clay. Similarly, within you, the well is an infinite source. The waters are coming from far away. Yet as long as you are on this earth, this well will never run dry. The flow of thought, feeling, image and word will always continue. The well of soul flows from the fracture in the circle of the mind. This is, in a sense, a frightening inner opening – anything can flow through from the distant and unknown mountains. Part of the wonder of living a real life is to make peace with this infinite inner opening. Nothing can ever close it. When you listen to the voices of your longing, you will begin to understand the adventure and the promise of life with which you are privileged.

Our longing for nature

eltic spirituality reminds us that we do not live simply in our thoughts, feelings or relationships. We belong on the earth.

19

The rhythm of the clay and its seasons sings within our hearts. The sun warms the clay and fosters life. The moon blesses the night. In the uncluttered world of Celtic spirituality there is a clear view of the sacrament of nature as it brings forth visible presence. The Celts worshipped in groves in nature and attended to the silent divinity of wild places. Certain wells, trees, animals and birds were sacred to them. Where and what a people worship always offers a clue to where they understand the source of life to be. Most of our experience of religion happens within the walled frame of church or temple. Our God is approached through thought, word and ritual. The Celts had no walls around their worship. Being in nature was already to be in the Divine Presence. Nature was the theatre of the diverse dramaturgies of the Divine Imagination. This freedom is beautifully echoed in a later lyric poem:

 h, blackbird it is well for you,
Wherever in the thicket be your nest,
Hermit that sounds no bell,
Sweet, soft, fairylike is your note.

(Translated by Myles Dillon)

The contemplative presence of nature is not ostentatious or cluttered by thought. Its majesty and

20

elegance drift into voice in the single, subtle note of the blackbird.

Ƈhe sanctuary of a favourite place

O awaken a sense of our ancient longing for nature can help us to anchor our longing. When we go out alone and enter its solitude, we return home to our souls. When you find a place in nature where your mind and heart find rest, then you have discovered a sanctuary for your soul. The West of Ireland landscape offers welcoming shelter to the soul. You can go to places in the limestone mountains where you are above the modern world; you will see nothing from the twenty centuries. There is only the subtle sculpture that rain and wind has indented on the stone. When the light comes out the stone turns white and you remember that this is living stone from the floor of an ancient ocean. Your eye notices how the fossils are locked into its solidification. Some of the stone, particularly at the edges, is serrated and shattered. In other places the long limestone pavement is as pure and clear as if it had just been minted. Swept clean by the wind, these pavements are smooth and certain. The eye is surprised at the still clusters of white, red and yellow flowers amidst the applause of rock. Moments of absolute blue startle the eye from the nests of gentian. Purple orchids sway elegantly in the breeze. Over the edge of the mountain you can hear the chorus of the ocean. Its faithful music has never abandoned this stone world that once lived beneath its waters. Perhaps nature senses the longing that is in us, the restlessness that never lets us settle. She takes us into the tranquillity of her stillness if we visit her. We slip into her quiet contemplation and inhabit for a while the depth of her ancient belonging. Somehow we seem to become one with the rhythm of the universe. Our longing is purified and we gain strength to come back to life refreshed, and refine our ways of belonging in the world. Nature calls us to tranquillity and rhythm. When your heart is confused or heavy, a day outside in nature's quiet eternity restores your lost tranquillity.

The longing of the earth

There is an ancient faithfulness in nature. Mountains, fields and shorelines are still to be found in the same places after thousands of years. Landscape is alive in such a dignified and reserved way. It can keep its memories and dreams to itself. Landscape lives the contemplative life of silence, solitude and stillness. It carries and holds its depths of darkness and

lonesomeness with such perfect eq
never falls out of its native rhythm. Rain
intensity and surprise. Winds rise and ke\
children, then grow still. Seasons build a\
with such sure completion, then give
nature never loses its sense of sequence. Tides clear
the shore and seem to push the sea out, then turn
and with great excitement adorn the shore with blue
again. Dawn and dusk frame our time here in sure
circles. Landscape is at once self-sufficient and
hospitable; we are not always worthy guests.

Though its belonging is still and sure, there is
also a sense in which nature is trapped in the one
place. This must intensify the longing at the heart of
nature. A little bird alights and fidgets for a minute
on a massive rock that was left behind in the corner
of this field by the ice thousands of years ago. The
miracle of flight is utter freedom for the bird; it can
follow its longing anywhere. The stillness of the
stone is pure but it also means that it can never
move one inch from its thousand-year stand. It
enjoys absolute belonging but if it longs to move it
can only dream of the return of the ice. Perhaps the
stone's sense of time has the patience of eternity.
There is a pathos of stillness in nature and yet all of
us, its children, are relentlessly moved by longing;
we can never enter the innocence of its belonging.
Where can we behold nature's longing? All we see

of nature is surface. Yet the beauty she sends to the surface could only come from the creativity of great and noble longing. The arrival of spring is a miracle of the richest colour. Yet we always seem to forget that all of these beautiful colours have been born in darkness. The dark earth is the well out of which colour flows. Think of the patience of trees. Year after year stretching up to the light, keeping a life-line open between the dark night of the clay and the blue shimmer of the heavens. Think of the beauti-ful, high contours of mountains lifting up the earth, the music of streams and the fluent travel of rivers linking the stolid silence of landmasses with the choruses of the ocean. Think of animals who carry in their dignity and simplicity of presence such refined longing. Think of your self and feel how you belong so deeply on the earth and how you are a tower of longing in which nature rises up and comes to voice. We are the children of the clay who have been released so that the earth may dance in the light.

The Irish writer Liam O'Flaherty was born in Gort na gCapall in Inis Mór in Aran. He left there as a young man and had never returned. Shortly before he died, he returned to that little village. A lifetime of changes had occurred, most of those he once knew were now dead. On his way into the village he saw the big rock which had been there for thousands of years.

O'Flaherty hit the old stone with his walking stick and said: '*A Chloich mhóir athním tusa,*' i.e. O great stone I recognize you. In silence and stillness the stone held the memory of the village. Stone is the tabernacle of memory. Until we allow some of nature's stillness to reclaim us, we will remain victims of the instant and never enter the heritage of our ancient belonging.

Our longing to know

When we emerged from the earth, not only were we given a unique inner well but we were also given a mirror in our minds. This mirror is fractured but it enables us to think about everything. Our thoughts can gather and ask themselves questions and probe mysteries until some new light is quarried. Because you are human you are privileged and burdened with the task of knowing. Our desire to know is the deepest longing of the soul; it is a call to intimacy and belonging. We are always in a state of knowing even when we do not realize it. Though the most subtle minds in the Western tradition have attempted to understand what it is that happens when we know something, no-one has succeeded in explaining how we know. We feel when we know something we come into a relationship with it. All our knowing is an attempt to transfigure the unknown – to complete the journey from anonymity to intimacy. Because each one of us lives behind the intimacy of a countenance, we long to put a personal countenance on our experiences. When we know what has happened to us, we will come closer to ourselves and learn more about who we are. Yet the world is not our mirror-image. Knowledge, including the knowledge we have of each other, does not abolish the strangeness. True knowledge makes us aware of the numinous and awakens desire.

Aristotle said in the first sentence of his *Metaphysics*: 'All men by nature desire to know.' This is the secret magic and danger of having a mind. Even though your body is always bound to one place, your mind is a relentless voyager. The mind has a magnificent, creative restlessness that always brings it on a new journey. Even in the most sensible and controlled lives there is often an undertow of longing that would deliver them to distant shores. There is something within you that is not content to remain fixed within any one frame. You cannot immunize yourself against your longing. You love to reach beyond, to discover something new. Knowing calls you out of yourself. Discovery delights the heart. This is the natural joy of child-hood and the earned joy of the artist. The child and the artist are pilgrims of discovery. When you limit your life to the one frame of thinking, you close out the mystery. When you fence in the desires of your heart within fixed walls of belief, morality and convention, you dishonour the call to discovery. You create grey fields of 'quiet desperation'. Discovery is the nature of the soul. There is some wildness of divinity in us, calling us to live everything. The Irish poet Patrick Kavanagh said: 'To be dead is to stop believing in/The masterpieces we will begin tomorrow.'

Discovery is the nature of the soul

he presence of a person who has stillness and contentment of heart engenders trust. They can sift from the chaff of talk and select what has weight and worth. Sometimes the dignity of their composure can bring the company of those present to a finer level of attention and worthiness. Conversely, you become uneasy in the presence of someone whose stillness and contentment are forced. Their composure only endures because it operates within a very limited frame of self-protection and denial. It is difficult to feel that you can be yourself in the company of such efficiently quelled longing. When you open your heart to discovery, you will be called to step outside the comfort barriers within which you have fortified

27

your life. You will be called to risk old views and thoughts and to step off the circles of routine and image. This will often bring turbulence. The pendulum will fix at times on one extreme; you will be out of balance. But your soul loves the danger of growth and, in its own wise trust, it will always return you to a place of real and vital equilibrium.

The very nature of the universe invites you to journey and discover it. The earth wants our minds to listen attentively and gaze wisely so that we may learn its secrets and name them. We are the echo-mirrors of contemplative nature. One of our most sacred duties is to be open and faithful to the subtle voices of the universe which come alive in our longing. Aristotle said that the reason we can know anything is that there is a morphic affinity between us and nature; this is the intimate and precise affinity of form. Animals, trees, fields and tides have other duties. For this alone have we been freed and blessed. Either we are in the universe to inhabit the eternity of our souls and grow real, or else we might as well dedicate our days to shopping and kill time watching talk-shows.

Life is a pilgrimage of discovery

deally, a human life should be a constant pilgrimage of discovery. The most exciting discoveries happen at the frontiers. When you come to know something new, you come closer to yourself and to the world. Discovery enlarges and refines your sensibility. When you discover something, you transfigure some of the forsakenness of the world. Nature comes to know itself anew in your discoveries. Creative human thought adds to the brightness of the world. Yet there is a strong seam of thought which has always de-animated nature and reduced the earth to a mere playground for the worst fantasies of human greed. Why is this? Such blind and destructive perception is often secretly driven by guilt. There is profound but subtle cosmological guilt in human beings. We even communicate guilt to our dogs! Yet the animal world often offers images of pure discovery. My neighbour's pony had a beautiful brown foal early in the spring. In the first days she followed her mother awkwardly on the uneven ground with her long, new, gangly legs. One afternoon as they were both lying down, the new foal got up and moved away on her own a little more confidently, and then more swiftly with every step. Suddenly, she found she could move faster and then

29

she discovered that she could run. It was a marvellous sight. She started to run so swiftly and gracefully, her head held high, circling round and round the stony field. She was utterly ecstatic at the discovery of her new swiftness. She would come back time and again and halt before her mother as if to say: 'Hey, see what I can do.' Each one of us has made a huge discovery that we have never got over. This is the discovery of the world. Our first journey was the journey to the earth and we are still travelling.

The first journey creates the traveller

WE ARE ALWAYS ON A JOURNEY FROM darkness into light. The journey from anonymity to intimacy is one we continually travel. Indeed, the human self, both body and mind, arrives in the world through this journey. We come out of anonymity into light. By some strange destiny seeds engage each other in the darkness of the womb. It is startling that the infinite intimacy of the human person begins in this unknown encounter between two individuals. Our parents set us on this journey when they make love and conceive us. We forget that our very conception emerged out of the passionate act of their longing for

30

each other. It is no surprise that we are filled with desire. Each of us is literally a child of longing. On its journey to humanity, the embryo actually travels through all the shapes of evolution. Each of these embryonic shapes becomes ever more personal until the blur of forms finally clarifies as the baby's body and the intimacy of a human countenance emerges. It is no wonder that we have such hunger to belong. The very formation of our tiny bodies as babies was itself a journey of the most precarious longing.

Already in you as a little dot of presence, some powerful longing knew how to guide original belonging to undertake the journey from nowhere towards the intimacy of becoming an individual with your own world within. Usually on a journey you leave a point and travel through a place until you arrive at an intended destination. Your journey into this planet was different to any other journey you will ever make. The journey actually created the one who travelled and created the inner landscape of mind and soul of the traveller. The elemental metamorphosed into the human. This is an instance of the astounding symmetry in nature. The inner sphere of the womb mirrors and completes the outer journey of evolution. There was some ancient preconscious sense of belonging alive in you which already felt enough connection with the mother to start on this dangerous path. Nothing remained the same, all the changes happened in the blind darkness, and the transition to each new stage entailed such complete transformation. The depth and poignant consistency of your hunger to belong can be traced to this forgotten journey between the worlds.

In the womb, something inside you already knew you were growing towards belonging. The hunger to belong is not merely a desire to be attached to something. It is, rather, sensing that great transformation and discovery become possible when belonging is sheltered and true. Belonging is a call to integrity and creativity. The structure of this call illuminates the very nature of belonging. The first belonging is to the body of the mother. Only when desire and destiny help realize this belonging does the embryo grow into self-identity and reach the threshold of belonging to itself. This first belonging is a blind and vulnerable struggle. It is a secret growth in the darkness. Without this primal longing to belong, no individual could ever come into being. When we normally think about people, we inevitably forget that each person actually grew out of this original impulse to belong. This preconscious longing grew to become the mind, body and spirit of a person. This belonging was not a static, fixed attachment. It was alive with desire and the wish to become the one you dreamed.

Even as a little micro-essence of tissue, you cling internally to the mother until you develop your own body to cross the next threshold into the distance-filled world. Despite all the scientific inventions that can provide information on the unborn child, the truth is, the really important things remain unknown. Something within you already knows the infinities that lie in wait outside the mother and recognizes that the only way of traversing them is to become a body. To be born is an incredible event, a great disturbance. You are cast out; thrown from the cave into the light. It is interesting that your first moment of experience is a moment of disturbance. In its abrupt dislocation, birth already holds the echo of death. The rhythm of this moment prefigures the subsequent rhythm of your life: parting and coming together. There can be no union without separation, no return without parting. No belonging is permanent. To live a creative and truthful life, it is vital to learn the art of being separate and the generosity of uniting.

Imagining the time before coming here

espite its endless and vital artistry, nature maintains great secrecy and reserve. When we see a pregnant woman, we know that some new person is coming here. Everything else remains unknown. Who that person is, what they will bring to their family and world, what kind of life he or she will have remain unknown to us and even to the mother, the carrier and the labyrinth of this creativity. This is one of the great privileges of woman, to be able to give birth. Mothers are the priestesses of the greatest Eucharist. In, and through, the mother empty space is changed into person. The anonymous water element becomes face, body, soul, life and inner world. To give birth can also be a great burden. Sometimes the weary face of a pregnant mother reveals how her essence is being rifled and her body and mind becoming implicated in the baby's destiny. A bond is being developed from which she will never be released. In a sense, she can never part from the one she has carried under her heart. To be involved in nature's most powerful mystery can also destroy all illusions and innocence. A friend told me recently that her moment of bleakest disillusionment was in hospital shortly before she went into labour with her first child. She walked out onto the hospital fire escape, looked into the night and realized her absolute isolation and saw opening before her a never-ending path of responsibility.

There is no other way into the universe except through the body of a woman. But where were you before you were conceived and entered the womb? This is one of the most fascinating in-between times in any life. It is also the one we know least about. Yet it is a journey that each of us has made. In the Western and Oriental traditions, we have a vast architecture of theory regarding life after death; there are bardos, purgatories, nirvana and beatific visions. There is a carefully thought out path of continuity, transfiguration and final homecoming after death. It is interesting to note the substantial absence, especially in the Christian tradition, of any geography of the time before we were conceived. Perhaps it sounds ridiculous to even explore this, since we did not exist before we were conceived. This may be true; but it is surely too simple to imagine that one moment there was no sign of you, everything was blank and empty, and then the next moment you had begun to be there. If you came out of somewhere, then you had to be somewhere before you came. There can be no such apparitions or pure beginnings. As well as having an 'afterwards' every person has a 'before'. The difficulty in imagining this is that the other world is invisible and all we have are intimations of our invisible past.

Each of us comes from somewhere more ancient than any family. Normally, if someone asks you where you are from, you can name a house, a street, a landscape. You have an address, parents and family. This is indeed where you are from now. But this information becomes weak when the question deepens to enquire as to where you are ultimately from. When you think about your parents, they had a whole life as strangers before they ever knew each other. You were not even a twinkle in their eyes then. Even when they came together, there was no sign, talk or notion of you. When you reflect further, you begin to see that your ultimate address is Elsewhere. Though you are now totally here, you are essentially not from here. You are a child of the invisible. You were not in any physical form before you were conceived. You emerged in seconds from the invisible and began to grow within darkness. This is why birth is always a surprise. It is the first sighting of the invisible one. Everyone wants to see the new baby. Suddenly, there is someone here who has never been seen before. In the excitement of the new baby's arrival, we often fail to notice the silent wound in the invisible world which allowed the new arrival to come through. We also forget the whole background which the new baby has had in the invisible world: the dream of its destiny, body, face, life and temperament. Many silent questions accompany a birth: why did this baby come here now, to this family? What changes will it bring? Who is this new person? In each new heart a bridge between the invisible and the visible world opens.

The invisible world is all around us

hat which we can see is visible, that which we cannot see is the invisible. Within us and around us there is an invisible world; this is where each of us comes from. Your relationship to the invisible influences so much of your life. When you cross over from the invisible into this physical world you bring with you a sense of belonging to the invisible that you can never lose or finally cancel. When you cross this threshold, you come into the gravity that rules the visible world. Space and time now set the frame for most of your experience. Once you come here you can never stop experiencing things. Every second of your life something new is going on: you notice a tree, remember a phrase someone said last night, daydream of holidays or wonder what is making you so uneasy. Every thing that you experience is now framed in a very definite way. All your experience happens some place and always at a definite time. As you live here, you build each day a new section of your biography. You trust what you see and know what you hear. You know your real life is happening here. Yet your longing for the invisible is never stilled. There is always some magnet that draws your eyes to the horizon or invites you to explore behind things and seek out the concealed depths. You know that the real nature of things is hidden deep within them. When you enter the world you come to live on the threshold between the visible and the invisible. This tension infuses your life with longing. Now you belong fully neither to the visible or to the invisible. This is precisely what kindles and rekindles all your longing and your hunger to belong. You are both artist and pilgrim of the threshold.

FORMS OF the INVISIBLE

he invisible is one of the huge regions in your life. Some of the most important things about you and your life are invisible. What you think and the way you think control how you feel, how you meet people and how you see the world. Yet your thoughts are invisible. One of the most fascinating questions about your thinking is why do you have the thoughts that you do and why do you link them together in these patterns? The secret bridges from thought to thought are invisible. No surgeon operating on a brain has ever found a crevice full of thoughts. What you believe about yourself determines how people treat you. Yet you can never see your beliefs. Belief is invisible. Your feelings make you sad or happy, yet the feelings are invisible too. The greatest presence, from whom all things come and who holds all things together, is also invisible too. No-one can see God. Because the invisible cannot be seen or glimpsed with human eyes, it belongs largely to the unknown. Still there are occasional moments when the invisible seems to become faintly perceptible. Sometimes, over a fire built out in the open, one can glimpse layers of air trembling. Or when a candle seems to make the air quiver. Maybe this is why we love colours. They bring the longing at the heart of the invisible to such passionate expression.

Under the guise of emptiness, the invisible keeps its secrets to itself. Yet the invisible remains the great background which invests your every gesture and action with possibility and pathos. The artistic imagination brings this out. We see this especially in sculpture. The shape of the sculpture evokes the shape of the emptiness around it. Also in dance we see how the body creates fluent sculpture in the air. It draws out the hospitality of the invisible. There is something quite courageous in the endurance of human presence against the vast canopy of the invisible. We endure the invisible by forgetting it – for as long as we can. When you become aware of the invisible as a live background, you notice how your own body is woven around your invisible soul, how the invisible lives behind the faces of those you love and how it is always there between you. The invisible is one of the most powerful forms of the unknown. It envelopes our every movement. It is the region out of which we emerged and the state we are destined for, yet we never see it. There is no map with which to discern territories of the invisible. It is without texture. This is probably why we long to ignore the invisible. There is a sense in which the invisible is also the home of fear. We tend to be afraid of what we cannot see or know.

The mystery of resemblance

N Connemara, when someone asks a child who they are, the child is not simply asked for their name. The question is: *Cé leis thú?* i.e. to whom do you belong? Already in the language there is a recognition that your identity is not merely your own personal marker. You are both an expression and extension of an already acknowledged family line. This tradition is further intensified in Connemara through the use of patronymics. If a person is called Seán O'Malley and his father was Tom and his grandfather was Páraich, he could be known as Seán Tom Páraich. His name becomes an articulation of the line of ancestry to which he belongs. The language is an echo of this belonging. Its constant use reinforces the reference and brings the presence of the ancestors to word. A long chain of belonging comes alive in the clink of a name.

The universe is full of differences. No two stones or flowers or faces are ever the same. There is such an intricate tapestry of differentiation in even the simplest places. On the seashore, no two seashells are ever quite the same. When you focus your attention, the texture and range of the differences in nature becomes more visible. Against this perspective the discovery of resemblance is startling, especially in human beings. Each individual carries a totally separate world in their heart. When you think of how differently you feel and think about life, it is a wonder that we can talk to each other at all. Even between the closest people, there are long bridges. This makes us attractive and fascinating to each other. To see a resemblance between people in the one family is interesting. Sometimes it is uncanny in a family how a child resembles an ancestor. For a moment, in a gesture, a way of walking, looking, responding or saying something, you glimpse the presence of an uncle or grandparent. Resemblance has a certain pathos. You behold the gesture, the looks of one person in another. However, each person is a different world. While the resemblance indicates continuity, it also reveals the distance of the two lives from each other. Resemblance remains, nevertheless, a startling index of the way in which two people can so obviously belong to the same clan. Often outside the family, you can be startled by resemblance. An old man I know who has been quite ill was making his first journey to Ireland recently. As his daughter picked him up at the airport, he pointed to a woman who seemed to be his recently deceased mother. When the woman turned around, the resemblance vanished. For a moment, the resemblance had startled both father and daughter.

Home as the cradle of destiny

There are many places of power in the world: the Pentagon, the Kremlin, the Vatican. Yet the most powerful place of all barely draws attention to itself. This is the family home. I remember one evening going for a walk. As I came home the light was ebbing away slowly. As the black tide of night was filling the valley, lights began to come on in the houses. The little lights seemed so fragile against the onrush of the night. This has always remained with me as an image of the vulnerability of human presence against the darkness of anonymity. Anywhere tenderness gathers itself, life often seems to assemble in threat about its nest. This is why all the major thresholds in human life have blessing structures around them in the religious traditions: birth, initiation, illness, marriage and death. There is a fragility and pathos in light when darkness encircles it. When you drive through a village at evening and the lights come on before the curtains are drawn, for a second you are allowed a glimpse into individual homes. The inhabitants become visible as they move about or sit down together to dinner. Within these walls a unique set of lives are framed and formed. Behind the guise of normal interaction they are having a huge influence on the hearts and minds of each other. While the home may be a powerful cradle influencing mind and personality, the lack of home is also a huge influence. So many children in poverty-stricken areas are homeless. Some are in institutional care. Imagine how difficult it must be for these little vulnerable ones to develop minds and hearts where they can rest and feel the warmth and shelter of self-belonging. Being deprived of intimate shelter at such a crucial time must cast a lonesome shadow over their future struggle to belong within society.

The family as Nest of belonging

he family is the most powerful structure of human belonging in the world. Within the limited compass of the home a wide range of energies are simultaneously awakening. Limited space inevitably forces form. Their belonging together offers an outer unity to the world. Among themselves the emergence of individuality is complex and always accompanied by either a latent or explicit struggle between them. Later in life, when one begins to explore one's identity, it is both surprising and shocking to learn how the roots of one's personality inevitably lead back to the unsuspecting home. The sources of your potential and the secrets of your blindness lie concealed there. The family is the first place where you stretch and test your essence. A family is not a monument to an extended egotism; it must be pervious, open in communication with the larger world. However, it is never a clear space where you can move as you wish. Family is a warm but cluttered space. Each family member must earn their own room in competition with the others. Yet amidst the cut and thrust of life, especially when times are difficult, it is great to know that you have your family.

A home is a place where a set of different destinies begin to articulate and define themselves.

It is the cradle of one's future. Home is the place where the stranger arrives, the place where you see things for the first time. Here you first begin to know that you have a body. You come to know smell, touch and hearing. Home is the place where your infant senses are fostered. You have been on a long journey: now you settle and learn to recognize things. Here you learn how to cry and begin to notice how the cry and the smile get you attention. Home is where you first notice others, where you first sense that you are separate and different. It is the place where you first recognize your own gender. The fascinating thing about home is how it functions, without the superintendence of consciousness. Yet, different gifts are being quietly received by each member of the family. Gifts that will take a full lifetime to unwrap and recognize.

Home is where you belong

he word home has a wonderful resonance. Home is where you belong. It is your shelter and place of rest, the place where you can be yourself. Nature offers wonderful images of home. It is fascinating in springtime to watch the birds build their nests. They gather the twigs and weave them into a nest. The floor and walls of the nest are padded with wool, moss or fur.

In the wall of a shed near my house every year a swallow returns from Africa and finds her way back into the opening between the same two stones under the side wall. There she builds her nest and hatches out her young. No journey is too long when you are coming home. In Irish we say: *Níl aon tinnteán mar do thinnteán féin*, i.e. there is no hearth like the hearth at home.

There is such wisdom in nature. Often it carries out its most miraculous work quietly under the veil of the ordinary. Sometimes we achieve the most wonderful things when we are not even aware of what we are doing. If we did know it, we might only paralyse ourselves and ruin the flow of natural creativity. If parents were fully aware of their effect, they could never act. If they could see the secret work of mind formation in the home and the harvest it will eventually bring, they could never achieve the neutrality which allows normal home life to happen in a natural way. Parents are generally wonderful people who give all their hearts and energy to the little people they have called into the universe. Parents must act in good faith – without excessive anxiety or self-rebuke. They must induct their children into the larger community.

Childhood as a Magic Forest

O a child, parents are gods. Children are totally vulnerable. They are still only at the threshold of themselves. During your life on earth, childhood is the time of most intense happening. Yet ironically, it is also the most silent time in your life. You are having these immense experiences of wonder, discovery and difficulty; yet the words and thoughts to name them have not yet arrived. This time of fermentation and change will influence so much of your later life, yet you have so little access to the integrating power of thoughts and words. Consequently, as a child, the depths of your experience remain opaque. Childhood is a forest which we never recognize while we are in it. Our minds and imagination and dreams constantly return there to explore the roots of our personality and presence. We try to unravel, from the forest of first-feelings and first-events, the secret of the patterns which have now become our second nature.

Childhood is an absolute treasure house of imagination. It is the forest of first encounters to which we can never again return. We have become too used to the world; wonder no longer animates us like it did then. There is so much that we can find out about the magic of our souls by revisiting these memories of first acquaintance. Never again have we experienced so directly and powerfully the surprise and the fresh tang of novelty. The forest of childhood is also the territory where our dreams, imagination and images were first seeded. So much happened to us there under the canopy of innocence. It was only later that we could notice that the shadows were present too. The memory of childhood is so rich that it takes a lifetime to unpack. Again and again, we remember certain scenes, not always the most dramatic, and gradually come to a kind of self-understanding and an understanding of our parents. When we are as old as they were when we first knew them, whose face do we see in the mirror – ours or theirs?

The belonging of childhood

NNOCENCE IS PRECIOUS AND POWERFUL. It is expected and acknowledged as a natural fact that a child is innocent. Yet innocence is more sophisticated than mere ignorance, lack of knowledge or experience. It is not accidental that the manner of our arrival in the universe is shrouded in innocence. This first innocence protects us from knowing the sinister negativity of life. It also immunizes us against recognition of how strange it is to be here, thrown into a world which is crowded with infinities of space, time, matter and difference. It should be frightening to be a child in such a vast and unpredictable universe, but the little child never notices the danger directly. Innocence is a state of unknowing and the readiness to know. The wisdom of the human mind, especially in the child, ensures that knowing the world happens in stages. The innocence of childhood never breaks completely in one vast bright or dark epiphany. It only gives way gradually to new recognitions and experiences. Even when severe trauma occurs, it is somehow integrated; though it does deep damage, it still rarely extinguishes the flame of innocence. There is a poignant sense in which the child must keep its innocence alive in order to continue to grow and not allow the darkness to swamp its little mind. Innocence minds us. It only lets us become aware of what we are able to handle. Innocence permits the child to belong in the world. This is the secret of the child's trust. The child assumes that belonging is natural and sheltering. Experiments have shown that young children who have been thoroughly cautioned against the danger of strangers can still be coaxed to walk off with a stranger in a public place while the parent is momentarily occupied. The innocence of childhood renews that of the parents and quickens their instinct to preserve it.

NNOCENCE has a lyrical continuity. A child cannot turn it on and off. The fractures in innocence are partial. In different moments, thresholds are crossed into experience. Yet innocence manages to hold off the full recognition of how broken the human journey will be. The innocence of the child is its immediacy and nearness to everything. Rilke says that in all our subsequent life we will never again be as close to anything as we were to our toys in childhood. The toy becomes your friend and closest confidant. Before and below words, you invest the delight and concern of your heart in the toy. If you are clearing out an attic and you come across one of your old toys from childhood, it can release a flood of memories. The child lives in the neighbourhood of wonder where innocence keeps mystery playful. Each new event and encounter is all-absorbing. No overall perspective on life is available. The child lives in the house of discovery. The unconscious innocence of the child assembles new experiences. It is their cumulative gathering which eventually signals the end of childhood. Brick by brick the house of innocence falls to ruins. Once that threshold into adulthood is crossed, one may never return again to the kingdom of innocence. Innocence always urges the child to explore and continues to pace and shelter this exploration until it is finally adult and ready to stand alone in its new knowing. In contrast to how a child belongs in the world, adult belonging is never as natural, innocent or playful. Adult belonging has to be chosen, received and renewed. It is a lifetime's work.

Childhood experience is deeply infused with longing. The adventure of being here is utterly engaging. There is longing to explore, to play and to discover. Because the sense and contour of the self are only coming into definition, the child's sense of longing is largely unrefined. This is often evident in the way children play with each other. Their play is never merely chaotic. It is inevitably governed by self-conscious and elaborate rules which they stipulate. Perhaps these delineate safe zones in which new experience becomes possible.

The longing of childhood is akin to dream

The imagination of early childhood has no limits. This is why children are fascinated by stories. A story has permission to go anywhere. Its characters can have any powers and do anything they like. The child rarely experiences the story as an observer. The child enters the story, it experiences its drama from within. Often a child will explicitly ask to be included as one of the characters in a story: 'Which am I, Daddy?' The wonder and imagination of the child are awakened and engaged. Perhaps the shape of story fascinates the child because it takes the child's longing to wild and dangerous frontiers where it cannot go in its day-to-day life. The story allows the child to act with a power and strength which is impossible in the limitation of its present little body. Anything and everything is possible in a story. The longing of the child lives in the realm of pure possibility. All doors are open. All barriers are down. Because it is a story with a beginning, middle and end, it offers a form of belonging where the full adventure of longing can be explored. Narrative is a dramatic form of continuity created by longing and it is also a place where human desire can come home. Great stories retain resonance because they embody the 'immortal longings' of the heart; our longing to enter them comes from the childlike side of our hearts.

Childhood's dark innocence

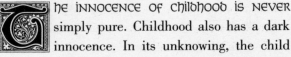 he innocence of childhood is never simply pure. Childhood also has a dark innocence. In its unknowing, the child senses the presence of negativity and evil. The

52

fascination with monsters and sinister goblins often grips the little mind. Children are not interested in stories which lack the dimension of fear. This accounts for the subtle depth of fairy tales.

Ϯhe Reꝺ bush of ancestry

s inꝺiviꝺuals, we are cut off from the dense and intricate networks of life within us. A simple instance of this is when you cut your finger and the surprise when you see your own blood flow. We forget the tree of bone and the bush of blood that flows within us. Blood is one of the most ancient and wisest streams in the universe. It is the stream of ancestry. An ancient bloodline flows from the past generations until it reaches and creates us now. Blood holds and carries life. From mythic times, it has been at the heart of sacrifice; life was offered both as plea and praise to the deities. The Catholic Eucharist still centres on the transfiguration of the wine of the earth into the divine blood of the redeemer. This consecration is not merely a memorial of the past event. The Divine Presence in the Eucharist is understood as an actual participation in the ongoing memory of God.

Superficially, a family might look like an accidental gathering of individuals called together by the chance meeting of a man and a woman who fell in love and wanted to express the depth of their love in procreation. At a deeper level, a family is an incredible intertwining of multiple streams of ancestry, memory, shadow and light. Each home hosts the arrival of history and assists the departure of new destiny. The walls of the home contain immense happenings that occur gradually under the subtle veil of normality. Though each family is a set of new individuals, ancient relics and residues seep through from past generations. Except for our parents and grandparents, our ancestors have vanished. Yet ultimately and proximately, it is the ancestors who have called us here. We belong to their lifeline. While they ground our unknown memory, our continuity bestows on them a certain oblique eternity. In our presence we entwine past and future. Virgil underlines the beautiful value of '*pietas*'. It means much more than duty; it is prospective as well as retrospective. Though Aeneas is utterly committed to his huge and painful destiny, he is concerned for his son as well as his father.

The loneliness and creativity of being a parent is the recognition that family is inevitably temporary. Good parenting is unselfish and, to encourage in-dependence in a child that has received unconditional love, acts to reinforce the sense and essence of belonging. Nothing, not even departure, can sever that intrinsic sense of belonging. Children are created to grow and leave the nest. Family provides the original and essential belonging in the world. It is the cradle where identity unfolds and firms. Such belonging outgrows itself. Home becomes too small and too safe. The young adult is called by new longing to leave home and undertake new discovery. The difficulty for parents is letting them go. In a certain sense parents and children never leave each other; this is a kinship that no distance can sever. However, in a substantial sense, part of the task of maturity is to become free of one's parents. Clinging to parents causes a destructive imbalance in one's life. One never achieves an integral sense of self-possession if one's parents continue to dominate large regions of one's heart. To grow is to come to know their fragility, vulnerability and limitation. There is great poignancy and pathos in parents' difficulty in letting go. Kahlil Gibran says: 'Your children are not your children. They are the sons and daughters of Life's longing for itself.'

Parents as memory holders

 arents have such incredible power to confirm and influence the inner life of the child. Identity is fashioned in the inner life. The child's sensibility is like a sponge. It absorbs everything. At that stage, without knowing it, we drink in the voices of our parents. We have not yet developed any kind of filter to sift the creative from the destructive. There is no such thing as perfect parents. Without wanting to, and often without knowing it, all parents leave some little trail of negativity for their children; this belongs naturally to life's ambivalence. There is never anything absolutely pure in the valley of tears. But we still love our parents in their imperfection, as Robert Frost says: 'We love the things we love for what they are.'

Children come here without knowing where they are landing. A little child has no power. In these times, terrible stories are emerging. Children have been violently abused both mentally and sexually. Outwardly, the home appeared normal, but it was in fact a quiet torture chamber. Sick and violent parents have turned their innocent little children into targets of their own demented psyches. Such violence marks a person for life. It shakes the inner ground of the psyche. This violation of the innocent is one of the most sinister forms of evil. It is a deeply troubling question. Why would a kind and loving Divine Power allow the innocent goodness of a child to be delivered into the hands of such twisted violence? It is a massive spiritual task for someone who has been abused to love and reclaim themselves. Abuse wants to turn the abused child against itself. To learn to break this inner reflex of violence is a task that can only be achieved with the help of a wise and caring healer and the kindness of grace. The abused child must learn to see itself as lovable by loving itself. And, in time, others. In a home where this love and space exists, a child has a wonderful introduction to life. You are encouraged and your gifts are awakened. For years you will be able to live from the perennial nourishment of this creative, initial belonging. You will be able to embrace and inhabit other styles of belonging demanded by the different stages of your journey.

Styles of belonging

We have suggested that the sense of belonging ultimately derives from place and persons. Landscape provides location; this makes it possible to know and approach things and peoples. If there were no place, there could be no thing. Family sets the focus of belonging during our first longings. We also suggested that the human body is the house of belonging; it is where we live while we are here. If there were no longing in us, we could subsist in listless indifference. We could be neutral about everything. Because we are always in different states and stages of longing, the ways we belong in the world are always diverse and ever changing. From the ways that longing and belonging crisscross each other we can identify different styles of belonging. Some continue to belong in the place they arrived on the first journey.

The Native

 Native is one who belongs to a place by virtue of birth. The term suggests that somehow your initial belonging to a particular place seeps into your heart in a way that can never be washed out again. This also recognizes that your first years in a place are the time when the main elements of your personality and presence are conditioned by the place, its inhabitants and the tonality of life and atmosphere of soul that were there. The native is also the one who remains in the place. Others who were born there moved away; the native is faithful to the place and continues the initial belonging. No-one knows the feel and memory of a place the way a native does. The one who remains knows the place from the inside and is attuned to the subtle world of longing which the native place holds. In past times there was a powerful intimacy between the native and the place; this belonging has been diluted by travel and the voices from outside which have come in through radio, TV and computer. The belonging has been loosened quite significantly. We are all moving more and more into the middle ground of nowhere in particular. The terrible sameness of the roads we drive has in part abolished place and space. We bypass place and lose the sense of journeying through space. Consequently, we now find articles and programmes about the particularity and richness of life among indigenous people so fascinating and even exotic. Ironically, together with this general dilution of what is native, there has been the most sinister resurgence of tribalism, for example in Yugoslavia, Northern Ireland and Russia. This is the darkest and most destructive expression of native identity. Belonging is defined narrowly and exclusively in terms of land and tribe. Those who embody anything contrary become targets of hate and violence. Such destructive creeds of belonging become poisonous. True belonging is hospitable to difference for it knows that genuine identity can only emerge from the real conversation between self and otherness. There can be no true self without the embrace of the other.

There is always a complex and subtle network of life among the natives of a place. It has a rhythm and balance of its own. To the arrogant outsider natives seem simple and naïve. This is always a massive over-simplification. It is only when the outsider comes in to live there that the subtlety and depth of the way of life become somewhat clearer. Given the immediacy of belonging among the natives there is usually a whole roster of unsaid and unexpressed life that never appears on the surface but which secretly anchors the way of life there. The limitation of the native way of life is that the code of belonging is often quite narrow and tight. Individuals who think differently or pursue a different way of life can be very easily identified, targeted and marginalized. Yet there are treasures preserved by the natives: ancient rhythms of perception and attunement to the world. This way of seeing life and practising belonging in the world finds unique expression in the language of the place. In the West of Ireland Gaeltacht, for instance, the old people are the custodians of the Gaelic language. Each one who dies takes a vocabulary to the grave with them that will never be replaced. The continual presence of the native underlines the temporary presence of the visitor.

The visitor

 he visitor is one who belongs some-where else, but is now here in the world of your belonging. The visit is a powerful and ancient theme. Regardless of the frequency of visits, the visitor remains essentially an outsider, an intruder from another area of belonging. We are made somewhat aware of our different identity through the visit. In earlier cultures where communities were more local and separate, the visitor brought news of a different world. Through the stories told of things seen and heard beyond the horizon, the prospect of other worlds became vicariously tangible. In the time of the oral tradition, the visit would have had an effect that would continue to ripple for a long time after. We who are native also become visitors elsewhere: the courtesies of giving and receiving are essential.

In the broad sense, because each of us lives in a body with so much clear space around us, a large portion of our life is awakened and altered by visitations that we have. Most of what happens to us in the world comes along the empty path to the house of belonging called the body. Great thoughts are not simply manufactured by the mind, they occur, i.e. they seem to come from Elsewhere. Sublime, illuminating and original thought seems to be inspired; or, as classical tradition has it, the visitation of the muse brings the original gift. Our origin in, and affinity with, the eternal is confirmed by the fact that what seems to come from the distance of Elsewhere turns out to be the most profound expression of our inner nature. The beyond holds the deepest secrets to here. Angels have always been received and understood as eternal visitors. The Christian story begins with such a visit. When the visitation comes from the eternal world, it disrupts the daily order; such a visitation breaks the predictable frame of experience and opens life up to new and more disturbing directions. This visitation can be dark and frightening. It can bring all the hidden vulnerability to the surface and expose a person to a future of loss and emptiness; this is explored in a sparse and penetrating way in Raymond Carver's precise and harrowing short story, 'A Small, Good Thing'.

Though the visit is always limited by time, it has a purpose. The visitor comes to see us for a reason. In society this is often the way a prophet appears. The vision and actions of a prophet visit a great unease on our comfort and complacency. It disturbs us in such a manner that we never regain the ease and amnesia of our old complacency. The prophetic voice disrupts our unreflective belonging and forces us to awaken the awkward questions. When they come alive, they retrieve the more humane longings of our nature and force us to disavow our strategies of false satisfaction. For the prophetic spirit, the longing for truth and justice puts every kind of belonging in question.

The visitor and the visitation are ancient motifs

and they derive their power from the simple fact that what is most precious to us in the world, namely, our life and presence here, is in the end but a mere visit. Each of us is a temporary visitor to the earth. We spend most of our lives deciphering the purpose and meaning of our visit here. Our time here will end in the embrace of the bleak and irreversible visitor called death. Meanwhile we live out our longings in the small world of belonging we call our neighbourhood.

The Neighbour

he Neighbour is an interesting presence in one's life. No great significance is ever ascribed to the neighbour. They are the people who happen to live adjacent to you. Yet in contrast to others outside the neighbourhood, we feel we somehow have a claim on the courtesy and friendliness of our neighbours. In former times when people were not such targets of pressure and impression, people were closer to their neighbours. People were poorer too and more dependent on each other. In Connemara, there is the phrase: '*Is fearr comharsa maith ná máilín airgid*', i.e. a good neighbour is better than a bag of money. Often when we need something or someone urgently, our friends and family may be far away;

the only ones we have near us are our neighbours. They are the individuals with whom we belong in a local place. In the fragmentation of contemporary life, people live in greater isolation and distance from each other. The old image of the neighbourhood as a group of local individuals who knew each other has vanished. A neighbour can be dead for weeks and we do not notice now. Our post-modern society is like the world of Leibniz monadology. Each individual, each home is an isolated monad with no bridge to the neighbour.

There is also the old phrase: good fences make good neighbours. Robert Frost in his poem 'Mending Wall' subverts this notion: 'something there is that doesn't love a wall'. Yet in the old phrase is the idea that a certain kind of neighbour can limit your independence and freedom and invade your privacy. Just because people dwell near you, they have no right to control your life in this way. The ideal neighbourliness means a balance between caring for those near you and keeping space free to engage and inhabit your own life. The atmosphere of the neighbourhood should never cripple the longing of the soul to wander.

The Wanderer

he wanderer is one who gives priority to the duties of longing over belonging. No abode is fixed. No one place is allowed finally to corner or claim the wanderer. A new horizon always calls. The wanderer is committed to the adventure of seeing new places and discovering new things. New possibilities are more attractive and intoxicating than the given situation. Freedom is prized highly. The wanderer experiences time and space in a different way than the native or the neighbour, who remains faithful to a place. Time is short and there is so much yet to be experienced. While each place has its own beauty, no particular place can claim to settle the longing in the wanderer's soul. Space and distance are never a barrier. Travel is the adventure. The purpose is never directed towards a specific destination. The journey is itself the ever changing destination. The wanderer travels light and carries none of the baggage of programmes or agendas. There is an openness and hospitality to new places and new people. The call of longing is always answered, often to the detriment of achieved belonging. At its extreme the wanderer can be like a butterfly. An obsession to explore things with an over-lightness of touch, the journey need not be a real journey;

merely a circular route around the same repetitions, each, of course, differently packaged than the last time.

The wanderer has been a great theme in literature and film. An old and innocent, but very subtle, film which explores this is *Shane*. He is a wandering cowboy who comes to work for a family – husband, wife and little boy. He helps them fight their enemies. He keeps to the honour of his task despite the warmth and attraction that is growing between him and the woman. When the difficulties are overcome, he wanders off again. Shane is wounded, a symbol of his awareness that he can never belong in the one place where he felt at home. A great number of Westerns have the hero riding into the sunset at the end. He is the modern version of the knight. He is honourable and courageous and remains completely dedicated to the adventure of the longing wherever it will take him. No one frame of belonging is large or flexible enough to contain him. Wandering is a very strong tradition in Ireland. In mythic times, there were fabulous journeys to strange lands; such a journey was known as an *immram*. In the early centuries Irish monks went into 'green exile'; many of them wandered the continent and laid down the basis for medieval civilization. Ireland has also suffered great depletion from the wandering called emigration.

The wanderer travels through a vast array of experience. The word wander derives originally from the verb 'to wind' and is associated with the word *wandeln*, to change. The wanderer does not find change a threat. Change is an invitation to new possibility. The wanderer is as free as the wind and will get into corners of experience that will escape the settled, fixed person. It is interesting that the word wander covers the movement of persons, animals, objects, thoughts and feelings. Wandering is the natural and indeed native movement of the majority of things in the world. The wind is the great elemental wanderer who roams the universe. In a fascinating passage in the Gospel of John the nature of spirit is described in terms of the unpredictable dance of the wandering wind:

he wind blows wherever it pleases;
You hear its sound,
But you cannot tell where it
comes from or where it is going.
This is how it is with all who are born
of the Spirit.

John 3: 8–9

The human body is a physical object held down by the force of gravity in a physical world; it is always in some one place. However, the vibrancy of

67

its presence is unmistakable. Thought is a permanent wanderer. No frontier is too far, no depth too deep. The body always belongs some one place; the ancient and ever-new longing of the soul can never find satisfaction in any one form of belonging. Delmore Schwartz has a poem where he calls the body: 'The Heavy Bear who goes with me'. It is a poem full of affection for the body, yet impatient with its awkwardness and gravity. The soul is full of wanderlust. When we suppress the longing to wander in the inner landscapes, something dies within us. The soul and the spirit are wanderers; their place of origin and destination remain unknown; they are dedicated to the discovery of what is unknown and strange.

The stranger

he stranger is an unknown person. One who has not been met before. The limitation of human individuality means that we know only a few people. Most of the world remains unknown to us. Most people remain strangers. This is one of the shocking things about travel; we can descend from the sky into a different country and people, right into the middle of an ongoing life. We know nothing of their names, lives or place. Yet into the journey of each person there is the occasional intrusion of the stranger. We immediately recognize the stranger as someone we have never encountered. When a stranger approaches, we usually exercise caution and keep them at a distance. This is the fascination of encounter. Humans are ancient creatures with millennia of experience in their blood. We are rational animals. The animal side of our nature knows the danger of the intruder, the stranger. Every friend was once a total stranger. The stranger can bring blessings and encouragement and can become *anam čara* or companion of our deepest intimacy. New life can come through the encounter with the stranger. Destruction and negativity can also arrive with the intrusion of the stranger. There is always danger in the stranger. Because we sense this, it usually takes a while before we open to let the stranger in. Strangers circle each other for a good while before familiarity begins to build. Each one of us enters the world as a total stranger. No-one had ever seen you before. You came without a name and yet you entered fully into the belonging of your life.

It is poignant to remember that even the most intimate *anam-čara* friendship cannot dissolve the strangeness between, and within, two people. The friend remains partly stranger. It is a naïve acquaintance that presumes that two people can ever know each other completely. Real soul-friendship acknowledges the mystery of the other person which can at times delight, and at other times, disappoint you. This strangeness keeps the passion and interest alive in a friendship. It is when two friends become predictable with each other that the kinship begins to fade. This is why space and freedom nourish and enrich a friendship. Each person remains always partly a stranger to themselves as well. Part of the wonder of being a person is the continual discoveries that you find emerging in your own self; nothing cosmically shattering, merely the unfathomable miracle of ordinary being. This is the heart of longing and what always calls us to new forms of belonging.

It is impossible to be on the earth and avoid awakening. Everything that happens within and around you calls your heart to awaken. As the density of night gives way to the bright song of the dawn, so your soul continually coaxes you to give way to the light and awaken. Longing is the voice of your soul; it constantly calls you to be fully present in your life: to live to the full the one life given to you. Rilke said to the young poet: 'Live everything.' You are here on earth now, yet you forget so easily. You travelled a great distance to get here. The dream of your life has been dreamed from eternity. You belong within a great embrace which urges you to have the courage to honour the immensity that sleeps in your heart. When you learn to listen to and trust the wisdom of your soul's longing, you will awaken to the invitation of graced belonging that inhabits the generous depths of your destiny. You will become aware of the miracle of presence within and around you. In the beginning was the dream, and the dream was Providence.

A blessing

 lessed be the longing that brought you here
and that quickens your soul with
wonder.

May you have the courage to befriend your eternal
longing.

May you enjoy the critical and creative
companionship of the question: 'Who am I?'
and may it brighten your longing.

May a secret providence guide your thought and
shelter your feelings.

May your mind inhabit your life with the same
sureness with which your body belongs in the
world.

May the sense of something absent enlarge your life.

May your soul be as free as the ever-new waves of the
sea.

May you succumb to the danger of growth.

May you live in the neighbourhood of wonder.
May you belong to love with the wildness of dance.
May you know that you are ever-embraced
in the kind circle of God.

chapter 2

Presence: The Flame of Longing

To realize that you are here

There is a lovely, disconcerting moment between sleep and awakening. You have only half-emerged from sleep and for a few seconds you do not know where you are, who you are or what you are. You are lost between worlds. Then your mind settles and you recognize the room and you take up your place again in your own life. And you realize that both you and the world have survived the crossing from night to reality. It is a new day and the world is faithfully there again, offering itself to your longing and imagination; stretching out beyond your room to mountains, seas, the countenances behind which other lives hide. We take our world totally for granted. It is only when we experience the momentary

73

disturbance of being marooned in such an interim that we grasp what a surprise it is to be here and to have the wild companionship of this world. Such disturbances awaken us to the mystery of thereness that we call presence. Often the first exposure to the one you will love or to a great work of art produces a similar disconcerting confusion.

Presence is alive. You sense and feel presence; it comes towards you and engages you. Landscape has a vast depth and subtlety of presence. The more attentive you are and the longer you remain in a landscape, the more you will be embraced by its presence. Though you may be completely alone there, you know that you are not on your own. In our relentless quest for human contact, we have forgotten the solace and friendship of nature. It is interesting in the Irish language how the word for the elements and the word for desire are the same word: *dúil*. As the term for creation its accent is on the elemental nature of creation. *Dúil* suggests a vital elementalism. It also means longing; *dúil a chur I gceol*, i.e. to get a longing for music. *Dúil* also holds the sense of expectation and hope. Could it be that *dúil* originally suggested that human longing was an echo of the elemental vitality of nature?

You feel the presence of nature sometimes in great trees that stand like ancient totem spirits night and day watching over a landscape for hundreds of years. Water also has a soothing presence and a seductive presence that draws us towards it. John Montague writes: 'Part order, part wilderness/Water creates its cadenced illusion.' Each shape of water: the well, stream, lake, river and ocean has a distinctive rhythm of presence. Stone, too, has a powerful presence. Michelangelo used to say that sculpture is the art of liberating the shape hidden and submerged in the rock. I went one morning to visit a sculptor friend. He showed me a stone and asked if I saw any hidden form in it. I could not. Then he pointed out the implicit shape of a bird. He said: 'For ten years I have been passing that stone on the shore and only this morning did I notice the secret shape of the bird.' Whereas human presence is immediate, the presences in landscape are mediate; they are subtle, often silent and indirect.

Presence is soul-atmosphere

RESENCE is the whole atmosphere of a person or thing. Presence is more than the way a person walks, looks or speaks. It is more than the shape of a tree or the colour of a stone. It is a blend of all these aspects but it is mainly the atmosphere of spirit that is behind them all and comes through them. This is why no two presences are ever the same. There are landscapes that are deeply still and consoling. Travel a half a mile further and you could be in a place that is brooding and sinister and you cannot wait to escape. You can often sense this in people's homes too. Houses now seem to resemble each other more and more. Years ago, as a child, one sensed how different each home was. Each one had a unique aura. It often seemed when a person came to visit that they brought the presence of their home with them. To a child's mind each neighbour's house was a different cave of presence. The furniture, colours and décor of each interior were different. In one, you can make yourself at home; in another, a brooding tension or hostility make you want to leave immediately.

There is a really distinctive and somewhat vulnerable presence to a home where someone lives alone. A family tends to fill up a house. The sounds of their conversations layer the walls and rooms with the texture of presence. When you come in, you walk into a vibrant web of presence. There are practically no clear spaces in a family home; every corner is packed with echo. In contrast, the home of the solitary person is never completely full. There is clearance and silence here. The silence belongs around one presence. Regardless of how cosy and welcoming the home may be, there is always a distilled quality of longing in a solitary person's home. Though the person is solitary, the home can often be full of presence and not at all lonely. Yet it is usually a more intimate event to visit such a home. There is none of the distraction and avoidance that meets you in a family home and that somehow protects both you and them from exposure. In the solitary home you have a certain access everywhere to the solitude of the inhabitant.

Presence has a depth that lives behind the form or below the surface. There is a well of presence within everything, but it is usually hidden from the human eye. This comes in different ripples to the surface. No two stages of presence are ever exactly the same. The flow of soul within means the surface is always different. When you know a place well, you can sense this. The fluent nuance of the light alters the presence of the landscape constantly. As the stream of feeling and thinking flows through you, it also alters your presence. Your presence is always in a subtle flow. When you are happy and at peace, your presence is gentle and approachable. When you are worried or anxious, there is a tension in your presence and it closes and tightens. If we were able to read presence, we could sense what is happening inside a person's mind. Some people have an open presence. They cannot hide anything, you know immediately what is haunting or delighting them. Others are adept actors at putting on a face. As T. S. Eliot says: 'to prepare a face to meet the faces that you meet'. The mask is always in place and it is exceptionally difficult to read what is happening within.

Presence is something you sense and know, but cannot grasp. It engages us but we can never capture its core; it remains somehow elusive. All the great art forms strive to create living icons of presence. Poets try to cut the line of a poem so that it lives and dances as itself. Poems are some of the most amazing presences in the world. I am always astounded that poems are willing to lie down and sleep inside the flat, closed pages of books. If poems behaved according to their essence, they would be out dancing on the seashore or flying to the heavens or trying to rinse out the secrets of the mountains. Reading brings the presence of other times, characters and cultures into your mind. Reading is an intimate event. When you read a great poem, it reaches deep into regions of your life and memory and reverberates back to you forgotten or invisible regions of your experience. In a great poem you find again lost or silent territories of feeling or thought which were out of your reach. A poem can travel far into your depths to retrieve your neglected longing.

Music as presence

RT has no interest in generalities. Art wants to create individuals. Music is perhaps the most divine of all the art forms in that it creates an active, living and moving form that takes us for a while into another world. There is no doubt that music strikes a deep and eternal echo within the human heart. Music resonates in and with us. It is only when you become enraptured in great music that you begin to understand how deeply we are reached and nourished by sound. The rush of our daily lives is dominated by the eye. It is what we see that concerns and calls us. 'You wish to see? Listen,' advised St Bernard. Generally we neglect almost completely the nourishment of listening to good and true sounds. The sound quality of contemporary life is utter dissonance and cacophony. We live in a world of mechanical noise which allows no spaces for silence to come through to enfold us. So much modern music is but a distraught echo of our hollow and mechanical times.

A human life is lived through a physical body. It is no wonder that we are so often tight with stress. We are forever being stoned by dead sounds. It is interesting in terms of architecture that one of the key building materials now is mass concrete. When you strike mass concrete with a hammer, the sound is muffled and dead and swallows itself. When you strike a stone an echo leaps from it; the stone is like an anvil; the music of the stone sings out. The sounds of our times have little inner music; all you hear is muffled hunger. When great music quickens your heart, brings tears to your eyes or takes you away, then you know that in its deepest hearth the soul is musical. The soul is sonorous, echoing the eternal music of the spheres.

It would be a gift to yourself to expose your soul to great music. Have a critical look at your music habits. Do you actually listen to any music at all? What do you listen to? Is the music that you hear too small for your growing soul? It is sad that classical music does not have a larger audience. We all need the wonder and magic of Mozart, Beethoven, Wagner and Brahms. I remember a cartoon in the *Süddeutsche Zeitung*. It was a simple, vacant sketch of a desert. Overhead it was the caption: *Eine Landschaft ohne Mozart*, i.e. a landscape without Mozart. Even if you never pray or visit a temple or church, you can come into vast presences of the Divine through the simple, mindful activity of bathing your soul in the wonderful tides of classical music. The friendship with this music is slow at the beginning. But like any great friendship, the more you let yourself into it, the deeper you belong. It calms the soul, awakens the heart and enriches your sensibility in a delightful way. It somehow manages to harbour in a simplicity of surface the greatest complexity of feeling and thought. Great music opens doorways into eternal presence. It educates and refines your listening; you begin to sense your own eternity in the echoes of your soul. Music is the perfect sister of silence. Georg Solti, the great conductor, said shortly before his death that he was becoming ever more fascinated with the silence at the heart of music and the depth structure it had. Music excavates the kingdom of silence until the eternal sound echoes in us; it is one of the most beautiful presences that humans have brought to the earth. It is one of the most powerful presences where the ancient and the eternal human longing comes to voice. Nietzsche said: 'The relationship between music and life is not only that of one language to another; it is also the relationship of the perfect world of listening to the whole world of seeing.'

The silence of sculpture

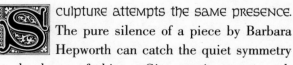 culpture attempts the same presence. The pure silence of a piece by Barbara Hepworth can catch the quiet symmetry at the heart of things. Giacometti creates such poignant shapes, long slender figures who seem to

be thinning out into the nothingness of the air and the gallery. It is almost as if they are inhabited by some mystical humility which urges them to let go. I remember once visiting an exhibition in the gallery in Köln. There was one special room for a piece by Josef Beuys; it was called The End of the Twentieth Century. It consisted of huge blocks of stone piled scatteredly on each other. Each column had a hole at one end. It was as if the stones had waited for millennia for the arrival and adventure of human presence that would bring voice, warmth and belonging to the earth. Human presence had indeed come. But something awful had gone wrong. They had destroyed themselves and all that were left now were huge stone columns used and abandoned. Beuys had so clearly anticipated the huge sadness that would issue from the placing and context of these stones. Sculpture is a powerful and wistful form of presence. There is an old anecdote that when Michelangelo was finished carving the sitting Moses, he was so enthralled with his presence that he tapped him on the knee with his chisel and said: 'Moses, get up.'

Within a fixed frame the artistic imagination strives to create or release living presence. The human imagination loves suggestion rather than exhaustive description of a thing. Often, for instance, one dimension of a thing can suggest the whole presence that is not there or available now. From the tone of a friend's voice on the phone, your imagination can fill in the physical presence perfectly. Imagination strives to create real presence. It is rarely drawn towards what is complacent or fixed. It loves to explore the edges where cohesion is breaking apart and where new things are emerging from difficulty and darkness. The imagination never presents merely the idea or the feeling but reaches deeply enough into the experience to find the root where they are already one. As beautiful and inspiring as art might be, it can never reach the power of presence naturally expressed in a baby's smile or the sinister glower that can cross an old woman's eyes. Human presence is different from everything else in the world. For fields, stones, mountains and trees we must be amazing creatures, utterly strange and incomprehensible. Because we ourselves are human presence, we are blind to its miracle. No concept, image or symbol can ever gather or hold down a presence. Indeed, the very existence of words, music, thoughts and art are the voices of longing which ripple forth from the shimmering depths of presence in us and in creation. Presence is longing reaching at once outwards and inwards.

The sanctuary of human presence

H. Lawrence's poems deal with the presence of nature: natural objects and creatures are not self-centred or self-pitying; they claim no privilege and do not intrude. It is the nature of humans to be present in a way that impinges on and engages others. Human presence is never neutral. It always has an effect. Human presence strikes a resonance. Colloquially, we refer to the chemistry of someone's presence. When two people discover each other, the way they look at and talk to each other indicates that they are enfolding each other in a circle of presence. Their style of presence evokes an affinity and calls them towards a voyage of discovery with each other. The echo of their outer presence calls them nearer and nearer so that they can begin to reveal the depth of inner presence which illuminates their physical presence. The opposite experience is also common. Two people meet and find that each other's presence pushes them away from each other. Outer presence has its own compass. Chemistry has a secret and powerful logic. We can never predict or plan whether we will move towards or away from another's presence. This is something that the occasion and the encounter will decide; it is a happening with its own freedom.

The human body longs for presence. The very structuring and shape of the body makes it a living sanctuary of presence. When a thing is closed, we only encounter its outer shell. The human body can never close off in such a hermetical way. The body is one of the most open and manifest presences in the world. Even from a person who is shy and always withdraws, presence still manages to seep forth. The human body is a language that cannot remain silent. The countenance is an intense and luminous icon of presence. Nowhere else in the world are you encountered and engaged as totally as by a human person. The human face is a miniature village of presence. Every dimension of the face expresses presence: the lines from which it is drawn, the curvature of the mouth, the shape of the face, the dome of the head and especially the eyes. All the aspects of the face combine to bring one individual life to expression. The face is the icon where all the atmosphere, feeling and thought of an individual life assemble visually.

The days and nights a person has lived seep into presence in the countenance. It is interesting that the Latin root of the word face is *'facies'* which means the shape or form of the head but is derived from the verb *'facere'* which means to make. This background confirms the artistic and active force of the face. Neither a surface nor a cover, the face is a doorway to the soul. When you gaze into someone's face, a pathway opens, resonant with their life and memory. You glimpse what life has made or unmade, woven or unravelled in that life. Each face fronts a different world. Merleau Ponty said: 'My body is the awareness of the gaze of the other.' We are animated through the presence of the other. Every face is a window outwards and inwards on a unique life. Of course, in dance and in theatrical activity the whole body becomes expressive. Because others can see us, our lives never remain merely ours alone. The openness of the face shows that we participate in the lives of others. Presence to each other is the door to all belonging. And there is nowhere in the universe where longing is so powerfully present as in the human countenance. From here all desire for dwelling and community issues.

The witness of hands

The whole structure of the human body anticipates and expects the presence of others. Hands reach out to embrace the world. Human hands are powerful images. Hands painted the roof on the Sistine chapel and the heavenly women on the wall of Sigeria; wrote the *Paradiso*; sculpted David; in Auschwitz hands rose to bless tormentors. Hands reach out to touch and caress the lover. Hands build walls, sow gardens and direct symphonies. Hands wield knives, pull triggers and press switches that bring terminal darkness. Hands write stories that deface people, strip lives bare. The whole history of our presence on earth could be gleaned from the witness and actions of hands. One of the great thresholds in human civilization was the development of tools with which we changed and civilized landscape. The use of simple tools still meant personal contact with nature. In these times we have crossed another threshold where the tool is replaced by the instrument. The instrument is a means of exercising a function. Instrumentalization is the whole functional world of the instrument as a means coming between us and life. With the development of instrumentalization, so much of our work and engagement with the world is no longer hands-on. Rather our hands press the key and the instrument expedites the action. Instrumentalization saves labour but at the cost of direct contact with the world.

The instrumentalization of contemporary life pushes us ever further away from nature. Even farmers now do not really get their hands dirty any more. Years ago when you looked at a farmer's hands, they were like miniature lexicons of the landscape. The hands were worn and roughened through contact with soil and stone. Often rib lines of clay insinuated themselves into the lines of the skin. It was a powerful image of living hands remembering that originally they were, and would again be clay. People dressed in their Sunday best going to Mass. Serving Mass, you would see perfectly dressed men come to the altar for Holy Communion. They would stand reverently and offer this pair of withered, earthened palms on which the white host would glisten: the Bread of Life on hands of clay. This is a vignette from a vanishing world. Generally it seems that when we lose individual contact with nature and with each other, we gradually lose our depth and diversity of presence. The world of function, instrument and image is a limbo where no presence lives, where no face is identifiable, where everything flattens into the one panel of sameness.

Styles of presence: the encouraging presence helps you to awaken your gift

 here are people whose presence is encouraging. One of the most beautiful gifts in the world is the gift of encouragement. When someone encourages you, they help you over a threshold you might otherwise never have crossed on your own. There are times of great uncertainty in every life. Left alone at such a time, you feel dishevelment and confusion like a gravity. When a friend comes with words of encouragement, lightness visits you and you begin to find the stairs and the door out of the dark. The sense of encouragement you feel from them is not simply their words or gestures; it is rather their whole presence enfolding you and helping you find the concealed door. The encouraging presence manages to understand you and put itself in your shoes. There is no judgement but words of relief and release.

Encouragement also helps you to engage and trust your own possibility and potential. Sometimes you are unable to see the special gift that you bring to the world. No gift is ever given for your private use. To follow your gift is a calling to a wonderful adventure of discovery. Some of the deepest longing in you is the voice of your gift. The gift calls you to embrace it, not to be afraid of it. The only way to honour the unmerited presence of the gift in your life is to attend to the gift; this is also a most difficult path to walk. Each gift is different; there is no plan or programme you can get ready-made from someone else. The gift alone knows where its path leads. It calls you to courage and humility. If you hear its voice in your heart, you simply have to follow it. Otherwise your life could be dragged into the valley of disappointment. People who truly follow their gift find that it can often strip their lives and yet invest them with a sense of enrichment and fulfilment that nothing else could bring. Those who renege on or repress their gift are unwittingly sowing the seeds of regret.

The blurred presence

OME people have a blurred presence. For some reason, so many thoughts and bands of feeling criss-cross simultaneously in their personality that you can never, finally, decide where you are with such a person. Their presence is distracted and confused. There is no line or contour you can finally follow. Such presences are usually self-absorbed and have neither clarity nor a sense of clearance around them to enable them to attend or engage with anyone else. When such a person is manager or chairperson of a group or company, there is neither vision nor an effective or clear resolution of anything.

The angry presence

NGER is a great flame of presence. It is difficult to mistake or ignore an angry presence. Usually anger is like fire, it starts with a spark and then multiplies in a rapid exponential rhythm. Anger wants to break out; it stops us in our tracks. Much of the time we avoid conflict; we put up with things. We let things go. When the flame of anger rises, it confronts things. Anger shouts stop! It can be a great force for change. It is so encouraging to hear the voice of righteous anger raised. It names and confronts injustice. It brings to light whatever is wrong and makes it clear to the perpetrators of injustice what they are doing. It is very interesting to notice how politically incorrect anger now is. Especially in these times, there are so many issues that should warrant great anger. James Hillmann remarks in his devastatingly incisive way that psychotherapy has managed to convert anger into anxiety. If one becomes angry on television, one immediately loses the trust of the audience. Whatever kind of subtle common denominator of propriety television exercises, it seems that an angry presence even when it is fully justified, still only manages to evoke sympathy for the target of the anger and the diminution of the presence of the angered one. Perhaps this only confirms even more trenchantly that television manages to depict only image and never real presence. Anger disrupts the fluent sequence of images and makes awareness awkward.

There are some people who seem to manage almost permanent anger. Every time you meet them, there is something new drawing their anger. Such people never relent. They are victims of a fire that started somewhere further back but continues to flare up on every new ground they enter. There are also people who are constantly nice; they are always pleasing and accommodating. They never lose their composure, they give nothing away. Yet if you really watch them, you will begin to detect a quiet fury behind the mask of niceness. It would be wonderful for them if, even once, they could unleash the fury with no concern for the situation in which they find themselves. It would limber up their personality and they would experience the immense relief of realizing they did not need to desperately court approval in the first place.

There are also individuals who use their anger as a brooding hostility to control those around them. There is a wonderful portrayal of this in John McGahern's novel *Amongst Women*. Moran, the father in a household of women, can use his silent anger as a massive controlling force which infests the home with a permanent undercurrent of tension. His wife is the mediating force who adverts to this ever-present hostility and ensures that Daddy is not disturbed. Related to this is the depressive presence. Sometimes the old definition of depression as inverted anger is accurate. The natural anger that should flame forth into the world is turned inwards on the self and used as a force of self-punishment. The outer presence is weary and passive but deep underneath somewhere a searing flame crackles in the self.

When you really inhabit your anger, you enter into your power as a person. This should not be a permanent necessity. But if you are in a situation where you are being controlled or bullied, the expression of your anger can liberate you. It is frightening how we often secretly believe that those who have power over us have right on their side and our duty is to comply. No-one can oppress you without some anger awakening in you, even covertly. If you listen to that anger, it will call you to a recognition of your right to an integrity of presence. And it will bring you to act and clearly show your strength. It is astounding how each day we give away so much of our power to systems and people who are totally unworthy of it. Ultimately anger points towards life. When your anger flames, it targets the falsity of expectation or tightness of belonging that is being inflicted on you. Anger breaks you free, suddenly.

The charismatic presence

ou really become aware of the force and light of human presence when you are in the company of a charismatic person. In theology, charisma means divinely conferred favour. A charismatic presence is one that inspires people. It has a natural balance between the personality and the vision which the person represents. In some way, the luminosity in the person is an aura that tangibly reaches out and affects others. In German one speaks of *'eine grosse Ausstrahlung'*, i.e. a great streaming forth of radiance. The charismatic person does have a radiance that stirs us. It is given to some people to be carriers of huge spirit. This is not something they have sought out or earned. It is not something that they have worked up in themselves. It seems to belong deeply in their nature. I remember once speaking to a friend about a family we both knew who had such spirit and he said: 'If you put one of them in a house on her own, you would fill it.' Charisma reminds us that there is no system or frame large enough to hold the secret immensity that is in each of us.

The truly charismatic presence is also to be distinguished from the overblown personality who fills a room with talk and bustle but manages to create more heat than light. When there is silence and poise anchoring the charismatic presence, there is a balance between what they are affecting outside and their own self-belonging and self-possession. If this anchorage is not maintained then such a presence is in danger of burning itself out. It is the art of belonging to one's soul that keeps one's presence aflame. From this belonging comes the light of inspiration and vision which cannot be manufactured, only received. Without such belonging the charismatic presence can, in extreme cases, become toxic. It can let in dark forces and inflame people with hatred, as in the case of fundamentalism and fascism; or numb them into passivity as in cults.

The anxious presence

There are anxious times in every life. These are times of trembling. Your confidence and security evaporate. What lies ahead of you seems brooding and threatening. Because we live in space, anything can approach and assail us. Because we live in time, there is always an interim period between us and what is coming. When we grow anxious, we fill up that interim with every imaginable disaster. Our fantasy turns wild and dark. Then when the dreaded event comes, it is never as bad as we have imagined and we are hugely relieved. We find again our natural poise. Some people, however, make a habit of anxiousness. Somehow, they have slipped into a mode of permanent worry. When they enter a room, they bring an aura of anxiousness that darkens the company and installs a certain gloom. If the others present attempt to continue their liveliness of presence, the anxious presence withdraws deeper into itself and looms in the room like an accusation. Such a person may have a great life, but they feel little of its joy or happiness. It is so difficult for such a person to find any inner distance from their anxiousness. To them it is serious and ultimate. There is no humour nor any sense of irony. Trying to force themselves out of it often only enforces it. Sometimes paying too much attention to it only confirms it as a condition for them. It is lovely to see a person liberate themselves from this. Somehow it dawns on them that it is not a condition at all; rather this anxiousness is something they do to themselves. With this recognition there is already a huge breakthrough achieved. When they explore further and ask why they need to punish themselves in this way, they are already on their way to peace. They stop punishing themselves and gradually the occasional smile begins to transform the anxious countenance. And laughter may not be far away!

DIGNITY OF PRESENCE

here is great beauty in dignity; it is a special quality of presence. It is wonderful to behold a person who inhabits their own dignity. The human body is its own language. Every gesture you make speaks about who you are. The way you hold yourself, how you walk, sit, speak and touch things tells of your quality of soul. Some people have a clear dignity of carriage and composure. You sense their self-respect and the ease with which they are at home in their own presence. There is no forcing of presence; they do not drive themselves outwards to impress or ingratiate themselves. Other people squander their dignity completely. They live a half-mile outside themselves, their personalities sprung in search of notice and affirmation. Your presence inevitably reveals what you think of yourself. If you do not hold yourself in esteem, it is unlikely that others will respect you either.

The beauty of dignity is its truth. When you were sent to the world you were given great freedom. This is a gift we forget. Regardless of how you appear to others, you are free to view yourself with affection, understanding and respect. While you depend on the affection and love of others to awaken your love for yourself, your sense of self should not depend on outside affirmation. When you have a worthy sense of your self, this communicates itself in your physical presence and personality. Outer dignity is gracious and honourable; it is the mirror of inner dignity. No-one else can confer dignity on you; it is something that comes from within. You cannot fake it or acquire it as you would an accent. Only you can receive the gift of dignity from your own heart. When you learn to embrace your self with a sense of appreciation and affection, you begin to glimpse the goodness and light that is in you and, gradually, you will realize that you are worthy of respect from yourself. When you recognize your limits but still embrace your life with affection and graciousness, the sense of inner dignity begins to grow. You become freer and less dependent on the affirmation of outer voices and less troubled by the negativity of others. Now you know that no-one has the right to tarnish the image that you have of yourself.

There is such a feeling of shame when you let yourself down, when you have acted beneath your dignity. There is something demeaning about having done something that is *infra dignitatem*. You would give anything to return to the point two minutes before the event and act differently. Having dignity of presence is not to be equated with being nice, always good or behaving conventionally. You can be as free as the wind in your views, beliefs and actions; you could be angry and awkward at times and still hold your dignity. Neither is dignity equivalent to stiffness or arrogant aloofness of personality. Dignity allows an immense pliability and diversity of presence but still holds the sense of worthiness and the honour of a larger horizon of grace and graciousness. Even in compromising and demeaning situations, you can still hold your sense of dignity. At such times your sense of dignity will keep a space of tranquillity about you. In the Third World one is often struck by the immense dignity of the poor. Even hunger and oppression cannot rob them of this grace of spirit. If you do not give it away, no event, situation or person can take your dignity away from you. The different styles of presence reveal how we belong to ourselves.

The architecture of belonging

 Canadian who recently visited Ireland for the first time remarked on landing at Shannon Airport how the patchwork of fields had humane proportion. Our world is indeed addicted to the vast expanse, be it the worldwide web or globalization. With this relentless extension, we are losing our sense of the humane proportion. When a thing becomes over-extended, it loses its individuality and presence and the power to speak to us. The landscape in the West of Ireland partly owes its intensity and diversity of presence to the proportion of its fields. Each field has its own unique shape and personality. When the walls frame a piece of land, they bring all that is in that field into sharp and individual relief: the stones, the bushes and the gradient of the field. Patrick Kavanagh speaks of 'the undying difference in the corner of a field'. The corner is always where a wall is most intense. The walls focus the field as an individual countenance in the landscape. No wonder so many of the fields have their own names and stories.

Where there is neither frame nor frontier, it is difficult to feel any presence. This is our human difficulty with air. It is invisible and always the same blank nothingness. The sky is a massive expanse but it is rarely the same blue all over; it is brindled with cloud and colour and framed by the horizon. The human mind loves proportion and texture. Though we are largely unaware of it, we always need a frame around an experience in order to feel and live. When you reflect on all the things you have known and experienced, you begin to see how each of them had its own different frame. Think of the time you met your partner and fell in love. This event happened at a certain time, in a certain place and at a very particular phase in your life. At any other time, it could not have happened in this way. In the landscape of memory there are many fields. Each experience belongs in its own field. This is what hurts and saddens us so profoundly about death. When we lose someone to death, they literally disappear. They vanish into thin air and become invisible to us. Our hearts reach towards them but their new presence has no frame and is now no longer to be located in any one place that we can know or visit. Our voices call to them, yet no echo returns.

All of human experience comes to expression in some kind of form or frame. It is literally impossible to have an experience that did not have a form. The frame focuses individuality and gathers presence. Without this frame, neither identity nor belonging would ever be possible. Belonging presumes warmth and intimacy. You cannot belong in a vast, nameless space. There is no belonging in the air except for birds who ride its currents. Belonging is equally difficult in the ocean; the vast expanse of water is anonymous. It has no face and only sailors who know it well can identify a particular place in its endless sameness. Where there is anonymity, there can be no real belonging. Of the four elements, the earth is the one with the greatest stable presence and thereness. Clay loves shape and texture. Of all the elements, the earth forms naturally into individual shapes, each of which is different. It is no wonder that, being made of clay, the human body is capable of such longing and belonging. The human self is intimacy. When we choose to give our hearts to, or belong with, someone, we only do it when we find a like echo in the intimacy of the other. Belonging seeks out affinity that has a definite form and frame. We feel we can trust that which has its own contour and individual autonomy of shape. This trust enables belonging.

The structures of our world bring the architecture of belonging to expression. In order to be, we need to belong. At work or among people, your social mask is on. When you come home, you are back where you belong, in your safe, sheltering space. Outside in the world, you have to temper your longing and obey convention. When you come back home, you can relax and be yourself. This recognition is caught in the old phrase: a man's home is his castle. At an exhibition in London some years ago, there was a minimalist Zen painting suggestive of great presence and shelter. Over the painting was the caption: all the holy man needs is a shelter over his head. The shelter of home liberates creativity and spirituality. When a person has lived in institutional spaces, there is great joy in privacy and celebration in the shelter of belonging. In a world where privacy is being eradicated, it is wonderful that we still have the shelter of our own homes, though modern technology has punctured that privacy. All belonging is an extension of the first and closest belonging of living in your own body. The body is a home which shelters you. All other forms of belonging continue this first belonging. You can see this continuity of belonging in the rooms you inhabit, the places you live, the office, the church, the shop, the pub. Each one of these spaces presents a different style of presence in the diverse architecture of belonging through which our lives move. There is a different level of belonging offered and required in each of these spaces. Different longings are met and mirrored in each of these different spaces. You always live in a space which frames your belonging but is yet unable to fully reflect your longing. This ambivalence gives such vitality and passion to human presence.

In the heart, the ache of longing

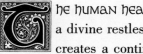he human heart is never still. There is a divine restlessness in each of us which creates a continual state of longing. You are never quite at one with yourself and the self is never fixed. There are always new thoughts and experiences emerging in your life; some moments delight and surprise you, others bring you onto

shaky ground. On the outside, your body looks the same. Your behaviour, work, home and circle of friends remain consistent and predictable. Yet behind this outer façade there is another life going on in you. The mind and heart are wanderers who are always tempted by new horizons. Your life belongs in a visible, outer consistency; your inner life is nomadic. Hegel says: 'Just this unrest that is the Self.' Your longing takes you frequently on inner voyages that no-one would ever guess. Longing is the deepest and most ancient voice in the human soul. It is the secret source of all presence and the driving force of all creativity and imagination: longing keeps the door open and calls towards us the gifts and blessings of which our lives dream.

Longing belongs to the word-family associated with the word *long*; it suggests either a spatial measurement or temporal duration. The crucial point here is that longing is a quality of desire which distance or duration evoke. In other words, your longing reaches out into the distance to unite you with whatever or whomsoever your heart desires. Longing awakens when there is a feeling that someone or something is away from you. It is interesting that the word desire comes from the latin '*desiderare*' which originally meant 'to cease to see'. This suggested a sense of absence and the desire to seek and find the absent one. Another version of the root of desire is '*de-sidus*': 'away from a star'. When you are in a state of desire, you are away from your star. Your heart yearns for the light and luminosity which are now absent. While we are in the world there is always a large area of the heart in exile. This is why we are suffused with longing. Deep down, we desire to come back into the intimate unity of belonging.

Celebration: when the moment blossoms

 elebration is one of the most intense and delightful forms of human presence. It is lovely to be able to celebrate. Some people never celebrate anything. They have no time. Others are too serious ever to think of celebrating. Some feel there is nothing to celebrate. Such people are prisoners who slog away in a secure and predictable routine. There are few surprises; and no surprise is allowed to interfere with the onerous burden of endurance and commitment. There is no time out for play or devilment. Other people are wonderful at celebrating. Even a small event can be an excuse for a celebration. There is a sense of joy and happiness in celebration. It is interesting that sadness generally drives us towards solitude whereas joy draws us together in celebration. Nothing does your heart so much good as real celebration. Laughter loosens all the tension in you. When you dance and sing your soul lifts and the lovely light of the eternal lifts you to a new lightness. Hegel said something fascinating about the True as a passionate festival: 'The True is thus the Bacchanalian revel in which no member is not drunk; yet because each member collapses as soon as he drops out, the revel is just as much transparent as simple repose.'

When we celebrate, we joyfully acknowledge and recognize the presence of some person, thing or achievement that delights us. The desire to celebrate is the longing to enter deeper into the mystery of actuality. Longing is no longer directed away towards an anticipated future. Now, the present moment has blossomed. You really want what you have. You know the blessings and gifts that are around you. Celebration is an attentive and gracious joy of presence. When you celebrate you are taking time to recognize, to open your eyes and behold in your life the quiet miracles and gifts that seek no attention; yet each day they nourish, shelter and animate your life. The art of belonging in, with and to your self is what gives life and light to your presence; it brings a radiance to your countenance and a poise to your carriage. When your heart is content, your life can always find the path inwards to this deep stillness in you. Rilke said so beautifully: *'Hier zu sein ist so viel'* i.e. to be here is so much. Real celebration is the opposite of contemporary consumerism. In fact, consumerism gradually kills both the desire and the capacity to celebrate. The turbo motor within the consumerist spirit ensures that enough is never, ever enough. The mind becomes slow and heavy; the effort to think differently is too demanding, the least stir in that direction already has us out of breath. Our minds are hugely overweight.

Functionalism kills presence

here is some technology which extends human presence over great distance and brings the absent one nearer; telephone and fax machine do this. Most technology, however, attempts to explain life in terms of function. Increasingly, when we approach something new our first question is never about the surprise of the thing but about how it functions. Our culture is saturated with information which stubbornly refuses to come alive with understanding. The more we become immersed in technology, the more difficult it is to be patient with the natural unevenness and unpredictability of living. We learn to close ourselves off and we treat our souls and minds no longer as presence but more in terms of

107

apparatus and function. Functionalist thinking impoverishes presence. The functionalist mind is committed to maintenance and efficiency. The priority is that things continue to work. In one's professional life, one can often experience this. You are called to the director's office for a chat. Whether you are to be promoted or demoted, you feel you are not being seen. What is at stake is either what the system can get out of you or no longer wants from you. If you have staked your identity in belonging to that system, you are now in deep trouble. There are so many disappointed people within companies and corporations and public-service jobs, people who were once idealistic but then reached the threshold of recognition where they discovered they were being treated as mere functionaries; they then lost confidence and belief in themselves.

Without reverence there is no sense of presence

unctionalism is lethal when it is not balanced by a sense of reverence. Without reverence there is no sense of presence or wonder. Functionalism eats into this necessary respect for otherness which makes us human. The functionalist mind is skilled in the art of using people and nature for its own projects and achievements. In contrast, the reverential mind is respectful of the presence and difference of each person and thing. This does not imply that the reverential mind stagnates in passive attention towards life. It is well able to engage and tussle with the world. But it continues to relate to life with a sense of mystery and respect. To engage life in a reverential way is to maintain a sense of proportion and balance. You acknowledge that there is a depth of presence in every person that should never be reduced in order to satisfy your own selfishness and greed. You cannot have a personal integrity of presence without recognizing and revering the presence of others. There is some strange, hidden symmetry in the soul. When you diminish another person, you diminish your self. When you diminish your self, you diminish others.

There is something deeply sacred about every presence. When we become blind to this, we violate nature and turn our beautiful world into a wasteland. We treat people as if they were disposable objects. We lament today the absence of God and the demise of the sacred. Yet it is we ourselves who have killed God. The world today is just as full of sacred presence as it was centuries ago. With the hardening of our minds, we are no longer able to feel and sense the ever-present sacred the way our ancestors did. Our arrogance and greed have killed the gods. Unknown to us, the suppression of Divine Presence costs a terrible price. Because nature and person lose their inner divinity when the gods depart. Past generations were often victims of a bleak, monolithic God who suppressed all creativity; we recognize the authority of no God and much of our creativity is monstrous. As Dostoyevsky said: 'If God does not exist, everything is permitted.' All the horizons become flattened and the wells dry up. We no longer walk the earth with wonder. We have purchased the fatal ticket. Instead of being guests of the earth, we are now crowded passengers on the runaway train of progress and productivity; the windows are darkened and we can no longer see out. The gadgets and games in each compartment are quite fascinating. There is constant theatre. Public relations experts offer sensational help in manicuring the image and searching out the best sound-bite. Even if we wanted to alight, no-one seems to be able to stop the train.

We desperately need to retrieve our capacity for reverence. Each day that is given to you is full of the shy graciousness of divine tenderness. It is a valuable practice at night to spend a little while revisiting the invisible sanctuaries of your lived day. Each day is a secret story woven around the radiant heart of wonder. We let our days fall away like empty shells and miss all the treasure.

The ascetical presence: the wisdom to subtract from the feast

unctionalism wants to acquire and control; its hunger is endless. The reverential mind can let things be and celebrate a person's presence or a thing's beauty without wanting something from them. There is an ascetical rhythm to experience. It is content to endure its own emptiness and does not need to rush to fill it with the latest distraction. It is interesting that asceticism has always been a key practice in the great religious traditions. In its most intense form the ascetical mind was very bleak and engaged in a radical denial of self and the world. Its more balanced expression recognizes and respects the otherness and the beauty of the world and endeavours to transfigure the desire to define oneself through possessions, achievements and power. Much of contemporary life suffers from a vast over-saturation. We have so much that we are unable to acknowledge or enjoy it. There is the obscenity of banks buying Van Gogh paintings as products and storing them in their dark vaults where no eye can enjoy them.

We would benefit greatly were we able to develop a more ascetic approach to our lives. As with all manner of spiritual discipline, we gain most when

111

we are willing freely to choose what is difficult. To include the ascetic as a vital dimension in our daily life would deeply enrich us. It would gain us a sense of space. It would help us make clearances in the exponential undergrowth of banality, sensation and exteriority which leaves us so distracted and overwhelmed. It is interesting that much of the modern fascination with mysticism is more self-indulgent than ascetic. We like to filter out the appealing insights or ideas and often choose to forget the ascetic demands of the mystics. Yet it is only through inner clearance of the ascetical that the insights can take root and grow in the clay of our lives. The writings of John of the Cross have the severance of asceticism at their core. The practice of ascetical longing clarifies all belonging.

o reach satisfaction in all
Desire its possession in nothing.
To come to possess all
Desire the possession of nothing.
To arrive at being all
Desire to be nothing.
To come to the knowledge of all
Desire the knowledge of nothing.

To come to be what you are not
You must go by a way in which you are not.

112

When you practise even some small asceticism, your experience gains a new sense of focus. Consumerist culture is not simply an outer frame which surrounds our lives. It is deeper and more penetrating than that. In fact it is a way of thinking which seeps into our minds and becomes a powerful inner compass. Consumerism and its greed are an awful perversion of our longing; they damage our very ability to experience things. They clutter our lives with things we do not need and subvert our sense of priority. They reduce everything to its functionalist common denominator. In contrast, the ascetical way clarifies our perception. It helps us to see clearly and sift the substance from the chaff. The fruit of even limited asceticism is clarity and discernment; you begin to recognize as chaff much of what you had held for the grain of nourishment.

Consumerism leaves us marooned in a cul-de-sac of demented longing, helpless targets of its relentless multiplication. The ascetical approach is selective and subtracts from the feast of what is offered in order to enjoy, explore and celebrate. The functionalist mind only multiplies everything. It fills its own house to the brim. Within its creed of acquisition, it becomes a helpless victim of the insidious multiplication of things until there is such a false fullness that the natural light of life cannot get in any more. As Milton says in Book 8 of

Paradise Lost: 'But man by number is to manifest/His single imperfection . . .' In the dreary liturgies of this creed, ascetism is anathematized or treated as treason. There is a driven desperation at the heart of functionalism. Deep down it is a craven desire for identity and poise; but it is also a desperate flight from oneself. At its root it is a fear of nothingness. It panics in the face of the creative and generous uncertainty at the heart of life. Any ascetical practice is difficult; you learn to walk a little on the path of self-denial. You could build into the rhythm of your week some little practice: it could mean fasting from food on a particular day, risking more regular and clearer meeting with your solitude, coming out from under the protection of your entrenched opinions or beliefs; visit a prison, hospital or old people's home once a fortnight or once a month. The intention of an ascetical discipline is not to turn you into a spiritual warrior but to free you for compassion and love towards others and towards yourself.

We cannot live without the infinite

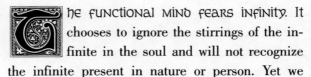he functional mind fears infinity. It chooses to ignore the stirrings of the infinite in the soul and will not recognize the infinite present in nature or person. Yet we

114

cannot live without some form of the infinite. St Augustine said: 'Thou hast created us for Thy self O Lord and our hearts are restless until they rest in thee.' The longing is ancient; it comes from Elsewhere. Our longing always stretches towards a further frontier. It is our nature to seek the infinite. Consequently, the functionalist mind constructs its own infinite out of things, possessions, achievements, stimulants and distractions. It is fixed on the treadmill of multiplication. This kind of addiction is portrayed with uncanny precision by Borges in his story 'The Book of Sand'; a man buys a book that is infinite and becomes a prisoner of the book. This is the cold anonymous infinite; it is without care, tenderness, mercy or mystery. It seems to awaken a longing that is repetitive and utterly obsessed with the single-destination kind of life. The wonder of human life is the generous diversity of presences that dwell in the house of the soul. While all of our inner presences belong together in the one intimacy, each presence is a different longing for a different destination. The cold infinite numbs our richness of longing and bundles all our longings until they make a magnetic projectile that draws our one life dementedly towards the palace of pale satisfaction. In contrast to the living and life-giving infinite, Hegel characterized this as *'die schlechte Unendlichkeit'*, i.e. bad infinity.

Some of the most sinister work of the cold infinite is apparent in the field of genetic engineering. Genetic intervention and manipulation allow unquestioned intrusion into the very identity of plant, animal and even human species. The world continues each day; we get up, go to work and put our hearts into the lives we live. Meanwhile the researchers work away secretly in laboratories we know nothing about. These powerful, anonymous, skilled strangers are literally reinventing creation; adding new and altered species to the earth. They are altering life in a frightening way and we are only faintly aware that what they call great developments are taking place. Suddenly then, one evening, an ordinary-looking sheep appears on our television screens. She bears the coquettish name Dolly. No other sheep in the world knows anything about her. She has never seen another sheep. It is astounding how those who control sinister change know how to parade their first product with such sickly in-nocence. Faust's dilemma is now ours. We have sold our souls for knowledge that is a dangerous in-trusion into realms where we have no right to trespass. The brilliance of the functionalist imagin-ation is its technical ability to invent objects to perform new functions. This ability has been central to the origin, evolution and definition of human society. We have learned to tame and harness the forces of nature. Now, however, at the end of this millennium, the functionalist mind is exerting an exclusive monopoly and sinister control over our lives. We invented the machine but now the high priests of the machine are reinventing us.

An infinite which ignores the sacred becomes monstrous. The sense of proportion disappears. In its most sinister sense anything is possible. Consumerism is the new religion. It is practised by increasing numbers of people in the Western world. Quantity is the new divinity; more and more products are offered. The more you have, the greater your status. The power of this divinity is its ability to reach you anywhere. The 'good news' of what it offers you is permanently coming towards you. Its messages flow right into your home through television. Advertising is its liturgy. Such advertisements sell themselves before they sell the product. There is no surplus with which the mind can conjure in advertisements. Everything is exactly divisible by the purposes of those who write copy. The fact that skill is involved does not make advertising into an art form any more than criminals who display skill and even courage deserve our admiration. Advertising is schooling in false desire.

We could never become consumers if we had no desire. It is poignant that despite maturity and judgement there remain visceral appetites within your heart which crave immediate satisfaction. Once awakened to a certain intensity, they race towards the object of desire. Your ability to discern or distance yourself from this drive becomes redundant. The adult returns almost to a childlike single-mindedness. In this sense, consumerist attitude is an obsessive and uncritical passion. It has a powerful and sophisticated ability to deconstruct all resistance. This new divinity is never abstract and does not insist on any major moral obedience. It touches our longing in a very concrete way. It ensures that it always targets the pocket as well as the heart. This is done with consummate skill so that we inevitably find ourselves magnetically attracted to the advertised icon, buying it and bringing it home. The advertisement is a tiny thought-package inserted deftly into the mind; once it opens and expands, its control over us is immense. At a broader cultural level, it is astounding to watch it unravel the complex network of the folk world. Within a few years this virus can penetrate to the very heart of an intricate way of life that had taken hundreds of years of history to construct. Before long a distinctive and unique way of life is rifled and the inhabitants exiled and drawn into the net of consumerist culture.

The blessings of desire

esire is one of the key forces in the origin, evolution and definition of identity. Blindly, but yet instinctively, it brought you out of the invisible world, sowed you in the womb and guided your way through a gallery of forms until you emerged as a baby. Instinctively, in the innocence of childhood, desire still directs your feelings and thoughts towards fulfilment. It leads you to explore new frontiers. When the innocence of childhood breaks and your consciousness becomes divided, your desire divides too. The belonging of childhood breaks; you feel confused and alone in a way you never were in childhood. New longings are surfacing and you can find little sense of belonging. Part of your desire becomes focused on what you want to do with your life. This is the task of realizing your life's dream. Your desire crystallizes in questions like: what do I want to do with my life? Where do I want to work? Who do I want to marry or do I want to marry? This is a complex and difficult time.

Deep down you desire the freedom to live the life you would love. Yet life itself will rarely give you exactly what you desire and seldom offers it to you in the form you would long for. Consequently, you learn the art of compromise. You learn to do with what you have. Destiny often deals us un-expected cards. Perhaps you have your dream profession, live in a lovely area and yet the person with whom you live has never managed to reach you. Often you look out at her/him from some place deep within and sadly acknowledge that despite the dignity and endurance of your daily affection and care for each other, that she/he will never want to travel that landscape to meet you. Or it could be the case that you find that you cannot give love at all; this is a worse hell than not receiving love. In relationships, the initial passion often settles in such a manner that you instinctively agree to meet on a certain level; other regions are to remain un-disturbed. Inevitably in life we end up walking one path. This demands choice and selection; we harness and limit the call of desire. Yet to live with a sense of balance, creativity and integrity so much depends on how and what we choose.

To keep the contours of choice porous

 hough choice deepens and incarnates a way of life, your soul and imagination have an immensity and diversity which can neither be reduced to or accommodated in your chosen path. If you neglect your own immensity,

120

your life-path itself becomes repressive and un-
natural. It cannot unfurl in its own natural rhythm.
You have to push your way through; your life
becomes over-deliberate. Every action and movement has to be forcibly chosen. You try to keep
yourself together. You do not feel that you have
taken a wrong path. No, this is the way life is. One
cannot drift endlessly. Eventually some direction
must be taken. That is all you have done. Yet you
feel disproportionately disappointed; it is as if you
have given up something which was unfairly
demanded of you. Eventually it becomes easier. You
have made that compromise that everyone seems to
have to make at a certain point. You do not have to
force yourself like you did at the beginning.
Gradually something seems to close off within you
and habit takes over so smoothly. Now it all happens
automatically. You have achieved cohesion and
stability in your life but you have paid an awful
price – the death of your longing and the loss of the
future you long for.

'Purity of heart is to will one thing'

A life's journey is made up of continual
daily choices. But there are moments of
profound choosing, when a partner, a life-
direction or a new way of being in the world is

chosen. This can be a wonderful time of focus and redirection. When such a moment of choosing is genuine, it is usually preceded by a time of gestation and gathering. Many different strands of your past experience begin to weave together until gradually the new direction announces itself. Its voice is sure with the inevitability of the truth. When your life decisions emerge in this way from the matrix of your experience, they warrant your trust and commitment. When you can choose in this way, you move gracefully within the deeper rhythm of your soul. The geography of your destiny is always clearer to the eye of your soul than to the intentions and the needs of your surface mind. Wordsworth says in *The Prelude:* 'Soul that art the eternity of thought.' The eye of the soul can see in all directions. When you truly listen to the voice of your soul, you awaken your kinship with the eternal urgency that longs to lead you home. The deepest call to a creative life comes from within your own interiority. It may be awakened or occasioned by a person or situation outside you, yet the surest voice arises from your own secret depth. The surest choosing grows out of the natural soil of experience. The Buddhists say: 'When the apple is ripe it falls of itself from the Tree.'

When we come to moments of profound choosing, we need to be careful about how and where we draw the lines of our choice. Even though a choice sets the fundamental direction of your life, it should not hermetically seal you off from the rest of life. The outer lines of choice should remain porous. Though we always end up having to choose, choice itself remains a mystery, utterly opaque, no matter how much we deliberate. Frost's poem 'The Road Not Taken' shows how, after the event, we achieve clarity and self-importance in dramatizing choices already made. But then, and indeed now, the choice we made is, was and remains mysterious. We are fashioned from the earth, clay shapes in human form. We are children of nature where borders are seldom sealed. Underneath our walls and city streets, left to itself the earth is still one ever-changing field. In order for life to flow, frontiers must remain porous. Nowhere is this more evident than the outer frontier of the human body, our skin. Skin is porous and in a constant interflow with nature. Were it to seal itself off in some hermetic act, it would kill the body. Similarly, the outer lines where we cut a clear choice or life-path should also remain porous in order to allow our other unchosen lives to continue to bless us.

Great choices need the shelter of blessing

uch moments of choosing are also moments of great vulnerability. Often there seems to be a dark side to destiny; it gathers to conspire against the freshly formed choice or chosen direction. The act of making a profound choice lifts one out of the level shelter of the crowd. There is the Daoist saying: the wind in the forest always hits the tallest trees. A choice creates clearance. In this new space the unknown has clear sights on the individual. No obstacles blur the target. Literary tragedy offers a profound exploration of this vulnerability. With passion, the tragic hero makes a choice. Unknown to him he stumbles against some divine law. The choice that opened the glimpse of a wonderful journey and possibility squeezes and tightens now like a noose around the protagonist's neck. The terrible consequences of the passionately chosen path begin to collapse underneath the hero and destroy him and his world. The transfiguration in tragedy is the recognition by the hero of the secret order which he unintentionally violated.

When beneath the frames of your chosen path, the garden of your unchosen lives has enough space to breathe and your life enjoys a vitality and a sense of creative tension. Rilke refers to this as 'the repository of unlived things'. You know that you have not compromised the immensity that you carry and in which you participate. You have not avoided the call of commitment; yet you hold your loyalty to your chosen path in such a way as to be true to the blessings and dangers of life's passionate sacramentality. No life is single. Around and beneath each life there is the living presence of these adjacencies. Often it is not the fact of our choosing that is vital but rather the way we hold that choice. In so far as we can, we should ensure that our chosen path is not a flight from complexity. If we opt for complacency, we exclude ourselves from the adventure of being human. Where all danger is neutralized, nothing can ever grow. To keep the borders of choice porous demands critical vigilance and affective hospitality. To live in such a way invites risk and engages complexity. Life cannot be neatly compartmentalized. Once the psyche is engaged with such invitation and courage, it is no longer possible to practise tidy psychological housekeeping. To keep one's views and convictions permeable is to risk the intake of new possibility which can lead to awkward change. Yet the integrity of growth demands such courage and vulnerability from us; otherwise the tissues of our sensibility atrophy and we become trapped behind the same predictable mask of behaviour.

To be faithful to your longing

o live in such a hospitable way brings many challenges. In marriage or with a life's partner, it demands trust and flexibility in the commitment. Many relationships die quietly soon after the initial commitment. They lose their passion and adventure. The relationship becomes an arrangement. This often happens because the couple renege on a plurality of other friendships as central to their lives. Even though you have one *anam čara*, one to whom you are committed, one who reaches you where no-one else can or will, this person cannot become the absolute mirror for your life. To expect any one individual to satisfy your life-longing is a completely unjust demand. No-one could live up to that expectation. The self is not singular. There are many selves within the one individual. Different friends awaken and reach different selves within you. Different gifts and different challenges come through your different friendships. To hold the borders of your commitment open allows you to give and receive from others without necessarily endangering the sacredness of your *anam-čara*bond. In fact it can enrich and deepen the primordial and permanent intimacy between you. To live with this porousness can at times lead to ambivalence but with discernment and integrity that need not become destructive. This art of living is vital in the workplace. This porousness often allows the alternative light to come through so that you do not have a blind faith in the system. You can still work committedly and creatively and yet recognize the surrounding functionalism and refrain from giving yourself totally and making yourself permanently vulnerable.

The addiction of distraction

hEN you choose someone or some way of life, you invest your heart. Choice becomes an invitation to commitment. When you commit, you deepen presence. Though your choice narrows the range of possibility now open to you, it increases the intensity of the chosen possibility. New dimensions of the chosen path reveal themselves; a new path opens inwards to depth and outwards to new horizons. Your choice has freed your longing from dispersing itself over a whole range of surface. When we avoid choice we often become victims of distraction. Like the butterfly we flit from one flower to the next, delightfully seduced by its perfume and colour. We remain secretly addicted to the temporary satisfaction and pleasure of immediacy. Kierkegaard divided the life-journey into stages and he saw the aesthetic stage as the wanderer whose longing is magnetized on the endless array of novelties. We celebrate the surface, unwilling to become acquainted with the depths where the darkness plies its slow and patient transfigurations. The colour and excitement of the surface, though delightful, are ultimately deceptive; it keeps us from recognizing the habit of our repetitions and the boredom and poverty which sleep there. When we choose a definite path or partner, we leave the endless array of beckoning surface. We go below the façade of repetition and risk the danger of encounter, challenge and responsibility. When you choose with discernment, integrity and passion, you submit yourself to the slow and unglamorous miracle of change.

IRONY AND RECOGNITION

HEN THE HERO IN A TRAGEDY ACTS OUT OF great passion and longing, he is often blind to the choice he is awakening. He participates in a sequence of action without ever dreaming where it is actually leading him. Often it may be clear to others but not to him. When one acts greatly one engenders great vulnerability. True recognition is withheld. The ground of realization prepares itself slowly. You are so close to what you are involved in that you literally cannot see it. This can often happen in relationships. The film *Fatal Attraction* portrayed a man who was guided totally by sexual passion and was blind to the nature of the person with whom he had become involved. It can also happen in a life over-committed to work. The workaholic is doing everything right to provide for the family but is blind to the fact that through his obsession with work he is already losing his family. They never see him; they are quietly becoming strangers to each other. When we spoil our children, we deprive them of learning the art of discipline and the recognition of boundaries. We think we are showing them love and support. Ironically, we are preparing great difficulties for them. Irony continues so long as you don't see. Then, when you suddenly see, you see through the whole sequence at once. You realize how the consequences had been building the whole time, unknown to you. Such recognition breaks your blindness; it also shows you clearly your own part in the story and your responsibility for what happened. It reveals that you have been obscurely complicit in your own downfall. Irony is the shy sister of such recognition.

It is vital that one's spiritual quest be accompanied by a sense of irony. To have a sense of irony ensures humility. Even in your moments of purest, honest intention, there is a sense in which you do not know and can never know what it is that you are actually doing. There is an opaque backdrop to even the clearest action. In everything we do and say, we risk encounter with the unknown. Often its ways are not our ways and it is only at the end that we see what it is that we have been doing. Certain longings want tenancy of your heart; when you succumb to these, you betray your deeper, eternal longing. You need to remain open, yet maintain discernment and critical vigilance. Critical openness is true hospitality and receptivity.

Longing keeps your sense of life kindled

The value of such openness is that it permits a crucial distance between you and the activity of your life in the world. It keeps a certain inner solitude clear so that you remain aware of a primordial longing of life rising in you. Longing in this sense is not a search for gratification or pleasure. This longing is the primal presence of your own vitality. It is the sense of life in you which makes you feel alive. It is rarely that psychology, philosophy or religion ever refer to the 'sense of life'. They concern themselves with the outer meaning of the world, the inner meaning of the soul and the threshold where both meet. This

130

search for meaning is as ancient as the awakening of the first question, it is as new and urgent as the question that is troubling you now. Without a sense of meaning life becomes absurd and surrealistic. In our times Camus, Sartre, Beckett and Kafka have explored the possibilities and consequences of any human action among the unpredictable chaos of life.

When your sense of meaning collapses or is violated, it becomes exceptionally difficult to remain creative or even to continue believing in anything. In the Siberian Gulag prisoners were forced victims of absurdity. They were made to do tasks which involved hard labour in the freezing cold. Regardless how minimal and slight a task might be, the human mind always desires that the task have some significance. The Gulag prisoners were often forced to move hundreds of tons of stones from a pile to another location some miles away. Every day, in the freezing cold, each prisoner filled and slowly wheeled barrow after barrow of rock to the other location. You can imagine their sense of satisfaction as over the weeks the new rock pile began to grow from the transported stone. Every stone was earned. On the very day that all the stones were transferred, the guards made the prisoners begin to bring the stones back again to reconstruct the original pile in the same place. This forced absurdity would eat into the coherence and break the secret belonging of any mind.

Each person incarnates longing

 UR QUEST FOR MEANING, though often unacknowledged, is what secretly sustains our passion and guides our instinct and action. Our need to find meaning is urged upon us by our sense of life. Normally, when we look at people, whether at work, on the street or in our homes, we inevitably think of them in practical terms. We experience other people very concretely. We notice the way they look, the role they play, clothes they wear, habits they have and especially the style of their personality.

Yet when you distance yourself from the particularities of individual lives, you begin to realize that no human person is here on earth accidentally or neutrally. Each person is a living world of longing. You are here not simply because you were sent here. You are here because you long to be here. A person is an incarnation of longing. Behind your image, role, personality, and deeper than your thoughts, there is a pulse of desire that sustains you in the world. All your thoughts, feelings and actions arise from a secret source within you which desires life. This is where your sense of life is rooted. Your

132

sense of life expresses itself in your convictions, intentions and passions. But it comes before them; it is prereflective, yet passionate and powerful. This secret presence of longing helps you endure the routine of the daily round; it emerges strongly when difficulty entangles you or when suffering strips away your networks of connection with the world. Your sense of life is not something you can invent or force with your mind. It is the wisdom of your clay and is eternally acquainted with awakening. As you discover the faithfulness of life within you, it transfigures your fear and assures you that you are more deeply rooted than you realize. It frees you for the adventure of solitude.

To find your true home within your life

 ach one of us is alone in the world. It takes great courage to meet the full force of your aloneness. Most of the activity in society is subconsciously designed to quell the voice crying in the wilderness within you. The mystic Thomas à Kempis said that when you go out into the world you return having lost some of yourself. Until you learn to inhabit your aloneness, the lonely distraction and noise of society will seduce you into false belonging where you will only become empty and weary. When you face your aloneness, something begins to happen. Gradually, the sense of bleakness changes into a sense of true belonging. This is a slow and open-ended transition but it is utterly vital in order to come into rhythm with your own individuality. In a sense this is the endless task of finding your true home within your life. It is not narcissistic; for as soon as you rest in the house of your own heart, doors and windows begin to open outwards to the world. No longer on the run from your aloneness, your connections with others become real and creative. You no longer need to covertly scrape affirmation from others or from projects outside yourself. This is slow work; it takes years to bring your mind home.

The human mind is an amazing gift. It delights in the activity of exploring, gathering and relating things. Because of its own inner belonging, its intimacy to itself, it is the most passionate and self-possessed difference in creation. Whereas stones or trees never seem bothered by their particular uniqueness, each human mind is powerfully conscious of its own difference; it has an intimate and unbreakable relationship with its own difference. This is what makes human individuality journey out of itself to explore and engage others; but it is also what makes each of us so deeply aware of our aloneness. In contrast to the rest of nature, the human mind makes us feel alone, aware of the distances we will never be able to cross. The mind cannot resist exploration because it always sees the world mirrored in itself. The huge longing of the human mind is to discover ever larger shelters of belonging.

The eros of thought

YOUR MIND is the double mirror of the outer world and of your inner world. It is always actively making pictures of things. If you lost your mind, you would lose your world as well. Your mind is so precious and vulnerable precisely because it holds your world. Thoughts are the furniture of the mind. They are the echoes and pictures which hold your world together. This is the fascinating adventure of perception. When you become aware of your thoughts and your particular style of thinking, then you begin to see why your world is shaped the way it is. It is an exciting and frightening moment when you realize your responsibility for your own thoughts. Then you know that you also have the freedom to think differently. Rather than having to travel always along predetermined tracks of thought, you now begin to realize the excitement of thinking in new directions and in different rhythms. You see that thinking has something eternal in it. In the Western tradition thought

135

has been understood as the place within the human person where we are most intimately connected with divinity. Thought is the place of revelation. The dance of thoughts is endless. In his essay on Donne, T. S. Eliot suggests that a thought to him was an experience as immediate as the scent of a flower.

Thought is a profound form of longing. Much of the thought that cripples us is dried out, dead thought. There is no warmth of longing alive in it. Thought that loses touch with feeling is lethal. This separation is the fracture from which fascism and holocaust emerge. Knowledge is intimacy. This is most evident in the activity of friendship. When the longing awakens between you and a stranger, you want to know them – to come close. Closeness without knowing can be either a fascination and reverence for mystery or the prostitution of longing. Spiritual longing is what first draws you close to a friend. This desire refines and deepens itself in coming to know them. Friendship is one of the most beautiful places where longing reaches initial fulfilment and is then further deepened, refined and transfigured. You can also see the longing of thought in the fascination of ideas. When you find yourself in a cul-de-sac in your life, and you feel lost and trapped, a new insight or awareness can come to you and you are able to free yourself.

Our longing is an echo of the divine longing

hought crosses fascinating thresholds when it engages mystery. Mystery cannot be unravelled by thought. Yet the most interesting thinking always illuminates some lineaments of mystery. It opens our minds to a depth of presence that cannot be rifled by even our brightest or most vigorous ideas. Mystery keeps its secret to itself. Through its reserve it invites us ever nearer to the hearth of truth and belonging. Mystery kindles our longing and draws us out of complacency into ever more refined and appropriate belonging. A life that has closed off mystery has deadened itself. Perhaps this is why modern discourse so often sounds inane; it is a forsaken language in which thought has lost its kinship with mystery. When this inner conversation is broken the sense of mystery dies. When we lose the guidance of mystery our culture becomes flat and at the end of these flat fields of thought there is no horizon, merely piles of negativity, an apocalyptic doom that darkens all hope.

Thought is the form of the mind's desire. It is in our thinking that the depth of our longing comes to expression. This longing can never be fulfilled by any one person, project or thing. The secret

137

immensity of the soul is the longing for the Divine. This is not simply a haunted desire for an absent, distant Divine Presence which is totally different from us. The desire of our hearts is so passionate and endless because of the Divine calling us home to presence. Our longing is an echo of the Divine Longing for us. Our longing is the living imprint of divine desire. This desire lives in each of us in that ineffable space in the heart where nothing else can satisfy or still us. This is what gives us that vital gift that we have called 'the sense of life'.

The wonder of presence is the majesty of what it so subtly conceals. Real presence is eternity become radiant. This is why the 'sense of life' in us has such power and vitality. But we are shadowed creatures; fear and blindness often trap us in inner prisons where belonging is cramped and longing becomes fixated. Yet our deepest longing is like a restless artist who tirelessly seeks to make our presence real in order that the mystery we harbour may become known to us. The glory of human presence is the Divine Longing fully alive.

A Blessing for Presence

*ay you awaken to the mystery of
being here and enter the quiet
immensity of your own presence.*
*May you have joy and peace in the
temple of your senses.*
*May you receive great encouragement
when new frontiers beckon.*
*May you respond to the call of your gift
and find the courage to follow its path.*
*May the flame of anger free you from
falsity.*
*May warmth of heart keep your presence
aflame and anxiety never linger about
you.*
*May your outer dignity mirror an inner
dignity of soul.*
*May you take time to celebrate the quiet
miracles that seek no attention.*
*May you be consoled in the secret
symmetry of your soul.*
*May you experience each day as a
sacred gift woven around the heart of
wonder.*

Chapter 3

Prisons We Choose to Live In

The beauty of wild distance

Outside there is great distance. When you walk out into the landscape the fields stretch away towards the horizon. At dawn the light unveils the vast spread of nature. Gnarled stones hold nests of fossils from a time so distant you cannot even imagine it. At night the stars reflect light from the infinite distance of the cosmos. When you experience this distance stretching away from the shore of your body, it can make you feel minuscule. Pascal said: 'The eternal silence of these infinite spaces [the heavens] frightens me.' There is a magnificent freedom in Nature; no frontier could ever frame her infinity. There is a natural wildness in the earth. You sense this particularly in wild places that have never been tamed

140

by human domestication. There are places where the ocean praises the steady shore in a continual hymn of wave. There are fresh, cold streams pouring through mountain corners which have a rhythm that never anticipated the gaze of a human eye. Animals never interfere with the wildness of the earth. They attune themselves to the longing of the earth and move within it as if it were a home rhythm. Animals have no distance from the earth. They have no plan or programme in relation to it. They live naturally in its landscapes, always present completely to where they are. There is an apt way in which the animal who always lives in the 'now' of time can fit so perfectly into the 'where' of landscape. The time and mind of the animal rests wherever it is. The poet Wendell Berry says: '. . . I come into the peace of wild things . . ./. . . For a time/I rest in the grace of the world, and am free.'

The house keeps the universe out

he human person is the creature that changes the wildness of the earth to suit the intentions of his own agenda. Hopkins argues against disturbing nature: 'Long live the weeds and the wilderness yet.' Humans are the one species which has deliberately altered the earth. One of the first ways this happened was through clearing trees and land to build homes. Humans wanted to come in from the great immensities of nature and the heavens. Homes provided shelter against marauding animals. They also provided shelters of belonging. Perhaps the awakening of the infinity in the mind demanded relief from the cosmos in the refuge of simple belonging. At another level, the home represents a certain limitation. It frames off the privacy of your life from the outside world. As cities expand octopus-like into the countryside, it is sad to see beautiful fields serrated with replica housing estates. An old neighbour of mine who rarely visited the city until recently was heard to remark as he looked at all the housing estates: 'The houses are all the same. How would a person find his way home in the evening?' A few minutes later the logic of his own musing had the solution: 'I bet you they are all numbered.'

A house can become a little self-enclosed world. Sheltered there, we learn to forget the wild, magnificent universe in which we live. When we domesticate our minds and hearts, we reduce our lives. We disinherit ourselves as children of the universe. Almost without knowing it, we slip inside ready-made roles and routines which then set the frames of our possibilities and permissions. Our longing becomes streamlined. We acquire sets of convictions in relation to politics, religion and work.

We parrot these back and forth at each other as if they were absolute insights. Yet for the most part these frames of belief can be viewed as self-constructed barriers, fragile clichés built around our lives to keep out the mystery. The game of society helps us to forget the unknown and subversive presence of the human person. The control and ordering of society is amazing; we comply so totally with its unwritten rules. In a city in the morning, you see the lines of traffic and the rows of faces all on their way to work. We show up. We behave ourselves. We obey fashion and taste. Meanwhile, almost unknown to ourselves, we are standing on wild earth at a crossroads in time where anything can come towards us. Yet we behave as if we carried the world and were the executives of a great plan. Yet everywhere around us mystery never sleeps. The same deep nature is within us. Each person is an incredibly sophisticated, subtle and open-ended work of art. We live at the heart of our own intimacy, yet we are strangers to its endless nature.

OUR FEAR OF FREEDOM: THE REFUGE OF FALSE BELONGING

N THE OUTSIDE A PERSON MAY SEEM contented and free, but their inner landscape may be a secret prison. Why do so many of us reduce and domesticate our one journey through this universe? Why do we long for the invisible walls to keep us in and keep mystery out? We have a real fear of freedom. In general, everyone is in favour of freedom. We fight for it and we praise it. In the practice of our lives, however, we usually keep away from freedom. We find it awkward and disturbing. Freedom challenges us to awaken and realize all the possibilities that sleep in the clay of our hearts. Dostoyevsky's legend of the Grand Inquisitor in *The Brothers Karamazov* is a haunting reflection on the idea of freedom. The story tells of Jesus coming back to sixteenth-century Seville during the Spanish Inquisition. They put him in prison and the Cardinal Inquisitor comes to interview Jesus: but he remains silent. The Cardinal complains to Jesus in a fascinating monologue: 'Why did you have to come back and interfere with our work?' He suggests that Jesus made a fatal mistake in overestimating humans. We are not capable of using the freedom that he attributed to and expected of them. The Cardinal says that the Church 'corrected' his work. Instead of the invitation to liberation and creativity, they choose to offer the people 'miracle, mystery and authority'. This is what they like and need. People are not capable of freedom.

The Cage of Frightened Identity

N the inner landscape of the soul there is a nourishing and melodious voice of freedom always calling you. It encourages you to enlarge your frames of belonging – not to settle for a false shelter that does not serve your potential. There is no cage for the soul. Each of us should travel inwards from the surface constraints and visit the wild places within us. There are no small rooms there. Each of us needs the nourishment and healing of these inner clearances. One of the most crippling prisons is the prison of reduced identity. The way we treat our own identity is often Procrustean. In Greek legend, Procrustes was a robber who stretched his victims until they fitted the length of his bed. Each one of us is inevitably involved in deciphering who we actually are. There is no other who can answer that question for you. 'Who are you?' is a surface question which has a vast, intricate rootage. Who are you behind your mask, your role? Who are you behind your words? Who are you when you are alone with yourself? In the middle of the night when you awake, who are you then? When dawn rescues you from the rain-forest of the night, who are you before you slip back safely beneath the mask and name by which you are known during the day? It is one of the unnoticed achievements of daily life to keep the wild complexity of your real identity so well hidden that most people never suspect the worlds that collide in your heart. Friendship and love should be the safe regions where your unknown selves can come out to play. Instead of holding your friend or beloved limited within the neat cage of frightened identity, love should liberate you both to celebrate the festival of complexity within you. We remain so hesitant and frightened to enjoy the beauty of our own divinity.

There are no manuals for the construction of the individual you would like to become. You are the only one who can decide this and take up the life-time of work that it demands. This is such a wonderful privilege and such an exciting adventure. To grow into the person that your deepest longing desires is a great blessing. If you can find a creative harmony between your soul and your life, you will have found something infinitely precious. You may not be able to do much about the great problems of the world or change the situation you are in, but if you can awaken the eternal beauty and light of your soul, then you will bring light wherever you go. The gift of life is given to us for ourselves and also to bring peace, courage and compassion to others.

The fixed image atrophies longing

E are no sooner out of the womb than we must begin this precarious unfolding and shaping of who we are. If we have bad or destructive times in childhood, we begin to fix on a survival identity to cover over and compensate for what happens to us. If we were never encouraged to be ourselves, we begin to construct an identity that will gain us either attention or approval. When we set out to construct our lives according to a fixed image, we damage ourselves. The image becomes the desperate focus of all our longing. There are no frames for the soul. Consequently, we are called, so far as we can, to live without an image of ourselves, or at least to keep the images we have free and open. When you sense the immensity of the unknown within you, any image you have built of yourself gradually loses its promise. Your name, your face, your address only suggest the threshold of your identity. Somehow you are always secretly aware of this. You know how you find yourself at times listening to someone telling you what you should do, or describing what is going on inside you, and you are whispering to yourself that they have not the foggiest idea who you actually are.

The Swiss writer Max Frisch describes something

of the mystery of acquaintance in one of his diaries: 'It is remarkable that in relation to the one we love we are least able to declare how he is. We simply love him. This is exactly what love is. The wonder of love is that it holds us in the flow of that which is alive; it maintains us in the readiness to follow this person in all his possible unfoldings. We know that every person feels transfigured and unfolded when we love them. And also for the one who loves, everything continues in the same unfolding, the things that are nearest and the things that are long familiar. We begin to see things as if for the first time. Love frees us from every image. That is the excitement and adventure and tension: we will never be finished with the one that we love as long as we love them and because we love them.' (Translation by the author.) As it continues to unfold, a loving relationship fosters the adventure of belonging. It also becomes a mirror for our thoughts and emotions, we can look at life from another's point of view and expand our horizons of imagination and perception; it rescues us from false limitation.

It may be more helpful to consider yourself in terms of symbol rather than image. A symbol is never completely in the light. It holds a vital line into the rootage in the dark. It has many faces. Paul Ricoeur says: 'A symbol invites thought.' The symbol does not nail thought to half-truth. A symbol is alive; it constantly nudges thought towards new windows of seeing. Because it is alive it mirrors most faithfully the subtle changes that are always happening in your soul. Though our outer lives retain a certain similarity – our faces, behaviour, friends, work, remain the same – there is an endless ebb and flow of newness inside you. This is the paradox of being a human. To look at your body, thoughts and feelings in a symbolic way enables you to inhabit more fully your presence and its freedoms. There is hospitality and space in a symbol for your depth and paradox. The self is not an object or a fixed point of reference. It is a diverse inner landscape too rich to be grasped in any one concept. There is a plurality of divine echoes within you. The *Tao Te Ching* says wryly: 'The Great Symbol is out of shape.'

To become free is everything

OMETIMES ideas hold us down; they become heavy anchors that hold the bark of identity fixated in shallow, dead water. In the Western tradition the idea of the sinfulness and selfishness of the self has trapped many people all their lives in a false inner civil war. Fearful of valuing themselves in any way, they have shunned their own light and mystery. Their inner world remained permanently off-limits. People were given to believe that they were naturally bad and sinful. They let this toxic idea into their minds and it gradually poisoned their whole way of seeing themselves. Sin was around every corner and probable damnation waited in any case at the end of the road. People were unwittingly drafted into blaspheming against their own nature. You could not let yourself go. Any longing to claim your nature or pursue your wildness would lead to ruin. This corrupted the innocence of people's sensual life and broke the fluency of their souls. Rather than walking the path with the encouraging companionship of your protecting angel beside you and the passionate creativity of the Holy Spirit at your deepest core, you were made to feel like a convict trapped between guilt and fear. It is one of the worst sins committed against people. So many good people were internally colonized with a poisonous ideology that had nothing to do with the kind gentleness and tender sympathy of God.

Yet despite being subjugated, there remains a deep longing in every person for self-discovery. No-one can remain continually unmoved by the surprising things that rise to the surface of one's life. It is a great moment when you break out of the prison of negative self-criticism and develop a sense of the inner adventure of the soul. Suddenly everything seems to become possible. You feel new and young. As you step through the dead threshold, you can hear the old structures of self-hate and self-torment collapsing behind you. Now you know that your life is yours and that good things are going to happen to you. At a Gospel Mass in New Orleans recently, the preacher invited each one of us to turn to our neighbour and say: 'Something good is going to happen to you.' It made me realize that there are such encouraging bouquets of words that we never offer each other. For days afterwards, I could see the chubby face and hear the gravel voice of this little boy beside me saying: 'Somethin' good's gonna happen to you.' His words became a kind of inner mantra that blessed me for days.

You were created to be free; within you there is deep freedom. This freedom will not intrude; it will not hammer at the door of your life and force you to embrace it. The greater presences within us do not act in this way. Their invitation is inevitably subtle and gracious. In order to inherit your freedom, you need to go towards it. You have to claim your own freedom before it becomes yours. This is neither arrogant nor selfish; it is simply moving towards the gift that was prepared for you from ancient times. As some German thinker said: *'Frei sein ist nichts/frei werden ist alles'*, i.e. to be free is nothing, to become free is everything. Albert Camus's story 'The Adulterous Woman' is a fine portrait of a woman who has fled from herself into the prison of a relationship with a man who is vacillating, demanding and lost. One night, during a listless and utterly frustrating business trip with him, she leaves the bedroom and goes out into the desert: 'Then with unbearable gentleness the water of the night began to fill Janine, drowned the cold, rose gradually from the hidden core of her being and overflowed in wave after wave, rising up even to her mouth full of moans. The next moment, the whole sky stretched over her, fallen on her back on the cold earth.' With sensuous and spiritual intimacy nature comes to find and free her by calling her suppressed nature to life.

Rousseau said: 'Man was born free, and everywhere he is in chains.' Each of us has a reservoir of unknown freedom. Yet our fear holds us back. The worst chains are not the chains which others would have you wear. The chains with which you manacle yourself cut deepest and hold you longest. In a certain sense no-one outside you can imprison you. They can only turn you into a prisoner if you assent and put on the chains they offer. There are no psychological police. Only you can step over that threshold into the prison of image, the prison of expectation or the prison of anxiety.

The mental prison

 MENTAL PRISON CAN BE AS BAD AS A physical prison. When you are trapped in a mental prison, the crippling idea or feeling robs you of all joy and freedom. You can see and feel little else. Your mind becomes a small room without light. You turn the wild mystery of your own mind into a shabby, negative little room; the windows are blocked and there is no door. The mental prison is devastatingly lonely. It is a sorrowful place because ultimately it is you who locks yourself up within a demented idea or feeling.

It is a helpless place to be trapped; all outside life lessens. There is a distance between you and everything else. It is difficult for anyone to reach you. You come to believe that the shape of the prison is the shape of reality. It is so difficult to leave the mental prison precisely because you cannot see beyond your pain. In other words, you are completely blind to the fact that it is you who construct it and you who decides to stay locked in there, that this punishment is mainly self-punishment. Inevitably, you tend to blame others and hold them responsible for whatever hurt put you away. It is only when you become aware of your own longing to be free that you realize how you allowed what happened to you to take away your power and freedom. You were so hurt that you were no longer able to distinguish your life from the hurt. It took you over completely. You acted in complicity with the hurt and turned against yourself.

We take upon ourselves the images made for us

t is astounding how we take on the violence that is directed towards us. When someone attacks you, it is practically certain that internally you will attack yourself. It would be great to have enough confidence in your self, and enough freedom and inner poise, that when hostility comes towards you, you could let it pass right over your shoulder. Someone assaults you verbally; points out your weaknesses and failures; testifies to the fact that the very sight of you is enough to make them want to reincarnate on the spot; and expresses the sincerest compassion with those who have to endure your blighted presence on a more frequent basis. Wouldn't it be lovely on such an occasion to be able to look that person in the eye and say from your heart: 'I am sorry that it disturbs you so much but, you know, right now I am just feeling so good. Can I get you a cup of coffee or anything?' What usually happens is that you are hurt and begin to use the ammunition that has been

154

just delivered against yourself. Such confrontation can burrow into you for weeks afterwards.

There is no-one outside who can open the door to release you from inner prison. The key is actually on the inside and it takes a long time to find the door and turn the key to come out onto the pastures where the wildflowers grow and the air is fresh and full. We are children of nature. Like the wind through the rich spring branches, thoughts should stir and lift you, opening you towards new horizons and not confine you to the stale, dead air of shabby inner rooms. Often in the New Testament people begged Jesus to cure them. Sometimes these were people who had lived inside the prison of illness for years. In his gentle yet incisive way, he often turned the question inwards and asked 'Do you want to be healed?' This is a great question to ask yourself when you notice that the changes you long for are not happening. Maybe you do not want to be free. Something in the inner confinement confirms something in you which you are not yet ready to let go. The mind does not have any internal police or prison guards holding you confined. You can be as free as your longing desires.

The prison of guilt

t is awful to feel guilty. Your mind and spirit become haunted. You keep on returning to some action or event in the past. You had acted dishonourably in some way. Perhaps it was some scalpel of a sentence that cut into someone's life or severed a friendship. Or something you did to someone that was wrong and has shadowed their life ever since. Perhaps it was something you did in ignorance or blindness; you only glimpsed the consequences later and by then it was too late. You can also carry a burden of guilt not because of any action but because of your non-action at a crucial juncture. If you had had the vision or courage to say or do something, then some-one else may have been spared great pain. Once you begin to see what your failure to act actually allowed, you feel guilty and ashamed.

There is hardly any life that is not shadowed in some place by guilt. There is always some little corner of even the most immaculate cupboard where there is the stain, if not the splinter, of a hidden skeleton. No-one lives a perfect life; there are places where we have been weak, ignorant and blind and the results have been damaging and destructive. The person who never made a mistake never made anything. We would be ashamed and humiliated if these failures were paraded before the public. Every life has some more or less burdensome secret. When you visit the corner in your heart where the secret lives, the guilt comes alive. When your burden of guilt is truthful to what actually happened and your part and responsibility in it, then the burden is appropriate. This is a very important condition and one that is difficult to judge. Sometimes we feel guilty about things in the past that should hold no guilt for us. Because we feel bad about something, we exaggerate our part in it and retrospectively ascribe more power and freedom to ourselves than we had in the actual situation.

Guilt in itself is useless. It belongs to the past and the past is over and gone. Regardless of how guilty you feel, you cannot return to that time, enter the situation and act as honourably as you now wish you had then. One of the great developments in modern culture is the way we have emancipated ourselves from the gnawing feeling of guilt that tormented past generations. When God and the system were harsh and culture was more uniform, good and innocent people felt scrupulously guilty about nothing. Now we are at the other extreme, where our rapid consumerist culture has lost all ability to feel guilt. Where there is no capacity for warranted and proportionate guilt, some terrible deadening of human sensibility has taken place.

When we treat a person wrongly or badly; when we hurt or damage someone, when we allow awful things to happen around us or in our name and we remain silent, when we buy goods that are products of the slavery and oppression of the poor; when we support institutions and policies that blight the unknown lives of those who have no voice; then, we definitely should feel a haunting guilt that should eat into our complacency and render our belonging uneasy.

When personal guilt in relation to a past event becomes a continuous cloud over your life, then you are locked in a mental prison. You have become your own jailer. While you should not erase your responsibility for the past, when you make the past your jailer, you destroy your future. It is such a great moment of liberation when you learn to forgive yourself, let the burden go and walk out into a new path of promise and possibility. Self-compassion is a wonderful gift to give yourself. You should never reduce the mystery and expanse of your presence to a haunted fixation with something you did or did not do. To learn the art of integrating your faults is to begin a journey of healing on which you will regain your poise and find new creativity. Your soul is more immense than any one moment or event in your past. When you allow guilt to fetter and reduce you like this, it has little to do with guilt. The guilt is

only an uncomfortable but convenient excuse for
your fear of growth.

Che prison of shame

hame is one of the most distressing
and humiliating emotions. When you feel
ashamed, your dignity is torn and compromised. Shame is a powerful emotion; it somehow
penetrates to the core of your soul. There is
inevitably a strong social dimension to shame. You
feel ashamed because you have acted dishonourably in some way. In some cultures the very
danger of incurring shame seemed to keep people
from stepping out of line. When someone did, then
the tribe cohered into one accusing eye glaring at
them in disgust and judgement. Such a person was
inevitably pushed out to the margins of isolation
and horrific emotional reprobation. Shame is a force
intended to put one outside all belonging. More
often than not, such one-sided conformity and its
conventions of judgement are factitious and secretly
corrupt. The one who does the forbidden thing
becomes the focus for all the anger of those who
would love to have done it too but are afraid of the
exclusion and shame.

Conventions that can wield the stick of shame are
immensely powerful. It is tragic to consider how

159

much women have endured under such conventions. Millions of women were burned at the stake on suspicion of being witches. Wouldn't it be lovely to see a religious leader visit one of these sites and go down on his knees to ask forgiveness from the women of the world for what was done to their sisters in the name of his religion?

Other women were denigrated for being pregnant. The act of bringing a child into the world is where woman works at the creative heart of the Divine; this sacred work for millions of women became a devastating occasion of shame for both themselves and their children. Their characters and reputations were blackened and they were driven out of belonging. The Irish poet and painter, Patricial Burke has contributed hugely to the acknowledgement and healing of this wound in Irish culture in her wonderful and devastating play *Eclipsed*.

We rarely think of the esteem and reputation we enjoy until we are in danger of losing it. This esteem allows us an independent and free space among people. There is no negative intrusion. We can get on with our lives. When you are shamed, the space around you is eviscerated. Now your every move draws negative attention. Hostility and disgust are flung at you. It is impossible from outside to even imagine the humiliation that shame brings. All the natural shelter and support around your presence is taken from you. All the imagination with which others have considered the different aspects of your presence stops. Everything about you is telescoped into the single view of this one shameful thing. Everything else is forgotten. A kind of psychological murdering is done. The mystery of your life is reduced to that one thing. You become 'a thing of shame'. Shame dehumanizes a person.

In ancient Ireland, words had incredible power. Invocations and curses could set massive events in motion. It is not surprising that poets at that time had great status. It was said that a bard could write an '*aor*', a satire about a person, that would cause 'boils of shame' to rise on their skin. Shame could not effect its punishment without language. The language of shame is lethal. Its words carry no hesitation or doubt. There is no graciousness or light in the language of shame. It is a language spoken without compassion or respect. The word of shame is put on you in a way reminiscent of how farmers used to brand cattle once. The brand is to mark you out. You are now owned by your 'shameful' deed.

Imagine how shame imprisons those who are on the target list of convention. Imagine the years of silent torment that so many gay people have endured, unable to tell their secret. Then, when they declare they are gay, the hostility which rises to

161

assail them. Think of the victims of racism: the people who are humiliated and tagged for hostility. The simple fact of their physical presence is sufficient to have a barrage of aggression unleashed on them. The intention of racism is to shame its victims into becoming non-persons.

Beyond its social dimension, shame also has a devastating personal complexity. When a person is sexually abused or raped, they often feel great shame at what happened to them. The strategy of such violence is to make the victim feel guilty and even responsible for what has happened. Sometimes this personal shame makes the victim silent and passive; consequently, the crime never becomes public. In some instances the threat of social shame further strengthens the decision to stay silent. Part of the essential work in healing such wounds is to help the person to see their own innocence and goodness and thus unmask the absolutely un-warranted violence of such intrusion and attack. When a person starts to see this, they often begin to awaken the force of anger within them in relation to what has happened to them. The fire of anger can be magnificent in burning off the false garments of shame.

The prison of belief

here is nothing in the universe as intimate as the Divine. When the image of the Divine we inherit is negative, it can do untold damage. When your God is a harsh judge, He forces your life to become a watched and haunted hunt for salvation. Like a sinister Argus, this God has eyes everywhere. He sees everything and forgets nothing. Such images of the Divine cripple us. If salvation and healing do not come lyrically as gifts, they are nothing. Belief should liberate your life. Anything that turns it into torment hardly merits the title salvation. The reduction of the wild eternity of your one life to a harsh divine project is a blasphemy against the call of your soul. People who inhabit the tormented prison of negative deity have awful lives. Tragically, they are partly responsible for keeping themselves locked in there; religion supplied the building material and they took up the task of their own self-incarceration. The spirit of a person is as intimate as their sexuality. When a person is theologically or spiritually abused, the pain can shadow the whole life. Spiritual abuse sticks like tar in the core of the mind. When you stay in the inner jail of harsh deity all the fun, humour and irony goes out of your life. Such a God has a fierce grip; he awakens everything fearful and negative in you and whispers to you that this is who you really are. Your presence becomes atrophied. Your face turns into a brittle, mask-like surface. You have become prisoner and warder in one.

When you turn your natural longing for the Divine into a prison, then everything in you will continue to ache. The prison subverts your longing and makes it toxic. Watched by a negative God, you learn to watch your self with the same harshness. You look out on life and see only sin. Your language becomes over-finished and cold. Others sense behind your eyes the ache of forsakenness that does not even know where to begin searching for itself.

The wildness of Celtic spirituality

he world of Celtic spirituality never had such walls. It was not a world of clear boundaries; people and things were never placed in bleak isolation from each other. Everything was connected and there was a sense of the fluent flow of presences in and out of each other. The physical world was experienced as the shoreline of an invisible world which flowed underneath it and whose music reverberated upwards. In a certain sense, they understood a parallel fluency in the inner world of the mind. The inner world was no prison. It was a moving theatre of thoughts, visions and feelings. The Celtic universe was the homeland of the inspirational and the unexpected. This means that the interim region between one person and another, between the person and nature, was not empty. Post-modern culture is so lonely partly because we see nothing in this interim region. Our way of thinking is addicted to what we can see and control. Perception creates the mental prison. The surrounding culture inevitably informs the perception. Part of the wisdom of the Celtic imagination was the tendency to keep realities free and fluent; they avoided the clinical certainties which cause separation and isolation. Such loneliness would have been alien to the Celts. They saw themselves as guests in a living, breathing universe. They had great respect for the tenuous regions between the worlds and between the times. The in-between world was also the world of in-between times: between sowing and reaping, pregnancy and birth, intention and action, the end of one season and the beginning of another. The presences who watched over this world were known as the fairies.

The lightness and imagination of the fairy world

o the contemporary mind any acknowledgement of the fairy world sounds naïve. Yet at a metaphoric level, it is recognition of the subtle presences which inhabit the interim places in experience, the edges of time and space impenetrable to the human eye. Our clear-cut vision imprisons us. The fairies were especially at home in the air element. There is nothing as free as the wind. In modern Ireland there is still a sense of their presence. Often at evening one sees a fog low in the fields. Usually fog is first on the mountains and then it comes down. In the gathering dusk this other fog collects in white streamers and clouds over the fields. It is almost as if a vaporous white wood suddenly stands suspended over the grass. All outlines are blurred; the interim kingdom becomes visible in a presence that is neither object nor light nor darkness. The ancient name still lingers. It is called *an ceo draíochta*: the fairy fog. On a still, clear day a few years ago a friend and I were visiting an old *cillín* or children's graveyard between two mountains. Suddenly, out of nowhere this powerful gust of a breeze threw itself out all over the *cillín*, bent the bushes low and just as abruptly vanished back into the seamless stillness of the day. It was as if all the sighs of the lost children unravelled for a moment from the quiet ground and came in a massive whoosh into our world. This is called the fairy breeze, *an Sí Gaoth*.

There are many stories in the Irish tradition of musicians who learned some of our most beautiful tunes from the fairies, e.g. *Port na bpúcaí*. This music often has a haunting beauty that seems to be inspired from beyond the limits of humans. A famous old fiddle-player in County Clare always played a special tune and claimed that the tune came in a visitation from the other world. The fairies might use a person's home while the whole family were in bed asleep. Humans were often brought into the fairy world. The fairies were invisible but if they allowed it, you could see them. There is an old story from the West of Ireland about a midwife who was called to tend a fairy woman who was giving birth. When the child was born, the fairies gave her some ointment to rub on the baby. By accident the woman rubbed her own eye with the ointment. When her work was finished, the fairies took her home. Some time afterwards the woman was at the market. Suddenly, she recognized one of the men at the market as one of the people from the fairy dwelling. She spoke to him and he realized that she could see him because of the ointment that had touched her eye. He was very angry to be visible to her. It was

167

said that he put his finger in her eye and blinded her. The invisible world is full of presences. They like to keep to themselves under the protection of invisibility. Through accident a mortal receives the unintended gift of seeing the invisible; it turns out to be an intrusion that has to be punished and the gift revoked.

There are many fantastic anecdotes about fairies. Long ago there was a man who lived near us who often went with the fairies. One night they went over to one of the islands with the intention of substituting a fairy child for a newborn there. They were up in the rafters of the house. Someone sneezed down below and the man uttered a loud blessing. The fairies dropped him and he fell onto the floor below among the people who realized at once that he had been there with the fairies. They chased him and he ran for the shore of the island. Catching an old plough he uttered an invocation: *'Molaim do léim a sheanbhéim céachta. Tabhair abhaile mé,'* i.e. I praise your leap, old beam of plough. Take me home. With that he gave a mighty leap over the ocean and landed home. The fairy world was not subservient to the normal laws of causality which regulate time and space. Their world had a lightness and playfulness. The fairy world was not merely adjacent to the mortal world, it seemed to suffuse it. Such a vital and fluent sense of

168

the world never permitted the notion of the Divine to become a sinister, crippling prison. The Celtic world was not a world of stolid fixation. It was a wild, rhythmic world where the unexpected and the unknown were constantly flowing on human presence and perception and enlarging them. When perception and culture are open to the possibility of surprise and visitation, it is more difficult for individuals to lock themselves away in mental prisons of forsaken thought and feeling. It is interesting to reflect that the Celts were not taken up with the construction of great architecture. They loved the vitality and magic of open spaces. Celtic spirituality is an outdoor spirituality. Living outside must make for a very different rhythm of mind!

Your vision is your home

Thought is one of the most powerful forces in the universe. The way you see things makes them what they are. We never meet life innocently. We always take in life through the grid of thought we use. Our thoughts filter experience all the time. The beauty of philosophy is the way it shows us the nature of the layers of thought which always stand invisibly between us and everything we see. Even your meetings with yourself happen in and through thinking.

The study of philosophy helps you to see how you think. Philosophy has no doctrines; it is an activity of disclosure and illumination. One of the great tasks in life is to find a way of thinking which is honest and original and yet right for your style of individuality. The shape of each soul is different. It takes a lifetime of slow work to find a rhythm of thinking which reflects and articulates the uniqueness of your soul.

More often than not, we have picked up the habits of thinking of those around us. These thought-habits are not yours; they can damage the way you see the world and make you doubt your own instinct and sense of life. When you become aware that your thinking has a life of its own, you will never make a prison of your own perception. Your vision is your home. A closed vision always wants to make a small room out of whatever it sees. Thinking that limits you denies you life. In order to deconstruct the inner prison the first step is learning to see that it is a prison. You can move in the direction of this discovery by reflecting on the places where your life feels limited and tight. To recognize the crippling feeling of being limited is to already have begun moving beyond it. As Heidegger said: 'To recognize a frontier is already to have gone beyond it.' Life continues to remain faithful to us. If we move even the smallest step out of our limitations, life comes to embrace us and lead us out into the pastures of possibility.

The East German philosopher Ernst Bloch has the following epitaph on his gravestone in Tübingen: '*Denken heisst überschreiten*', i.e. to think is to go beyond. Thinking that deserves the name never attempts to make a cage for mystery. Reverential thought breaks down the thought-cages that domesticate mystery. This thinking is disturbing but liberating. This is the kind of thinking at the heart of prayer, namely, the liberation of the Divine from the small prisons of our fear and control. To liberate the Divine is to liberate oneself. Each person is so vulnerable in the way they see things. You are so close to your own way of thinking that you are probably unaware of its power and control over how you experience everything, including yourself. This is the importance of drama: it provides you with the opportunity to know yourself at one remove, so to speak, without threatening you with annihilation. Your thinking can be damaged. You may sense this but put it down to how life is. You remain unaware of your freedom to change how you think. When your thinking is locked in false certainty or negativity, it puts so many interesting and vital areas of life out of your reach. You live impoverished and hungry in the midst of your own abundance.

171

The haunted room in the mind

N Ireland there are many stories of
haunted houses. There may be a room
where one senses a presence or hears
footsteps or a strange voice. Such haunted places
remain uninhabited. People are afraid to go in
there. The place is forsaken and left to deepen ever
further into the shadow of itself. The way you think
about your life can turn your soul into a haunted
room. You are afraid to risk going in there any more.
Your fantasy peoples this room of the heart with sad
presences which ultimately become disturbing and
sinister. The haunted room in the mind installs a
lonesomeness at the heart of your life. It would be
devastating in the autumn of your life to look back
and recognize that you had created a series of
haunted rooms in your heart. Fear and negativity
are immense forces which constantly tussle with us.
They long to turn the mansions of the soul into
haunted rooms. These are the living conditions for
which fear and negativity long and in which they
thrive. We were sent here to live life to the full.
When you manage to be generous in your passion
and vulnerability, life always comes to bless you. Had
you but the courage to acknowledge the haunted
inner room, turn the key and enter, you would
encounter nothing strange or sinister there. You

would meet some vital self of yours that you had banished during a time of pain or difficulty. Sometimes when life squeezes you into lonely crevices you may have to decide between survival or breaking apart. At such times you can be harsh with yourself and settle for being someone other than who you really long to be. At such a time you can do nothing else; you have to survive. But your soul always remains faithful to your longing to become who you really are. The banished self from an earlier time of life remains within you waiting to be released and integrated. The soul has its own logic of loyalty and concealment. Ironically, it is usually in its most awkward rooms that the special blessings and healing are locked away. Your thinking can also freeze and falsify the flow of your life's continuity to make you a prisoner of routine and judgement.

The shelter of continuity

ontinuity is one of the great mysteries of life; it is essential to identity. When you look at the waves on the shore, one after the other, in perfect pleated sequence, they unfold. From the break of dawn the day arises until the height of noon and then gradually falls to gather in the coloured shadow-basket of twilight. The seasons, too, follow the melody of forward unfolding.

173

One of the most beautiful images of continuity and sequence is the river. Always in motion towards the ocean, it continues to look the same. As Heraclitus said: 'You cannot step twice into the same river.' In a matter of seconds both you and the river are different. The river is the ideal of continuity. It preserves the fluency of continual change and yet holds the one form. The river is so interesting because it offers a creative metaphor of the way the mind flows in and through experience. Your life is made up of a sequence of days. Each day brings something new and different. The secret of time's intention and generosity depends on how your days follow each other. Every yesterday prepares you for today. What today brings could not have reached you yesterday or a hundred days ago. Time is more careful in its sequence than we often notice. Time ripens according to its hidden rhythm. In its heart, time is eternal longing.

Regardless of how you look back on your life, you cannot force it out of the order in which it has unfolded. You cannot de-sequence your life. The structure of your life holds together. That is the unnoticed miracle of memory; it is the intimate mirror of the continuity of your experience and presence. While you sleep, your memory continues to gather and store up every moment. If your memory had forsaken you moments before you awoke this morning, you would not recognize your family. And when you looked in the mirror the face of a stranger would have looked back at you. If your memory were wiped, your world would evaporate. Continuity is difficult to grasp because it is hidden and subtle. In a sense, we are powerless ever to break continuity. Even the severest and most shocking change insists on its belonging to the moments that preceded it. Then, even that shocking change in its turn builds the next bridge to the future. We try to understand and control continuity by calling it causality. We claim that every event has a cause. We attempt to understand the parts of the sequence in a clear and linear way. The difficulty here is our tendency to jump to conclusions about how one time or thing grows out of another in our lives. When we make the connections too easy for ourselves, we let the mystery, like sand, slip through the openings.

CERTAINTY FREEZES THE MIND

 love the radical novelty of the Scottish philosopher David Hume, who proclaimed on looking inside his own mind that he could see no sign of a self anywhere. Neither could he see any such thing as a cause. Hume's theory is bold and provocative and, as with the most interesting philosophical theories, it brings great difficulties. It is refreshing that he torpedoed the notion of causality. We do have a deadening desire to reduce the mystery of continuity to a chain of causality. We bind our lives up in solid chains of forced connections which block and fixate us. This silences the voices within us that are always urging us to change and become free. Our sense of uncertainty and our need for security nail our world down. We pretend that we live in a ready-made house of belonging. We walk through its halls, open its doors and shelter inside its walls as if it were a fixed house and not the invention and creation of our own thinking and imagination; a flimsy nest of belonging swinging on a light branch that tempts the unknown storms. Like the birds, each one of us is an artist of the invisible. No more than them, we leave no traces on the invisible air.

Each time we go out, the world is open and free; it offers itself so graciously to our hearts, to create something new and wholesome from it every day. It is such a travesty of possibility and freedom to think we have no choice, that things are the way they are and that the one street, the one destination, the one role, is all that is allotted to us. That we are lucky with so little. Certainty is a subtle destroyer.

We confine our mystery within the prison of routine and repetition. One of the most deadening forces of all is repetition. Your response to the invitation and edge of your life becomes reduced to a series of automatic reflexes. You know how you are so used to getting up in the morning and observing the morning rituals of washing and dressing. You are still somewhat sleepy, your mind is thinking of things you have to do in the day that lies ahead. You go through these first gestures of the morning often without even noticing that you are doing them. This is a disturbing little image because it suggests that you live so much of your one life with the same automatic blindness of adaptation. After a while, unknown to you, a wall has grown between you and the native force of your experiences. You go through things only half-aware that they are actually happening to you. This subtle conditioning becomes so effortless that you are only half present in your life. Sometimes you are lucky and destiny wakes you up abruptly, you stumble and trip into love or some arrow of suffering pierces your armour. These routines of repetition are often most evident in your work. You somehow manage enough concentration to get the motions right, so that hardly anybody suspects that you really live elsewhere or that you have got badly lost in some bland Nowhere. It also often happens in our emotional life with the person with whom we live. Time and again, we find ourselves back at the same point in the circle of repetition with each other. The same difficulty

177

repeats itself in an uncanny echo of the past.

Habit is a strong invisible prison. Habits are styles of feeling, perception or action that have now become second nature to us. A habit is a sure cell of predictability; it can close you off from the unknown, the new and the unexpected. You were sent to the earth to become a receiver of the unknown. From ancient times these gifts were prepared for you; now they come towards you across eternal distances. Their destination is the altar of your heart. When you allow your life to move primarily along the tracks of habit, the creative side of your life diminishes. There is an old story from Russia about a prince who lived with a large retinue in a huge palace. One of the key rules in palace life was that no-one could sleep two consecutive nights in the same room. The prince insisted on this constant changing about to keep alive their sense of being pilgrims here on earth. The true pilgrim is always at a new threshold.

Cħe ᴅᴀɴɢᴇʀ ᴏꜰ ᴛħᴇ ɴᴀᴍᴇ

 ᴀɴɢᴜᴀɢᴇ ɪꜱ ᴏɴᴇ ᴏꜰ ᴛħᴇ ᴍᴏꜱᴛ ꜰᴀꜱᴄɪɴᴀᴛing presences in the world. The discovery and use of language are a unique human achievement. Words become the mirrors of reality. Imagine if tomorrow the veil of language fell away

178

from us. We would not be able to think, understand or communicate. Consciousness would be wiped clean. Words are the unnoticed treasure houses of discovery and meaning. Wittgenstein said: 'The limits of my language mean the limits of my world.' Without language the world would fade away from us. Words keep things present. Language has a secret life, an undercurrent murmuring away, audible in rhymes and rhythms, ambiguities and assonances. Most certifiable uses of language are hostile to this undercurrent. The poetic use of language honours these possibilities, keeps them alive and sometimes reanimates the 'ordinary' language we speak without thinking. Yet often our language is over-finished and cripplingly tight. Language is a great power. When something flows in to the shore of your life, one of your first responses is the attempt to name it. A name should never trap a thing. In the Jewish tradition, for instance, if you knew the name of a thing, you had an inkling of its secret and mystery. The name was a doorway of reverence. When you name a dimension of your experience, one of your qualities or difficulties, or some presence within you, you give it an identity. It then responds to you according to the tone of its name. We need to exercise great care and respect when we come to name something. We always need to find a name that is worthy and spacious.

When we name things in a small way, we cripple them. Often our way of naming things is driven by our addiction to what is obviously visible. Celtic spirituality is awakening so powerfully now because it illuminates the fact that the visible is only one little edge of things. The visible is only the shore-line of the magnificent ocean of the invisible. The invisible is not empty but is textured and tense with presences. These presences cannot be named; they can only be sensed, not seen. Names are powerful. Sometimes in folk-culture people are quite '*pisreógach*' or superstitious about telling their own name. This is illustrated by a story I heard from a priest who was appointed to a rural area. During his first months there, he visited the whole parish. One day, he noticed an old man digging a garden. He said hello and the man came up, rested his arms on the wall and held a most interesting and quite personal conversation with the new priest. As the conversation was about to end, the priest asked him his name. The old man glowered at him and said: 'That is something I never told anyone in my life,' and went back to dig his garden.

Many of the places in our lives where our growth has arrested are places we have carried out negative baptisms. We have put the wrong names on many of our most important experiences. We have often caricatured and shown disrespect to some of our most faithful desires. We have kept some of our most beautiful longings as prisoners in our hearts, falsely imprisoned simply because of mistaken identity. Pablo Neruda has a poem called 'Too Many Names':

 ondays are meshed with Tuesdays
And the week with the whole year.
Time cannot be cut
With your exhausted scissors,
And all the names of the day
Are washed out in the waters of night.

No-one can claim the name of Pedro,
Nobody is Rosa or Maria,
All of us are dust or sand,
All of us are rain under rain.
They have spoken to me of Venezuelas,
Of Chiles and Paraguays;
I have no idea what they are saying.
I know only the skin of the earth
And I know it is without a name . . .

The wildness of the invisible world is nameless. It has no name. A first step towards reawakening respect for your inner life may be to become aware of the private collage of dead names you have for your inner life. Often, the experiences of wilderness

181

can return us to the nameless wildness within. Some time, go away to a wild place on your own. Leave your name and the grid of intentions and projects and images which mark you out as citizen Z. Leave it all, and let yourself just slip back into the rhythms of your intimate wildness. You will be surprised at the lost terrains, wells and mountains that you will rediscover, territories which have been buried under well meaning but dead names. To go beyond confinement is to rediscover yourself.

The limit as invitation to the beyond

he prisons we choose to live in are closely connected to our experience of limit and frontier. We often remain passively within our inner prisons because we believe the limitations are fixed and given. It is strange how being caught makes you lose the sense of outside and beyond. You become trapped one side of a wall; after a while you learn to see only what cages you; you begin to forget other views and possibilities. It is the lonely struggle of the prisoner to continue to remember that he belongs to life and not to limitation. Limitation is, of course, real and factual, but it is meant to be temporary. A limit is meant to call you beyond itself towards the next new field of experience. We usually view limitation

182

not as a calling to growth, but as confinement and impossibility. Something begins to change when we can see exactly where the walls of limitation stand in our lives. There is a poem by Cavafy called 'Walls' that describes how the walls that lock us in are secretly built. You hear nothing and you notice nothing.

hen they were building the walls,
How could I not have noticed?
But I never heard the builders,
Not a sound,
Imperceptibly they closed me off
From the outside world.

Cavafy articulates something that happens to all of us. Your complicity with other people's images and expectations of you allows them to box you in completely. It takes a long time to recognize how some key people on your life's journey exercise so much control over your mind, behaviour and actions. Through the image they project onto you, or through the expectations they have of you, they claim you. Most of this is subtle and works in the domain of the implicit and unstated subtext; it is, of course, all the more powerful for not being direct and obvious. When you become conscious of these powerful builders and their work of housing you in, something within you refuses to comply, you begin to send back the building materials. There is no planning permission here, thanks for the kindness! Such projection and expectation is based on their fear and the need to control. Expectation is resentment waiting to happen. In contrast, friendship liberates you.

The delicate art of freeing yourself

eal friendship is a powerful presence in helping you to see the prisons within which you live. From inside your own life it is so difficult to gain enough distance to look back on yourself and see the outer shape of your life. This discernment is often easier for your friend than it would be for you. A real friend will never come with a battering ram to demolish the prison in which they see you. They know that it could be too soon. You are not yet ready to leave. They also know that until you see for yourself how and where you are caught, you cannot become free. If they destroy this prison cell, you will inevitably build a new one from the old material. True friendship attunes itself with care to the rhythm of your soul. In conversation and affection, your friend will only attempt something very modest, namely, to remove one pebble from the wall. When that pencil of light shines in on your darkness, it arouses your longing to become free. It reminds you of the freshness and fragrance of another life that you had learned to forget in your cell. This dot of light empowers you and then, brick by brick, you will remove the walls you had placed between the light and yourself. True friendship trusts the soul to find the light, to loosen one pebble in the wall and open the way to freedom. Massive inner structures begin to loosen and break when the first pencil-light of recognition hits us.

Often others may judge you to be in a prison whereas in actual fact you were never more free and creative. True knowing goes beyond projection, impression and expectation. There is a whole moral question here regarding the nature and timing of disclosure and intervention. If you show someone bluntly that they are caught in a prison, you make them aware of their confinement. If they are incapable of liberating themselves, then you have left them with a heavier burden. There is a telling story of a British anthropologist who came to a village in India where the natives wove the most beautiful shawls. The art of weaving was highly prized there. The workers wove the shawls amidst conversation with each other about local events and old stories. Weaving was their secret skill and its methods were instinctive. The anthropologist observed them for weeks. Then one morning he came there and told them that he had worked out exactly how they did it. He made explicit the implicit skill they exercised. He showed them the secret of their artistry. In that disclosure, he robbed their artistry of all its magic. With that he changed them from surprised artists of emergent beauty into helpless, impoverished workers. This story could stand as a metaphor for the massive transformation in the modern world. The natural and ancient creativity of soul is being replaced by the miserable little arithmetic of know-how.

Creativity is rich with unexpected possibility. Know-how is mere fragmented mechanics which lacks tradition, context and surprise. Analysis is always subsequent to and parasitic on creativity. Our culture is becoming crowded with analysts and much of what passes for creativity is merely clever know-how. When creativity dries up, the analysts turn on themselves and begin to empty out the inner world; this has contributed to the terrible loss of soul in our culture. It is wise to recall that analysis comes from the Greek word '*analuein*' which means to break something complex into its simple elements. When the embrace and depth of creativity are absent, analysis becomes destruction. It can break things apart but there is nothing now to put them back together again. Nature always maintains this balance between breakage and new life.

The true shelter of the porous wall

MONG the most delightful features in the West of Ireland landscape are the stone walls. These walls frame off the fields from each other. They bestow personality and shape on the fields. These walls are more like frontiers than hermetic boundaries. When you see a wall on the mountain, you see the different styles of openings between the stones. Each wall is a series of different windows of light. Rabbits, hares and foxes have favourite windows in these walls through which they always cross. Each wall is a frontier and simultaneously a labyrinth of invisibility. Often as children, if we were herding cattle on the mountain, we would shelter during showers by these walls. When you looked out from one of these windows between the stones, you would see the whole landscape beneath you in a new way; everything was framed differently. These walls are also often shelters for all kinds of growth, grasses, plants, briars. It was called *foíseach* in Irish. It became home to a whole subculture of insects, bees, birds and animals. Because of the shelter and kindness of the walls you would often find the sweetest grasses there. Sheep and cattle were never slow to find out the sweetest grass. Wouldn't it be interesting if, instead of hermetically sealed barriers, the areas of beginning and ending in our hearts and lives could be such rich and latticed frontiers? They would be windows to look out on alternative possibilities; in other words, the freshness of other styles of being and thinking could still be somehow present even if they were not directly adjacent or even engaged. The natural shelter which grows on both sides of such frontiers would be left alone, to grow according to its own instinct. The most trustable shelter around the human mind and heart is the one that grows naturally there.

Every life has its own natural shelter. So often our severity with ourselves cuts that to shreds. Then we wonder why we feel so naked and unsheltered when the storm comes. The wisdom of folk-culture always recognizes that when the storm of suffering rages one should not go out there into single combat with it. Rather one should lie in and shelter close to the wall until the storm has abated. There is a humility in the idea of lying low and sheltering. It recognizes that the storm comes from the penumbral unknown; it has a mind and direction of its own and the vulnerable individual can but shelter until the time of tranquillity returns. The modern tendency to safari into subjectivity to find the cause of everything was alien to the folk mind.

To roll the stone off the heart

he Christian story is about the subversive transformation of all barriers which confine or imprison. Jesus never advocated a life which confined itself within safe, complacent walls. He always called people into the beyond: 'I have come that you may have life and have it more abundantly.' The Resurrection is frightening because it is a call to live a life without the walls of crippling definition or false protection. The huge stone over his tomb was rolled away. The cave of dying was ventilated and freed. It is a powerful image of smashing open the inner prison. The confined, the exiled, the neglected, are visited by the healing and luminosity of a great liberation.

On a farm the season of greatest change is spring-time. Everything is in the flourish of growth. You often notice where a large flat rock has fallen onto the grass. All around the rock is growth. Beneath the rock, the grass has turned yellow and sour. In every life there are some places where we have allowed great slabs of burden to remain fallen on our heart. These slabs have turned much of our inner world sour and killed many of the possibilities which once called us: the possibilities of play, of having holidays, of seeing something new and un-expected in our lives, of going to new places within

189

and without, of living life to the full. When these
slabs are pulled off our hearts, we can move freely
again and breathe and feel alive. Wouldn't it bring
such calmness and freedom to your life if your
thoughts about yourself, your feelings and your
prayer could become a window which would look
inward on the presence of the Divine?

If you cannot forgive, you are still in jail

N an article in the *New York Times*
shortly before he died Joseph Brodsky
wrote about prison literature. He said: in
prison you have limited space and unlimited time.
This is the exact context in which your mind could
unravel. You can do terrible things to your mind. It
is lonely that you cannot be protected from your
self. It would bring relief to give your tormenting
self a holiday away from your life so that you could
find peace. In such times you are a prisoner of your
worst self. Prisoners have to be very careful about
minding their inner world. One should pray for
those in prison that, though they have lost the outside world, the mystery of the inner world might
open for them. When you have unlimited time with
yourself, the danger is that you will tear yourself
apart. As Nietzsche said: 'In a time of peace the

warlike person attacks himself.' This happens also, of course, to communities: they go to war with themselves in the absence of enemies. It is, however, a permanent companionship of some lives. There are people this morning whose lives were never better. There is peace around them. Objectively their conditions are very good. Yet they are totally tormented. They have scraped away the last vestiges of shelter from their souls. There is nothing significantly wrong here. It is just that these demented people have designated their minds to become their tormentors. Their hostility is now focused on everything about themselves. They have become prisoner and torturer in one.

Forgiveness is one of the really difficult things in life. The logic of receiving hurt seems to run in the direction of never forgetting either the hurt or the hurter. When you forgive, some deeper, divine generosity takes you over. When you can forgive, then you are free. When you cannot forgive, you are a prisoner of the hurt done to you. If you are really disappointed in someone and you become embittered, you become incarcerated inside that feeling. Only the grace of forgiveness can break the straight logic of hurt and embitterment. It gives you a way out because it places the conflict on a completely different level. In a strange way, it keeps the whole conflict human. You begin to see and understand the conditions, circumstances or weakness which made the other person act as they did. I remember once reading an interview with a leading Czech dissident during the communist dictatorship. The authorities often arrested and jailed him. He was asked in the interview how he kept his poise. He said he never allowed himself to forget during interrogation that his interrogators were human like himself. He said that were he to caricature them as monsters he would have lost his freedom and shelter in the situation. To keep them human helped him stay human too.

A friend from East Germany spent a lot of time in jail there. The communist regime saw him as a subversive who kept raising awkward questions about the system. He says that one of the first things he had to learn in jail was not to resent the prison guards. If he had, he could not have endured the jail. He was friendly with them in so far as that was possible and never allowed his mind to destructively focus on them. Walking this emotional tightrope, he managed to keep his balance and freedom during his years of imprisonment. Years afterwards, when he was out of jail, he happened to meet one of his former fellow prisoners. They talked of their years in jail. This man began to tell him of the hatred he still harboured for the prison guards and, if he ever met any of them, what he would do to them. My friend said to him: 'The sad thing about what you are saying is that it shows that you are still in prison.' If you cannot forgive you are still in jail. When you forgive those who have wronged you, you let yourself out of prison. You take from your own heart the hook that has dragged you along behind them across fields of years.

Why are we so reluctant to leave our inner prisons? There is the security of the confinement and limitation that we know. We are often willing to endure the searing sense of forsakenness and distance which it brings rather than risking the step out into the field of the unknown. It used to be common that long-time prisoners when released often gravitated back towards the jail; the daylight hurt their eyes and it was so long since they had had to live in the outside world. This reluctance is captured powerfully in Pär Lagerkvist's novel *Barabbas* which imagines Barabbas being released from jail; his future life is poignantly haunted by the shadow of the young man who was crucified in place of him. The Greek poet Cavafy has another poem called 'Windows'. It describes living inside hungry days in confinement: '. . . I wander round and round/trying to find the windows . . .' Without the grace and encouragement of the eternal, we would be forever confined.

Our secret companions and liberators

F the human person were alone, then it would be exceptionally difficult to liberate oneself from such inner prisons. However, in the Celtic tradition there was a strong sense that each of us has an invisible companion who walks the road of life with us. Our secret companions in the invisible world are the angels. One of the poverties of modern life is the loss of belief in such presences. The Christian tradition says that when you were sent here to the earth, a special angel was chosen to accompany your every step, breath, thought and feeling. This is your guardian angel, who is right beside you, as near as your skin. The Irish poet Denis Devlin says: 'It is inside our life the angel happens.' The imagination of the tradition understands that your angel has special responsibility for your life, to watch over you and keep a circle of light around you, lest any negativity damage you in any way. Your angel is as ancient as eternity itself and has a memory that is older than the earth. Your angel was there when the eternal artist began to dream you. Your angel is wedded to the dream and possibility of your life, and wishes to keep your life from becoming fixated in any inner prison.

Your angel is aware of the secret life that sleeps

194

in your soul. Without you even knowing it, your angel is always at work for you. It is possible to sense this if you consider for a moment the key thresholds in your life. You may feel that you should contact an old friend or someone you haven't seen for a while. You set out to do this and you discover that the friend really needs you. The visit could never have been more opportune. There are also the times when someone comes into your mind and the next thing they are at your door or on the phone. This is the secret world of association and inspiration which can never be explained. Artists could never create without the inspiration which the angel brings. It is the gift of the angel to watch over that threshold where your invisible world comes to visible form. Any art, belief or spirituality that lacks inspiration is ultimately dry and mechanical. Something inspired has the surprise, vitality and warmth of the eternal in it. The Irish word for angel is '*aingeal*'. This was also the word for a burnt-out cinder taken from the fire. It was often given to a child going out in the night for protection; it was said to represent an angel. The word '*aingeal*' shows how our tradition fused a spirituality of the elements with that of the angels.

I imagine the angels are spirits of light and playfulness. They are often depicted as playing musical instruments. They have none of the seriousness or narrowness that often accompanies dead religion. Angels are specially present around young children. In the West of Ireland people always recognized that the angels were near children. Fresh from the eternal world, babies are often said to be able to see their own angels. To know that you have a strong and individual spiritual companion is great encouragement not to linger for false shelter in unnecessary prisons. In your angel, you have as much shelter as you need. You are not on your own. If you could see your path with the eyes of your soul, you would see that it is a luminous path and that there are two of you walking together, you are not alone. When loneliness or helplessness overcomes you, it is time to call on your angel for help and courage. This is the tender region of the heart where your angel is especially competent and helpful. There are lovely prayers which the Celts said to their angels:

SOUL-SHRINE

 hou angel of God who hast charge of me
From the fragrant Father of
mercifulness,
The gentle encompassing of the Sacred Heart
To make round my soul-shrine this night,
Oh, round my soul-shrine this night.

Ward from me every distress and danger,
Encompass my course over the ocean of truth,
I pray thee, place thy pure light before me,
O bright beauteous angel on this very night,
Bright beauteous angel on this very night.

Be Thyself the guiding star above me,
Illume Thou to me every reef and shoal,
Pilot my barque on the crest of the wave,
To the restful haven of the waveless sea,
Oh, the restful haven of the waveless sea.

Carmina Gadelica

(Translated by Alexander Carmichael)

The angel of attraction and inspiration

he angel keeps a circle of light around
your life and your angel is particularly
active in the region of friendship and
relationship. One of the mysteries of friendship is
the attraction between two people. Where does it
come from? What animates this attraction? How do
two people meet? How do they manage to be in
the same place at that particular moment so that the
whole adventure of longing and belonging can come
awake between them? Had they missed that

197

moment, would they have remained strangers? Or would some other moment have gathered them towards this beginning? There is a whole arena of secret preparation and gathering here that we cannot penetrate with our analytical or conscious minds; perhaps this is the domain of angelic creativity. Perhaps the attraction between two people is not accidental; could it be that their ancient angels know how much they have to bring each other and without this their lives cannot become true? The angels are artists in the subtle chemistry of spirit. If you are in difficulty in your friendship, it is wise to go to your mutual angels for the gifts and blessings that you both need. Because your friendship is now paralysed you cannot give anything to each other. When the metallic distance of pain cripples the sacred space between you and the one you love, it is wise to ask the spirits of light and inspiration to make a path for you towards each other.

The angels awaken the sacred melodies of inspiration and brightness and beauty in the soul. A friendship with one's angel is a choice for each of us. If we do not open this up, the angel continues to work for us anyway. To make this explicit is to come into a new depth and sense of presence. It releases you from the grey walls of the inner prisons where life gets lost and stale. In a certain sense, your angel is the voice and presence of ancient divine longing within you. This urges you forth from all false belonging until you come into the divine rhythm where longing and belonging are one.

The angel as artist of your transfiguration

N our post-modern, consumerist culture anything is marketable. With the yawning abyss of spiritual hunger opening, any little relic of the sacred is for sale. There is a huge market for things of the spirit that can be easily digested. The angels are now in fashion. They are talked about in the idiom of magic and apparition. It is important to recall that the sacred has both a silence and a secrecy about it. Divine intimacy has a crucial reserve and shyness. Your friendship with your angel is ancient. It is intimate in a way that concerns the very essence of your identity and destiny. A person should never reduce the mystery of their invisible world to the clichéd descriptions of external banter. The very nature of angelic presence is totally alien to this garish, neon attention. Perhaps such empty and undignified talk drives away our invisible companions. It disrespects their reverential and eternal shyness. In the Celtic world there was such a lyrical and natural sense of these divine presences without any of the garishness or voyeurism of the disappointed contemporary mind.

When you begin to awaken to your incredible freedom, the walls of your inner prisons gradually become the thresholds of your new life, your new place of growth. The old walls can become the thresholds of new belonging which is hospitable to the depths and directions of longing within you. Your angel can liberate your soul from the false, tight spaces where fear, limitation, negativity, bitterness and disappointment hold you. The angel is the inner artist of transfiguration, adept at opening and structuring new configurations of spirit where longing and belonging live in the most creative tension with each other. Your angel can see your invisible world and knows where you have been imprisoned, where the lost and forsaken parts of your life are locked away. Your angel is the custodian of your deep and ancient memory. In this way, nourishment, courage and strength are brought from the harvest of your memory to meet the hungry places in your present time. Your angel works in and through your imagination. The divine imagination offers you all the gifts that you need and particularly those blessings for the broken areas of contradiction, suffering and pain. You could ask your angel to go to the places of nourishment to assuage your present hunger and thirst.

There is a lovely poem by Kathleen Raine which links the images of angels, birth and renewal:

 ear angel of my birth,
All my life's loss,
Gold of fallen flowers,
Shells after ebbing wave
Gathered on lonely shores
With secret toil of love,
Deathless in memory save
The treasures of my grave.

Your angel is the spirit of renewal and transfiguration. Celtic mythology had a wonderful sense of novelty. There was no such thing as a prison in the Celtic mind. You could see that so powerfully in the way that things continued to change shape and take on other different forms. There was no fixed boundary between the visible and the invisible. Without warning or preparation, things could appear suddenly out of the invisible air. This happens often in the Irish epic, *The Táin*: a presence coagulates itself and comes out and is standing there giving advice or warning or prophecy. The Celts inhabited a rich imaginative landscape. At the heart of Celtic spirituality is the fire, force and tenderness of the Celtic imagination. All spirituality derives from the quality and power

201

of the imagination. The beauty of Celtic spirituality is the imagination behind it which had no boundaries. The essence of a thing or person was never confined in any prison of definition or image. Celtic spirituality is an invitation to a wonderful freedom. The recovery and awakening of the invisible world is as wild and free as the immeasurable riches of the earth. W. H. Auden in his poem 'In Memory of W. B. Yeats' has the following beautiful verse:

n the deserts of the heart
Let the healing fountains
start,
In the prison of his days
Teach the free man how to praise.

In prayer your angel can help you to praise and sing the song of freedom from your heart. Your angelic presence can convert a dead world into a new world of mystery, potential and promise. The British poet Philip Larkin has a poem called 'First Sight' about lambs born in the snow. On a farm it is exciting to see new lambs finding the world during their first few hours here. Larkin's poem describes the snow-covered landscapes into which these new lambs arrive. They see and know nothing except snow. They have landed in a white world; before them every hill and bush is white. Larkin then suggests the absolute novelty that is still concealed. Waiting for them is:

 arth's immeasurable surprise,
  They could not grasp it if they
    knew,
What so soon will wake and grow
Utterly unlike the snow.

This poem marks and articulates an unnoticed and surprising threshold of recognition. Similarly, outside the walls of the inner prison in which you are now locked, there is the gift of the earth's immeasurable surprise awaiting to bless and enlarge your spirit. You were born for life, you were born for eternal life. No fear or false conviction should confine you in any crippled emotional or thought space that is unworthy of the springtime that sleeps so lightly in the clay of your heart. Winter always precedes spring and is often a time of suffering. In the prisons we build for ourselves, our belonging becomes crippled and our longing haunted. When we suffer, our sense of belonging is broken.

A blessing

ay you listen to your longing to be
free.
May the frames of your belonging be
large enough for the dreams of your soul.

May you arise each day with a voice of blessing
whispering in your heart that something good
is going to happen to you.

May you find a harmony between your soul and
your life.

May the mansion of your soul never become a
haunted place.

May you know the eternal longing that is at the
heart of time.

May there be kindness in your gaze when you
look within.

May you never place walls between the light
and yourself.

May your angel free you from the prisons of
guilt, fear, disappointment and despair.

May you allow the wild beauty of the invisible
world to gather you, mind you and embrace
you in belonging.

chapter 4

Suffering as the Dark Valley
of Broken Belonging

Our secret kinship with
the darkness

Regardless of how lucky, blessed or
privileged one might be, there is no life
that is not called at some time to walk
through the bleak valley of suffering. This
is a path without hope, without shelter and without light. When suffering comes into your life, it
brings great loneliness and isolation. Your life
becomes haunted: your belonging breaks. Suffering
and pain can assail us with such ferocity because
darkness is so near us; within this darkness our
longing is numbed and calls out for release and
healing.

Though you live and work in the light, you were
conceived and shaped in darkness. Darkness is one

of our closest companions. It can never really surprise us; something within us knows the darkness more deeply than it knows the light. The dark is older than the light. In the beginning was the darkness. The first light was born out of the dark. All through evolution the light grew and refined itself, until, finally, a new lamp was lit with the human mind. Before electricity came to rural areas, the candle and the lamp brightened the home at night. There was one special lamp with a mirror fitted behind it to magnify the light. If you looked into the light at an angle, you could catch a heart-shaped light reflected in the mirror. It was as if the light wished to see itself. Of all previous brightness in creation, this was the new secret of the light of the mind: it was a light that could see itself. The mind brought a new quality of light which could acknowledge and unveil mystery and create mysteries of its own.

Its eternity of patience rewarded, infinity discovered at last its true mirror in the human soul. For the first time there was someone who could see the depths and reflect the glimpses. In a certain sense, all of human action, thought and creativity makes mirrors for life to behold itself. Yet the closer our acquaintance with the mystery, the more the mystery deepens. Brightness only reinforces the opaque soul of the darkness. We forget so easily

that all our feelings, thoughts and brightness of mind
are born in darkness. Thoughts are sparks of
illumination within the dark silence and stillness of
our bodies. We have an inner kinship with darkness
which nothing can dissolve. This protects us from
allowing too much outside light into the secret centre
of our minds. The immensity and slow beauty of the
inner life need the shelter of the dark in order to grow
and find their appropriate forms.

Light has many faces – the dark has one

here is a touching innocence in the
mystery of the human self. Even after
thousands of years of experience and
reflection, we still remain a mystery to ourselves. In
the so-called ordinary person there is something
deeply unpredictable and unfathomable. We have
never been able to definitively decipher the secret
of our nature. Of course every secret delights in the
dark and fears the light. Regardless of how you
might force the neon light of analysis on your self, it
can never penetrate. It remains on the surface and
creates tantalizing but ultimately empty images.
Even when you approach your self tenderly, with the
candle of receptive and reverential seeing, all you
achieve is a glimpse. There is something in the

207

sacred darkness of the mind that does not trust the facility and quickness of light. Darkness resists the name. Darkness knows the regions which the name can never reach or hold or dream. The dark must smile at the proud pretence of words to hold networks of identity and meaning. But the dark knows only too well the fragile surface on which words stand. Darkness keeps its secrets. Light is diverse and plural: sunlight, moonlight, dusk, dawn and twilight. The dark has only one name. There is something deep in us which implicitly recognizes the primacy and wonder of the dark. Perhaps this is why we instinctively insist on avoiding and ignoring its mysteries.

The human eye loves the light. Feasts of colour and varieties of shape continually draw towards the shore of its vision. Movement excites and attracts the eye. So much of our understanding of ourselves and the world finds expression in metaphors of vision: awareness, seeing, clarity, illumination and light. To become aware is to see the light. It is interesting that, outside of poetry, there is little corresponding geography of differentiation or appreciation of darkness. Darkness is the end of light. We are confronted by the unknown. Though we peer deeply into its anonymity, we can see little. We speak of darkness as the domain of mystery. Darkness resists the eye. It is where all our vision and seeing becomes qualified and revised. Marina Tsvetayeva has an amazing long poem called 'Insomnia' in which she recognizes the ancient presence of the night:

lack as – the centre of an eye,
the centre, a blackness
That sucks at light. I love your
vigilance.

Night, first mother of songs, give me
the voice to sing of you
In those fingers lies the bridle of the
four winds.

Crying out, offering words of homage
to you. I am
Only a shell where the ocean is still
sounding.

But I have looked too long into human
eyes.
Reduce me now to ashes – Night, like a
black sun.

(Translated by Elaine Feinstein)

The bright Night of the earth

Yet the eye can become accustomed to
the dark. Country people know this well.
When a city person moves to a rural
region, she is often overwhelmed at the darkness of
the night. Houses shine out like beacons but all
roads and fields are buried in pitch darkness. She
discovers how bright and magical the night sky
shines through. With no light pollution the stars and
moon perforate the night with such lucid brighten-
ings. When you leave a lighted room and go out into
the night, you are almost totally lost and blind at first.
Then as your eyes grow more accustomed to the
night, the outlines of things begin to loom more
clearly; shadowed presences become visible. There
is an inner depth and texture to darkness that
we never notice until we have to negotiate the
absence of light.

It is no wonder then that Nature supplies the
most trustable metaphors for the spiritual life of the
mind. The fecundity of such metaphors is their
capacity to disclose the slow creativity of the dark.
The darkness is the cradle of growth. Everything
that grows has to succumb to darkness first. All
death is a return to darkness. When you sow seeds,
you commit them to the dark. It must be a shock for
seeds to find themselves engulfed in the black

smother of clay. They are helpless and cannot resist the intricate dissolution which the earth will practise on them. The seed has no defence; it must give way, abandoning itself to the new weave of life that will thread forth from its own dissolving. A new plant will gradually rise observing the ancient symmetry of growth: root further into darkness and rise towards the sun. When the new plant breaks the surface of the ground, it is a gift of the hidden wisdom of the clay. She knows the mystery of growth. This wisdom finds such solid expression in trees.

The tree as artist of belonging

There is something so sure and dignified in a tree's presence. The Celts had a refined sense of the worthy wonder of trees. For them many trees were sacred. Near their holy wells there was often either an ash or oak tree. The Yugoslavian poet Ivan Lalich captures the secrets of wisdom and guidance that direct the tree's growth. In his poem 'What Any Tree Can Tell You', he follows the patience of the tree as it navigates the dark. The tree knows how to avoid the stone and knows where to seek the water:

> *. . . should it not act so,*
> *to foster its own loss, its branches*
> *   will be stunted,*
> *its upward effort hunched . . .*

(Translated by Francis Jones)

The tree rises from the dark. It circles around the 'heart of darkness' from where it reaches towards the light. A tree is a perfect presence. It is somehow able to engage and integrate its own dissolution. The tree is wise in knowing how to foster its own loss. It does not become haunted by the loss nor addicted to it. The tree shelters and minds the loss. Out of this comes the quiet dignity and poise of a tree's presence. Trees stand beautifully on the clay. They stand with dignity. A life that wishes to honour its own possibility has to learn too how to integrate the suffering of dark and bleak times into a dignity of presence. Letting go of old forms of life, a tree practises hospitality towards new forms of life. It balances the perennial energies of winter and spring within its own living bark. The tree is wise in the art of belonging. The tree teaches us how to journey. Too frequently our inner journeys have no depth. We move forward feverishly into new situations and experiences which neither nourish nor challenge us because we have left our deeper

212

selves behind us. It is no wonder that the addiction to superficial novelty leaves us invariably empty and weary. Much of our experience is literally superficial; it slips deftly from surface to surface. It lacks rootage. The tree can reach towards the light, endure wind, rain and storm, precisely because it is rooted. Each of its branches is ultimately anchored in a trustable depth of clay. The wisdom of the tree balances the path inwards with the pathway outwards.

When we put down our roots into the ground, we choose from life's bounty, we need to exercise a tender caution about where the roots should go. One of the vital criteria of personal integrity is whether you belong to your own life or not. When you belong in yourself, you have poise and freedom. Even when the storm of suffering or confusion rages, it will not unhouse you. Even in the maelstrom of turbulence some place within you will still anchor you faithfully. These inner roots will enable you later to understand and integrate the suffering that has visited. True belonging can integrate the phases of exile.

Che suffering of self-exile

 any people sense a yawning emptiness at the centre of their lives. This secretly terrifies them. They become afraid that if they engage the emptiness, they will lose all control over their life and identity. This fear drives them towards permanent flight from any possibility of real self-encounter. They keep conversations always on safe ground. Often they are the humorous figures who constantly joke and will not allow any question through their subtle protection shields. They labour valiantly to be accepted by others, but no-one, not even themselves, ever gets near them. A phalanx of language and movement keeps them hidden. It is as if their every word and gesture strain desperately into the safe middle distance. Yet they long all the while to enter the door of their own hearts but fear has hidden the key. This is a neglected and unattended region of suffering, the secret suffering of the permanently self-exiled. They are always circling within inches of home, yet they seem never to be able to get there. They are somehow forlorn and their presence is dislocated. The suffering here is the exile from true inner belonging. It is the voice of forlorn longing. It is as if a secret limbo has opened in that region between a person's intimate heart and all their actions and connections in the outer world. In the intense whirr of dislocation and fragmentation which assails modern consciousness, this limbo has become ever more extensive. There is a consuming loneliness which separates more and more individuals from each other and from their own inner life.

Post-modern culture is deeply lonely. This loneliness derives in large part from the intense drive to avoid suffering and pain and the repudiation of commitment. People relentlessly attempt to calm their inner turbulence by all manner of therapy and spirituality. They seek refuge in each new programme or method as if it offered final resolution. Yet so many of these programmes have no earth beneath the seductive surface. They can offer no growth, nor enable a person to identify the pain at the root of identity. Such external tamperings never manage to reach or embrace the inner loss which is a natural part of being a human person. Every heart has to manage the emptiness of its own dark. Jung suggested that neurosis was unmet suffering. This dialogue with your inner loss is slow and painful. Yet to avoid or sidestep this necessary pain only brings a slow, seeping sense of loneliness which continues to shadow and haunt your life. The Romanian philosopher E. M. Cioran said: 'Suffering is the cause of consciousness. (Dostoevsky) Men belong to two categories: those who have understood this, and the others.'

Why are you so vulnerable?

hy is the individual so easily a target of suffering and pain? Why are we so exposed and vulnerable? First, we are vulnerable because each of us is housed in a body. This little clay tent is a sacramental place. The body is in constant conversation with creation; it allows us through our senses to smell the roses, see the waves and stars and read forever the hieroglyphics of the human countenance. The body is also very unsheltered. You are surrounded by infinite space without physical shelter. This is why, from the very beginning, humans have sought secure belonging in caves and then in houses. The desire for strong physical shelters mirrors and reveals how space is open and anything can approach the temple of your life from any side. Home offers shelter from the threat of contingency. Yet home too is vulnerable. No walls are strong enough to keep the destructive visitations abroad. The human body is a fragile home.

Second, you are vulnerable because you are an individual. To be an individual is to be different. Each individual is separate. There is a dark logic to experience which often seems to target individuality. Suffering is suffering because it is an anonymous and destructive force. It has a darkness which vision cannot penetrate. Suffering happens when this bleak and opaque anonymity invades your individuality. A dark force of pain surrounds the unique signature of your presence. Suffering would be more manageable if its pain were restricted merely to the surface of one's life or at least to some one corner of one's individuality. Some religious theories suggest that suffering belongs only to the area of the non-self. If this were true, it would lessen the fever of pain that suffering brings. Alas, however, one's individuality is not constructed in such convenient compartments. Your heart, mind and body are a unity, each place within you is intimately one with every other. Pain in one part of the body affects every other. Your nervous system is the miracle that makes all the different parts one living and feeling presence. There is something about pain and suffering that is pervasive. It suffuses your full presence.

Third, we are vulnerable because we live in time. We cannot control time. The tides of time can throw absolutely anything up on the shore of your life. It is amazing how successfully we repress the recognition of our total vulnerability. We have learned to forget that any moment can bring an abrupt and irreversible change of destiny. As you are reading this, there are people who woke up happy this morning and are now receiving news that will utterly change their lives. Suddenly, death is a gathering presence. Others are coming under the blade of disappointment. For ever more, they will remember this day as the day that divided their life in two. The time before will be looked back on as a time of unrealized contentment, the time after as the time of carrying a new loss that turned meadows of possibility into a desert.

Fourth, we are vulnerable because of the destiny that is given to each of us. Each person who walks through this world is called at some time to carry some of the weight of pain which assails the world. To help carry some of this pain a little further for others is a precious calling. It is, however, a lonely, sad and isolating time in one's life. Yet often when the suffering has lightened, you may glimpse some of the good that it brought. We are all deeply connected with each other. In some strange way we all belong with each other in the unfolding and articulation of the one human story. Each of us is secretly active in weaving the tapestry of spirit. When you see a Persian tapestry, it looks beautiful. Yet, underneath, the tapestry is a mesh of various rough threads. Perhaps this is part of our difficulty in understanding the sore weave of pain that often sears our life. In terms of understanding, we remain at the back and see only the raw weave. Perhaps there is something beautiful being woven but we are unable in this life to see much of the secret aesthetic of pain.

The pain of exposure

ulnerability is an infinitely precious thing. There is nothing as lonely as that which has become hardened. When your heart hardens, your life has become numb. Yeats says: 'Too long a sacrifice can make a stone of the heart.' Though vulnerability leaves one open to pain, one should somehow still be ultimately glad of vulnerability. Part of our origin lies in the Darwinian kingdom of species competition and adaptation. Some instinct within us knows that we must be careful about exposure. We cannot let the heart be too easily seen or we will get hurt. Everyone gets hurt. The extreme response to hurt is to close the heart. Yet to make yourself invulnerable is to lose something very precious. You put yourself outside the arena of risk where possibility and growth are alive. Vulnerability risks hurt, disappointment and failure. Yet it remains a vital opening to change and to truth. We should not see our vulnerability as something that we need to hide or get over. The slow and difficult work of living out your vulnerability holds you in the flow of life. It is great when we can learn to behold our vulnerability

219

as one of the most important gates of blessing into the inner world. It is in giving love that we are most human and most vulnerable.

The loss of spontaneity

N the Bible it is apparent that practically all the real points of novelty, change and growth are related to points of vulnerability. When you are vulnerable, you are exposed externally; what comes towards you can really hurt you. When you are in harmony, you can take untold pressure. You can carry many burdens with grace. When you suffer, your sense of rhythm deserts you. Perhaps it is only then you become aware of how deeply your life is normally blessed by unnoticed spontaneity. A natural spontaneity always holds you in the dance of your soul. When that spontaneity dries up, you fall out of the embrace and onto the rough gravel of deliberateness. You can no longer depend on your natural presence. When you really suffer, you learn the awful necessity of deliberateness. Even the smallest act must be willed and it costs you disproportionate energy. It is the last straw that breaks the camel's back. I heard this as a child and it always struck me as quite incredible that one more straw could have such a destructive effect on the strong back of the camel. The last straw was surely no heavier than all the prior straws. It was the fact of the camel's vulnerability and the cumulative weight of all the prior straws that were so destructive. When you carry a great weight of pain, you can be knocked over by a feather. Cut off from your spontaneity, it is extremely difficult to stand at all on your own ground. It takes a constant renewal of energy to hold yourself to your own routine. After a day of suffering you are totally exhausted and empty and most probably you cannot look forward to the ease of sleep either. The serpents of anxiety never sleep; they poison the innocence of the night.

The point of equilibrium

 t is lonely to carry a burden. A burden is always heavy. If you learn how to carry it, you can lessen weight and awkwardness. It takes time to learn this; you must experience the weight of the burden and then you discover its secret. At home we had a garden up the mountains. There was no water in the garden and the well was quite distant. To keep blight away the potatoes had to be sprayed with bluestone. The water had to be carried in buckets to fill the barrel of spray. If you had only one bucket to carry, it was very awkward. Though two buckets of water were heavier, they were far easier to carry. The burden was heavier but each side balanced the other and could be endured for the long distance over rough ground. Similarly with the burden of suffering. When in patience and prayer we painstakingly manage to discover the point of equilibrium within our burdens, we are able to carry them more easily.

People who do physical labour know the secret of balanced endurance. One summer, I worked on the buildings in Connecticut. I was working with Swedish and Norwegian carpenters. My job was to carry long heavy planks of timber over to the new houses and then pull them up onto the roof so that the carpenters had them ready to hand. I will never forget my first day. It was pure slavery. Fifty times I promised myself silently that they would not see me tomorrow. However, by evening, I was beginning to manage the art of carrying huge planks twenty or thirty feet long on my shoulder. Once I learned to judge where the point of equilibrium at the centre of the plank was, I could carry the weight easier. If you do not learn how to carry it, even a small burden can tread you into the ground. Only through listening to the burden that has come to you will you be able to discover its secret structure. No-one else can help you here. This is something that you must find out for yourself. Each burden is different. You alone know what it is like from underneath. While you are suffering, you live each day in the harsh and bruising presence of your burden. You know its inner configuration. No burden is uniform; it is made up of many different strands and materials. If you attend to it, the point of equilibrium will gradually reveal itself.

WHEN YOU STAND IN THE PLACE OF PAIN, YOU ARE NO-ONE

UFFERING IS FRIGHTENING. It UNHOUSES and dislocates you. Suffering is the arrival of darkness from an angle you never expected. There are different kinds of darkness. There is the night where the darkness is evenly brushed. The sky is studded with the crystal light of stars and the moon casts mint light over the fields. Though you are in the darkness, your ways are guided by a gentle light. This is not the darkness of deep suffering. When real suffering comes, the light goes out completely. There is nothing but a forsaken darkness, frightening in its density and anonymity. The human face is the icon of creation. In this countenance creation becomes intimate. Here, you are engaged by immediate presence. There is something in suffering that resents the human face. Suffering resents the shelter of intimacy. The dark squall of suffering dismantles belonging and darkens the mind. It rips the fragile net of meaning to shreds. Like a dark tide it comes in a torrent over every shoreline of your inner world. Nothing can hold it back. When you endure such a night, you never forget it.

When you stand in the place of pain, you are no-one. There is a poignant line from Virgil's *Aeneid* describing one of the heroes found dead in anonymous circumstances: '*corpe sine nomine*' i.e. a body without a name. Belonging is shredded. You are visited and claimed by a nothingness which has neither contour nor texture. Suffering is the harrowing and acidic force of anonymity. You are utterly unhoused. Now you know where Nowhere is. No-one can reach you. Suffering seems to be a force of primal regression. It almost wipes your signature as an individual and reduces you to faceless clay. Suffering is raw, relentless otherness coming alive around you and inside you.

Suffering's slow teachings

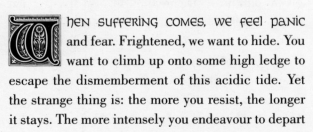 hen suffering comes, we feel panic and fear. Frightened, we want to hide. You want to climb up onto some high ledge to escape the dismemberment of this acidic tide. Yet the strange thing is: the more you resist, the longer it stays. The more intensely you endeavour to depart

the ground of pain, the more firmly you remain fixed there. It is difficult to be gentle with yourself when you are suffering. Gentleness helps you to stop resisting the pain that is visiting you. When you stop resisting suffering, something else begins to happen. You begin to slowly allow your suffering to follow its own logic. The assumption here is that suffering does not visit you gratuitously. There is in suffering some hidden shadowed light. Destiny has a perspective on us and our pathway that we can never fully glimpse; it alone knows why suffering comes. Suffering has its own reasoning. It wants to teach us something. When you stop resisting its dark work, you are open to learning what it wants to show you. Often we learn most deeply and receive profoundly from the black, lonely tide of pain. We often see in nature how pruning strengthens. Fruit trees look so wounded after being pruned, yet the limitation of this cutting forces the tree to fill and flourish. Similarly, with drills of potatoes, when they are raised, earth is banked up around them and seems to smother them. Yet as the days go by the stalks grow stronger. Suffering can often be a time of pruning. Though it is sore and cuts into us, later we may become aware that this dark suffering was secretly a liturgy of light and growth. Wordsworth suggests that 'suffering . . . shares the nature of infinity'.

It is lonely to acknowledge that it is often

suffering alone that can teach us certain things. There is subtle beauty in the faces of those who have suffered. The light that suffering leaves is a precious light. One often meets people who have had the companionship of suffering for forty or fifty years. It is humbling to see how someone can actually build a real friendship with suffering. Often these people are confined to bed. They are forsaken there. Yet I often think that such people are secret artists of the spirit. Perhaps their endurance is quietly refining the world and bringing light to the neglected and despairing. The call to suffering can be a call to bring healing to the world and to carry light to forsaken territories. The way you behold your pain is utterly vital in its integration and trans-figuration. When you begin to sense how it may be creative in the unseen world, this can help the sense of purpose and meaning to unfold. Gradually your sense of its deeper meaning begins to bring out the concealed dignity of suffering.

There is a belief nowadays that true growth can only happen when all the optimum conditions prevail. If a person has had a difficult childhood or has been hurt, there is a presumption that their life is eternally shadowed and their growth severely limited. Someone once asked a wonderful actress from which well she drew her creativity and how it was that she never got lost in the Hollywood glitter.

She said: 'All my life I have had the blessing of an extremely hard childhood behind me.' Not to wish difficulty on anyone or naïvely to praise it, yet if we can embrace difficulty, great fruits can grow from it. The lovely things that happen bless us and confirm us in who we are. It is, however, through difficulty and opposition that we define ourselves. The mind needs something against which it can profile and discover itself. Opposition forces our abilities to awaken; it tests the temper and substance of who we are. Difficulty is a severe looking-glass; yet in it we often glimpse sterling aspects of our soul which we would otherwise never have seen or even know that we possessed. It is not what happens to us that is in the end decisive but rather how we embrace and integrate it. Often the most wonderful gifts arrive in shabby packaging.

In terms of history, all people go through terrible times of suffering. Irish history carries a great weight of pain. It is difficult to come to terms with such lonely cultural memory. J. B. Metz speaks of the 'dangerous memory' of suffering. There is a tendency now in revisionist history to explain the past in terms of movements and trends of the contemporary time. This is inevitably reductionist. The suffering of the people is forgotten; they become faceless, mere ciphers of a trend or dynamic of history. To sanitize history is to blaspheme against memory. Equally, to become obsessed with the past is to paralyse the future.

The sense of meaning vanishes

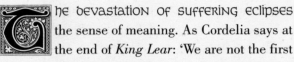he devastation of suffering eclipses the sense of meaning. As Cordelia says at the end of *King Lear*: 'We are not the first who with best meaning have incurred the worst.' People who are sent on to the dark ground of suffering know how all the normal certainties collapse. Painstakingly, you have to begin again to reconstruct some minimal shelter for your burdened heart and your cleft soul. Pain breaks your innocence. It shatters your trust in the world you knew. Now you know how destructive and lonesome life can become. No-one shouts for joy when they feel the ground of pain opening beneath them and exclaims: 'God, I know exactly why this came now. Is it not wonderful that I am totally miserable? I will carry this for a few weeks. Afterwards, I will be happier than I have ever been.' If you can do that, then it is not suffering at all, or else you have actually broken through to sainthood!

Suffering seems to be a frightening totality. When it comes, it puts you in the place of unknowing. All the old knowing of the conscious mind becomes redundant. The leave-taking of your surface

228

knowing often allows the deeper knowing within you to emerge. The experience of suffering can free a person to be in the world in a completely fresh and vital way. The intention of suffering may be to break the shell of ego with which each of us deftly surrounds ourselves. That we spin a coccoon around us is completely understandable. We are so small and fragile. The universe is too big for us. Our inner worlds are too immense. The possibilities are endless and the dangers too frightening. Even if you had kind parents and a magic childhood, there are still places in your heart that have grown hard in the rough and tumble of experience. There are few people walking through the world without the shell of ego. Suffering makes an incision in that shell and breaks it open so that a new hidden life within can actually emerge.

Farm life often shows how shells give way to reveal new life. We had hens at home. They would hatch every year. As a child, I always found it fascinating to see the eggs when the little chicks were ready to come out of the shell. At that time you would hear the tiniest twitter of knocking against the wall of the shell from within. Then, ever so slowly, the new little wet chick would force its way out and gradually break the shell that was its womb so that it could come out into the new world which awaited it. Similarly, suffering helps us break the shell of ego from within; then we can release a new dimension of ourselves which is now too large and too bright for the small darkness in which it has been growing; it could no longer breathe and live there. Real suffering breaks open the smallness within you and liberates you into larger and more hospitable places in life. It enlarges your belonging.

'When sorrows come, they come not single spies, but in battalions'

UFFERING always brings a myriad of questions which we cannot answer. Why me? What did I do to deserve this? Why was what was so precious in my life so abruptly taken from me? Will I be able to survive this at all? How will I live from now on? When you are standing in the place of pain none of these questions can be answered. Suffering often resembles fire. The flames of pain sear and burn you. The metaphor of the flame is illuminating because suffering often exhibits the exponential rapidity of flames; the pain can suddenly multiply within you. Like fire, suffering is a swift and powerful force. There is no distance between the spark and the flame. There is a hunger and passion in fire which totally take over; it can transform something that was solid and stable into powdered ashes. Often the flame of pain can have a cleansing effect and burn away the dross that has accumulated around your life. It is difficult to accept that what you are losing is what is used, what you no longer need. The Daoist tradition has a wonderful understanding that in the human body and spirit there is always a wintertime, when something is dying and falling away. There is always simultaneously a springtime, when something new is coming to life. When you allow your soul to work on that threshold, where the old can fall away and the new arrive, you come into rhythm with your destiny.

The new window is open

UFFERING is the sister of your future possibility. Suffering can open a window in the closed wall of your life and allow you to glimpse the new pastures of creativity on which you are called to walk and wander. But this window often only opens when the suffering begins to recede. While you are going through the dark valley, it is almost impossible to understand what is happening to you. The light that suffering brings is always a gift that it leaves as it departs. While you are in pain, you can see and understand nothing. The flame of suffering burns away our certainties, it also burns out the falsity within us. Each of us lives

231

with a certain set of illusions that are very dear to us. We use these illusions as consoling lenses through which we view the world. But an illusion is always a false lens; it can never show us the truth or reality of a situation. Suffering cleanses us of the falsities that have accumulated in our hearts. So often our minds are like magpies. We pick up and take on everything that glitters even though it may have no substance. In a magpie's nest, one finds random collections of colourful but useless debris. The fire of suffering cleanses completely the falsities to which our longing has attached itself. This liberates us from the emptiness of false belonging and allows us to belong in a real and truthful way in our lives again. Truth is difficult to reach and endure; but it is always the doorway to new freedom and life. As Shakespeare says in *Othello*: 'this sorrow's heavenly/It strikes where it doth love.'

How is the hard-earned harvest divided?

NE of the most haunting questions is: how are the fruits of suffering divided? This question touches on the old question of the one and the many. Though there are billions of people in the world we are all part of the one individuality. We are all one. Each of us is intimately linked with every other person. Though most of the others are strangers to us, who knows the secret effect that we have on each other? 'No-one lives for himself alone,' the Bible says. The pathways of causality and continuity are hidden and subtle in the world of soul. Perhaps the visitation of suffering in your life is bringing healing and light to the heart of someone far away, whom you will never know or meet. When lonely suffering is courageously embraced and integrated, it brings new light and shelter to our world and to the human family. This is the invisible work of the Great Spirit who divides and distributes the precious harvest of suffering. Gifts and possibilities unexpectedly arrive on the tables of those in despair and torment. This perspective brings some consoling meaning to the isolation of pain. When the flames of suffering sear you, you are not suffering for yourself alone. Though you feel like a nobody and you are locked into a grey nowhere, you were perhaps ironically never nearer to the heart of human intimacy. When we receive the courage to stand gracefully in the place of pain, we mediate for others the gifts that help heal their torment. Through the fog of forsakenness a new shoreline of belonging becomes clear.

There is a haunting poem by Pessoa which captures the searing uncertainty of pain.

I know, I alone

 know, I alone
*How much it hurts, this
   heart*
With no faith nor law
Nor melody nor thought.
Only I, only I
And none of this can I say
Because feeling is like the sky –
Seen, nothing in it to see.

The mystery of transfiguration

 art of the beauty of Christianity is the
utter realism with which it engages
suffering. At the heart of Christianity
there is suffering embraced and transfigured. There
is a depth of meaning to the term 'transfiguration'. It
means so much more than mere change. When a
thing 'changes', there is the suggestion that it is no
longer itself. A thing 'transfigured' is more fully
itself than ever, and more: it is irradiated with
beauty, whether it is a vase painted by Cézanne or a
turn of phrase that comes to new life in a great
poem. Often you see this in a simple gesture; a
great actor can utterly transfigure such a gesture.
Often in the films of Kieslowski the camera moves

234

from the biography of the drama to focus on an old person, possibly a beggar shuffling laboriously along a street. In the context the moment becomes a deft window into an unknown and unrecognized world. At its most sublime intensity, transfiguration is utter vision; no-one can stay long on the mountain of transfiguration, but if you have ever been there, you cannot suppress this seeing without damaging yourself. For thousands of years, the cross has been a symbol of the transfiguration of pain. It is a powerful, touching and sacred symbol. In its time the Cross was a sign of shame. People were crucified as criminals. The glory, light and healing of Christianity earns their way through the fire-path of great suffering. This is the profound tension; here light and dark, suffering and healing are sistered. The fire-path of suffering is the final gathering-place of all the ideas and intentions of Jesus.

Jesus is a fascinating man. The book I would give anything to read has never been written: the auto-biography of Jesus. What was his life really like? What did he dream of? What happened on the day that it finally dawned on him that he was from the heart of the Divine? What did he do for the rest of that afternoon? Jesus had a beautiful mind and a wonderful imagination. He was deeply creative; he was a carpenter and a poet. His practice of compassion was subversive. He never judged anyone. I

235

always imagine that Jesus had beautiful eyes. Anyone he gazed upon must have felt the infinite gentleness of the Divine suffusing their hearts. T. S. Eliot speaks of 'some infinitely gentle . . . infinitely suffering thing'. There was something about his presence which offered people a new life. Religion has often forgotten this and fashioned an image of God which only brings fear and guilt on us. Given the defensive and self-perpetuating tendency of all institutions, it is doubtful if any system could ever embody his infinite gentleness and subversive perception.

There is hardly any other figure in the Western tradition who has been so thoroughly domesticated as Jesus. He was a free spirit who had a wildness in him. Every time the Church of the time tried to box him in, he danced away from their threats and trick questions effortlessly. It is enthralling that there are twenty-six or -seven years of his life about which we know nothing. It was only in the last couple of years of his life that he began to present himself as God. It would be fascinating to have the possibility of excavating the inner landscapes of his solitude to see what was dawning on him. How such tender and wild light was brightening in the clay of his heart. There must have been great disturbance and excitement in his mind in those days of such inner quickening. His decision to take it on, to let his life and individuality be driven by this, must have had the inevitability of destiny. Could he glimpse the lonely consequences this choice would have? He would take on his young body, gentle face and unique mind, the pain, loneliness and suffering of the world. He would become a thing with no beauty – which would bring sadness to every eye that looked upon it. He would become the suffering servant of life's most merciless negativity. And thus achieve a beauty beyond conventional understanding to which poets, artists and mystics have responded for two millennia.

He would come into this destiny not as a victim or accidental martyr. No, through choice he gathered into the circle of his heart the pain of the world. This is horribly evident in his inner torture and fear in Gethsemane. Something awful happened in that garden. He sweated blood there. He was overcome with doubt. Everything was taken from him. Here the anguished scream of human desolation reached out for Divine consolation. And from the severe silence of the heavens, no sheltering echo returned. This is what the Cross is: that bleak, empty place where no certainty can ever settle. His friends betrayed and abandoned him. Christ explores the endless heart of loss with such gentle and vulnerable courage.

Behind the dark a subtle brightening

he Stations of the Cross are poignant places of pathos. They are a series of icons which show how pain focuses in human life. The cross is a unique axis in time. It is where time and timelessness intersect. All past, present and future pain were physically carried up the Hill of Calvary in this Cross. This darkness is carried up the Hill so that it could face the new dawn of resurrection and become transfigured. In essence, the Cross and the Resurrection are the one thing. They are not subsequent to each other. The Resurrection is the inner light hidden at the heart of darkness in the Cross. On Easter morning this light explodes onto the world. This is the mystery of the Eucharist. The Eucharist is a fascinating place; it embraces Calvary and Resurrection within the one circle. In Christian terms there is no way to light or glory except through the sore ground under the dark weight of the Cross.

The Cross is a lonely forsaken symbol. Good Friday is always deeply lonesome. There is an eerie and disturbing sadness at the heart of this day. On Good Friday, the pain of the world is returning to the Cross, awaiting transfiguration again. The Cross is an ancient symbol. Expressed lyrically, there is cruciform structure to every pain, difficulty and sadness. In this sense, the Cross is not an external object that belongs far away on a hill in Jerusalem. Rather the shape of the Cross is internal to the human heart. Every heart has a cruciform shape. When you look at the different conflicts in your life, you find that they are places where the contradictions cross each other. At the nerve of contradiction, you have the centre of the Cross, the nail of pain where two intimate but conflicting realities criss-cross. To view the standing Cross is to see how it embraces all directions. The vertical beam reaches from the lowest depth of clay to the highest zenith of divinity, the horizontal beam stretches the breadth of the world. The promise to each of us is that we will never be called to walk the lonely path of suffering without seeing the footprints ahead of us which lead eventually over the brow of the hill where Resurrection awaits us.

Behind the darkness of suffering a subtle brightening often manifests itself. There are two lines which echo this in a poem by Philippe Jaccottet: 'Love, like fire, can only reveal its brightness/on the failure and the beauty of burnt wood.' There is consolation and transfiguration here. The fires of suffering are disclosures of love. It is the nature of the lover to suffer. The marks and wounds that suffering leave on us are eventually places of beauty. This is the deep beauty of soul where limitation and damage, rather than remaining forces that cripple, are revealed as transfiguration.

Sweet honey from old failures

UFFERING MAKES US DEEPLY AWARE OF our own inability. It takes away our power; we lose control. The light of our eyes can see nothing. Now it is only the inner light in the eye of the soul that can help you to travel this sudden, foreign landscape. Here we slowly come to a new understanding of failure. We do not like to fail. We are uncomfortable in looking back on our old failures. Yet failure is often the place where suffering has left the most precious gifts. I remember some time ago speaking to a friend who was celebrating his fiftieth birthday. He told me that this milestone made him reflect deeply on his life. He was surprised and excited on looking back at his life to discover that much of what he had understood as the successes in his life did not hold their substance under more critical reflection. As against that, what he had always termed his failures now began to seem ever more interesting and substantial. The places of failure had been the real points of change and growth. This is often true in our own experience. Sometimes a person puts their heart and soul into their career. They make huge sacrifices, putting their family in second place. Then, when the key position becomes available someone else walks into it. At the crucial moment, through no fault of his own, he has failed and the opening will not come again. Initially, this is a devastating experience. Finding understanding and support in the bosom of his family, he slowly begins to see through his life. He is shocked to realize that he hardly knows his family at all; he has been absent so much. As his withdrawal from the drug of career becomes surer, he sees things differently. The failure could not actually have come at a better time. If this had not happened now, his grown-up children would have left home without his really knowing them. This experience of discovery also often happens when a person retires or is made redundant; they learn to reclaim and enjoy the life they never knew they had lost. There is a beautiful verse from Antonio Machado:

ast night I dreamed
– blessed illusion –
that I had a beehive here
in my heart
and that
the golden bees were making
white combs and sweet honey
from my old failures.

(Translation by Robert Bly)

241

Failure is the place where destiny swings against our intentions. What you wanted and worked for never came. Your energy and effort were not enough. Failure also happens in the inner world, the times when your own smallness and limitation ruined things; you reached deep into yourself for something kind or creative and caught only small-ness. Failure often gnaws most deeply in the territory of relationships. Times when you have caused damage. Failure also includes personal weakness. This is often where literature evokes great feeling. This was a theme that haunted Joseph Conrad in his novels *Heart of Darkness* and *Lord Jim*. Conrad explores failure in the challenging area of affinity. One character sees himself in another and the other's failure gnaws at him and threatens to unravel a life built on standards and achievement. In *Heart of Darkness*, Marlow only catches glimpses of Kurtz but he has foreknowledge of his failure in him-self. Failure is then often the place where you suffered unintentionally. Reflection on our failures brings home to us the hidden secrets of our nature. Failure is the place where longing is unexpectedly thwarted. This often brings interesting discovery and reintegration.

Unconscious suffering

elow the surface in the night side of your inner world, there is also suffering happening. Given that suffering usually causes pain, it sounds strange to suggest that you might actually be suffering without knowing it. Yet there seems to be something in this idea the more one thinks about it. There is a vast area of the human soul that is totally unknown to us. Let us not equate it simply with the subconscious. This holds us too firmly within the idiom of psychoanalysis. In that unknown region there are many things happening of which you are afforded no glimpse. It is probable that quite a lot of suffering happens there that never ascends to the surface of your mind. Quietly in the night of our souls, everyone suffers. This suffering can be at work, refining, tempering and balancing your presence here in the world. Patiently it turns the charred icon of your falsity into the luminous icon of real presence. Perhaps this perspective can open a little window into the dark mystery of how children suffer. There is the awful reality of children who are suffering horribly in the world through abuse, poverty and wars. Yet there is also the fact that in some way all children suffer. Under the playful world of every child there is some unconscious darkness deciphering itself and working itself through. Every child carries even in its innocence some of the burden of the pain of the world. This is akin to the unknown suffering in which every adult also participates. There is something in the very nature of suffering that loves the darkness of the unknown and that hurts us and lessens us even without our being fully conscious of it.

Suffering in the Animal Kingdom

HERE ARE DIFFERENT FORMS OF SUFFERING. There is also much suffering in the world that humans are too unrefined to carry. This is where our more ancient sisters and brothers, the animals, come in to carry part of the world's pain. This pain for which our minds are as yet too coarse. Sometimes when you look into an animal's face, you see great pain. This is not pain brought about by the consciousness negatively targeting itself. Animal consciousness is more lyrical and free. An animal does not burden itself in the way a human can.

Many of our burdens are false. Animals do not spend years inventing and constructing burdens for themselves. You do not walk into a field and encounter a cow who is seriously self-analysing and in deep turmoil because she is failing to connect with her inner calf! It is highly improbable that you will ever meet a cow who is swamped by the fact that her project of self-improvement has unleashed this huge ancestral cow thing in her life, and now she can hardly walk because she knows she is carrying all the cow karma of her ancestry! Neither will you find a cow who is fatally depressed because she has discovered that on the night she was born the astrological structure of her destiny was negatively set and she is just reluctantly grazing in the sweet grass knowing that soon the very fields will rise up against her! As far as we know cows are not burdened in this manner by ultimate questions. Nevertheless, you often encounter such loneliness in animal presence; they seem to receive it from elsewhere. It belongs somehow to the intimate pain of the world. An animal's face can often be an icon of profound lonesomeness. It is said that once, before one of his major breakdowns, Nietzsche was walking down the street in Turin. Coming up the street against him was a horse and cart. He looked deeply into the horse's face and went up and put his arms around its neck and embraced it. The sadness in the old horse's face was a perfect mirror of his own torture. Every form of life participates in the light of soul and also in the darkness of suffering. A kind of voluntary kinship is made possible through suffering.

Suffering brings compassion

NE OF THE GREAT FRUITS OF SUFFERING IS compassion. When you have felt and experienced pain, it refines the harshness that may be in you. Tolstoy said that our great duty as humans was to sow the seed of compassion in each other's hearts. This happens in friendship. If you are in pain and your friend knows pain, you feel the kinship and understanding that can really shelter you. Understanding is one of the few shelters that are capable of standing in the suffering place. I was in China once and I visited many Buddhist temples. My favourite Buddha was one I discovered at the back of the altar in one of the temples, a Buddha with hundreds of hands and in each hand there was an eye. I asked a young Buddhist monk who this Buddha was. The monk explained that this was a Buddha who had lived a wonderful life. He had reached such a level of soul-refinement that he was about to go into nirvana. He took one look back before crossing this threshold and saw that there was still one person suffering in the world. He was then given the choice, either to go into nirvana or go back to help the suffering one. He chose to come back. The very moment that he made that choice, he was raised immediately into nirvana. He was given a hand to help everyone who was suffering and an eye in each hand to see where the help and shelter were needed. This Buddha is a beautiful image of compassion which has strength, wisdom and enlightenment within it.

Illness: the land of desolation

hen suffering comes, the darkness has arrived. The light is out. Even your faith falls away. When you are at the heart of great pain, you enter a land of sheer desolation. There is a strange and strong poem by the Connemara poet Caitlin Maude which captures this:

etween the rosary
And the thirty acres
The pearl of your belief fell
On a land without blessing.

(Translation by the author)

The land of suffering feels like a land that blessing has never touched. Illness is a form of suffering that quickly takes us into the land without blessing. Illness is a terrible visitor. We never value or even see some things in our lives until we are just about to lose them. This is particularly true of health. When we are in good health, we are so busy

247

in the world that we never even notice how well we are. Illness comes and challenges everything about us. It unmasks all pretension. When you are really ill, you cannot mask it. It also tests the inner fibre and luminosity of your soul. It is very difficult to take illness well. Yet it seems that if we treat our illness as something external that has singled us out and we battle and resist it, the illness will refuse to leave. On the other hand, we must not identify ourselves with our illness. A visit to a hospital often shows that very ill people are more alive to life's possibilities than the medical verdict would ever allow or imagine.

When we learn to see our illness as a companion or friend, it really does change the way the illness is present. The illness changes from a horrible intruder to a companion who has something to teach us. When we see what we have to learn from an illness, then often the illness can gather itself and begin to depart. A friend of mine has been through awful illness in the past three years. It was a strange viral illness. He lost his ability to walk and his sight for a period. I was overwhelmed by the gentleness with which he was able to meet this hostile destroyer. Of course he focused his mind firmly on the horizon of healing and tried to shelter in the luminosity of his soul. However, he did not constantly quarrel with the illness or turn it into an unworthy enemy. Sometimes when you see a thing as the enemy, you only reinforce its presence and power over you. He befriended his illness; he travelled with it, remaining very mindful and holding on as far as he could to the shelter of blessing. Well, the illness took him on an amazing journey, over mountains that he could never have anticipated. He has returned now and has entered health again. But he is a changed person. He has learned so much. His soul now enjoys a quiet depth; his gentleness has grown. His presence enriches you when you meet him.

To befriend the places of pain

When different places within us are in pain, we should extend the care of deep friendship towards them. We should not leave them isolated under siege in pain. A friend of mine went to hospital to have a hysterectomy. A priest friend came to visit her on the evening before her operation. She was anxious and vulnerable. He sat down and they began to talk. He suggested to her that she have a conversation with her womb. To talk to her womb as a friend. She could thank her womb for making her a mother. To thank it for all her different children who had begun there. The body, mind and spirit of each child had been

249

tenderly formed in that kind darkness. She could remember the different times in her life when she was acutely aware of her own presence, power and vulnerability as a mother. To thank her womb for the gifts and the difficulties. To explain to it how it had become ill and that it was necessary for her continuing life as a mother to have it removed. She was to undertake this intimate ritual of leave-taking before the surgeons came in the morning to take her womb away. She did this ritual with tenderness and warmth of heart. The operation was a great success. Her conversation with her womb changed the whole experience. The power was not with the doctors or the hospital. The experience did not have the clinical, short-circuit edge of so much mechanical and anonymous hospital efficiency. The experience became totally her own, the leave-taking of her own womb. When a part of your body is ill, it must be a lonely experience for it. If we integrate its experience and embrace it in the circle of recognition and care, it alters the presence of the illness and pain. Externally, we should endeavour to remain alert to others and their distress at our condition. How often do we see how sick people comfort their comforters?

The dark visitation of illness needs to be carefully encountered, otherwise the illness can become a permanent tenant. A friend of mine was involved in a terrible car accident and was badly injured.

One of her legs was damaged. She told me of being in hospital: she began to feel that her body and life were terminally damaged. The darkness of this realization gripped her totally. She spent days locked into the prospect of her bleak future. She became addicted to the wounding of her body. She felt that she would never again be able to shake herself free of this burden. Then one day, almost like a ray of light through a dark sky, she realized that this was the wound that would make her a life prisoner. When she began to see the power it was assuming, she realized with desperation that she could not permit it permanent tenancy. So she began to distance herself from the wound. Gradually, over a period, she regained her confidence and poise and came back to healing. There is, perhaps, a moment in every life when something dark comes along. If we are not very careful to recognize its life-damaging potential before it grips us, it can hold us for the rest of our lives. We can become addicted to that wound and use it forever as an identity card. We can turn that wound into sorrow and forsaken-ness, a prison of crippled identity. It is difficult to be objective and gracious about your wounds because they can hurt and weep for years. Wounds are not sent to make us small and frightened; they are sent to open us up and to help graciousness, compassion and beauty root within us. Wounds offer us unique gifts but they demand a severe apprenticeship before the door of blessing opens.

The vulnerability and mystery of the body

All our knowing is tenuous and shadowed. Our bodies, too, are so fragile. An accident can suddenly visit a life and completely change one's world. In one split second in a car crash your whole world could be taken from you. You then have to enter the world of illness and pain and begin to learn how to reside there. Your body is your only home in the universe. When you become ill or injured, you have to become used to your body as a new dwelling. All of a sudden it is strange, vulnerable and injured. Up to now it worked with you and for you; now it hesitates, it must be encouraged and often it just squats there unable to move or partake. There is a desperate poignancy in the presence of a sick body. A friend of mine who now has the companionship of illness and cannot be left alone says: 'I have had to get used to living with this third thing that is always there now between me and everything.'

The body is such an intricate and complex place. The more you become aware of what a nuanced inner network it is, the more you wonder how it

252

actually continues to function in secrecy and silence. The heart is the great warm centre of your life. All emotion and feeling lives here. Think of the faithfulness of your heart that has never once stopped. In every moment of work, relaxation, thought, pain and sleep, it continues to keep your life flowing. Your heart reflects the movement of your experience. The heart is the place of great departure in the body. From here all your blood flows out to every inner territory. The heart is also the place of great return, the place to where all the tired blood returns to be reinvigorated.

Though the body is splendid and mysterious, it is fragile too. Joy and blessings, trouble and turbulence can reach us because we are in these visible tents of clay. We live on an unseen threshold. The name of that threshold is fragility. Our courage breaks here 'like a tree in a black wind', as Yeats puts it. Consequently, we need the shelter and blessing of prayer. Our language instinctively expresses this. The greeting 'Hello' expresses surprise and delight that you have survived since the last meeting. 'Goodbye' means that a blessing be around you until we meet again. These rituals of greeting and valediction are secretly meant to appease the deities and invoke blessing on us. Yeats adverts to this hidden seam of vulnerability when he says:

ome away human child!
To the waters and the wild
With a fairy hand in hand
For the world's more full of weeping than
you can understand.

No wound is ever silent

 here is no-one — regardless of how beautiful, sure, competent or powerful — that is not damaged internally in some way. Each of us carries in our hearts the wound of mortality. We are particularly adept at covering our inner wounds. No wound is ever silent. Behind the play of your image and the style you cut in the world, your wounds continue to call out for healing. These cuts at the core of your identity cannot be healed by the world or medicine, or by the externals of religion or psychology. It is only by letting in the divine light to bathe these wounds that healing will come. The tender kindness of the Divine knows where the roots of our pain are concealed. The divine light knows how to heal their sore weeping. Every inner wound has its own particular voice. It calls from a time when we were wronged and damaged. It holds the memory of that breakage as pristine as its moment of occurrence. Deep inner wounds evade time. Their soreness is utterly pure.

These wounds lose little of their acid through the natural transience of chronological time. If we dig into ourselves with the fragile instruments of analysis we can destroy ourselves. Only the voice of deep prayer can carry the gentle poultice inwards to these severe crevices and draw out the toxins of hurt. To learn what went on at the time of such wounding can helps us greatly; it will show us the causes, and the structure of the wound becomes clear. Real healing is, however, another matter. As with all great arrivals in the soul, it comes from a direction that we often could neither predict nor anticipate.

Celtic recognition and blessing of the dark side

he Celtic tradition recognized that we need to invoke blessing on our suffering and pain. It is wrong to portray Celtic spirituality as a tradition of light, brightness and goodness alone; this is soft spirituality. The Celtic tradition had a strong sense of the threat and terror of suffering. One of the lovely rituals was the visit to the holy well. These wells were openings in the earth-body of the goddess. The land of Ireland was the body of the Goddess Eriu. Wisdom and cures were to be found in the holy wells. In our valley there are three such wells. Two have cures for sore eyes. All kinds of personal things were left here as 'thanks offerings' for the cure. Many of these wells are in the mountains. It is quite a poignant thing in a bleak, stolid landscape to find these little oases of tenderness bedecked with personal mementoes, sacred places where people have come for centuries to the goddesses of the earth looking for healing. These wells were places where the water element was used to bless and heal. In the Irish tradition there is a wonderful respect for holy water. People put little bottles of holy water in the walls of their farms to keep away evil and sickness. Some carry it in their cars to prevent accidents. Others sprinkle it at night for the holy souls and for absent friends and loved ones. There is a sense of how the water element can bring protection. The human body has a huge percentage of water. Blessing with water is beautiful; it is as if the innocent water of the earth which has flown wild and free in rain and ocean comes to bless its embodied human sister.

The Celtic tradition had a great sense of how the powers of Nature could also be stirred to bring pain and destruction. There are many such stories. For instance, a woman who had special powers could cause a storm at sea by stirring water violently in a vessel. Or a fisherman at sea could raise wind by whistling for it. There are also many stories of people who had charms to cure animals. They could diagnose intuitively what was wrong with the animal and then use the charm to bring the animal back to health. Certain people also had the charm to cure people. In the invisible network of suffering, it is amazing how some have the power to heal us and others help us carry the burden.

Co help carry the suffering of another

The loneliness of suffering targets each person individually. When you suffer, no-one can really experience what it is like for you. Beneath this isolation of the individual is there some way in which suffering contributes to the light and creativity of creation? The poet and theologian Charles Williams had a theory of Co-inherence. He understood creation as a web of order and dependency between all of us and God: 'the web of diagrammatized glory'. Within this belonging there is a secret exchange of spirit continually flowing between us. A person has, then, the choice to take on the sufferings of another and carry them. In modern times, this courageous kindness is exemplified in the action of Maksymilian Kolbe, a Polish priest who was prisoner in Auschwitz. A prisoner had escaped from Block 14. The Lager

Kommandant said that ten would die for the one who had escaped. He chose ten men. One of them cried as he was chosen, he knew he would never see his wife and children again. Maksymilian Kolbe stepped up and asked the Kommandant if he could take the man's place. He was allowed. They were thrown in a death cell and starved to death. This is a powerful story of the courage and kindness of taking the Cross from the shoulder of another. The Celtic tradition had similar beliefs. This was practised, for instance, when a woman was in the throes and torture of childbirth. She might offer a waistcoat or some other item of clothing belonging to her man in the belief that she could transfer her pains to him. Or alternatively the man might go out onto the farm and do some excruciatingly hard work in order to take some of the pain from his woman. Creation seems to have a secret symmetry in which we all participate without being aware of it. Suffering seems to awaken this and break our belonging. Yet, perhaps ironically, we are nearest then to the heart of intimacy.

Out of the Winter a New Spring

Parenthood is an ever-changing mystery. One of its most neglected regions is the time when the parents are old. Perhaps, in the last years of their lives, parents do actually carry some of the pain their children are now enduring in their own lives. There is a tendency in us to underestimate parents when we have outgrown them; they are old now and do not understand us. We tend to lock them inside the images they present externally. They circle around the same old stories, habits and complaints. Perhaps there is something deeper going on behind the façade of ageing and helplessness. They hold our images in their hearts and maybe they carry us in a tender way through certain difficulties and pain without our ever suspecting it.

In the land of suffering there is no certainty. We cannot understand suffering because its darkness makes the light of our minds so feeble and thin. Yet we trust that there is great tenderness at the root of pain, that our suffering refines us, that its fire cleanses the false accretions from the temple of the soul. Out of the winter ground a new springtime of fresh possibility slowly arises. In its real presence suffering transfigures and enlarges human beings. We must, however, be careful to distinguish it from the fabricated, self-imposed burdens which we create out of our own falsity. Such burdens bring us nothing. They keep us circling in the same empty rooms of dead fact. They never open us to the fecundity of possibility. Real suffering calls us home in the end to where our hearts will be happy, our energy clear and our minds open and alive. Furthermore, the experience of suffering calls our hearts to prayer; it becomes the only shelter. In this sense, suffering can purify our longing and call us forward into a new rhythm of belonging which will be flexible and free enough to embrace our growth. Real suffering is where the contradictions within us harmonize, where they give way to new streams of life and beauty. As the Zen monk said: 'When one flower blooms, it is spring everywhere.'

A blessing

 ay you be blessed in the holy names of those who carry our pain up the mountain of transfiguration.

May you know tender shelter and healing blessing when you are called to stand in the place of pain.

May the places of darkness within you be surprised by light.

May you be granted the wisdom to avoid false resistance and when suffering knocks on the door of your life, may you be able to glimpse its hidden gift.

May you be able to see the fruits of
suffering.
May memory bless and shelter you with the
hard-earned light of past travail, may
this give you confidence and trust.
May a window of light always surprise you.
May the grace of transfiguration heal your
wounds.
May you know that even though the storm
might rage not a hair of your head will
be harmed.

chapter 5

Prayer: A Bridge between Longing and Belonging

The human body gathered in prayer configures our need

ne of the most tender images is the human person at prayer. When the body gathers itself before the Divine, a stillness deepens. The blaring din of distraction ceases and the deeper tranquillity within the heart envelops the body. To see someone at prayer is a touching sight. For a while they have become unmoored from the grip of society, work and role. It is as if they have chosen to enter into a secret belonging carried within the soul; they rest in that inner temple impervious to outer control or claiming. A person at prayer also evokes the sense of vulnerability and fragility. Their prayer reminds us that we are mere guests of the earth, pilgrims who always walk on unsteady ground, carrying in earthen vessels multitudes of longing.

We look up to what is above. We look up in wonder and praise at the sun. At night our eyes long to decipher the faces of the moon. Cathedral spires reach to the heavens and call our eyes towards the silent immensity of the Divine. Mountains and horizons lure our longing. We seem to believe that true reality could not be here among us; it has to be either above us or beyond us. In human society we adopt the same perspective. We place our heroes and heroines on pedestals. They have power, charisma, beauty and status. They are the ones we 'look up to'. Yet pedestals are usually constructed with the most fragile psychological materials. Once we have elevated someone, we begin to chip away at the pedestal until we find the fissures that will eventually topple the hero. The popular press perfectly illustrates this point; it unmakes the idols it has made. Despite the desire to look up and to elevate people, one of the most touching and truthful configurations of human presence is the individual gathered in prayer.

To sit or kneel in prayer is visually our most appropriate physical presence. There is something right about this. It coheres with the secret structure of existence and reality, namely that we have a right to nothing. Everything that we are, think, feel and have is a gift. We have received everything, even the opportunity to come to the earth and walk awake in this wondrous universe. There are many people who have worked harder than us, people who have done more kind and holy things than us and yet they have received nothing. The human body gathered in prayer mirrors our fragility and inner poverty and it makes a statement recognizing the divine generosity that is always blessing us. To be gathered in prayer is appropriate. It is a gracious, reverential and receptive gesture. It states that, at the threshold of each moment, the gift of breath and blessing comes across to embrace us.

There is such beauty and goodness in the world. In our times, it is fashionable to paint everything first in its darkest colours. The darkness becomes so absorbing that we never reach the colour and light. To concentrate exclusively on the negative makes us feel powerless and victimized. It is only fair to underline the joy that is in creation too. Joy is a dignified presence; if we insist on being morose and depressing, it will not interrupt us or intrude on us. There is a subtle rhythm to joy. Until you break forth to embrace it, you will never know its power and delight. Every day of your life there is joy waiting for you, hidden at the heart of the significant things that happen to you or secretly around the corner of the quieter things. If your heart loves delight, then you will always be able to discover the quiet joy that awaits to shine forth in many situations. Prayer should help us develop the habit of delight. We weight the notion of prayer with burdens of duty, holiness and the struggle for perfection. Prayer should have the freedom of delight. It should arise from, and bring us to, humour, laughter and joy. Religion often suffers from a great amnesia; it constantly insists on the seriousness of God and forgets the magic of the Divine Glory. Prayer should be the wild dance of the heart too. In the silence of our prayer we should be able to sense the roguish smile of a joyful God who, despite all the chaos and imperfection, ultimately shelters everything.

Prayer is ancient longing

 RAYER IS AN ANCIENT LONGING; it has a special light, hunger and energy. Our earliest ancestors knew and felt how the invisible, eternal world enveloped every breath and gesture. They recognized that the visible world was merely a threshold. Their very first representations on the walls of caves express the desire to name, beseech and praise. To the ancient eye, the world was a mystery independent in its own rhythm and poise. Nature was a primal mother with an unfathomable mind; she could be tender or cruel. The force and surface of nature were merely the exterior visage which concealed a wild, yet subtle mind. For the ancients prayer was an attempt to enter into harmony with the deeper rhythm of life. Prayer tempered human arrogance; it became the disclosure point of the deeper, eternal order. In post-modern society the isolated individual has become the measure of all things. It is no surprise that, in our loss of connection with nature, we have forgotten how to pray. We even believe that we do not need to pray.

PRAYER IS THE NARRATIVE OF THE SOUL

RAYER ISSUES FROM THAT THRESHOLD where soul and life interflow; it is the conversation between desire and reality. It is not to be reduced to the intermittent moments when we say prayers in words. Prayer is a deeper and more ancient conversation within us. In this sense, the inner life of each person is prayer that commences in the first stir in the womb and ends with the last breath before return to the invisible world. In a similar sense one could consider prayer as the soul-narrative of a people issuing from that threshold where the desire of a people negotiates

266

the constraints and sufferings of its history. This is echoed in the haunted prayer of Lear: 'Poor naked wretches, wheresoe'er you are,/That bide the pelting of this pitiless storm,/How shall your houseless heads and unfed sides,/Your looped and windowed raggedness, defend you/From seasons such as these? O I have ta'en/Too little care of this.'

Near us, there is the ruin of an old penal church. It is a two-roomed, limestone ruin set in a hazel wood on the side of the valley. It is called *coilltín phobail* i.e. the little wood of the people. This was the church where our people gathered to pray in penal times when there was a war against the faith. There was a price on the head of every priest. My father often told us that during the Mass watchmen kept lookout at different points on the horizon. The priest celebrated the Mass in one of the rooms but never showed his face to the congregation. Remaining unknown, he protected both himself and his people. This little penal ruin stands as a poignant metaphor of resistance and desire for the Divine which an empire could not kill. Prayer is often the space where the poor and the oppressed retrieve and express their nobility and graciousness. Prayer awakens the soul and opens doors of possibility. In bleak and brutal times, it keeps the dream and longing of the heart alive. It is the only refuge of belonging in extreme times.

One Sunday morning in Manhattan, a friend took me to a gospel community in Harlem. As an outsider I felt that we might be intruding on their sacred space. But there was a wonderful, warm welcome. Up front, on the altar, over fifty people in vestments led the congregation in singing the liturgy. The gospel singing was magnificent. The ebb and flow of its easy rhythm brought us gently and gradually into deeper tranquillity of soul. Yet there was such poignancy to the singing because one realized that these were some of the songs that had kept the souls of these people's ancestors alive in the brutal times under the slave owner's whip. These deep-hearted, earth-resonant prayer songs kept meaning in the kingdom of the heart. Though their bodies were owned as objects, prayer kept their souls free and their minds dreaming of a time when the new day would break and the shadows flee.

Prayer and the desire to survive

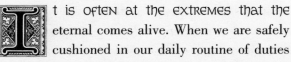t is often at the extremes that the eternal comes alive. When we are safely cushioned in our daily routine of duties and expectations, we forget who we are and why it is that we are here. When suffering chooses you, the fabric of self-protection tears. The old familiarities and securities fall away as if they had never been

there. The raft of desires which guided daily life become utterly insignificant. Suddenly they seem like fantasies from another era. Every ounce of energy gathers into one intention: the desire to survive. In some subtle, animal sense, we always secretly know how precarious and vulnerable our presence here is. Suffering absolutely unveils this fragility. E. M. Cioran writes: 'Without God, all is night, with him light is useless.' Our desire to endure and survive is a powerful instinct and it shows how desperately we long to belong to life. It takes immense pain to dislodge that ancient desire to belong. Yet when that desire is driven to the edge of its own endurance, it can often endure there when it turns to its own depth and takes the form of prayer. The prayer which calls out of this wilderness is one of the deepest cries of the human heart. Often this prayer is answered excruciatingly slowly. At the first stage, just enough light is released to enable you to hold on at the edge of the cliff. Then, over time, a stronger light gathers to guide you back to shelter. Such suffering radically refines the way you belong in your life. The true essence of your life becomes present to you. Real prayer opens the heart of desire, at a level below your image, words and actions. Real prayer is the liberation of that inner voice of the eternal.

A prayer is never wasted

RAYER is never wasted. It always brings transformation. When you really want to pray for something and you do not receive it, you tend to believe that your prayer was not answered. Such prayer has a powerful intentionality; and it is true that at times your prayer is not answered in a direct way. You do not receive what you long for. Unknown to you, that prayer has secretly worked on another aspect of the situation and effected a transfiguration which may become visible only at a later stage. Unknown to you, prayer is always at the service of destiny. Your days and ways are never simply as they appear on the surface. Human vision is always limited and selective and you never see the whole picture. However, the providence which weaves your days sees the greater horizon and knows what your life needs in order for you to come fully to birth as the person you are called to be. Prayer refines you so that you may become worthy of your possibility and destiny. The irony of being here is that sometimes it is precisely what you want to avoid that brings you further towards creativity and compassion. The intensity of rejection is the index of need.

In prayer we learn to see with the eyes of the soul

hrough prayer we learn to see with the eyes of the soul. Your normal vision is always conditioned by the needs of the ego. Prayer helps you to clearer vision. It opens you up to experiences you would never otherwise entertain. It refines your eyes for the unknown narrative which is quietly working itself through your words, actions and thoughts. In this way prayer issues from, and increases, humility. The normal understanding of humility made it out to be a passive self-depreciation in which any sense of self-worth or value was diminished. Humility has a more profound meaning. Humility is a derivative of the Latin word *humus* meaning 'of the earth'. In this sense, humility is the art of being open and receptive to the inner wisdom of your clay. This is the secret of all natural growth: as the Bible says, 'unless the seed dies it remains but a single seed'. Meister Eckhart, in speaking of the original Creation, says: 'The earth fled to the lowest place.' Clay is not interested in any form of hierarchy; it is immune to the temptation and competition of the vertical line. Under the convenient guise of not being noticed and being the lowest ground, it operates a vast sacramentality of growth which nourishes and sustains all of life. In our misguided passion for hierarchy, we put first things first and other things nowhere.

The earth welcomes difficulty as invitation to novelty and freshness; the earth is full of all kinds of individualities. Yet no individuality ever becomes isolated. Each remains somehow porous, receiving and returning growth. The humility that prayer brings educates your spirit in the art of inner hospitality. You slowly learn to lose your defensiveness. You enter more deeply into the wisdom of your clay, your humus nature. You learn not to be uneasy or afraid. When your deeper nature awakens and is allowed to work, you discover a new flexibility. You do not need any more to define yourself negatively in terms of avoidance. Humility brings a new creativity. You begin to glimpse possibilities in situations and experiences which up to now you had considered closed.

Humility also brings you a new self-possession. You no longer feel the need to vocalize in the current jargon, at every moment, what is going on inside you. Language itself is wedded to silence. Now, like the silent earth, the cradle of all growth, you too can watch the stirrings of a new springtime in the clay of your heart. You gain more courage. You become surer about who you are and you no longer need to force either image or identity. When you come into rhythm with your nature, things happen of themselves.

The deepest prayer happens silently in our nature

t is important to acknowledge that our deepest prayer happens in our nature. Prayer is not the monopoly of the pious; neither is it to be restricted to the province of those who are religious or spiritual. Conversely, neither can we say that those who have no religion or belief are not in prayer. Neither is prayer to be equated with prayers – the sequence of holy words with which we attempt to reach God. Were the spiritual life to be reduced to what we can see and the categories we put around people, no-one could ever be deemed spiritual. Prayer is the activity of the soul. The nature of each soul is different. The eternal is related to each of us in a unique way. Frequently, our outer categories of holiness are mere descriptions of behaviour. They are not able to mirror or reflect the secret and subtle way in which the Divine is working in the individual life. The words we use to describe the holy are usually too nice and sweet. Sometimes, the Divine is awkward and contrary. God might be most active in an individual who just at that time invites our disappointment, judgement or hostility. The prayer of the soul voices itself in each life differently. One of the wonderfully consoling aspects of the world of

spirit is the impossibility of ever making a judgement about 'who' someone is in that world. You may
know 'who' a person is in the professional or social
world, but you can never judge a person's soul or
attempt to decipher what their destiny is or what it
means. No-one ever knows what divine narrative
God may be writing with the crooked lines of someone's struggles, misdeeds and omissions. We are all
in the drama, but no-one has seen the script.

Deep below the personality and outer image, the
soul is continuously at prayer. We need to find new
words to help name the unusual and unexpected
forms of the Divine in our lives. When we divide life
into regions, we lose sight of the most interesting
places where the Divine is alive in us. It is difficult
to trust most spiritual or pious talk; it inevitably
seems to have either a dead or a domesticated God
as its reference. The Divine Presence slips through
the crevices between our words and judgements.
Wall-to-wall spiritual talk leaves no oxygen for a
living God to breathe or for the danger of the soul to
quicken. Words map the world. When we attempt
to name the Divine we need words which illuminate
its seamless and hidden presence. The Divine has
no frontiers. Our fear and limitation invent the
barriers that keep us locked out from our divine
inheritance. That kind of banishment makes you a
victim of your own loss. To the Divine Eye, creation

in its diversity is one living field. Often where we consider the Divine to be absent, it is in fact present under a different form and name. Spiritual discernment is the art of critical attention that is able to recognize the Divine Presence in its expected and unexpected forms. The Divine prayer sustains all life; it never ceases, in every place and in every moment its embrace is there.

The prayer of being

N the Christian tradition there have been many different theories of prayer. One predominant explanation tended to consider prayer as withdrawal from the world. Away from distraction and confusion, prayer is the stillness of pure attention to the Divine. In its extreme form this tendency encourages passivity and quietism. The other main theory understands prayer as action and engaged presence: *laborare est orare*, i.e. to work is to pray. Perhaps we do not need to choose between them because they may be false alternatives. Everybody should attempt both these forms of prayer, particularly the form they find uncongenial. Exclude nothing. Maybe it would also be possible to bring them together if we speak of the prayer of being. At its deepest level creation is continuously at prayer. The most vital and creative prayer is always happening within us even though we never fully hear it. Now and again we catch the echoes of the music of inner prayer.

What is it that prays in us?

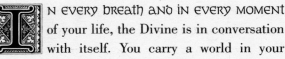N every breath and in every moment of your life, the Divine is in conversation with itself. You carry a world in your mind, which you only catch glimpses of on occasions. Your own mystery is never fully present to you. This means that your prayers in wishes and words are always partial and often blind. Yet the deep prayer of the heart continues within you in a silence that is too deep for words to even reach.

One of the fascinating things to ask about prayer is: what do you pray with? Put more tenderly: what is it that prays within you? If prayer is but the voice of the superficial mind, the result is endless inner chatter. Prayer goes deeper. More precisely: prayer issues from an eternal well within you. The presence that prays within you is your soul. It is interesting to read in the New Testament how the soul is always seen as a continuation of the Holy Spirit. Nowhere does it ever say that we should pray *to* the Holy Spirit. The Holy Spirit is not different from the activity of your prayer. You pray *in* the Holy Spirit. The little preposition suggests how you are suffused with the Holy Spirit. Your body is the temple of the Holy Spirit and the deepest level in you is spirit.

One of the deepest longings in the human heart is the longing for a foundation to things. Because we sense how fragile and uncertain life can be, we long for a foundation that nothing can shake. The first stage in building a house is to dig out the foundation. If the house were simply built on surface ground, the walls would crack and come away from each other. Yet the irony is that we never penetrate past the surface layer. Being on earth, we feel we are on solid ground. Yet at its deepest foundation the earth rests again on the nothingness of the empty air – but it is held there by the invisible force fields of gravity. It is appropriate in the inner world that the deepest foundation of the mind and the heart also rests on the invisible nothingness of the soul. The roots of all intimacy and belonging are planted powerfully in the invisible spirit. You belong ultimately to a presence that you cannot see, touch, grasp or measure. When you forget or repress the truth and depth of your invisible belonging and decide to belong to some system, person or project, you short-circuit your longing and squander your identity. To have true integrity, poise and courage is to be attuned to the silent and invisible nature within you. Real maturity is the integrity of inhabiting that 'immortal longing' that always calls you to new horizons. Your true longing is to belong to the eternal that echoes continually in everything that happens to you. Real power has nothing to do with force, control, status or money. Real power is the persistent courage to be at ease with the unsolved and the unfinished. To be able to recognize, in the scattered graffiti of your desires, the signature of the eternal. True prayer in the Holy Spirit keeps the graciousness and splendour of that vulnerability open.

Prayer and wonder: the art of real presence

 Prayer is the art of presence. Where there is no wonder there is little depth of presence. The sense of wonder is one of the key sources of prayer. Wonder at the adventure of being here is one of the special qualities of humans. Plato said, 'All thought begins in wonder.' Even our older sisters and brothers, the animals, often seem to be enthralled in silent wonder at creation. Sometimes in humans, profound wonder can only be expressed in silence. Perhaps the huge silence of the animal world is their expression of wonder at creation. It certainly seems that the excitement of being here often overcomes them. Animals at play express pure joy. When you see young foxes tussle and tumble with each other or a brace of lambs frisk and canter in the spring, you sense the innocent delight of the animal world. Animals often seem so contemplative in their presence. Often when one goes out to the mountains to herd cattle, one comes upon them grazing slowly on the tough mountain grass. They raise their heads and look lingeringly into the middle distance. That still gaze resembles the human gaze of wonder. At times they look at us not just with wonder but in amazement. How strange we must seem to them, so full of talk and trembling restlessness.

Wonder is a beautiful style of perception; when you wonder at something, your mind voyages deep into its possibility and nature. You linger among its presences. You do not take it for granted and are not deceived or blinded by its familiarity. The sense of wonder keeps experience fresh and original. It is lovely to see a relationship that even after years has still retained its wonder. When the person you love still causes you to wonder, you are still alive to their mystery. Wonder is the child of mystery. It calls your heart to thanks and praise.

WONDER AWAKENS US TO THE MAGIC OF THE WORLD

ONDER ENLARGES THE HEART. When you wonder, you are drawn out of yourself. The cage of the ego and the railtracks of purpose no longer hold you prisoner. Wonder creates a lyrical space where thought and feeling take leave of their repetitive patterns, to regain their original impulse of reverence before the mystery of what is. Such a tiny word, yet *is* confers the highest dignity and mystery. Most other words have such personal colour and promise. *Is* looks so tight; it is a little splinter of language. Yet the word *is* holds all reality and is the dividing line between existence and non-existence, truth and falsity. To say something *is* means that it has real presence, it is not a fantasy nor a mere notion. The greatest distance in the world is the distance between *is* and *is not*.

One has often had the experience of driving somewhere, your mind absorbed. The next thing you come over a hill and suddenly the wild ocean is there. When you leave the room on a frosty winter's night to go outside and find the dark heavens braided with starlight and the silent moon presiding over the sleeping fields and mountains; sometimes we abruptly wake up to the magic of things!

The Shawshank Redemption is a film about

friendship in a depressing prison setting. Every kind of brutality operates there. In that prison the sounds are sinister and the silence is eerie. One day a prisoner who is working in the library manages to get into the main office. He locks the door and puts on a piece of wonderful classical music, a duet from Mozart's *Marriage of Figaro*, and plays it over the loudspeaker into the prison yard. As if from the eternal spheres, like an invisible manna, this beautiful music falls onto all the haunted lives in this dreary place. All the prisoners stop, entranced, and listen. There is pure silence and stillness to receive the full visitation of the music. This is a moment of pure epiphany. The visit of the music is such a surprise. In the lovely shock of its beauty, the lost grandeur of creation is suddenly present. This is a moment of pure wonder in a black world.

Wonder never rests on the surface of a fact or situation. It voyages inwards to discover why something is the way it is. In this sense wonder kindles compassion and understanding. When you meet someone with a difficult or abrasive personality, you move away from them. If you begin to wonder what made them like that, you may become more open to the hidden story that has shaped their awkward presence.

Wonder invites mystery to come closer

he sense of wonder can also help you to recognize and appreciate the mystery of your own life. There is always a vitality and excitement about a person who has retained a sense of their own mystery. They have passion to explore and discover new aspects of themselves. Such a person is a living presence. It is deadening to be trapped in the company of someone who has a predictable and ready-made reaction to everything. Conversation is carefully framed and directed. Should you risk taking the conversation into uncharted areas, you draw a blank. It is as if a whole inner domain has been robbed of its natural resonance. One gets the same feeling from people who have explored their inner world and describe their identity in terms of whichever syndrome is in vogue at the moment. The words they use to describe their self-discoveries are all borrowed.

This jargon has no colour and no resonance of any mystery, opaqueness or possibility. Real wonder about your soul demands words which come from the more submerged inner thresholds where different forces meet. These words would be stamped with the unique signature of your presence. They would be imaginative and suggestive of the depths of the unknown within you. Unlike the fashionable graffiti of fast-food psychology, they hold the reverence to which mystery is entitled. Respect is a close companion of wonder.

Wonder, as the child of mystery, is a natural source of prayer. One of the most beautiful forms of prayer is the prayer of appreciation. This prayer arises out of the recognition of the gracious kindness of creation. We have been given so much. We could never have merited or earned it. When you appreciate all you are and all you have, you can then celebrate and enjoy it. You realize how fortunate you are. Providence is blessing you and inviting you to be generous with your gifts. You are able to bless life and give thanks to God. The prayer of appreciation has no agenda but gracious thanks. Nothing is given to you for yourself alone. When you receive some blessing or gift, you do it in the name of others; through you, they, too, will come to share in the kindness of providence.

You cannot step outside your life

HE UNKNOWN EVOKES WONDER. If you lose your sense of wonder, you lose the sacramental majesty of the world. Nature is no longer a presence, it is a thing. Your life becomes a dead cage of fact. The sense of the eternal recedes and time is reduced to routine. Yet the flow of our lives cannot be stopped. This is one of the amazing facts about being in the dance of life. There is no place to step outside. There is no neutral space in human life. There is no little cabin down at the bottom of the garden where the force and familiarity of life stop, and you can sit there in a space outside your life and yourself and look in on both. Once you are in life, it embraces you totally. This is most evident in the mystery of thinking. You cannot step outside your own thought. As Merleau Ponty says: 'There is no thought to embrace all thought.' Most of the time we are not even aware of how our thinking encircles everything. When we wake up to how our thoughts create our world, we become conscious of the ways in which we can be blind and limited. Yet even when we decide to be critical and objective towards our own thinking, thinking is still the instrument we use in the practice of this criticism. We live every moment of our lives within this relentless reflexivity. Even when we are tired and weary of the patterns of our own thinking, they still shape our vision and guide our actions.

ONDER at the unknown also calls forth prayer. The unknown is our closest companion; it walks beside us every step of our journey. The unknown is also the place where each of us has come from. From ancient times, prayer is one of the ways that humans have attempted to befriend the unknown. Prayer helps us to build an inner shelter here. Nature is the kind surface, the intimate face of a great unknown. It is uncanny to behold how boldly we walk upon the earth as if we are its owners. We strut along, deaf to the silence in the vast night of the unknown that lives below the ground. Above the slim band of air which forms the sky around our planet is the other endless night. Wonder makes the unknown interesting, attractive and miraculous. A sense of wonder helps awaken the hidden affinity and kinship which the unknown has with us. Ancient peoples were always conscious of the world underneath. Special sacred places could be doorways into that numinous region. Odysseus and Aeneas, the two mystical voyagers of classical antiquity, knew where to go in order to enter the world underneath. In Celtic mythology, this is where the *Tuatha de Dannan* secretly lived. They were residents at the

285

roots of the earth. They controlled all fertility and growth. Offerings and libations were regularly made to them. In ancient culture, nature always had an elemental divinity which demanded respect and reverence. While holding its reserve, the unknown revealed dimensions of its numinosity. Places can be numinous but so can people.

The Celtic art of approaching the unknown and nature

he Celtic tradition was powerfully aware of the numinous power of the unknown. It had refined rituals for approaching it. The Celts had no arrogance in relation to mystery. The people who mediated the unknown were called druids. They helped the people to understand that the elemental divinities were not anonymous or impersonal. The earth was a goddess and all the elemental forces took on personality. The druids offered gifts to the gods and the goddesses. They interceded for the people and initiated them into the rhythm of belonging which the Celtic deities required. The druids often worshipped in sacred groves. They are associated with sacred trees, especially the oak. They were also skilled in the art of interpreting the dreams of the people. They frequently undertook shamanic feats.

They were able to change into different shapes and they could enter smoothly into the air element and escape from all forces of gravity. They lit the sacred fires and watched to see how the flames would turn; in this way they were able to divine the future of the people. The Celtic world had a deep sense of the appropriateness of approach to the unknown. The lyricism and sacredness of the approach drew from the unknown the blessings which the people needed.

Nature is always wrapped in seamless prayer

 eltic wisdom was deeply aware that Nature had a mind and spirit of her own. Mountains have great souls full of memory. A mountain watches over a landscape and lures its mind towards the horizon. Streams and rivers never rest; they are relentless nomads who claim neither shape nor place. Stones and fields inhabit a Zen-like stillness and seem immune to all desire. Nature is always wrapped in seamless prayer. Unlike us, nature does not seem to suffer the separation or distance which thought brings. Nature never seems cut off from her own presence. She lives all the time in the embrace of her own unity. Perhaps, unknown to us, she sympathizes with our relentless dislocation and distraction. She certainly knows how to calm our turbulent minds when we trust ourselves into the silence and stillness of her embrace. Amongst Nature, we come to remember the wisdom of our own inner nature. Nature has not pushed herself out into exile. She remains there, always home in the same place. Nature stays in the womb of the Divine, of one pulse beat with the Divine Heart. This is why there is a great healing in the wild. When you go out into nature, you bring your clay body back to its native realm. A day in the mountains or by the ocean helps your body unclench. You recover your deeper rhythm. The tight agendas, tasks and worries fall away and you begin to realize the magnitude and magic of being here. In a wild place you are actually *in* the middle of the great prayer. In our distracted longing, we hunger to partake in the sublime Eucharist of nature.

Prayer: a clearance in the thicket of thought

N Prayer we come nearest to making a real clearance in the thicket of thought. Prayer takes thought to a place of stillness. Prayer slows the flow of the mind until we can begin to see with a new tranquillity. In this kind of thought, we become conscious of our divine belonging. We begin to sense the serenity of this clearing. We learn that regardless of the fragmentation and turbulence in so many regions of our lives, there is a place in the soul where the voices and prodding of the world never reach. It is almost like the image of the tree. The branches can sway and quiver in the wind, the bark can drum to the frenzy of rain and yet all the while at the core of the tree, there pertains the stillness of its anchorage. In prayer, thought returns to its origin in the infinite. Attuned to its origin, thought reaches below its own netting. In this way prayer liberates thought from the small rooms where fear and need confine it. Despite all the negative talk about God, the Divine still remains the one space where thought can become free. There we will be liberated from the repetitive echoes of our own smallness and blindness. Prayer sets our feet at large in the pastures of promise. When you pray, the eternal submerged melody in the clay of your heart rises from the silence to infuse with blessing your life and your friendships in the seen and the unseen world. Blessed be God who made us limited and gave us such longing! This is where prayer can heal thought. Prayer can make us aware of the clusters of presence which make up our secret companionship. Prayer is the path to the secret belonging at the heart of our other lives.

Prayer and the Voices of Longing

Prayer is the voice of longing; it reaches outwards and inwards to unearth our ancient belonging. Prayer is the bridge between longing and belonging. Longing is always at its most intense in the experience of vulnerability. There is a frightening vulnerability in being a human. Culture and society are utterly adept at masking this. Humans behave generally as if the world belongs to them. They exercise their roles with such seriousness. Life is guided by rules of action and power. Some people gain a certain control over our lives. We are very conscious of them and careful that they receive the necessary attention and affirmation. Sometimes you find yourself at civilized gatherings of those worthy ones; the conversation and behaviour observe such a careful pattern of mannered unreality that you have to work at stifling the surrealistic inner voice that wants to declare some wild absurdity to stop the games and offer some respect to the concealed vulnerability. When it is present in its raw form, in poverty or pain, we prefer to look the other way. The sight of extreme and unsheltered vulnerability makes us afraid that our good fortune too could turn. It also makes us feel guilty; we do so little for the abandoned and forgotten. Underneath all our poise and attempted control of life there is a gnawing sense of vulnerability.

Mystical prayer as a mosaic of presence

ecause we are so limited, it is difficult for us to understand who we are and what happens to us. No human can ever see anything fully. All we see are aspects of things. Being human is like being in a room of almost total darkness. The walls are deep and impenetrable; but there are crevices which let in the outside light. Each time you look out, all you see is a single angle or aspect of something. From within this continual dark you are unable to control or direct the things outside this room. You are utterly dependent on them to offer you different views of themselves. All you ever see are dimensions. This is why it is so difficult to be certain of anything. As the New Testament says: 'Now we see in a glass darkly, then we shall see face to face.'

Most of the time we are so rushed in our daily routine that we are not even aware of how limited our seeing actually is. In this century the Impressionist and Cubist painters attempted to paint what an object might look like if it were seen simultaneously from all perspectives. Picasso and

Kandinsky often take simple objects like guitars or animals and portray them in fascinating multiplicity of different visions. If you could only step back from your life and view it from different angles, you would gain a whole different sense of yourself. Aspects of you that may disappoint and sadden you from one perspective may be perfectly integrated in the image of you as seen from another angle. Sometimes things that really belong in your life don't seem to fit because the way you view them is too narrow. We see a good illustration of this in friendship. You have different friends. No two of your friends see you in exactly the same way. Each one brings a different part of your soul alive. Even though your friends all like you, they may not like each other at all. This is one of the sad and joyful things about a wake. Different friends have diverse stories of the departed. A funeral involves the creation, in a stricken community, of a narrative whose ending makes a beginning possible. All the stories are like different pieces that combine to build a mosaic of presence. All the stories go to make up the one story. This is like mystical prayer. This wholesome and inclusive seeing, where all the differences can be seen to belong together, is what mystical prayer brings. Mystical prayer brings you into the deepest intimacy with the Divine. Your soul receives the kiss of God. Such closeness has great beauty and frightening tenderness. Embraced in this belonging, all talk and theory of the Divine seem so pale and sound so distant.

Mystical prayer is never trapped. Most of our viewpoints are trapped like magnets to the same point on the surface. Mystical prayer teaches us a rhythm of seeing that is dynamic and free and full of hospitality. Far below and beyond the fear and limitation of the ego, mystical prayer teaches us to see with the wild eye of the soul. It sees the secret multiplicity of presences that are active at the edge of our normal field of vision. In this kind of prayer you will find what Paul Murray describes as:

 ground within you no-one has ever seen, a world beyond the limits of your dream's horizon.

PRAYER AS THE DOOR INTO YOUR OWN ETERNITY

HERE ARE NO WORDS FOR THE DEEPEST things. Words become feeble when mystery visits and prayer moves into silence. In post-modern culture, the ceaseless din of chatter has killed our acquaintance with silence. Consequently, we are stressed and anxious. Silence

293

is a fascinating presence. Silence is shy; it is patient and never draws attention to itself. Without the presence of silence, no word could be ever said or heard. Our thoughts constantly call up new words. We become so taken with words that we barely notice the silence. But the silence is always there. The best words are born in the fecund silence that minds the mystery. As Seamus Heaney writes in 'Clearances': 'Beyond silence listened for'. When the raft of prayer leaves the noisy streams of words and thoughts, it enters the still lake of silence. At this point, you become aware of the tranquillity that lives within you. Beneath your actions, gestures and thoughts there is a silent tranquillity. When you pray, you visit the kind innocence of your soul. This is a pure place of unity which the noise of life can never disturb. You enter the secret temple of your deepest belonging. Only in this temple can your hungriest longing find stillness and peace. This is summed up in the line from the Bible: 'Be still and know that I am God.' In stillness, the silence of the Divine becomes intimate.

On that day you will know as you are known

he shape of each soul is different. No-one else can ever get inside your world and experience first hand what it is like to be you. This is at once the mystery of individuality and its great loneliness. Those close to you can best sense and imagine what it is like to be you, but they can never feel, see or know your life from the inside. The deeper ground of individuality is to be sought in the originality of the Divine Imagination, manifest in the relish of beginnings. The Divine Artist is utterly creative, makes each thing new and different. Each individual expresses and incarnates a different dimension of divinity. Each one of us comes from a different place in the circle of the Divine. Consequently each one of us prays out of a different inner world and each one of us prays to a different place in the Divine circle. This is the place we left to come here. This is the empty nest in the Divine where the secrets of our origin, experience and destiny are stored. When we pray, we pray to that space in the Divine Presence which absolutely knows us. This could be what is suggested in that moment in the New Testament when the Lord says of our return to the invisible world: 'On that day you will know as you are known.'

All of our time here, we are on a constant threshold between the Divine and the human. The Divine knows us totally. We only know ourselves partially. When we return home this disproportion and blindness will be healed. Then our knowing will be equal to the Divine knowing of us. This recognition confers great permission on the individuality of prayer. You can only pray through the unique lens of your individuality. There is no need for you to be in any way guilty about your reluctance or inability to mimic the formal prayers of your religion or the pious prayer of others. If you listen to the deep voice of your heart, that voice is at one with the unique melody of your soul. Your deepest prayer is the prayer of your essence. When you move deeper into the inner world and enter the temple of your essence, your prayer will be of one pulse beat with the Divine Heart.

The soul is the home of memory

PRAYER helps us to belong more fully in our own lives. Ingeborg Bachmann said: 'It takes so long to learn to take your place in your own life.' The more we come to recognize the subtle adjacencies in our lives, the more easily they can enter our belonging. The more we recognize the neglected and unseen dimensions of our lives, the more enriched and balanced we become. It takes a lifetime's work to belong fully in your life. It is almost as if each event, encounter and experience is a pathway to be explored and lived. Then the wisdom of the soul harvests it and brings its treasures back in along that pathway until they belong to the deepest circle of your self. Each day we voyage outwards and at evening our souls bring home what we have suffered, learned and created. The soul is more ancient than consciousness and mind. Each day your soul weaves your life together. It weaves the opaque and ancient depth of you with the actual freshness of your present experience. The soul is the home of memory. When you pray, you enter that sanctuary where the repository of unlived and lived things opens to embrace the mystery of what you now live. You cannot break into this place inside you. All attempts to force entry will be circumvented by your wily soul. However, when you pray into your own depths, they might open for a moment to offer you a glimpse of the eternal artistry that is at work in you. This eternal longing is put beautifully by Fernando Pessoa:

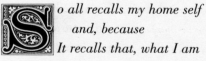 *o all recalls my home self*
and, because
It recalls that, what I am
aches in me.

Because prayer comes from such a deep space within you, it can afford you glimpses of yourself. Prayer satisfies the longing of the unknown to find you. It helps transfigure the barriers to your inner world. You come to discover that there is no distance between you and the deepest core of your being.

To breathe in your soul light

VEN though the body may kneel or words may be said or chanted, the heart of prayer activity is invisible. Prayer is an invisible world. Normally, when we look at something, we see it empirically. We notice its shape, colour and limits. In prayer we see with the eye of the soul. We see in a creative and healing way. A lovely way to pray is to engage this light of the invisible world. Because the body is in the soul, all around your body there is an embrace of subtle soul light. When you pray with your breath, you breathe this soul light into the deepest recesses of your clay body. When you feel isolated or empty or lonesome, it is so nourishing to draw the eternal shelter of soul light deep into you. This helps to heal you and returns you to inner tranquillity. When you come in to a rhythm of breathing, you go deeper than the incisions of thought and feeling which separate you. This prayer restores your belonging at the hearth of divinity, a belonging from which no thought or act can ever finally exile you.

Praise is like morning sun on a flower

he Bible respects and extols particularly the prayer of praise. It is interesting to ask why the prayer of praise is honoured. Perhaps the reason is to be discovered in a consideration of the nature of praise. There is a lovely saying in Irish: '*Mol an óige agus tiocfaidh sí*', i.e. praise youth and it will blossom. Praise issues from recognition and generosity.

It has nothing to do with the politics and manipulation of flattery. Praise is truthful affirmation. God has no need of your praise. Yet the act of praising draws you way outside the frontiers of your smallness. To praise awakens the more generous side of your heart. It draws out the nobility, the *Úaisleacht*, in you. When the soul praises, the life enlarges. We know as individuals how encouraging praise can be. It is like watching nature on a spring morning. At first the flowers are all closed and withdrawn. Then, ever so gradually, as the rays of the sun coax them, they open out their hearts to praise the light. The diminishing of praise is an acute poverty in post-modern culture. With the swell of consumerism and technology and the demise of religion, we are losing our ability to praise. We replace praise with banal satisfaction. The absence of praise reduces culture to a flat monoscape; the magic of its creative and imaginative curvature gets lost. A culture that cannot praise the Divine becomes a bare, cold place. The demise of religious and spiritual practice has contributed hugely to this flattening.

One can understand how a culture that has come of age can find little shelter or resonance in the way many of the rituals of institutional religion are practised. Increasing numbers of people stay away. Others attempt to develop their own rituals. The difficulty here is that a deeply resonant ritual emerges over years, out of the rhythms of longing and belonging in a community. Great ritual creates an imaginative and symbolic frame which can awaken the numinous otherness, the tenderness and the danger of the Divine. It is a subtle and infinitely penetrating form. Scattered, isolated individuals cannot invent ritual. Consumerism has stolen the sacred ritual structures of religion and uses them incisively in its liturgies of advertising and marketing. Meanwhile the post-modern soul becomes poorer and falls even further from the embrace and practice of sacred belonging. The great thing about a community at prayer is that your prayer helps mine – as mine helps yours. This makes no consumerist sense but it is one of the most vivid enhancements of Being available to us. Individualism of the raw competitive kind is ignorant of this dimension.

Prayer changes space

NOTHER beautiful thing about prayer is the way it changes space. Physical space is full of distance. It is distance that separates people and things. Even between two people who love each other and live with each other, the short distance between their bodies is the colossal distance between two different worlds. The magical thing about prayer is that it creates spiritual space. This alters physical distance. In spiritual space there is no distance. A prayer offered for someone in New Zealand reaches them as swiftly as the prayer offered for someone right beside you. Prayer suffuses distance and changes it. Prayer carries the cry of the heart innocently and immediately over great and vast distances. William Stafford evokes this in his poem 'An Afternoon in the Stacks'. He describes the aftermath of reading a book. The act of reading becomes a wild symbiosis of the reader's longing and the wise configuration of words. Stafford knows that the reverberation of this intimacy will continue: 'the rumour of it will haunt all that follows in my life/A candle flame in Tibet leans when I move.' In spiritual space, the trail of intimacy can traverse any distance and still retain the intensity and belonging.

Graced Vision Sees Between Things

PRAYER REVEALS A HIDDEN WORLD. THE WAY we see things is heavily conditioned. The eye always moves to the object. In a landscape, the eye is drawn at once to a stone, a tree, a field, a wave or a face. The eye has great affection for things. Only infants or adults lost in thought gaze lingeringly into the middle distance. These are moments when we literally look at nothing. This perennially neglected nothing is precious space because it provides the medium and the trail of connection between all the separate, different things and persons. Anish Kapoor, reflecting on his fascinating exhibition at the Hayward Gallery, says: 'The void is not silent. I have always thought of it more and more as a transitional space, an in-between space. It's very much to do with time. I have always been interested as an artist in how one can somehow *look* again for that *very first moment* of creativity where everything is possible and nothing has actually happened. It's a space of becoming . . .' This middle distance is not empty; it is a vital but invisible bridge between things. Distance is necessary to sight: bring a thing too close and it blurs to invisibility. If our vision were graced and we could really see between things, we could be surprised at the secret veins of connection which join all that is

302

separate in the one embrace. We are a family of the one presence. This is the concealed belonging which prayer helps to unveil.

It is so important that prayer happens in the world, every day and every night. It is consoling to remember that there are old and feeble nuns in forgotten convents who live out their days by creating little boats of prayer to ferry nourishment to a hungry world. There are also monks in monasteries in cities and in lonesome mountains whose wonderful chorus of prayer keeps life civilized and somehow still balanced. In our precarious and darkening world, we would have destroyed everything long ago were it not for the light and shelter of prayer. Prayer is the presence that holds harmony in the midst of chaos. Every time you pray, you add to the light and harmony of creation. If you do not pray, if you do not believe in prayer, then you are living off the prayers of other people. Each day when we wake and each night when we gather ourselves in sleep, we should gently send the light of prayer from our hearts. It is important that some light of prayer emanates from each individual. Prayer is the most beautiful poem of longing. Martin Buber said: 'Prayer is not in time but time is in prayer.' Prayer is eternity and, therefore, time inhabits prayer.

'Behold, I am the Ground of thy Beseeching'

RAYER is a light that once lit will never fail. All prayer opens the Divine Presence. When you sit in prayer, the purest force of your own longing comes alive. Julian of Norwich has a wonderful poetic insight into prayer as longing. The Lord whispers to her: 'Behold, I am the Ground of thy Beseeching.' In other words, your longing for God is not a thrust through empty distance towards a removed God. The actual longing for God is not a human invention; rather it is put there by God. The longing for God is already the very presence of God. Our longing for God brings the kiss of the Divine to the human soul. Prayer is the deepest and most tender intimacy. In prayer the forgiving tenderness of God gathers around our lives. God infects us with the desire for God.

You can pray any time and anywhere. You do not have to travel to some renowned spiritual guide to learn how to pray. You do not need to embark on a fifty-five-step spiritual path until you learn how to say a proper, super prayer. You do not have to sort out your life so that you can be real with God. You do not have to become a fundamentalist, and hammer away your most interesting contradictions

304

and complexities, before you can truly pray. You need no massive preamble before prayer. You can pray now, where you are and from whatever state of heart you are in. This is the most simple and honest prayer. Many of our prayer preparations only manage to distract and distance us from the Divine Presence. We always seem to be able to find the most worthy of reasons for not just being quite ready to pray yet; this means that we never get to prayer. Prayer is so vital and transforming that the crucial thing is to pray now. Regardless of what situation you are in, your heart is always ready to whisper a prayer. We are always in the Divine Presence, every second, everywhere. In prayer the Divine Presence becomes an explicit companionship that warms, challenges and shelters us. We do not have to skate over vast, frozen lakes of pious language to reach the shore of the Divine. God is not so deadeningly serious. We need to be gentle and smile, as Hopkins so beautifully writes: 'My own heart let me more have pity on; let/Me live to my sad self hereafter kind.' God is wild and must also have a subtle sense of irony. In the lyrical unfolding of our days, we remain in the Presence. The simplest whisper of the heart is already within the Divine Embrace.

The Celtic tradition always had a very refined sense of the protective closeness of God. Prayers like this: 'No anxiety can be ours, the God of the

Elements, the King of the Elements, the Spirit of the Elements closes over us eternally.' There was no distance between the individual and God. There was no need to travel any further than the grace of your longing in order to come into the Divine Presence. The Celtic imagination enfolded the prayer of nature into the heart of their conception of God. It is the God of sun, moon, stars, mountains and rivers. The earth is the ever-changing theatre of Divine Presence. God has a dwelling in the earth and the ocean. He inspires all things, he quickens all things, he supports all things and creates all things. Celtic spirituality is imbued with a powerful fluency of longing and a lovely flexibility of belonging. It is the exact opposite of fundamentalism.

Prayer is critical vigilance

PRAYER is the liberation of God from our images of God. It is the purest contact with the wildness of the Divine Imagination. Real prayer has a vigilance that is constantly watching and deconstructing the human tendency towards idolatry. Despite our best sincerity, we still long to control and domesticate the Divine. Meister Eckhart says that the closer we come to God, the more it ceases to be God. He says God '*entwird*', i.e. God un-becomes. In other words,

God is only our name for it. Elsewhere he writes: 'Therefore, I pray to God that he may make me free of "God", for my real being is above God if we take "God" to be the beginning of created things.' Idolatry is the worship of a dead God. It is ironic that every human needs some God on the inner altar of the heart. We cannot live without some deity, whether it is Jesus, the Trinity, Allah, Mohamed or the Buddha. The deity could also be money, power, greed, addiction or status. The critical vigilance of real prayer endeavours to ensure that it is the flame of the living God that burns on the altar of our hearts. Such prayer longs for the real warmth of divine belonging. Real prayer helps you to live in the beauty of truth. It is a visitation from outside the frontier of your own limitation. The great Irish poet Seán O'Ríordán says: '*Níl aon bhlas ag duine ar a bhlas féin*', i.e. no-one can taste his own tasting. Though you are the closest and nearest person in the world to yourself, you cannot taste your own essence. When it comes to truly enfolding yourself you remain a stranger. Only in the embrace of prayer are you able to unfold and enfold yourself in truth, affection and tenderness.

A generous heart is never lonesome

t is important to pray for those who are given into our care in the world. Each person walks a unique pathway through the world. You have your own work, gifts, difficulties and commitments. In order to take your place and contribute to the light of the world, you need to honour all these different dimensions of your life. Adjacent to all your activity in the world, there is also present in your life a small group of people who are directly in your care. They are usually family and some intimate friends who come to dwell at the centre of your life. These people are sent to you with gifts and challenges. In turn you have a duty to look out for them. These people are in your soul-care. When someone is really close to you, you are in each other's soul-care. Because of the calling of your own life, you cannot be continually there. Yet in the affection of prayer, you can carry the icons of their presence on the altar of your heart. Often unknown to the world, you secretly carry these friends in your heart and from heart to heart you bless, mind and care for each other. In the Celtic tradition it was always recognized that if you sent blessings out from your heart, they multiplied and returned again to bless your own life. A generous heart is never lonesome. A generous heart has luck. The lonesomeness of contemporary life is partly due to the failure of generosity. Increasingly we compete with each other for goods, image and status. The one can only ascend if the other is put down; there is only so much room on the pedestal. The old class system may have largely vanished but our new system has a more subtle but equally lethal need for hierarchy. We forget that competition is false. An old rule in thought is that you can only compare like with like. No two individuals in the world are alike. Consequently, it is false to compare people and continue to foster such destructive ideology of competitiveness. We damage the sanctuary of each other's presence by building such false standards of comparison and competition. We have been seduced by competitiveness. And so easily. Because of the bogus certainties it supplies.

The beauty of the prayer gift

t is a wonderful gift when a person prays for you. One of the greatest shelters in your life is the circle of invisible prayer that is gathered around you by your friends here and in the unseen world. When you are going through difficult times or marooned on some lonesome edge in your life, it is often the prayers of your friends that bring you through. When your soul turns into a wilderness, it is the prayers of others that bring you back to the hearth of warmth. I know people who have been very ill, forsaken and damaged; the holy travellers that we call prayers have reached out to them and returned them to healing. The prayer of healing has wisdom, discernment and power. It is unknown what prayer can actually achieve. When you meet someone at the level of prayer, you meet them on the ground of eternity. This is the heart of all kinship and affinity. When you journey in there to meet someone, a great intimacy can awaken between you. I imagine that the dead who live in the unseen world never forget us; they are always praying for us. Perhaps this is one of the ways that they remain close to our hearts; they extend the light and warmth of prayer towards us. Prayer is the activity of the invisible world, yet its effect is actual and powerful. It is said that if you pray beside a flower it grows faster. When you bring the presence of prayer to the things you do, you do them more beautifully.

To frame each frontier of the day with prayer

 fter the absolution of night, the dawn is a new beginning. All the mystical traditions have recognized that the dawn is a special time. They all have had rituals of prayer for beginning the day. They do not greet the day with worry or the anxiousness of how many items are on the agenda before twelve. They literally take time to welcome the new day. Acknowledging the brevity of our time on earth, they recognize the huge, con-cealed potential of a day for soul-making. This space to recognize each unique day invests the day with a sense of the eternal. The monastic tradition blesses this beginning with prayer. As children we were taught to say the 'morning offering' prayer. Though quite traditional, this was an admirable prayer of care for the new day. It would be lovely, in the morning, if you could give thanks for the gift of the new day, and recognize its promise and possibility, and, at evening, gather the difficulties and blessings of the lived day within a circle of prayer. It would intensify and refine your presence in the world if you came into a rhythm of framing your days with prayer.

A wonderful teacher and inspiration in the West of Ireland has, as a motto for his school, the axiom: 'The mind altering alters all.' This is a powerful dictum to have as central to the vision of a school. The mind is the eye of the world. When the mind changes, the world is different. In a transferred sense, the prayerful presence transfigures every-thing. We will never understand the power of our prayer to effect change and to bring shelter to others. We should pray also for those who suffer each day: those in prison, hospital, mental institutions, refugees, prostitutes, the powerful, the destroyers. There are so many broken places where our prayer is needed each day. We should be generous with our prayer. It is important to recognize the extent and intensity of spirit that prayer awakens and sends out. Prayer is not about the private project of making yourself holy and turning yourself into a shining temple that blinds everyone else. Prayer has a deeper priority which is, in the old language, the sanctification of the world of which you are a privileged inhabitant. By being here you are already a custodian of sacred places and spaces. If you could but see what your prayer could do, you would always want to be in the presence that it awakens. There is a poem by Fernando Pessoa which articulates this:

To be great, be entire

o be great, be entire:
   Of what is yours nothing
   exaggerate or exclude
Be whole in each thing. Put all that
   you are
Into the least you do
Like that on each place the whole moon
Shines for she lives aloft.

312

This is a beautiful prayer poem; to put all that you are into the least that you do. When you hold back, you avoid the truth of situations, you diminish what a friendship or an experience can become. There are many people who love and belong with each other but their disappointment with one another, or the wounds they have caused, holds them out of reach from each other. Wouldn't it be great if they could risk again coming in on a wave of new hope to the shore of each other's lives? The greatest gift you can give is the gift of your self; it is a huge gift. The sun is the mother of life. She gives her light so generously and evenly all over the earth. Like the sun each one of us should share the light of our souls with generosity.

To create your own prayer that speaks your soul

O pray is to develop and refine the light of your life. It smooths the coarseness in your vision. It brings you closer to the homeland of your heart. There are many wonderful ancient and classical prayers from the tradition. Yet there is something irrevocably unique and intimate about your own individual prayer. It would be wonderful to create your own prayer. Give yourself time to make a prayer that will become the prayer of your soul. Listen to the voices of longing in your soul. Listen to your hungers. Give attention to the unexpected that lives around the rim of your life. Listen to your memory and to the inrush of your future, to the voices of those near you and those you have lost. Out of all of that attention to your soul, make a prayer that is big enough for your wild soul; tender enough for your shy and awkward vulnerability; that has enough healing to gain the ointment of divine forgiveness for your wounds; enough truth and vigour to challenge your blindness and complacency; enough graciousness and vision to mirror your immortal beauty. Write a prayer that is worthy of the destiny to which you have been called. This is not about any kind of self-absorbed narcissism. It is about honouring the call of your soul and the call of eternity in you. Take as much time as you need to find the shape of the prayer that is appropriate to your essence. It might take a month or a year. When you have it shaped, memorize it. When you have it learned off by heart, you will always carry this gracious prayer around the world with you. Gradually it will grow into a mantra companion. It will be the call of your essence, opening you up to new areas of birth; it will bring the wild and tender light of your heart to every object, place and person that you will meet.

chapter 6

Absence Where Longing Still Lingers

The subtle trail of absence

EVERYONE WHO LEAVES YOUR LIFE OPENS a subtle trail of loss that still connects you with them. When you think of them, miss them and want to be with them, your heart journeys out along that trail to where they now are. There are whole regions of absence in every life. Losing a friend is the most frequent experience of absence. When you open yourself to friendship, you create a unique and warm space between you. The tone and shape of this space is something you share with no-one else. Your friend struck a note in the chamber of your heart that no-one else could reach. The departure of the friend leaves this space sore with loss, some innocence within you is unwilling or unable to accept that one you gathered so close is now gone. It is the longing for the departed friend that makes the absence acute. Absence haunts you and makes your belonging sore. Absence is never clear cut; it reveals the pathos of human being. Physically each person is a singular, limited object. However, considered affectively, there are myriad pathways reaching outwards and inwards from your heart. The true nature of individuality is not that of an isolated identity: it is this active kinship with the earth and with other humans. When distance or separation opens, this connection is not voided – rather, the departed friend is now present in a different way. They are no longer near physically, in touch, voice or presence. But the sore longing of their absence somehow still keeps them spiritually near. Longing holds pathways open to the departed; it does not erase people. Absence is one of the loneliest forms of longing and when you feel the absence of someone, you still belong with them in some secret way. There is a subtle psychic arithmetic in the world of belonging.

Absence and presence are sisters

he ebb and flow of presence is a current that runs through the whole of life. It seems that absence is impossible without presence. Absence is a sister of presence. The opposite of presence is not absence but vacancy; where there is absence there is still energy, engagement and longing. Vacancy is neutral and indifferent space. It is a space without energy. It remains blank and inane, untextured by any ripple of longing or desire.

By contrast absence is vital and alert. The word absent has its roots in Latin *'ab–esse'* which means to be elsewhere. To be away from a person or a place. Whatever or whoever is absent has departed from somewhere they belong. Yet their distance is not indifferent to the place or the person they have left. Though now elsewhere, they are still missed, desired and longed for. Absence seems to hold the echo of some fractured intimacy.

And the earth knew absence

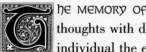he memory of the earth shrouds our thoughts with depth and mystery. In each individual the earth breaks its silence. In human gesture its primal stillness becomes fluent. Because we are so driven by thought we often forget our origin. We are seldom sensitive and patient enough to recognize in the mirror of thought the shadow of clay. The mind echoed back the earth's deepest dreams and longing, yet its original break

from the earth must remain the earth's deepest experience of absence and loss. In us the earth experiences absence. Certain moments in nature seem to crystallize this loneliness. Often at night, when you hear the wind mourning around the house, it seems to be an elegy for us, its vanished children. Among animals the experience of loss often comes to poignant expression. When the calves were weaned from the cows on our farm, they would cry all night: the long wail of grief for their lost calves. Nature is elemental longing. The ancient stories of a culture frequently offer insights into absence and how it crosses all boundaries between the elements, the animal and the human.

The legend of Midhir and Etain

 NE of the most beautiful stories in the Irish tradition on the theme of the ebb and flow of presence and absence is the story of Midhir and Etain. The fairy prince Midhir fell in love with Etain. His wife Fuamnach was furious and with the help of a druid changed Etain into a butterfly and raised a storm that buffeted the butterfly for seven years up and down the country. One day, a gust of wind blew her into the palace of Aengus the god of love. Even in butterfly form he recognized her but he was not able to remove the

318

spell. But she did manage to change into a woman from dusk until dawn. He had a garden with the most beautiful flowers and he put invisible walls around her so that she could enjoy the garden. But Fuamnach found out and sent a storm that buffeted Etain around the country again. Meanwhile, Midhir was not able to bear her absence. He searched every corner of the land for her. One day she was blown in through the window of the king's palace. She fell into a goblet of wine that the queen was drinking. After nine months she was born again as the king's daughter and named Etain again. She grew up to be a very beautiful woman and the high king took her for his wife. Midhir came to the great assembly at Tara and recognized her again, but she did not remember him. Beating the high king at a game of chess, all he asked was that he would receive one kiss from Etain. After meeting Midhir, Etain began to dream of her former life. Little by little, she began to recall all she had forgotten and she pined and fretted for Midhir. On the evening that he was to return for the kiss, Tara was armed against him like a forest of steel. Magically, he appeared in the midst of the banqueting hall and he embraced Etain. The alarm was raised. The king and his army rushed out after him but there was no sign of them in front of the castle. They all looked up to see two white swans circling in the starry sky over the palace.

The structure of this story is fascinating in what it reveals about the longing that lingers so potently at the heart of absence. When they fall in love, they create a unique space with each other, a special echo in each other's hearts. The intensity of this claim on each other sets the whole direction of the story from this point on. Once she is changed into a butterfly and driven away, Midhir is haunted by her absence. His life becomes one long search for her who awakened his heart and then vanished. Her metamorphosis as a new child of the king erases her memory of him. But the longing at the heart of the absence he feels, ensures that his power of recognition stays alert and patient. He finds her in a totally unexpected place and in the most extreme form of otherness, namely, in the form of a completely different person. Yet he still recognizes her. After the initial encounter, her former life begins to return in dream. This becomes an intense and exclusive longing. Transformed finally into swan shape, they are now united as graceful artists of the air; the sweet irony here is that this was precisely the element which had so tortured Etain and insured her demented absence and separation from her lover. Now it is the element of their escape and unification.

The longing for real presence

he deeper the intimacy and belonging, the more acute the sense of absence will be. It seems that real intimacy brings us in out of the bleakness of exile. Intimacy is belonging. We come in out of the distance and grow warm at the hearth of the friend's soul. Now there are places within us that are no longer simply our own. Rather they are inhabited with the taste and colour of the friend's presence. When the friend departs, the inner house of belonging falls to ruins; this is why absence holds such acute presence and poignance. True belonging alters and recreates your identity. When that belonging is fractured or lost, something of our deepest self departs. To open yourself is to risk losing yourself. Emily Dickinson says:

bsence disembodies
so does Death
hiding individuals from the
Earth.

Absence hides the one you love. You desire to be with the beloved, to see her, hear her, rest in her presence. But she is hidden from your eyes though not hidden from your heart. Letters and photographs are no longer objects of joy to raise your heart; now they are filled with pathos. You find yourself in places you were together and your heart is seared with absence.

We are vulnerable to absence because we so deeply desire presence. Some writer, referring to another, said: 'He has quite a delightful presence but a perfect absence.' Obviously, happiness increased when the other was absent! The mind separates us, makes us absent from the earth. The privilege of the mind is its capacity for presence. There seems to be nothing else in nature that can focus in such conscious presence. The deepest longing of the mind is for real presence. Real presence is the ideal of truth, love and communication. Real presence is the ideal of prayer here and the beatific vision in the hereafter. Somewhere deep in the soul, our longing knows that we break through to the eternal when we are gathered in the shelter of presence. There are the moments of our deepest belonging. For a while the restlessness and hunger within the heart grows still. The sense of being an outsider, a stranger here, ceases. For a while we are home. This is such a satisfying and refreshing experience; it nourishes us to the roots.

Yet the experience of presence always remains fleeting and temporary. Not often do hunger, readiness and grace conspire to bring our souls home; and when they do the visit is inevitably short. The mind and time are doomed to move relentlessly onwards. All we achieve is the glimpse, the taste; we are not allowed to linger. We plunge forth again into the ever diverse fields of new experience. Presence becomes broken, scattered and fragmentary. We endeavour to be real. Yet so much of our presence is diminished by our role and its functions. Behind our many intricate and necessary social masks, we often secretly wonder who we are and daydream of letting everything derivative and second hand fall away and living the life we love. We dream of leaving the daily round where absence rather than presence seems to control and determine things. Most of our social world is governed by a sophisticated and subtle grammar of absence. In post-modern culture we tend increasingly to inhabit virtual reality rather than actual reality. More and more time is spent in the shadowlands of the computer world. The computer world is all foreground but has no background. There are many people who have to earn their living in the world of function. Imagine someone in a factory assembly line who has to hit the same bolt every twenty seconds for the rest of their working life. You could not stay present in that kind of work unless you were a saint or a Zen mystic. In your heart, you would have to be elsewhere. This work makes you absent. This is the absence that Karl Marx referred to as alienation.

Much of modern life is lived in the territory of externality; if we succumb completely to the external, we will lose all sense of inner and personal presence. We will become the ultimate harvesters of absence, namely, ghosts in our own lives.

Che homeless mind

IN POST-MODERN CULTURE the human mind seems particularly homeless. The traditional shelters no longer offer any shelter. Religion often seems discredited. Its language and authority structures seem to speak in the idiom of the distant past and seem powerless to converse with our modern hunger. Politics seems devoid of vision and is becoming more and more synonymous with economics. Consumerist culture worships accumulation and power; it establishes its own gaudy hierarchies. In admiring the achievement and velocity of these tiger economies, we refuse to notice the paw marks of its ravages and the unglamorous remains of its prey. All these factors contribute to the dissolution of real presence. The homeless mind is haunted by a sense of absence that it can neither understand nor transfigure. Indeed, in its desperation it endeavours to fill every moment with some kind of forced presence. Our poor times suffer from unprecedented visual aggression and cacophony.

There is a great story about the loss of belonging in Gershon Scholem's book on the *Major Trends in Jewish Mysticism*. In the eighteenth century, there arose in Eastern Europe a remarkable mystical movement called Hasidism. Its founder was known as the Baal Shem Tov, and he was a religious genius and pioneer. One day, a calamity threatened the community in which he lived, and so he called his chief disciple and said, 'Come, let us go out into the woods.' They went to a certain special spot that the master seemed to know about, and he built a particular kind of fire and offered a prayer. He said, 'Oh, God, Thy people are in dire need. Please help us in this moment of distress.' Then to his disciple he said, 'It is all right now. Everything will be all right.' They went back and found that, indeed, the calamity which had been impending somehow had been averted. The master died and in the next generation, this disciple became the leader of the same group. And in his day, another major disaster threatened to wipe out the community. Now, he took his chief disciple and they set out for the woods, but he had forgotten just where the exact place was, though he did remember how to light the fire. So he said, 'Oh, God, I don't know where the place is, but you are everywhere, so let me light the fire here. Your people need you, calamity threatens. Please, help.' After the prayer he turned to his disciple and

said, 'It is all right now.' And when they returned
to the town, they were greeted with the joyful news
that the threat had been removed. Well then, that
disciple became the master in the next generation
and, once again, some catastrophe was imminent.
This time he went out with his disciple. He no
longer knew the place, and he had forgotten how to
make the fire, but he still knew the prayer and he
said, 'God, I don't know this place very well but you
are everywhere. I don't know how to make the fire
but all the elements are in your hands. Your people
need you. We ask for your help.' Then he turned to
his disciple and said, 'Now it is all right. We may go
back.' They went back and everything indeed was
all right. The story concludes by stating that today,
we don't know the place, we no longer know how to
make the fire, we don't even know how to pray. So
all we can do is to tell the story, and hope that somehow the telling of the story itself will help us in this
hour of need.

Psychology and self-absence: talking ourselves out

 UR culture is fragmented; the old
shelters are gone and around us there is
the severe cold breeze of isolation. This
has made our desire for belonging all the more

intense. We search continually for connection. Today many people find this in therapy and psychology. If you find a wise guide to lead you on the inner quest, you are a fortunate person. It is dangerous to open your self to another in such a total way. Opening your soul to an unworthy guide can have negative consequences. When you really tell how and who you are, you offer your listener a key to the temple of your life. You allow them a huge voice in your conversation with yourself. Listening is such an underrated activity. In fact it is hugely subversive. Because when we listen deeply, we take in the voice of the other. The inner world is so tender and personal and the voices that really enter assume great power.

I like to think of psychology as soul searching: you search your soul and you also search for your soul; and, of course, on the quest your soul is searching with you. The journey has diverse paths and different voices surface suggesting a real adventure and the possibility of awakening and healing. Good soul searching refines and heals your presence. It helps you to belong more honestly to yourself. If you are driven by needs and inner forces of which you are unaware, then your behaviour and actions are not free; you only partly belong to yourself. To bring these subtle forces into the light helps change their negative control over you. The magic of psychology is how powerfully it underlines the effect that awareness can have. When you come to know yourself, you come home to yourself and your life flows more naturally. As you become more integrated, your integrity deepens. You inhabit the heart of your life; you become the real subject of your life rather than being its target or victim. I remember when the wall came down in Germany meeting a friend who had been in Berlin that week. She said, '*Man erlebt sich als reines Subjekt*', i.e. in Berlin these days you experience your self as pure subject. This was a statement of the immense personal power of feeling, thinking and seeing that is in each of us. When the run of life and possibility is with you, you feel as if you are riding a wave of energy. Unfortunately, much of the time we are not gathered in the grace of such inner fluency. More often than not we are split asunder within, one part fighting against the other. To learn the art of being the subject of your own life and experience enlarges your spirit. It would be great as we grow older to become more free and fluent. You often see old people who have grown into this grace. Though their bodies are old, their presence is as majestic and swift as a ballet dancer. They have somehow entered the mystery of true unity. They are at one with themselves. It is interesting to hyphenate the religious ideal as at-one-ment. This unity is the heart of all belonging; without this hidden unity of everything, no belonging would be possible. The unity is also the secret Elsewhere that now holds the presence of those who have vanished from our lives; it ensures that absence is not vacancy.

Good soul searching helps you to sift the past. Often you only begin when you find yourself in crisis. The word crisis comes from the Greek word *krinein* and means 'to sift'. When you take time to search your soul and its past you will know more clearly what belongs to you and what does not. When you sift your soul, you are better able to identify the host of various longings which you carry. When you listen to your longings coming to voice, you can discern which horizons they have in mind. You understand that to pursue certain longings would probably destroy you. Certain voices would love to seduce you. It is interesting that at the source of the Christian tradition, in the Genesis story, the future of creation is determined by longing. The desire to eat of the fruit of the tree of good and evil caused the rupture in creation. When Adam followed his longing, its immediate effect was the loss of the ideal belonging of Paradise. In Christian mythic terms, the perennial tension between longing and belonging is to be traced back to this fracture. Expelled from the harmony of Paradise, our belonging will always be fractured and temporary. Our longing will be permanent and full. Towering over the Greek tradition is the longing of the wanderer to return home. The huge longing of Odysseus is going in the other direction. He is already an exile, he wants to return to the belonging of his home and homeland. The true search for soul brings longing and belonging into a creative tension of harmony. Mediocre therapy could haunt your soul with absence by reducing each inner presence to a function.

Brittle language numbs longing

 t is a testimony to the relevance of a science when it finds its way into the heart of a culture. In this crossing, the science is often vulgarized. Contemporary culture is riddled with psychologese. So many people speak of themselves now in the brittle clarity of disembodied psychological terms. One such powerful term is 'process': 'I am looking at my own process', or 'let us try and process that for a while'. In many cases 'processing' has become a disease; it is now the way in which many people behave towards themselves. This term has no depth or sacredness. Processing is a mechanical term: there are processed peas and beans. The tyranny of processing reveals a gaping absence of soul. The only wisdom now required is managing to get the right emotional components and complexes onto the appropriate assembly line, so that they can go through the solidifiers and emerge in the correct packaging and can be 'dealt' with. A 'deal' is a business or contractual arrangement; it is also an experience that cards have, especially in casinos. When you hear someone say: 'I am having to "deal" with this feeling right now', you may wonder if the emotion has been secretly absent for a while doing a crash course in Wall Street and is now forcing its 'owner' into an unexpected corner. Such terminology is blasphemous; it belongs to the mechanical world. When you use psychologese on your inner life, it 'formats' your holy wildness. You become an inner developer, turning the penumbral meadows of the heart into a concrete grid. No wonder the tone of the modern soul sounds like the prison language of a ghetto. Such brittle, cold language numbs your longing and unravels the nuance and texture of your presence; it can turn you into a ghost in your own life, a custodian of absence, a grey visitor of vacancy.

The obsession with such turgid analysis betrays how suspicious we have become of our own experience. We treat our experience, not as the sacramental theatre of our numinous lives, but rather as if it did not belong to us at all or as if it were merely public property. Unless you trust your experience and let it happen, you cannot be present to yourself or anything else in a natural way. When you lose this hospitality to yourself, there is no longer any welcome for the surprise and wonder of new things. Your experience becomes poor and, ironically, the poorer it gets, the more obsessive is the desire to analyse it to bits. When your experience is rich and diverse, it has a beautifully intricate inner weaving. You know that no analysis can hold a candle to the natural majesty and depth of even the most ordinary moment in the universe. Every moment holds a gallery of sacred forms. Soul searching is the activity of respectful and critical wonder at the drama of your biography. As with any worthy story, it has its own inner destiny and form independent of its author. When you keep scraping at your soul, you damage your very ability to experience anything. If you loot your sensibility, you have nothing to open the door to welcome the world.

Beyond being an observer – becoming a participant

When you become an interfering observer in your own life, you cease to be a living participant. Much modern therapy trains people to be rigid observers of themselves. They never sleep on the job. Like heroic cowboys, they manage to sleep with one eye open. It is, then, extremely difficult to let yourself become a whole-hearted participant in your one beautiful, unrepeatable life. You are taught to police yourself. When you watch a policeman walk down a street, he does it differently. He is alert, his eyes are combing everything. He does not miss anything. When you police yourself, you are on the beat alone, you are so alert that the usual inner suspects inevitably surface and suddenly you are in your element, you can exercise your full authority. You will put them through the full process: identification, arrest and conviction. You know how to 'deal' with them. Such an approach to the self highlights the modern reduction of the 'who' question to the functionalism of the 'how'. We need a new psychology to encourage us and liberate us to become full participants in our lives; one that will replace self-watch with self-awakening. We need a rebirth of the self as the sacred temple of mystery and possibility; this demands a new language which is poetic, mystical and impervious to the radiation of psychologese. We need to rediscover the wise graciousness of spontaneity. The absence of spontaneity unleashes us negatively on ourselves.

Certain cultures practise wholesome spontaneity, others are somewhat more rigid and considered in their behaviour. An Irish friend lived in Berlin for a while in the Eighties; at this time punk culture was still strong. One day, he was walking down a street and there were two disciples of punk ahead of him. Each had an architecture of hair that must have taken months to perfect, a series of unbelievable shapes and colours. He walked faster and reached the pedestrian light first. It was still on red; he looked up and down the street, there was no traffic coming. Having a functional rather than sacred attitude to such objects, he crossed the street on red and continued along the other side. He looked over his shoulder to see how far behind him the punks were now. But he could not see them. When he looked further back, he saw that they were still waiting on the other side for the green light. It struck him that the programming had penetrated far below the hairline. And these were the anarchists! When spontaneity is absent, longing and belonging rigidify. Who we are and what happens to us in the world occur spontaneously. Meister Eckhart says: '*Deus non habet quarum*', i.e. God does not have a why. There is huge spontaneity in the divine which graces life. God is no functionalist driven by the mechanics of a gender or programme. As our lives flow into the absence of the past, it is the spontaneity of memory which we can neither control nor force which gathers and keeps that absence for us.

MEMORY IS FULL OF THE RUINS
OF PRESENCE

S WE JOURNEY ONWARDS IN life, increasingly spaces within us fill with absence. We begin to have more and more friends among the dead. Every person suffers the absence of their past. It is utterly astonishing how the force and fibre of each day unravel into the vacant air of yesterday. You look behind you and you see nothing of your days here. Our vanished days increase our experience of absence. Yet our past does not deconstruct as if it never was. Memory is the place where our vanished days secretly gather. Memory rescues experience from total disappearance. The kingdom of memory is full of the ruins of presence. It is astonishing how faithful experience actually is; how it never vanishes completely. Experience leaves deep traces in us. It is surprising that years after something has happened to you, the needle of thought can hit some groove in the mind and the music of a long-vanished event can rise in your soul as fresh and vital as the evening it happened. Memory provides such shelter and continuity of identity. Memory is also fascinating because it is a subtle and latent presence in one's mind. The past seems to be gone and absent. Yet the grooves in the mind hold the traces and vestiges of everything that has ever happened to us. Nothing is ever lost or forgotten. In a culture addicted to the instant, there is a great amnesia. Yet it is only through the act of remembrance, literally re-membering, that we can come to poise, integrity and courage. Amnesia clogs the inner compass and makes the mind homeless. Amnesia makes the sense of absence intense and haunted. We need to retrieve the activity of remembering, for it is here that we are rooted and gathered. Tradition is to the community what memory is to the individual. The absence of the past remains subtle yet near.

Ruins: temples of absence

he human heart longs to dwell. The root of the word 'dwelling' includes the notion of lingering or delaying. It holds the recognition of our pilgrim nature, namely, the suggestion that it will only be possible to linger for a while. From ancient times, we have carved out dwelling places on the earth. Against the raw spread of nature, the dwelling always takes on a particular intensity. It is a nest of warmth and intimacy. Over years and generations, a large aura of soul seeps into a dwelling and converts it in some way into a temple of presence. We leave our presence on whatever we touch and wherever we dwell. This presence can never be subsequently recalled or wiped; the aura endures. Presence leaves an imprint on the ether of a place. I imagine that the death of every animal and person creates an invisible ruin in the world. As the world gets older, it becomes ever more full with the ruins of vanished presence. This can be sensed years and years later, even more tangibly, in the ruins of a place. The ruin still holds the memory of the people who once inhabited it. When the ruin is on a street, its silence is serrated because it endures the import of surrounding echoes. But when a ruin is an isolated presence in a field, it can insist on its personal signature of presence in contrast to the surrounding nature. A ruin is never simply empty. It remains a vivid temple of absence. All other inhabited dwellings hold their memory and their presence is continually added to and deepened by the succeeding generations. It is consequently quite poignant that a long since vacated ruin still retains echoes of the presence of the vanished ones. Hölderlin captures this unstated yet perennial presence of the echo of touch in abandoned places:

 hen night is like day
And over slow footpaths,
Dense with golden dreams,
Lulling breezes drift.

The abandoned place is dense with the presence of the absent ones who have walked there. Another region of absence is the absence of what is yet to come.

The absence of the future

here is also a whole region of the absent which embraces not the vanished but that which has not yet arrived. On the pathway of time the individual is always somehow in the middle. There are events, persons, thoughts and novelties ahead which have not yet arrived. This is the territory of the unknown. We are always reaching forward with open gestures into the future. Much of our thinking endeavours to invite the unknown to disclose itself. This is especially true of questions. The question is the place where the unknown becomes articulate and active in us. The question is impatient with the unrevealed. It reaches forward to open doors in the unknown. The question attempts to persuade absence to yield its concealed presences. All perception works at this threshold. Unknown to ourselves we are always unveiling new worlds that lie barely out of reach. This is where the imagination is fully creative. All language, thought, creativity, prayer and action live out of that fissure between word and thing, longing and fulfilment, subject and object. There are invisible furrows of absence everywhere.

Towards a philosophy of loss

 ife is rich and generous in her gifts to us. We receive much more than we know. Frequently life also takes from us. Loss is always affecting us. Like the tide that returns eternally to rinse away another wafer of stone from the shoreline, there is a current of loss that flows through your life. You know the sore edges in your heart where loss has taken from you. You stand now on the stepping stone of the present moment. In a minute it will be gone never to return. With each breath you are losing time. Absence is the longing for something that is gone. Loss is the hole that it leaves. The sense of loss confers a great poignancy on your longing. Each life has its own different catalogue. Some people are called to endure wounds of loss that are devastating. How they survive is difficult to understand. Each of us in our own way will be called at different times to make its sore acquaintance. From this angle, life is a growth in the art of loss. Eventually we learn to enter absolute loss at death. In Connemara when someone is dying, they often say: '*Tá sí ar a cailleadh*', i.e. literally, she is in her losing.

In a certain sense, there can be no true belonging without the embrace of loss. Belonging can never be a fixed thing. It is always quietly changing. At its core, belonging is growth. When belonging is alive it always brings new transitions. The old shelter collapses; we lose what it held, now we have to cross over into the beginnings of a new shelter of belonging that only gathers itself slowly around us. To be honest and generous in belonging to the awkward and unpredictable transition is very difficult. This happens often in friendship and love. Your relationship may be changing or ending. Often the temptation is to suppress this, avoid it or cut it off in one brutal, undiscussed stroke. If you do this, you will not belong to the changing and you will find yourself an intruder on the emerging new ground. You will not be honourably able to rest in the new belonging because you did not observe the dignity of painfully earning your passage. Loss always has much to teach us; its voice whispers that the shelter just lost was too small for our new souls. But it is hard to belong generously to the rhythm of loss.

The beauty of loss is the room it makes for something new. If everything that came to us were to stay, we would be dead in a day from mental obesity. The constant flow of loss allows us to experience and enjoy new things. It makes vital clearance in the soul. Loss is the sister of discovery; it is vital to openness; though it certainly brings pain. There are some areas of loss in your life which you may never get over. There are some things you lose and, after the pain settles, you begin to see that they were never yours in the first place. As the proverb says: what you never had you never lost. Loss qualifies our whole desire to have and to possess. It is startling that you cannot really hold onto anything. Despite its intensity, the word 'mine' can only have a temporary and partial reference. Ironically, sometimes when we desperately hold onto something or someone, it is almost as if we secretly believe that we are going to lose them. Holding on desperately cannot in any way guarantee belonging. The probability is that it will in some strange way only hasten loss. True belonging has a trust and ease; it is not driven by desperation to lose yourself in it or the fear that you will lose it. The loneliest wave of loss is the one that carries a loved one away towards death.

Grief: longing for the lost one

A s a child you think death is so strange. You anticipate that when it comes it will be accompanied by major drama. Yet so often death arrives with uncanny quiet. It steals into a room and leaves an awful silence. A loved one is

341

gone. The first time that death takes someone close to you, it breaks your innocence and your natural trust in life. It is strange to lose someone to death. The shock should paralyse you but the disturbing quiet somehow makes everything sufficiently unreal and the force of the loss is dissipated. Unlikely as it may sound, though death has indeed occurred and you were there, you do not truly know yet that your friend has died. You go through the funeral days, their drama and sympathy buoyed up by the certainty and shelter of rhythm which this whole ritual provides. It is only later, when the new silence gathers around your life, that you realize your awful loss. You have been thrown out of the shelter of a belonging where your heart was at home.

The time of grief is awkward, edgy and lonesome. At first you feel that it is totally unreal. With the belonging severed, you feel numbed. When you love someone, you are no longer single. You are more than yourself. It is as if many of your nerve endings now extend outside your body towards the beloved and theirs reach towards you. You have made living bridges to each other and changed the normal distance that usually separates us. When you lose someone, you lose a part of yourself that you loved, because when you love it is the part of you that you love most that always loves the other. Grief is at its most acute at death. There is also a whole, unacknowledged grief that accompanies the break-up of a relationship. This indeed can often be worse than death, at least initially, because the person is still around and possibly with someone else. The other is cut off from you. Grief is the experience of finding yourself standing alone in the vacant space with all this torn emotional tissue protruding. In the rhythm of grieving, you learn to gather your given heart back to yourself again. This sore gathering takes time. You need great patience with your slow heart. It takes the heart a long time to unlearn and transfer its old affections. This is a time when you have to swim against the tide of your life. It seems for a while that you are advancing, then the desolation and confusion pull you down and, when you surface again, you seem to be even further from the shore. It is slow making your way back on your own. You feel so many conflicting things. You are angry one minute; the next moment you are just so sad. After a death there are people around you, yet you feel utterly isolated: no-one else has the foggiest notion of your loss. No-one had what you had, there-fore, no-one else has lost it. Yet when friends try to gently accompany you, you find yourself pulling back from them too. In a remarkable collection of modern elegies to mourn the loss of his wife, the Scottish poet, Douglas Dunn, ends his poem 'The Clear Day' with this verse:

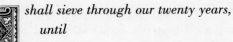 shall sieve through our twenty years,
        until
    I almost reach the sob in the intellect,
The truth that waits for me with its loud grief,
Sensible, commonplace, beyond understanding.

Because your loss is so sore, something within you expects the world to understand. You were singled out. Now you are on your own. Yet life goes on. That makes you angry: sometimes, you look around at your family or the others who have been hit by this loss; it does not seem to have hurt them as much. But you remember that behind the façade they are heartbroken too. You have never experienced anything like this. During grief, the outer landscape of your life is in the grip of grey weather; every presence feels ghostly. You are out of reach. You have gone way into yourself. Your soul lingers around that inner temple which is empty now save for the sad echo of loss.

Grief is a journey that knows its way

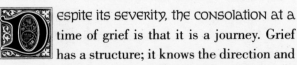espite its severity, the consolation at a time of grief is that it is a journey. Grief has a structure; it knows the direction and it will take you through. It is amazing how time and again, one of the most consoling factors in

experience is that each experience has a sure structure; this is never obvious to us while we are going through something. But when we look back, we will be able to pick out the path that offered itself. Experience always knows its way. And we can afford to trust our souls much more than we realize. The soul is always wiser than the mind, even though we are dependent on the mind to read the soul for us. Though travel is slow on the grief journey, you will move through its grey valley and come out again onto the meadow where light, colour and promise await to embrace you. The loneliest moment in grief is when you suddenly realize you will never see that person again. This is an awful shock. It is as if all the weeks of sorrow suddenly crystallize in one black bolt of recognition. You really know how total your loss is when you understand that it is permanent. In this life there is no place that you will ever be able to go to meet again the one who has gone. On the journey of grief this is a milestone. You begin thereafter to make your peace with the shock.

We grieve for ourselves

 radually, you begin to understand more deeply that you are grieving primarily over your own loss. The departed one has gone home and is gathered now in

345

the tranquillity of the Divine Belonging. When you realize that it is for yourself that you are grieving, you begin to loosen your sorrowful hold on the departed one. Part of what has had you holding on so desperately is the fear that if you let go, you would lose them for ever. Now you begin to glimpse the possibilities of being with them in a new way. If you loosen the sad grip of grief, a new belonging becomes possible between you. This is one of the most touching forms of belonging in the world: the belonging between us and our loved ones in the unseen world. It is a subtle and invisible belonging for which the crass obviousness of modern culture has no eye. Yet this invisible belonging is one in which so many people participate. Though the silent weeping of your heart lessens, you get on, more or less, with your life, a place is kept within you for the one who is gone. No other will ever be given the key to that door. As years go on you may not remember the departed every day with your conscious mind. Yet below your surface mind, some part of you is always in their presence. From their side, our friends in the unseen world are always secretly embracing us in their new and bright belonging. Though we may forget them, they can never forget us. Their secret embrace unknowingly shelters and minds us.

The bright moment in grief is when the sore of

absence gradually changes into a well of presence. You become aware of the subtle companionship of the departed one. You know that when you are in trouble, you can turn to this presence beside you and draw on it for encouragement and blessing. The departed one is now no longer restricted to any one place and can be with you any place you are. It is good to know the blessings of this presence. An old woman, whose husband had died thirty years earlier, told me once that the last thing she did each night before sleep was to remember him. In her memory she went over his face detail by detail until she could gather his countenance clearly in her mind's eye. She had always done this since he died because she never wanted him to fade into the forgetfulness of loss.

While it is heartbreaking to watch someone in the throes of grief, there is still a beauty in grief. Your grief shows that you have risked opening up your life and giving your heart to someone. Your heart is broken with grief because you have loved. When you love, you always risk pain. The more deeply you love, the greater the risk that you will be hurt. Yet to live your life without loving is not to have lived at all. As deeply as you open to life, so deeply will life open up to you. So there is a lovely symmetry and proportion between grief and love. Connemara is a dark landscape full of lakes and framed with

347

majestic mountains. If you ask a person here how deep a lake is, they say that they have often heard their ancestors say that the lake is always as deep as the mountain near it is high. The invisible breakage of grief has the same symmetry. Meister Eckhart said: 'Depth is height' and there is a haunting poem from the third century BC by Callimachus which imaginatively captures grief and the richness of absence as memory:

hey told me, Heraclitus,
They told me you were dead.
They brought me bitter news
    to hear
And bitter tears to shed.
I wept as I remembered,
How often you and I
Had tired the sun with talking
And sent him down the sky.
But now that you are lying,
My dear old Carian guest,
A handful of grey ashes,
Long, long ago at rest.
Still are your gentle voices,
Your nightingales, awake –
For death he taketh all away
But these he cannot take.

(Translated by William Cory)

348

The imagination and the altars of absence

N contrast to the discursive mind, the imagination seems more at home in its portraiture of absence and loss. This should not surprise since the hallmark of the imagination is suggestion rather that description. The imagination offers you only the most minimal line in order to permit and encourage you to complete the picture for yourself. Consequently, the most enthralling part of a poem or a story is actually that which is omitted or absent. It is often at the very end of a short story that the threshold is reached which would lead into the real story. The writer has not cheated you but rather brought you to a door that you must open yourself. You are invited to people this absence with your own imagined presences. Your imagination begins to take you into a shape of experience which calls you beyond the familiar, the factual and the predictable. Through acquainting you with places from which you have been absent, it enlarges and intensifies your presence. This often happens magically when you visit an art gallery. Art galleries are temples to colour. Art reminds one of what Keats said so memorably: 'I am sure of nothing but the holiness of the heart's affections and the truth of the imagination.'

The imagination teaches us that absence is anything but empty. It also tries to mirror the complexity of the soul. In order to function, society always tries to reduce things to a common denominator or code. Politics, religion and convention are usually committed to looking away from the raging complexity that dwells under the surface in every human heart. The penumbral and paradoxical world of the soul is taken for all practical purposes as absent. The external world deals with the individual by first engaging in this act of subtraction. Consequently, we depend desperately on the imagination to trawl and retrieve our poignant and wounded complexity which is forced to remain absent from the social surface. The imagination is the inspired and incautious priestess who, against the wishes of all systems and structures, insists on celebrating the liturgy of presence at the banished altars of absence.

In this sense the imagination is faithful and hospitable to everything that lives in the house of the heart. It is willing to explore every room. Here the imagination shows courage and grace. Literature's most fascinating and memorable characters are not saints or cautious figures who never risked anything. They are characters who embody great passion and dangerous paradoxical energy. In this way, the imagination mirrors and articulates that constant companion dimension of the heart that by definition and design remains perenially absent, namely, the subconscious. Absence is such a powerful theme and presence precisely because such a vast quantity of our identity lies out of reach in this unknown and largely unknowable region. Though predominantly absent from our awareness, the rootage of the subconscious accounts for so much of what happens above in the days of our lives. Because the imagination is the priestess of the threshold she brings the two inner territories together. The imagination unifies the inner presence and the inner absence of our lives – the daylight outside the self by which we are known and the inner night-time self whose dimensions remain unknown even to ourselves. The artist is the one who is committed to the life of the imagination.

The artist as permanent pilgrim

OR most roles in life there are structures of study and apprenticeship to acquire the skill to function in that profession. Though there are certain structures there for training in the arts, the artist is different. The artist trains himself; it can be no other way. Each artist is animated by a unique longing. There are no outer ready-made maps for what the artist wants to create. Each is haunted by some inner voice that will not permit any contentment until what is demanded is created. The artist cannot settle into the consensus of normal belonging. His heart pushes him out to the edge where other imperatives hold sway. There is great lonesomeness in becoming implicated in the creation of something original. Rimbaud said: 'I have no ancestors.' In a sense the artist is called not so much from outside but from the unknown depths within.

The invitation to create comes from elsewhere. Artists are the priestesses and priests of culture. They coax the invisible towards a form where it becomes faintly visible, silence towards voice and the unknown towards intimacy. Artists help us to see what is secretly there. No artist stands alone in a clear space. Every artist works from the huge belonging to the tradition but yet does not repeat anything. The artist belongs in a strange way. He inhabits the tradition to such depth that he can feel it beat in his heart but his tradition also makes him feel like a total stranger who can find for his longing no echo there. Out of the flow of this intimate foreignness something new begins to emerge.

The artist is fiercely called to truth. Despite all the personal limitation and uncertainty, he has to express what he finds. Sometimes the findings are glorious. Rilke's poetry gladdens the heart and makes you aware of the secret eternity of everything around you. The music of Beethoven gives huge voice to the dense cadences of creation. At other times, the artist has to name and portray the crippling and poisonous forms of belonging which we settle for: Kafka's meticulous articulation of the surrealism of bureaucracy; Beckett's portrayal of the famine of absence that can never be warmed or filled. In this way the artist calls us to freedom and promise. In art we see where the lines of our belonging have become tight and toxic.

The artist is always faithful to longing first. This willingness to follow the longing 'wherever it leads' demands and enables all kinds of new possibilities of belonging. Hölderlin says: '*Was bleibt aber stiften die Dichter*', i.e. what endures the poets create. The creation of such permanence is the result of following longing to the outposts, beyond every cozy or settled shelter, until some echo of the eternal belonging is sounded. There are large numbers of our brothers and sisters who are also at the outposts we never visit.

The ONES WE NEVER hEAR FROM

 his absence works also at the social level. Society is coming more and more to mirror the media. Yet the media is no

353

innocent surface or screen on which anything and everything is welcome to appear. The media works with a powerful selectivity. It constructs its world around carefully chosen and repetitive and loud chronicles. Yet there are so many that we never hear from. We never read of them in the papers. We never hear of them in the news. A whole range of people are absent. They are usually the poor, the vulnerable, the ill and prisoners. Their voices would be slow and direct and would gnaw at our comfort and endanger our complacency. Most of us who are privileged live quite protected lives and are distant from and blind to what the poor endure. Out of sight – out of mind. What is absent from our view does not concern us.

Addiction: obsessed longing

 NE of the terrible metaphors of post-modern society is the drug. The addiction to drugs is arguably one of the greatest problems facing Western society. When drugs hook you, they make your longing captive. The depth and complexity of your life telescopes into one absolute need. Regardless of the presence of others who love you, the gifts that you have, the life that you could have, your life now has only one need, the drug. The longing of the addict is a craving for which he will

354

sacrifice all other belonging. It is astounding how the inner world of the human heart has a capacity for such absolute single-mindedness. Addiction is longing that is utterly obsessed. There is no distance any more between the longing and the drug. The longing determines the life. The drug has the power of a sinister God; it awakens absolute passion and demands absolute obedience.

A drug is an anonymous and unattractive piece of matter. For the addict, however, this banal stuff shines like the most glorious diamond imaginable. When the eye sees it, the longing is already travelling in the direction of pure joy; no wonder they choose names like ecstasy. The addict has no memory. All time is now; either the now of joy or the tortured now of longing for the fix. Far away from the dingy streets where the addict moves, probably out in the most scenic and beautiful area of the city, live the suppliers. They make their wealth from the misery of those poor demented ones for whom the city streets are an underworld. The suppliers work international routes which are the same as the international routes for arms. At a broader cultural level, drug addiction is a profound metaphor for contemporary society. The marginalized addicts are the scapegoats for the collective addiction in contemporary society. The obsessive nature of our culture comes to expression in the addict. The addict is visible, tangible and vulnerable. The addict is always on the margins of belonging. A group who also have to endure absence through losing or giving up belonging are the emigrants.

Τhe emigrants

ontemporary society is deeply unsettled. Everywhere there is the emergence of a new diaspora due to hunger and poverty. The subjects of this diaspora are the emigrants. Exile is difficult and disconcerting. You are uprooted. Something within us loves the continuity, shelter and familiarity of our home place. Among your own people you can trust the instinctive compass of your words and actions. You move in a natural rhythm that you never notice until you are away. Exile is difficult because you find yourself among strangers. And it is slow work to find a door into the house of their memory.

While at university I worked a summer on the buildings in America. I met an old man from our village in the West of Ireland. He was over eighty and had left home at eighteen and never returned. He talked so wistfully of home. He could remember the name of every field and well. As he intoned the litany of Gaelic place-names, his eyes kindled in the warmth of belonging. Even though he had lived

356

in exile all his adult life, there was a part of his heart which never left home. I imagine that he withdrew into this private sanctuary of memory when times were raw and lonely. Those in exile understand each other. You'd see it in the way they meet and talk. What they can presume about each other. How easily they slip into the rhythm of companionship. You'd see it in the Irish in a Kilburn pub, a group of Turkish people sitting by a river at the weekend in a German town, or the Filipino girls who gather near a bridge in Hong Kong every Sunday to talk of home. When you emigrate, you fracture your belonging to the language of your homeland.

Language and belonging

ach language has a unique memory. The thoughts, whispers and voices of a people live in their language. Gradually, over time, all the words grow together to build a language. The sound of the wind, the chorus of the tides, the silence of stone, love whispers in the night, the swell of delight and the sorrow of the darkness, all came to find their echoes in the language. As it fills out, the language becomes the echo-mirror of the people and their landscape. No-one knows the secret colour and the unique sound of the soul of a people like their language does. A language is a magical presence. It is utterly alive. Because we use it every minute, to feel and think and talk, we rarely stop to notice how strange and exciting words are. It is like the air we cannot live one moment without it, yet we rarely think of it. The most vital centre of your life is your mind. Your world is moored to your mind. Now there is no power that awakens and opens the mind like language does. Words form our minds and we can only see ourselves and the world through the lenses of words. As they age over centuries, words ripen with nuance and deeper levels of meaning. The memory of a people lives in the rich landscape of its language. The destructive things done by them and to them live there too.

When someone intrudes and takes over what is not their own, everything in the place reminds them that they do not belong there. Their guilt and unease can be assuaged by making the takeover as clean and thorough as possible. They must control everything. This is what a colonist does. Our Irish language was targeted in this way. The flow between the feeling and the language was broken. Your own language fits your mind. Ancestral memory and nuance break on the shores of thought.

A philosophy of Dúcas

he longing of a people is caught in the web of their language. Dreams and memories are stored there. A language is the inner landscape where a people can belong. When you destroy a people's language through colonization or through the more subtle, toxic colonization of consumerism, you fracture their belonging and leave them in limbo. It is fascinating how a language fashions so naturally the experience of a people into a philosophy of life. Sometimes one word holds centuries of experience; like a prism you can turn it to different angles and it breaks and gathers the light of longing in different ways.

In the Irish language, there are no specific substantive nouns of longing and belonging. This must mean that the Irish mind never saw them as fixed, closed realities nor as separate things. Both belong together in a wider, implicit sense of life and living. The word *dúcas* is the larger embrace. *Dúcas* captures the inner sense and content of belonging in that it means one's birthright and heritage. This brings to expression the particular lineage of belonging which one became heir to on entering the world. The act of birth brings possibility and limitation but it also confers rights. *Dúcas* also means one's native place. This is where you were born and the networks of subtle belonging that will always somehow anchor you there. There are many deep and penumbral layers to the way we belong in the world. There is none more dense and difficult to penetrate than the time and place of our first awakening as children. In the Irish tradition, there was a deep sense of the way a place and its soul-atmosphere seep into you during that time.

The phrase '*ag fillead ar do dúcas*' means returning to your native place and also the rediscovery of who you are. The return home is also the retrieval and reawakening of a hidden and forgotten treasury of identity and soul. To come home to where you belong is to come into your own, to become what you are, to awaken and develop your latent spiritual heritage. *Dúcas* also means the nature of the relationship you have with someone when there is a real affinity of soul between you both. When you have *dúcas* with someone, there is a flow of spirit and vitality between you. The echo of each other's longing brings and holds you both within the one circle of belonging. In this sense, *dúcas* is what enables and sustains the *anam-cara* affinity.

Dúcas also refers to a person's deepest nature. It probes beneath the surface images and impressions of a life and reaches into that which flows naturally from the deepest well in the clay of the soul. It refers in this sense to that whole intuitive and quickness of longing in us that tells us immediately how to think and act; we call this instinct. An old Irish proverb believes that instinct is a powerful force within us. It may remain latent for ages but it can always break out: '*Briseann an dúcas amac trí súile an cait*', i.e. *dúcas* will break forth even through the eyes of the cat. This is often used to interpret, explain or excuse something in a person. 'He cannot help it – he has the *dúcas* for that.' In some sense, *dúcas* seems to be a deeper force than history. You belong to your *dúcas*; your *dúcas* is your belonging. In each individual there is a roster of longing that nothing can suppress. *Dúcas* suggests the natural wildness of uninhibited nature. There is also the proverb which says *dúcas* is impervious to outside training: '*Is treise an dúcas ná an oillúint*', i.e. *dúcas* is stronger than education or upbringing. *Dúcas* shows the faithfulness of memory but accents the inevitable results of instinct. Yet without an awareness of *dúcas*, we are blind to what we do. Soul searching is the excavation of the *dúcas* in and around us in order to belong more fully to ourselves and to participate in our inner heritage in a critical and creative way. Given the sense of homelessness in modern life, there is anxiety and fear and a tendency to prescribe a style of belonging that has no self-criticism and wants to corral longing in fixed, empirical frames. This is fundamentalism.

Fundamentalism: false longing and forced belonging

Nable to read or decipher the labyrinth of absence, the homeless mind often reverts to nostalgia. It begins to imagine that our present dilemma rather than being a new threshold of possibility, is in fact a disastrous fall from an ideal past. Fundamentalism laments the absence of the time when everything was as it should be. Family values, perfect morality and pure faith existed without the chagrin of question, critique or the horror of such notorious practices as alternative lifestyles or morality. Such perfection, of course, never existed. Neither experience nor culture has ever been monolithic. Fundamentalism is based on faulty and fear-filled perception. It constructs a fake absence, i.e. the absence of something that never in fact existed in the first place. It then uses this fake absence to demand a future constructed on a false ideal. It pretends to have found an absolute access-point to the inner mind of the mystery. Such certainty cannot sustain itself in real conversation that is critical or questioning.

Fundamentalism does not converse or explore. It presents truth. It is essentially non-cognitive. This false certainty can only endure through believing that everyone else is wrong. It is not surprising that such fundamentalism desires power in order to implement its vision and force others to do as prescribed. Fundamentalism is dangerous and destructive. There is neither acceptance nor generosity in its differences with the world. It presumes that it knows the truth that everyone should follow. There is often an over-cozy alliance between it and official religion. Disillusioned functionaries sometimes see fundamentalism as the true remnant which has succeeded in remaining impervious to the virus of pluralism. When people on the higher rungs of hierarchy believe this, the results are catastrophic. Blind loyalty replaces critical belonging. The creative and mystical individuals within an institution become caricatured as the enemy; they become marginalized or driven out. Some of the most sinister forms of fundamentalism are practised in cults.

Cults and sects

 pirituality which cuts itself off from religion can go totally astray and become entangled in the worst networks of deception, illusion and power. We are all aware of the horror stories of individuals whose minds have been taken over by cults and sects. These individuals are offered emotional warmth and belonging. The price is the handing over of the individual mind. Cults are instinctively adept at mind-altering. They seduce and exploit the natural longing for the spiritual. Unlike a great religious tradition which demands and requires the critical loyalty and inner opposition of its theologians, a cult has no theology. The counter-questions are neither invited nor allowed. The cult manages to hold you prisoner while making you feel and believe that you are liberated and free. You could even feel pity and worry for those outside the cult, the lost ones who haven't yet seen your light. The cult operates an efficient dualism which separates mind and heart and splits self and society. It captures your longing in a sinister trap. The rise of cults testifies to the awful loneliness of post-modern culture. They are attractive because they seem to present a way of belonging which offers consolation, certainty and purpose. Even though they do not actually deliver any of these possibilities in a real or truthful sense, their following certainly invites us to look at the crisis of belonging in our society and religions.

Our longing for community

ach one of us wants to belong. No-one wants to live a life that is cut off or isolated. The absence of contact with others hurts us. When we belong, we feel part of things. We have a huge need to participate. When this is denied us, it makes us insecure. Our confidence is shaken and we turn in on ourselves and against ourselves. It is poignant that we are actually so fragile inside. When you feel rejected, it cuts deep into you, especially if you are rejected by those whose acceptance means a lot to you. The pain of rejection only confirms the intensity of our longing to belong. It seems that in a soul sense we cannot be fully ourselves without others. In order to *be*, we need to *be with*. There is something incomplete in purely individual presence. Belonging together with others completes something in us. It also suggests that behind all our differences and distances from each other, we are all participating in a larger drama of spirit. The life and death of each of us does indeed affect the rest of us. Not only do we long for the belonging of community but at a deeper level we are already a community of spirit.

There is a providence which brought us here and gave us to each other at this time. In and through us, a greater tapestry of creativity is being woven. It is difficult for us to envisage this. We live such separate and often quite removed lives. Yet behind all the seeming separation, a deeper unity anchors everything. This is one of the powerful intimations of the great religious traditions. The ideal of community is not the forcing together of separate individuals into the spurious unity of community. The great traditions tell us that community somehow already exists. When we come together in compassion and generosity, this hidden belonging begins to come alive between us. Consequently, a community which is driven by power, or too great a flurry of activity and talk, will never achieve much more than superficial belonging. The attempt to force community usually drives the more creative and independent people away. We do not build community as if it were some external and objective structure. We allow community to emerge. In order for community to emerge, we need time, vision and a certain rhythm of silence with each other. At its heart, it is impossible to grasp what makes community. We often hear the phrase 'community spirit' and that recognizes that community is not so much an invention or construction of its members but a gift that emerges between them and embraces them. We do not make community. We are born into community. We enter as new participants into a drama that is already on. We are required to maintain and often reawaken community.

Perhaps community is a constellation. Each one of us is a different light in the emerging collective brightness. A constellation of light has greater power of illumination than any single light would have on its own. Together we increase brightness. Yet no star can move away outside the constellation in order to view the overall brightness. It is interesting how perspective is such a powerful force in determining what we see and what we miss. Many of the astronauts who have voyaged into space have had amazing experiences. As they moved further and further away from the earth, many of them were overcome with emotion and affection for that diminishing little blue planet called earth. Raised infinitely out of their individual communities, they gradually had a total view of the earth. Looking through the accelerating infinity of space, their hearts were touched with tenderness for home. Similarly with us, within the solitude of our own individual light, we can never glimpse our collective brightness. All we see are frail candles, stuttering in the wind and the dark. Yet this should not make us insensitive to the embrace and the potential of our greater light. What kind of luminous view the dying must have as they slowly ascend to leave here?

Che shelter of community

 NE OF THE GREAT OREAMS OF HUMANITY iS the founding of a perfect community where longing and belonging would come into sublime balance. From Plato's *Republic* to the

Basic Community, in Latin America, of contemporary times, the realization of this ideal has continually called the human heart. In the Christian story, it is the dream of the realization of the Kingdom of God. The perfect community would be a place of justice, equality, care and creativity. Humans have wonderful abilities and gifts. Yet our ability to live together in an ideal way remains undeveloped. All community life seems to have its shadows and darkness. In contrast to many communities in nature, human intensity in its brightness and darkness makes it difficult to envisage an ideal community.

The ideal of creation is community, i.e. a whole diversity of presences which belong together in some minimal harmony. It is fascinating to lift a stone in a field to find a whole community of ants in such active rhythm. Though we would not suspect it, ants also have their shadowed order whereby some colonies actually have their own slave-ants to work for them. Who would ever suspect that such negative hierarchy can be found in miniature under a stone! Nature is a wonderful community that manages to balance light and dark, destructiveness and creativity with incredible poise. Think of the sequence of the seasons and the waves and the force fields that hold planets in rhythm. When you examine closely any piece of a field or bog, your eyes slowly begin to discern the various communities of insect, bird, animal and plant life that coexist together. What to the glance seemed to be just another bit of a field reveals itself as a finely tuned, miniature community. Each little self has its own space and shelter. It is an organic and diverse community. If humankind could only let its fear and prejudice go, it would gradually learn the inestimable riches and nourishment that diversity brings. Community can never be the answer to all our questions or all our longings. But it can encourage us, provoke us to raise questions and voice our desires. It cares for us, whether we know it or not.

Rural communities have a special, distinctive essence. In bygone days here in Connemara when a person got married the whole village would gather and build a simple but sufficient house for the couple in one day. In our village, neighbours would work in groups to get the harvest in. One day everyone would gather at our farm to bring home the hay or turf, or to cut the corn; the next day we would go to another farm. This is the old Irish notion of the *Meitheal*: the community gathered as an effective group to do the work for each other that an individual working alone could not have done.

Each one of us is a member of several communities simultaneously: the community of colleagues at work, neighbours, family, relations and friends.

Such communities develop naturally around us. No individual can develop or grow in an isolated life. We need community desperately. Community offers us a creative tension which awakens us and challenges us to grow. No community we belong to fits our longing exactly. Community refines our presence. In a community no one person can have their own way. There are others to be considered and accommodated too. In this way, we are taught compassion and care. We learn so much from community without ever realizing how totally we absorb its atmosphere. The community also challenges us to inhabit to the full our own individuality. No community can ever be a total unity which embraces and fulfils all the longing of its individuals. A community can only serve as a limited and minimal unity. Community becomes toxic when it pretends to cover all the territories of human longing. There are destinations of longing for each individual which can only be reached via the path of solitude.

The most intimate community is the community of understanding. Where you are understood, you are at home. There is nothing that unites or separates us like the style and species of our perception. Often in a close friendship, the different ways of seeing are what bring most hurt, not the things that each person does. When the perceptions find a balance in their own difference, then the togetherness and challenge can be wonderfully invigorating. When there is an affinity of thought between people and an openness to exploration, a real community of understanding and spirit can begin to grow. Where equality is grounded in difference, closeness is difficult but patience with it brings great fruits. Such community is truthful and real. There is a deep need in each of us to belong to some cluster of friendship and affinity in which the games of impression and power are at a minimum and we can allow ourselves to be seen as we really are, where we can express what we really believe and where we can be challenged thoroughly. This is how we grow; it is where we learn to see who we are, what our needs are and the unsuspecting effect our thinking and presence have on other lives. The true realization of individuality requires the shelter of acceptance and the clear pruning blade of criticism. Our post-modern culture has enshrined the cult of individualism as authenticity. The irony here is that the pursuit of individualism is abstract and empty. Real individuality in all its bright ambivalence is forgotten. Individualism is the enemy of real individuality. The true path of in-dividual longing always avoids the fast highway and travels the solitary boreens which traverse the true landscapes of creativity, difficulty and integration.

Our world desperately needs to come in from the lost islands of desiccated individualism and learn to stand again on the fecund earth where vibrant and vital interaction can happen between people. Arnold speaks of islands separated by the 'unplumbed, salt, estranging sea'. Our world is facing so many crises ecologically, economically and spiritually. These cannot be overcome by isolated individuals. We need to come together. There is incredible power in a community of people who are together because they care, and who are motivated by the ideals of compassion and creativity. When such a community develops and maintains its own vision, it will not fall into the trap of being the prisoners of reaction and begin to resemble more and more the opposition. It will not deconstruct in the introverted power games but maintain its care and critical focus. When such a prophetic community is nourished by prayer and animated by divine longing, it is unknown the harvest of creativity and belonging which it can bring. True community transfigures absence.

Towards a new community

 ur culture is complex and fast moving. We have a sharp eye for authoritarianism and control in their direct and obvious forms. We are, in ironic contrast, almost completely blind to the huge control and subtle authoritarianism of consumerist image culture. On the one hand we are warriors for the free view and simultaneously absolute disciples of the god of quantity. Our crisp cynicism and compliant greed have meant that we have unwittingly severed huge regions of the invisible tissue which holds community and civility together. Our society is addicted to and incessantly nourishes and inflates the spectacular. The invisible tissue which sustains real belonging is never spectacular; it is quiet and unostentatious. In order to survive as a planet and as a society, we need to reawaken and retrieve these lost and forgotten capacities of ours. Such virtues may heal our absence from our true nature.

One of these quiet virtues is honour. Contemporary psychology and spirituality speak of 'honouring your gifts'; the focus is inevitably subjective and sometimes narcissistic. Honour is a broader and deeper presence. The Irish word '*Úaisleacht*' means nobility; it also carries echoes of honour, dignity and poise. A person can be wild, creative and completely passionate and yet maintain *Úaisleacht*. This is in no way an argument for some kind of code of honour; such codes inevitably become external and arrogant. It is more a plea for the retrieval of a sense of honour. This reawakening would gradually ensure the lessening of our tabloid convention and obsession. The sense of honour would also begin to reveal the vast fissures in and the hollowness of the huge kingdom of image and PR. Television might cease to be a soap kingdom. At evening, the empty screen might indeed become some kind of genuine mirror for our real concerns. Some of the huge questions which now confront us might actually begin to come alive in our homes instead of the pursuit of fake questions which further nothing but gossip and passivity. Imagine a programme called 'The Awkward Question' which would genuinely pursue many of the fundamental questions that media avoids. A sense of honour in the way we relate with each other would invite the return of respect; the recognition that every person is worthy of respect. No-one should have to earn respect. It could also mean a re-awakening of our sense of courtesy. There is something very fine about a courteous person. Our times are so vulgar.

Compassion is another such quiet virtue. There is a huge crisis of compassion in contemporary society. This crisis has nothing to do with our in-ability to feel sympathy for others. It has more to do with the numbing of our compassion through our image exposure to so many of the horrors that are happening around the world. We feel overwhelmed and then hopeless. It is important to remember that a proportion of our numbness is convenient. We avoid the harrowing images or allow ourselves to be immediately overwhelmed. Most of us continue our privileged lives within our complacent cocoons. Outside of the normal pain and difficulties of our lives and those of our friends, we rarely come into contact with the hungry, the destitute and the oppressed. Their convenient absence from our lives means that we can never follow through and make the connection between the way we live and the awful lives to which our more helpless and vulnerable sisters and brothers are condemned. Not far from any of us, there are the poor, the homeless, the prisoners, the old people's homes and the addicts. Because we are privileged, we have great power. We have a duty to speak out for those who have no voice or are not being listened to. The practice of compassion would show us that no sister or brother deserves to be excluded and pushed onto the bleak margins where life is sheer pain and endurance. We should at least begin to have some conversations with these members of our human family. It would open our eyes. When our compassion awakens, our responsibility becomes active and creative. When we succumb to indifference, we blaspheme against the gifts that we could never earn that have been so generously given to us. The duty of privilege is absolute integrity.

Hope is another quiet virtue. We live in a culture where information is relentlessly meted out to us in abstract particles. So much of our information is a series of facts about how disastrous everything is. When we listen to the voices of doom, we become helpless and complicit in bringing the doom nearer. It is always astounding to see how willing humans are to give away their power and become disciples of helplessness. This accounts for the chromatic cynicism which reigns in our times. Cynicism is very interesting. Behind the searing certainty of the cynic, there is always, hidden somewhere, disappointed longing. It takes a good deal of energy to be a committed cynic. Time and again, life offers opportunities and possibilities. Time cannot help being a door into eternity. Within even the most cynical heart, eternity is a light sleeper. It takes considerable energy to continually quell the awakening invitation. Argument with a cynic merely serves this sliced certainty. A more subtle approach that addresses not the argument but the residue of disappointed longing can bring change. Our world is too beautiful and our human eternity too magnificent that we should succumb to hopelessness and cynicism. The human heart is a theatre of longings. Under every hardened and chromatic surface – be it system, syndrome or corporation – there is a region of longing that dreams as surely of

376

awakening to a new life of freedom and love as winter does of the springtime.

There are many other quiet virtues like care, sympathy, patience, confidence and loyalty. A new sense of community could gradually surface if we called upon some of these virtues to awaken. The great religious traditions advocate these as ideals. Increasingly the custodianship and representation of these traditions have fallen into the hands of frightened functionaries who can only operate through edict and prescription. Few of them have the sensibility and imagination to address our longings in a way that respects our complexity and wildness of soul. They are unable to invite our sense of freedom and creativity to awaken and begin the new journey towards belonging. We need to take back our own power and exercise our right to inhabit in a creative and critical way the traditions to which we belong. We have allowed the functionaries to persuade us that they have the truth and that they own our traditions. A great tradition is a spacious and wonderful home for our nobility of soul and desperation of longing. We need to exercise our belonging in a new and critical way.

Divine longing transfigures absence

NE of the things about longing is that it is not merely an abstract concept. Every heart has longing. This means that longing is always full of feeling. There is great concentration now on 'getting in touch with your feelings' and 'expressing your feelings'. There is often more than a whiff of narcissism about these projects. In this practice we have increasingly lost sight of the beauty and wholesomeness of feeling itself. Feeling is a powerful disclosure of our humanity. A person who can rely on feeling things is fully in touch with their own nature. Such a nature is difficult to grasp and define, but we do know that we can trust someone who has it. When we say 'there is great nature' in a person, we mean that there is a presence of feeling in them that is passionate, deep and caring. We can trust that even in awkward times of confusion and conflict the pendulum of nature will eventually come to rest in truth and compassion. It also suggests a deeper substrate of presence than personality, role or image. When we lose touch with our nature, we become less human. When we discover our own nature, we find new belonging.

The feeling of longing in your heart was not put there by yourself. We have seen how each of us was conceived in longing and every moment here has been a pilgrimage of longing. Your life is a path of longing through ever-changing circles of belonging. Your longing echoes the Divine Longing. The heart of transcendence is longing. God is not abstract or aloof. We have done terrible damage to the image of God. We have caricatured God as an ungracious moral accountant: we have frozen the feeling of God and drawn the separated mind of God into war with our own nature. God has not done that. Our thinking has; the results have been terrible. We have been abandoned in an empty universe with our poor hearts restless in a haunted longing; furthermore this has closed the door on any possibility of entering into our true belonging. We are victims of longing and we cannot come home. The thinking that has invented and institutionalized this life has damaged us; we are at once guilty and afraid. Of such a God E. M. Cioran writes: 'All that is Life in me urges me to give up God.' Our vision is our home. We need to think God anew as the most passionate presence in the universe – the primal well of presence from which all longing flows and the home where we all belong and to which all belonging returns. God is present to us in a form that endlessly invites our longing, namely, in the form of absence. Simone Weil said: 'The apparent absence of God in this world is the actual reality of God.'

God has a great heart. Only a Divine Artist with such huge longing would have the beauty and tenderness of imagination to dream and create such a wonderful universe. God is full of longing: every stone, tree, wave and human countenance testifies to the eternal and creative ripple of Divine Longing. This is the tender immensity of Jesus. He is the intimate linkage of everything. As Blake said: 'Christ the Imagination'. This is why there is always such hope of change and transfiguration; the deepest nature of everything is longing. Beneath even the most hardened surfaces longing waits. Great music or poetry will always reach us because our longing loves to be echoed. Neither can we ever immunize ourselves against love; it knows in spite of us exactly how to whisper our longing awake. It is as if, under the clay of your presence, streams of living water flow. Great moments always surprise you. The routine is broken and unexpected crevices appear on the safe surface of your life. Such moments dowse you – they make you recognize that within you there is eternity.

You should never allow any person or institution to own or control your longing. No-one has a right to deny you the beautiful adventure of God by turning you into a serf of a cold and sinister deity. When you let that happen, it makes you homeless. You are a child of Divine Longing. In your deepest nature you are one with your God. As Meister Eckhart says so beautifully: 'The eye with which I see God is God's eye seeing me.'

That circle of seeing and presence is ultimate belonging. It is fascinating that Jesus did not stay on the earth. He made himself absent in order that the Holy Spirit could come. The ebb and flow of presence and absence is the current of our lives; each of them configures our time and space in the world. Yet there is a force that pervades both presence and absence; this is spirit. There is nowhere to locate spirit and neither can it be subtracted from anything. Spirit is everywhere. Spirit is in everything. By nature and definition, spirit can never be absent. Consequently, all space is spiritual space and all time is secret eternity. All absence is full of hidden presence.

In the pulse beat is the life and the longing, all embraced in the great circle of belonging, reaching everywhere, leaving nothing and no-one out. This embrace is mostly concealed from us who climb the relentless and vanishing escalator of time and journey outside where space is lonesome with distance. All we hear are whispers, all we see are glimpses; but each of us has the divinity of imagination which warms our hearts with the beauty and depth of a world woven from glimpses and whispers, an eternal world that meets the gaze of our eyes and the echo of our voices to assure us that from all eternity we have belonged and to answer the question that echoes at the heart of all longing: while we are here, where is it that we are absent from?

A Blessing for Absence

ay you know that absence is full of tender presence and that nothing is ever lost or forgotten.

May the absences in your life be full of eternal echo.

May you sense around you the secret Elsewhere which holds the presences that have left your life.

May you be generous in your embrace of loss.

May the sore of your grief turn into a well of seamless presence.

May your compassion reach out to the ones we never hear from and may you have the courage to speak out for the excluded ones.

May you become the gracious and passionate subject of your own life.

May you not disrespect your mystery
    through brittle words or false belonging.
May you be embraced by God in whom
    dawn and twilight are one and may
    your longing inhabit its deepest dreams
    within the shelter of the Great
    Belonging.

Vespers

As light departs to let the earth be one with night
Silence deepens in the mind and thoughts grow
   slow;
The basket of twilight brims over with colours
Gathered from within the secret meadows of the day
And offered like blessings to the gathering Tenebrae

After the day's frenzy may the heart grow still
Gracious in thought for all the day brought,
Surprises that dawn could never have dreamed,
The blue silence that came to still the mind,
The quiver of mystery at the edge of a glimpse,
The golden echoes of worlds behind voices.

Tense faces unable to hide what gripped the heart,
The abrupt cut of a glance or a phrase that hurt,
The flame of longing that distance darkened,
Bouquets of memory that gathered on the heart's
   altar,
The thorns of absence in the rose of dream.

And the whole while the unknown underworld
Of the mind turning slowly in its secret orbit.

May the blessing of sleep bring refreshment and
    release
And the angel of the moon call the rivers of dream
To soften the hardened earth of the outside life,
Disentangle from the trapped nets the hurt and
    sorrow
And awaken the young soul for the new tomorrow.

Suggested further Reading

Gaston Bachelard, *The Poetics of Space*, Boston, 1969.

Jean Baudrillard, *Fatal Strategies*, New York, 1990.

Wendell Berry, *Collected Poems*, North Point Press, 1984.

Saint Bonaventure, *The Journey of the Mind to God*, (trans. by P. Boehner, O.F.M.), Hackett, 1993.

Jorge Luis Borges, *The Book of Sand*, London, 1980.

Ian Bradley, *The Celtic Way*, London, 1993.

Albert Camus, *Exile and the Kingdom*, Vintage, 1991.

Alexander Carmichael, *Carmina Gadelica*, Edinburgh, 1994.

Liam de Paor, *Saint Patrick's World*, Four Court's Press, 1996.

William Desmond, *Being and the Between*, New York, 1995.

Myles Dillon, *Early Irish Literature*, Dublin, 1994.

Robert Graves, *Greek Myths*, BCA, 1993.

Séamus Heaney, *The Haw Lantern*, London, 1987.

Philippe Jaccottet, *Selected Poems* (trans. by Derek Mahon), London, 1988.

K. Kavanagh, O.C.D. and O. Rodriguez, O.C.D. (trans.) *The Collected Works of John of the Cross*, ICS, 1979.

Thomas Kinsella (trans.), *The Táin*, Oxford, 1986.

Ivan V. Lalić, *The Passionate Measure* (trans. by Francis R. Jones), Dedalus, 1989.

Mary Low, *Celtic Christianity and Nature*, Edinburgh, 1996.

Iris Murdoch, *Metaphysics as a Guide to Morals*, London, 1992.

Gerard Murphy, *Early Irish Lyrics*, Oxford, 1996.

P. Murray, ed., *The Deer's Cry: A Treasury of Irish Religious Verse*, Dublin, 1986.

Pablo Neruda, *Selected Poems* (trans. by N. Tarn), London, 1977.

Noel Dermot O'Donoghue, *The Mountain Behind the Mountain: Aspects of the Celtic Tradition*, Edinburgh, 1993.

John O'Donohue, *Person als Vermittlung: Die Dialektik von Individualität und Allgemeinheit in Hegels 'Phänomenologie des Geistes'. Eine Philosophisch-theologische Interpretation*, Mainz, 1993.

Anam Ċara: Spiritual Wisdom from the Celtic World, London, 1997.

Echoes of Memory, Dublin, 1994/1997.

Daithi O'Hogain, *Myth, Legend and Romance: An Encyclopaedia of the Irish Folk Tradition*, New York, 1991.

Fernando Pessoa, *Selected Poems*, (trans. by J. Griffin), Penguin, 1982.

M. Merleau Ponty, *Phenomenology of Perception*, London, 1981.

Kathleen Raine, *The Lost Country*, Dolmen Press, 1971.

On a Deserted Shore, Dolmen Press, 1973.

Rupert Sheldrake, *The Rebirth of Nature*, London, 1990.

Cyprian Smith, *The Way of Paradox: Spiritual Life as Taught by Meister Eckhart*, London, 1987.

George Steiner, *Real Presence*, London, 1989.

David Whyte, *The Heart Aroused*, New York, 1995.

Esther de Waal, *The Celtic Way of Prayer*, London, 1996.

ANAM ĊARA
by John O'Donohue

'Words of wisdom . . . A heady mixture of myth, poetry, philosophy . . . Profound and moving'
Independent

When St Patrick came to Ireland in the fifth century AD he encountered the Celtic people and a flourishing spiritual tradition that had existed for thousands of years. He discovered that where the Christians worshipped one God, the Celts had many and found divinity all around them – in the rivers and hills, the sea and sky, and in every kind of animal – an ancient Celtic reverence for the spirit in all things which survives to this day.

Irish poet and scholar John O'Donohue uses an intuitive approach to spirituality and shares the secrets of this ancient world. Here you will learn how to reconnect with the treasures that lie hidden in your own soul, how to discover your individual nature and understand the 'secret divinity' in your relationships.

'This book is a phenomenon . . . A book to read and reread forever'
Irish Times

A Bantam Paperback
0553 50592 0

CONAMARA BLUES
by John O'Donohue

A new collection of poetry by the author of *Anam Cara*.

Conamara in the West of Ireland is a strange and beautiful landscape – a place of intense contrasts that is uniquely dependent on light and shade. In this exquisitely crafted collection of poetry, John O'Donohue evokes the vital energy and rhythm of Conamara, engaging with earth, sky and sea, and the majestic mountains that quietly preside over this terse landscape.

Written with penetrating insight and a deftness of touch, *Conamara Blues* offers a unique, imaginative vision of a landscape of hope and possibility that is at once both familiar and unknown.

Available in Doubleday Hardcover
0385 601514